THE
CHESS
MACHINE

ROBERT LÖHR

*Translated from the
German by* ANTHEA BELL

THE PENGUIN PRESS
New York
2007

THE PENGUIN PRESS
Published by the Penguin Group

Penguin Group (USA) Inc., 375 Hudson Street, New York, New York 10014, U.S.A. • Penguin Group
(Canada), 90 Eglinton Avenue East, Suite 700, Toronto, Ontario, Canada M4P 2Y3 (a division of Pearson
Penguin Canada Inc.) • Penguin Books Ltd, 80 Strand, London WC2R 0RL, England • Penguin Ireland,
25 St. Stephen's Green, Dublin 2, Ireland (a division of Penguin Books Ltd) • Penguin Books Australia Ltd,
250 Camberwell Road, Camberwell, Victoria 3124, Australia (a division of Pearson Australia Group Pty Ltd) •
Penguin Books India Pvt Ltd, 11 Community Centre, Panchsheel Park, New Delhi – 110 017, India •
Penguin Group (NZ), 67 Apollo Drive, Rosedale, North Shore 0745, Auckland, New Zealand
(a division of Pearson New Zealand Ltd.) • Penguin Books (South Africa) (Pty) Ltd,
24 Sturdee Avenue, Rosebank, Johannesburg 2196, South Africa

Penguin Books Ltd, Registered Offices: 80 Strand, London WC2R 0RL, England

First American edition
Published in 2007 by The Penguin Press, a member of Penguin Group (USA) Inc.

Copyright © Robert Löhr, 2005
Translation copyright © Anthea Bell, 2007
All rights reserved

Originally published as *Der Schachautomat* by Piper Verlag GmbH, Munich. English translation published in
Great Britain under the title *The Secrets of the Chess Machine* by Fig Tree, an imprint of Penguin Books Ltd.

Publisher's Note
This is a work of fiction. Names, characters, places, and incidents either are the product of the author's imagination or are used fictitiously, and any resemblance to actual persons, living or dead, business establishments,
events, or locales is entirely coincidental.

LIBRARY OF CONGRESS CATALOGING IN PUBLICATION DATA
Löhr, Robert.
[Schachautomat. English]
The chess machine : a novel / Robert Löhr ; translated from the German by Anthea Bell.
p.   cm.
ISBN 978-1-59420-126-4
1. Chess—Fiction.   I. Bell, Anthea.   II. Title.

PT2712.O47S3313   2007
833'.92—dc22
2006052456

Printed in the United States of America
1   3   5   7   9   10   8   6   4   2

Designed by Marysarah Quinn

THE CHESS MACHINE

Neuchâtel: 1783

ON THE WAY FROM VIENNA TO PARIS WITH HIS FAMILY
Wolfgang von Kempelen stopped in Neuchâtel, where on 11 March 1783,
at the inn on the marketplace, he presented his legendary chess machine,
an android in Turkish robes that could play chess. The Swiss did not give
Kempelen and his Turk a warm welcome. The automaton makers of the
principality of Neuchâtel, after all, were considered the best in the world,
and now along came an imperial civil servant from the Hungarian
provinces—a man who built clockwork devices just as a hobby, not for
a living—and who had successfully taught his automaton to *think*. An
intelligent machine. An apparatus consisting of springs, cogwheels, cables, and cylinders that had beaten almost all its human opponents at the
Game of Kings. Compared to Kempelen's extraordinary chess machine,
the Neuchâtel automata were merely outsize clockwork toys, a frivolous
amusement for noblemen with more money than was good for them.

In spite of local resentment, however, the chess-playing automaton's
performance was sold out. Those who could not get seats had to watch
standing behind the rows of chairs. The people of Neuchâtel wanted to
see how this miracle of technology worked; secretly, they were hoping
that Kempelen was a fraud and that under their expert scrutiny the most
brilliant invention of the century would turn out to be an ordinary con-

juring trick. But Kempelen frustrated their hopes: when, with a confident smile, he showed them the internal arrangements of the device at the beginning of the performance, all that could be seen was its mechanism, and when that mechanism was wound up and the Turk began playing chess, it did so with the unmistakable movements of a machine. The Neuchâtel patriots had to acknowledge that Kempelen was nothing short of a genius in the field of mechanics.

The Turk defeated its first two opponents, the Mayor and the President of the Neuchâtel Chess Club, in a humiliatingly short space of time. Then Kempelen asked for a volunteer to play the third and last game of the day. A few minutes passed before anyone finally offered. Kempelen and the audience looked around for the volunteer, but he could be seen only when he emerged along the path cleared for him as the spectators moved aside—for the man was so small that he came only just above waist-level of the others present. Wolfgang von Kempelen took a step back and put one hand on the chess cabinet for support. The sight of the dwarf had visibly shaken him, and he went as pale as if he had seen a ghost.

Gottfried Neumann—for such was the dwarf's name—was a watchmaker himself and had come to Neuchâtel from neighboring La Chaux-de-Fonds especially to see the Mechanical Turk play. The dwarf's hair was black with a few strands of silver-gray, tied back in a Prussian queue at the nape of his neck, and his eyes were chestnut brown, like the eyes of the chess-playing Turk. His expression was severe. His forehead seemed naturally furrowed, and the dark brows above his eyes might have been frowning since his birth. He was about the height of a six-year-old boy but clearly stronger. It was as if too much body had been fitted into too little skin. He wore a close-fitting dark green coat tailored to his special measurements and had a silk cravat around his neck.

A murmur filled the hall as Neumann approached Kempelen. None of the audience had ever seen Neumann play chess. The President of the Chess Club asked for other volunteers, men known to be good chess players, hoping that the automaton might yet be forced into a draw, but he was hissed down: yes, the Turk had proved itself unbeatable, but at least a match between a machine and a dwarf would be well worth watching.

Kempelen did not pull out the chair for the little watchmaker as he had for his two predecessors. Like them, Neumann sat at a separate table with a separate chessboard, leaving the audience a clear view of the Turk. Kempelen waited until the dwarf was seated, then cleared his throat and asked the audience to be quiet and pay attention. Meanwhile Neumann was looking at the chessboard and the sixteen red chessmen in front of him as if he had never seen their like before. His shoulders were hunched; he was sitting on his hands like a child.

Kempelen's assistant wound up the chess automaton with a crank, and the clockwork began to move, creaking. The Turk raised its head, moved its left arm over the chessboard, and with three fingers placed a pawn in the middle of the board—the opening that it had used in the other two games. The assistant copied the move on Neumann's chessboard, but the dwarf did not react. He didn't even look up. He just examined every one of his chessmen like old friends whom he had long thought dead. The audience began to shift restlessly.

Wolfgang von Kempelen was about to speak when Neumann finally bestirred himself. He moved his king's pawn two squares forward, challenging the Turk's white pawn.

Venice: 1769

On an anonymous November day in the year 1769 Tibor Scardanelli had woken up in a windowless prison cell, with encrusted blood on his swollen face and a splitting headache. He groped in vain for a jug of water in the dim light. The reek of alcohol on his ragged clothes turned his stomach. He dropped back on the straw mattress and leaned against the cold lead of the wall. Certain experiences in his life were obviously bound to recur—he was destined to be cheated, robbed, beaten, arrested, and left to starve.

On the previous evening the dwarf had been playing chess for money in a tavern, and he spent his first winnings on brandy instead of a proper meal. So he was already drunk when the young merchant challenged him to play for a stake of two guilders. Tibor was winning the game easily, but when he bent to pick up a dropped coin, the Venetian put his queen back on the board, although she had been taken long ago. Tibor protested, but the merchant wouldn't give way—much to his companions' amusement. Finally he offered the dwarf a draw and took back his stake, amid the laughter of the spectators. The alcohol had clouded Tibor's reason. He seized the merchant's hand as it clutched his money. In the ensuing scuffle he and the Venetian both fell to the floor. Tibor was getting the better of it until one of the merchant's companions smashed the brandy jug over his head. Tibor did not lose consciousness, even when the Venetians took turns beating him up. After that they handed him over to the carabinieri, explaining that the dwarf had cheated them at play and then attacked and robbed them. Thereupon the carabinieri took him to the nearest prison, the leaden chambers of the *piombi* at the top of the Doge's palace. Tibor's assailants had left him neither what little money he had nor his chessboard, but at least his amulet of the Madonna was still around his neck. He clutched it with both hands and prayed to the Mother of God to get him out of this hole.

Before he had come to the end of his prayer, the jailer opened his cell door and let a nobleman in. The man was about ten years older than Tibor, with an angular face and dark brown hair receding at the temples. He was dressed à la mode, without aping the foppishness of the Venetians: a nut-brown frock coat with lace-trimmed cuffs, breeches of the same color tucked into tall riding boots, and a black cloak over these garments. On his head he wore a three-cornered hat, now wet with rain, and he had a rapier at his belt. He didn't look like an Italian. Tibor remembered seeing him the night before among the guests in the tavern. The nobleman was carrying a jug of water and a crust of bread in one hand, and in the other a finely worked traveling chess set. The jailer brought him a candlestick and a stool, on which he seated himself. The man put the bread, water, and his hat down beside Tibor's mattress, and without a word he opened the chessboard out on the floor and began setting up the chessmen. When the jailer had left the cell again, closing the door behind him, Tibor could bear the silence no longer and spoke to the newcomer.

"What do you want?"

"You speak German? Good." He took a watch out of his waistcoat pocket, flipped it open, and placed it beside the chessboard. "I want to play a game against you. If you can defeat me within a quarter of an hour, I'll pay your fine and you're a free man."

"Suppose I lose?"

"If you lose," replied the man, when he had put the last chessman on the board, "I'd be disappointed . . . and you would have to forget you ever met me. But if I may offer you a piece of advice: make sure you win, because there's no other way you'll get out of this place. They've fitted a few more gratings here since the Chevalier Casanova's time."

With these words, the stranger picked up his knight and held it above the pawns. Looking at the board, Tibor noticed a gap in his own ranks. His red queen was missing. Tibor glanced up, and the nobleman anticipated his question. He patted his waistcoat pocket, where the queen was tucked away.

"It would be too easy with the queen."

"But without a queen how am I supposed to . . . ?"

"That's up to you."

Tibor made his first move. His opponent riposted at once. Tibor made five quick moves before he finally had time to turn his attention to the bread and water. The nobleman was playing an aggressive game. Intent on taking advantage of his superior numbers of chessmen to decimate Tibor's ranks, he deployed a chain of pawns and moved into Tibor's half of the board. But Tibor held his ground. His opponent's pauses for thought grew longer.

"Your thinking is costing me time," protested Tibor, when five minutes had passed by the watch.

"You'll just have to play faster."

And Tibor did play faster: he leaped over the line of white pawns and drove the king into a corner. Five minutes later he could see that he was going to win. His opponent nodded, put his king aside, and sat back on his stool.

"Giving up?" asked Tibor.

"I'm calling a halt. You know I can't win now. So I can make better use of your last five minutes in captivity. Congratulations. You played well." He offered Tibor his hand. "I'm Baron Wolfgang von Kempelen, from Pressburg."

"Tibor Scardanelli, from Provesano."

"Pleased to meet you. Tibor, I want to make you an offer. I must go a little way back in time in my story here: I am in the service of Her Majesty Empress Maria Theresia of Austria and Hungary. She has entrusted a number of tasks to me since I took up my position as a civil servant attached to her court, and I've carried them all out to her complete satisfaction. But other good men could have done them equally successfully. I, however, want to do something *out of the ordinary*. Something that will raise me higher in her eyes . . . and may even make me immortal. Do you follow me?"

Wolfgang von Kempelen waited for Tibor's nod, then went on.

"A few weeks ago the French physicist Pelletier showed off some of his experiments at court: he was playing around with magnetism—hocus-pocus, nails flying through the air, coins apparently moved over a piece of paper by an invisible hand, hair suddenly standing on end, that sort of thing. Dr. Mesmer's already curing people with his knowledge of magnetism, and now along comes this French conjuror with his tricks, wasting my valuable time—and the Empress's too. After the performance Maria Theresia asked me what I thought of Jean Pelletier, and I spoke my mind: I told her that science had already progressed much further, and I myself, even without studying at the Académie like Pelletier, could show her an experiment that would make his act look like mere mumbo-jumbo. That aroused her curiosity, of course. She took me at my word . . . and gave me leave of absence from all my duties for six months to prepare this experiment."

"What sort of experiment?"

"I didn't know myself at the time, but I'd already made up my mind to construct some extraordinary kind of machine. I must tell you that I'm not just a civil servant; I also have a good knowledge of mechanics. My original plan was to build the Empress a machine that could speak."

"But that can't be done," Tibor instinctively protested.

The Baron smiled and shook his head, as if many others before Tibor had already reacted in the same way. "Of course it can be done. I shall build the world a device that speaks as distinctly as a human being, and in every language too. But six months, as I realized, isn't long enough for such a herculean labor. There just isn't time to get hold of all the materials and test them. And one doesn't keep an empress waiting. So I'm going to build a different sort of machine." Kempelen took the red queen out of his waistcoat pocket and put her down with the other chessmen. "A *chess machine*."

Kempelen stopped to relish Tibor's inquiring expression, then went on. "An automaton that plays chess. A thinking machine."

"It can't be done."

Kempelen laughed as he took a sheet of paper out of his waistcoat and unfolded it. "You said that before. And this time you're right. No machine will ever be able to play chess. In theory, yes, it's possible, but in practice . . ."

He handed Tibor the paper. It was the sketch of someone sitting at a table, or rather at a cabinet with several closed doors. Both the figure's arms rested on the tabletop, and a chessboard lay between them.

"That's what the automaton will look like," explained Kempelen. "And since it can't function of its own accord, it needs a human brain."

Tibor shuddered at the idea, and Kempelen laughed again. "Never fear, I'm not going to saw anyone's skull open. What I mean is, someone will guide the automaton from inside." Kempelen placed one finger on the closed cabinet.

And now at last Tibor understood why the Hungarian Baron had sought him out and followed him here, why he sounded so friendly, and why, above all, he was prepared to buy his freedom. Kempelen crossed his arms over his chest. Tibor was shaking his head long before he answered.

"I won't do it."

Kempelen raised his hands in a conciliating gesture. "Take it easy, take it easy. We haven't even discussed terms yet."

"What terms? It's a fraud."

"It's no more or less of a fraud than magnetizing a couple of pieces of iron and talking about 'magical attraction.'"

"Thou shalt not bear false witness."

"Thou shalt not play for money either, if you're going to throw the Bible up at me."

"People will examine the machine and find out the deception."

"They'll examine it, yes, but they won't find anything. That's *my* part of the business."

Tibor was still unconvinced, but he could think of no more reasons.

"Just *one* performance in front of the Empress," said Kempelen, "and then I'll dismantle the machine. Even great sensations have only a short lease of life these days. I want to impress Maria Theresia just once, and then my fortune's made. She'll back my other projects. And by the time I unveil my speaking machine, the chess automaton will be long forgotten."

Tibor looked at the sketch of the android.

"Listen to my offer: you'll get generous wages, with good board and lodging until the performance. And then you'll be playing chess in front of the Empress, perhaps even *against* her. Not many people can say that."

"It won't work."

"And suppose it doesn't, what do you have to fear? I may be censured, but you? You keep your wages and make yourself scarce. You can only gain by the deal."

Tibor said nothing for a while, then looked at the watch. Time had run out. "If I don't do it . . . will you still pay for my freedom?"

"Of course I will. I gave you my word. Just as I give you my word that our chess automaton will be an unprecedented success."

Tibor carefully folded up the sketch and handed it back. "Thank you very much. But I don't want any part in a fraud."

Kempelen gazed into Tibor's eyes until he looked away. Only then did he take the paper.

"A pity," said Kempelen, and began packing the chessmen away. "You're missing a unique opportunity to take part in a great venture."

WOLFGANG VON KEMPELEN said a brief goodbye on the steps outside the Doge's palace, giving Tibor the name of his inn, just in case. Tibor watched him as he walked over the Piazza San Marco and disappeared from sight. The Hungarian made it look as if Tibor had been only one of many candidates for this strange assignment.

It had started to rain again: a fine, cold, persistent November rain. Tibor went back down the deserted alleys to the tavern on the Rio San Canciano, where the landlord and his two barmaids were still busy clearing up. The landlord was not pleased to see the troublemaker back. He told Tibor that the merchant had taken Tibor's stake and his chess set away as souvenirs. When Tibor asked for the Venetian's name and address, the landlord sent him packing.

Outside the tavern Tibor stood in the rain, undecided, until the two barmaids put their heads around the door. They'd tell Tibor the man's name and address, said one of them, but in return they wanted a look at his prick, because yesterday evening they'd been wondering if it was really true that dwarves have bigger cocks than ordinary men. Tibor was left speechless, but he had no choice. Without his chess set, he was finished. He made sure they were alone, then briefly exposed himself. The delighted barmaids giggled and gave Tibor the address.

TIBOR SPENT the rest of the day keeping watch outside the Venetian's palazzo. He was soon drenched by the rain, but the advantage of the weather was that the citizens—and most important of all, the carabinieri—hurried past and took no notice of him. With his hood over his head, he looked like a lost child.

Tibor had to possess his soul in patience until evening. Then the merchant came out of his house. He was wearing a black cape over a showy frock coat, with a plumed hat to keep the rain off. Tibor followed him at a suitable distance. In spite of the rain, the Venetian's sweet perfume was so strong that Tibor wouldn't have lost track of him even blindfolded. When they had walked down several streets, Tibor caught up with him. The merchant was surprised to see the dwarf again and put one hand to the hilt of his rapier to make sure it was at the ready. He did not stop, and Tibor had difficulty in keeping up.

"Go away, you little monster."

"I want my stake and my chess set back."

"How you managed to get out of the *piombi* I don't know, but I can make sure you go back there in no time at all."

"*You* should be shut up there! Give me my chess set!"

The merchant put a hand inside his cape and brought out Tibor's set. "This one?"

Tibor lunged for it, but the Venetian held it out of reach. "I'm off to play a few games with my lady friend. We have our own chess sets, of course, one pewter, one very valuable with marble chessmen, but this one"—and he shook Tibor's shabby chess set so that the chessmen inside rattled—"this one will give the whole thing a rustic touch. More personal."

"I can't live without my chess set!"

The merchant put the set away again. "All the better."

Tibor tugged at the man's cape. With one swift movement the Venetian had freed himself, drawn his sword, and held the blade to Tibor's throat. "Any aesthete would be grateful to me for slitting your throat, so don't give me an excuse."

Tibor raised his hands in a placatory gesture. The Venetian pushed the sword back into its sheath and walked away, laughing.

BY THE TIME the Venetian left his mistress's house just before morning to retrace his steps home, Tibor had spent eight hours imagining the two of them in the warm, surrounded by delicious food and wines and silken cushions, playing amateurish chess and then making love, laughing all the time at the thought of the inebriated, well-thrashed dwarf who now, in wet clothes and without a roof over his head, was longing to have his pathetic chessboard back. Tibor was prepared: he was ensconced in a narrow alley beside the canal on the Venetian's way home, hidden among the construction materials on a building site. He had found a rope and tied one end to a basket full of bricks standing at the side of the canal.

When the merchant came along, Tibor stretched the rope. His enemy fell to the ground, and Tibor was on him at once, tying his hands behind his back. Tibor had never stolen anything in his life; he just wanted to recover his own property. He would even forgo his stake. Once the merchant realized what was happening, he shouted for help. One of Tibor's hands closed over his mouth. With his other hand the dwarf tugged the chess set out from under the man's cape. But then the Venetian suddenly reared and threw Tibor off his back. The chess set dropped to the ground and fell open. The chessmen were scattered over the paving stones, and some of them fell into the water of the canal.

The Venetian was faster than Tibor. Since his arms were still pinioned, he gave Tibor a powerful kick. As the dwarf fell, his back hit the basket of bricks and sent it toppling over the edge into the canal. The rope stretched taut, hauling the merchant over the paving stones by his bonds. He screamed in horror as the weight of the bricks pulled him into the canal. Tibor, lying in his path, was dragged into the water with him.

No sooner was Tibor immersed than he started swimming, paddling vigorously like a dog. Under water a violent kick from the merchant connected with him. Tibor's clothes, which had been soaked immediately, dragged him down. His head hit a wall, and he felt his way up it. Back on the surface, he spat out the filthy-tasting canal water and clung to a projecting ledge.

Only after he had taken a couple of breaths did he realize that the merchant had not come up with him—and that the bricks and the rope were anchoring the man to the bottom. Motionless, Tibor watched as the ripples and rising air bubbles subsided. A last set of bubbles burst on the surface, and then all was still, except for Tibor's own gasping breath.

Tibor worked his way along the wall to the nearest ladder. As he moved along, he struck the drowned man's head with his foot. The contact filled him with sheer horror, and he expected the dead body to grasp him and pull him down any moment now. In panic, he grabbed the rungs of the ladder and hauled himself out of the water.

When Tibor had solid ground under his feet again, he stared at the black waters of the canal. He thought he saw a rat swimming on the surface, but it was only one of his chessmen. The Venetian's silly plumed hat was drifting past the opposite wall like a garishly colored duck. Nothing else was left of him. Tibor rapidly retrieved some of his chessmen, but the set was incomplete. In his haste, he threw the whole game into the water and realized too late that neither the board nor the pieces would sink. Then he ran for it.

. . .

THE NEAREST CHURCH was San Giovanni Elemosinario, but its doors wouldn't open. San Polo and San Stae were locked too. Tibor saw the rosy sky of dawn through the gap between two palazzi. He felt as if the sun were the eye of God and he must hide from it at any price. He wasn't going to face the light of day again until he had confessed his dreadful deed before an altar.

Finally the oak door of Santa Maria Gloriosa gave way, and Tibor breathed a sigh of relief when he was alone in the church. The smell of candle wax and incense calmed him. He dipped his fingers in some holy water and anointed his wet forehead. Then he went along the side aisle straight to the altar of the Virgin Mary, for he couldn't bear the sight of Jesus on the cross just now. The Savior in his bonds reminded him too vividly of what the Venetian would now be looking like in the canal.

Tibor fell on his knees before the mourning Madonna, repented of his sin, and prayed. Occasionally he glanced up, and from time to time it seemed to him that Mary was smiling a little more understandingly. Now that the tension was ebbing away from his body, Tibor began to freeze with cold. The chill crept up from the stone slabs into his wet clothes, and soon he was shaking all over. He wished himself in the warm arms of the Mother of God, where the naked baby Jesus now lay. But it was right that he should suffer: he had just killed a man.

EVEN IN THE WAR Tibor had remained free of that sin. At the age of fourteen, when he had been chased away from his parents' farm, his native village of Provesano, and the Republic of Venice because the neighbors made out that the little goblin was molesting village girls, he was picked up near Udine by a regiment of Austrian dragoons passing through. The soldiers were on their way north to take Silesia back from the thieving Prussians, and they recruited Tibor as boot-boy and lucky mascot.

So in the spring of 1759 Tibor found himself in the middle of the

Seven Years' War, which at this point had been raging for three years. The boot-boy accompanied his regiment to Silesia by way of Vienna and Prague, and the dragoons ascribed the defeat of the Prussian troops at Kunersdorf to his influence as a lucky charm. Tibor was present during the occupation of Berlin and led a reasonably good life in the army camps and occupied cities. He learned German, had a little uniform made to fit his small body, was well fed, and sometimes joined the soldiers in their drinking sprees.

But luck deserted the Austrians in November 1760. At the battle of Torgau, Tibor's regiment was wiped out by the Prussians. Although he had not been involved in the fighting, he took a musket ball in his thigh, so he didn't get far during the retreat by night. Mounted soldiers took him prisoner. Since the Prussian cuirassiers had lost more than half of their own men on the battlefield, they were bent on vengeance. The dwarf was an unusual item of loot, too good to be wasted in a quick execution. So the Prussians emptied a provisions barrel of the salt fish it had contained, stuffed Tibor inside it instead, nailed the lid back on the barrel, and threw the unfortunate dwarf into the river Elbe.

Tibor was imprisoned there for two days and two nights. He couldn't move, let alone free himself. The wound in his thigh had been only sketchily bandaged, and the icy waters of the Elbe seeped through a crack between the staves of the barrel. Tibor either had to caulk the leaky place or get it up above his head to keep from drowning. The barrel was both a prison and a lifeboat to him, for he couldn't swim. At first the overpowering smell of fish made him vomit, but two days later, starving, he was licking the salt from inside the staves. The exhausted dwarf shouted for help until his voice failed him. Then he remembered the medallion of the Virgin around his neck, and he sought salvation in prayer, promising Mother Mary never to touch a drop of drink again if she would free him from this floating dungeon. Six hours later he also promised her his virginity, and three hours later still he vowed to go into a monastery.

If he had waited one more hour he would have been saved anyway, even without that oath, for by now the barrel had reached Wittenberg. It was here, of all places, that some ferrymen fished Tibor out of the Elbe and freed him, and here of all places, in Luther's own city, he fell to the ground, covered it with kisses, and stammered Catholic prayers of gratitude—as if a salted dwarf stinking of fish and wearing a bloodstained dragoon's uniform weren't a strange enough sight in itself.

Tibor was taken into custody, his wound was tended, and his evil-smelling uniform burned. He quickly recovered and equally quickly grew impatient: he had given the Virgin Mary his word, and he wanted to put his vow into practice as soon as possible. But he had to wait three months before he was released. Then, although the war was still in full swing, keeping Tibor a prisoner was costing the Prussians more than anything he could be worth to the Austrians.

A free man again, Tibor joined a group of traveling showmen on their way to Poland. That was the quickest way back to Roman Catholic soil.

WHEN THE SOUND of bells roused Tibor from his devotions, the stone beneath his knees was dark with canal water. A few morning church-goers had assembled in the pews and outside the confessional. Tibor lit a candle for the dead man, said a prayer for his soul, and set off for Wolfgang von Kempelen's inn.

But the Hungarian Baron had already left. Even as Tibor was trying to quell his sense of panic, however, the porter added that Kempelen had been going to stop off to see a glassblower on the island of Murano before traveling home.

Tibor crossed to Murano and despite his disreputable appearance was taken to Signor Coppola's study at once. A servant led him through the glassworks to a door on which he knocked three times. While the two of them waited for some signal from within, the servant looked Tibor up and down, or rather one of his eyes looked Tibor up and down, for the other was still staring fixedly at the door as if it had a life of its own. And as if that wasn't enough, one of his eyes was brown and the other green. Tibor was toying with the idea of turning back when a voice inside the room told them to come in. Thereupon the squinting servant opened the door for Tibor.

Coppola's study looked like an alchemist's workshop, except that here the various jars, flasks, and vials themselves, not their contents, were the objects of interest. Wolfgang von Kempelen was sitting at the only table left clear in the middle of the room, which had no windows in its walls, and opposite him was Coppola, a portly, chinless man wearing a leather apron. A flat box lay on the table between them. Kempelen did not seem particularly surprised to see Tibor again.

"You've come at just the right moment," he greeted him. "Sit down."

Coppola nodded toward a stool, which Tibor drew up beside Kempelen. The master glassblower said nothing; nor did he seem much discomposed by Tibor's unusual build. However, he looked once into his eyes so penetratingly that Tibor blinked and had to glance away.

With a wave of his hand, Kempelen requested the stout Venetian to carry on. Coppola turned the box toward Kempelen and Tibor with its clasp facing them and ceremoniously opened it. Inside, embedded in small eye sockets lined with red velvet, lay twelve eyes—six pairs—with all their pupils staring at Tibor. It was such a shock that Tibor visibly started and crossed himself. Kempelen broke out laughing, and Coppola hoarsely joined in.

"Excellent!" Kempelen praised the glassblower in faultless Italian. "You could hardly ask for a better testimonial to your work."

Drawing a fabric glove over his fingers, Coppola picked a deep blue eye out of its velvet socket and placed it on a piece of cloth in front of Kempelen. Kempelen picked the eye up with rather less ceremony and turned it in his hand, so that the pupil kept peering out between his fingers. Then he put the eye back on the velvet lining beside its companion, but at such an angle that the lifeless pair of eyes now squinted horribly. Coppola handed Kempelen more eyes.

Tibor realized that they were made of glass and were not preserved eyes taken from dead bodies, as he had initially supposed. That, however, didn't make the sight of those six pairs of eyes much more tolerable.

When Kempelen had seen enough, he asked Tibor, "And which pair will be your eyes?"

"My . . . ?"

"For the automaton. Which would you choose for it?"

Tibor pointed to the squinting blue glass marbles. Coppola grunted approvingly, but Kempelen shook his head. "A blue-eyed Turk? The Empress would feel really cheated."

WOLFGANG VON KEMPELEN was in a hurry to get back to Pressburg, and that suited Tibor very well. Sometime or other a gondola was going to bump into the merchant's body, and then people would start looking for the dwarf. Kempelen didn't ask why Tibor had changed his mind so quickly. On the mainland, in Mestre, he bought him new clothes, and they climbed into a barouche.

The next day Tibor had a bad attack of influenza. Kempelen provided medicine and blankets for the invalid but did not interrupt their journey. Meanwhile he negotiated the terms of their contract with Tibor. Kempelen was offering a weekly wage of five guilders, with free board and lodging, and an extra bonus of fifty guilders if the performance before the Empress was a success. Tibor was so overwhelmed by these figures that he never even dreamed of haggling.

TIBOR HAD last held a steady job in the summer of the year 1761, in the Polish monastery of Obra, to which he had fled from Prussia. He worked as a gardener, learned to read and write, and daily thanked God the Father, the Savior, and above all the Holy Mother of God for the safety of the monastery walls. He did not become a monk, but then he hadn't actually promised the Virgin Mary to take vows.

In fact Tibor's time in the monastery lasted not forever but only four years. A small group of novices indulged in playing chess, in defiance of the abbot's ban on it, and Tibor was initiated into the "Game of Kings" himself. One of the novices explained the rules to the dwarf, and from his first game on Tibor defeated all his opponents. It seemed incredible that he had never played chess before. Over the weeks he became a great attraction: more and more monks were admitted to the secret chess club, played against this newly discovered chess genius, and lost to him. The dwarf enjoyed the admiration of the brothers, until one bad loser alerted the abbot to the gaming going on within his walls. A scapegoat was required, and the lot fell on Tibor. With one accord, all the novices swore that the dwarf had tempted them to play, and he had to leave Obra. He was paid his wages and given the chess set, for after all—or so the novices told the abbot—he had smuggled it into the monastery himself.

In the autumn of 1765, then, Tibor was on the road once more, and as it was a cold autumn, he decided to go south. It took him three more years to get back to the Venetian Republic. The chess set had cost him his job in the monastery, and now it was to earn him a living: he made money in the taverns along his way by winning his opponents' stakes. Often he would play for payment in kind: a meal here, a bed for the night there, a seat in the mail coach. He could undoubtedly have earned more in towns, but he avoided places of any size. It was bad enough to have a whole village gawping at him.

The small chess player was a sensation in the villages, but he was never popular, certainly not when he won the villagers' money. Tibor sought comfort from their hostility in praying to the Madonna, and he took time off to visit every roadside shrine and every chapel along his way. But the remote Mother of God wasn't always there for Tibor, so he found another and far more physical comfort: brandy. Since he spent most of the time when he wasn't on the road in hostelries, strong liquor was readily available. One night, on the border of the Venetian Republic, the inebriated Tibor was beaten and robbed on the road by villagers from whom he had won over forty guilders the day before.

Now aged twenty-four, he returned to his native land in the summer of 1769—on foot, in rags, a drunk. A few months later he left it again in Kempelen's fine carriage, wearing good clothes and with a purse full of coins.

BARON WOLFGANG VON KEMPELEN and Tibor Scardanelli reached their journey's end on the afternoon of St. Nicholas's Day. Shortly before they came to the bridge over the Danube leading to Pressburg on the far side of the river, Kempelen had the carriage halted on a slight rise. Gentle snow was falling, but it melted as soon as it touched the ground.

When Tibor had urinated, he scrutinized the city. By comparison with Venice, Pressburg appeared almost boring: a neat, tidy place that had spilled beyond its original town walls, with the huts of fishermen and ferrymen in front of it, and vineyards stretching away behind. Only St. Martin's Cathedral with its green tower really caught the eye. To the left rose Castle Mount, with the bulky shape of the castle lying on it like a table turned upside down, its four corner towers reaching into the gray sky like the table legs.

The Danube rolled lethargically past Pressburg and on along its course, divided by an island in the middle of it. Kempelen came up beside Tibor and pointed to a pontoon bridge linking the two banks. "See that? A floating bridge. If ships want to get past, the two halves of the bridge come apart and join up again later."

"A floating bridge?"

"Exactly. Extraordinary structure, don't you agree? Now ask me who built the bridge."

"Who did build the bridge?"

"Wolfgang von Kempelen. And a man who can build a floating bridge over the biggest river in Europe will surely be able to hide a dwarf in a piece of furniture." Kempelen knelt down beside Tibor and put a hand on his shoulder. "Take a good look at the city, because you won't be seeing much of it for the next few months."

"Why not?"

"Simple. Because none of the people of Pressburg must ever set eyes on you."

"What?"

"A man of your height who's also a brilliant chess player is living in the Kempelen household, and a few months later Baron Wolfgang von Kempelen unveils a chess-playing machine . . . don't you think someone might put two and two together?"

Tibor's eyes lingered on St. Martin's Cathedral. He would very much have liked to see the Madonna there, just once.

"I'm sorry, but those are my conditions. Don't forget, I have far more to lose than you." Kempelen clapped Tibor encouragingly on the back. "But never fear, my house is a city in itself. You'll lack for nothing there." Kempelen stood up again, brushed the soil off his knees, and went back to the carriage. He stood there like a footman, holding the door open for Tibor, and sketched a bow.

"Now, your first rehearsal in keeping out of sight, please."

Tibor clambered into the barouche, and a little later the two of them crossed the river over Kempelen's pontoon bridge.

Pressburg, Donaugasse

KEMPELEN'S HOUSE LAY JUST OUTSIDE THE CITY WALLS, not far from the Lorenz Gate, where Klemensgasse led into Donaugasse. It had three stories, and unlike the neighboring houses it had bars over not only its ground-floor windows but the windows on the first floor too. Darkness had already fallen, so no one saw the small, dwarfish figure climb out of the carriage and enter the house. As soon as they were in the front hall, Kempelen asked Tibor to go ahead up to the workshop on the top floor. Tibor climbed the dimly lit staircase, taking off the scarf, cap, and heavy coat that Kempelen had bought him. Portraits and maps hung on the walls, and he saw the family emblem on the first-floor landing— a tree above a crown. Up on the top floor Tibor opened the double doors leading into the Baron's workshop.

The room where Tibor was to spend almost every waking hour during the coming months was about eight paces long and six wide. The left-hand wall had three tall windows in it, and since the curtains were not drawn over them, a little light from the streetlamps outside fell into the workshop. Two doors, one in the right-hand wall and one at the far end of the room, opened into other rooms beyond them. Countless books stood on oak shelves, most of them behind glass doors to protect them from the dust of the workshop. The tools of the joiner's, metalworker's, and watchmaker's trades lay on two tables and a workbench—T-squares, planes, hammers, drills, chisels, gravers, scissors, knives, clamps, rasps, and, above all, files and pliers in every imaginable size, as well as other instruments that Tibor had never seen before, and finally magnifying glasses and mirrors that reflected the faint light from the street. Materials were stacked under the tables and along the walls: boards and battens, paint, wires, cables and cords, iron pins and nails, thin metal disks, and many different kinds of textiles. Where the walls had no furniture against them, the French wallpaper was almost entirely covered by engravings and drawings. Most of these sketches were construction designs that Tibor didn't understand, but in the twilight he could also make out several more representational drawings which reminded him of the sketch that Wolfgang von Kempelen had shown him in his prison cell in Venice.

But Tibor saw all this only out of the corner of his eye. What held him spellbound from the first was the object in the middle of the room, covered with a linen cloth and waiting for its maker's return. The shapes outlined under the fabric told Tibor that it was the chess machine. He could make out a head and shoulders, and the tabletop for the chess-board in front of them. Tibor approached the automaton with care, as if approaching a corpse, and just as one might draw back a winding-sheet, Tibor lifted the linen.

The sight made him shudder. The chess player sitting on a stool behind the cabinet with his legs crossed—or perhaps her legs, for the sex of this artificial human being could not yet be determined—was no more than a mutilated skeleton. Its breast and back were open, revealing not ribs and muscles but battens and cables; its left arm ended just above the wrist, as if someone had chopped its hand off, and three cables stuck out of the stump. Most horrible of all, however, was the chess player's face, or rather its head, because there was no face at all. There was the end of a tube where the mouth should have been, and instead of eyes two strings ended in the eye sockets like useless optic nerves. The skull in the shadows behind the sockets was empty. Tibor was so spellbound by the sight of this wooden monstrosity that it was a long time before he remembered to cross himself.

Suddenly the door that Tibor had closed behind him opened, and a man who wasn't Kempelen came in with an oil lamp. Was Tibor supposed to hide from him? As his head hardly came above the top of the chess cabinet, the man didn't see him. He was lighting all the oil lamps in the room, his back turned to Tibor. He was slender, his untidy dark-blond hair almost flopped into his eyes, he wore a pair of spectacles, and he had gloves with their finger-ends cut off on his hands. He was probably about Tibor's own age. A floorboard creaked under Tibor's weight. The man spun around and saw the dwarf. The sight startled him so much that he clutched at his heart with his free hand and swore.

For a moment the two of them scrutinized each other in silence, and then a smile spread over the face of the man looking at Tibor. He started roaring with laughter and seemed unable to stop.

"Amazing," said the man, once he had pulled himself together. "You really are a . . . a small sensation." He laughed again at this joke and went on laughing until Kempelen joined them.

"Ah, so you two have met! Tibor, this is my assistant Jakob. Jakob, meet Tibor Scardanelli from Provesano." Reluctantly, Tibor took the proffered hand. The assistant shook hands vigorously.

"You'll be spending a lot of time together," said Kempelen. "Jakob is helping me to design the chess player. He made the cabinet, now he's going to build the Turk too."

"The Turk?"

"Yes, first we planned our automaton as a young woman, a charming creature with porcelain skin and a silk dress, but then we changed our minds." Kempelen laid a hand on the unfinished android's shoulder. "This will be no pretty mademoiselle but a fierce Mussulman. A Saracen, the terror of the Crusaders, murderer of Christian children, answerable only to himself and Allah. We want to scare our opponents a little. And after all, the game of chess comes from the Orient. So who should be master of it if not an Oriental?"

Jakob moved to take Tibor's topcoat from him. "That's enough talking. Let's see how his brain fits into the skull."

"Not now, Jakob. We have a long journey behind us, and we don't want to let our guest out of one box and force him straight into another. Take him to his room."

Jakob led Tibor into a small room opening off a corridor behind the door on the right. It was furnished with the necessities, a bed, table, chair, and washbasin, and there was a small window looking out on the inner courtyard, but even a man of normal height could have seen out of it only by standing on tiptoe. Kempelen's assistant brought Tibor bedclothes and a chamber pot, and a little later Kempelen himself came in carrying a tray laid with Tibor's supper: some brown bread and ham, hot tea, and two glasses. As they drank, Kempelen told Tibor about the rest of the household.

"My wife and child and three servants live in this house. I'll soon introduce my wife to you, but you're not likely to be seeing the domestic staff. My manservant gives me no cause for concern, but the maid and the cook are simple folk, and women at that. The fair sex isn't exactly known for its discretion, so they mustn't find out anything about you. They have instructions to enter my living quarters only by permission, and to keep out of the workshop entirely, so you won't see them up here at all. If you want to take a bath or relieve yourself, you'll have to do it at night. And if there's anything you need, ask Jakob first. He has lodgings near the castle, but when he's working late, he often sleeps in the workshop. I'm not afraid of spies; it's the ordinary people of Pressburg, the peasants, the servants, the Slovaks—they all have the bad habit of curiosity, which is outdone only by their superstition." Kempelen sipped his tea. "I'm sorry to have to burden you with so many rules and regulations, but this is an ambitious project, and I can't afford to let it fail. One careless mistake could ruin everything."

Tibor nodded.

"Are you happy with your room? Is there anything else you need?"

"A crucifix."

Kempelen smiled. "By all means." Then he rose to his feet. "Goodnight, Tibor. I look forward to working with you. I feel sure that our meeting will prove very advantageous to both of us."

"Yes. Goodnight, Signore Kempelen."

IN THE MORNING LIGHT next day Tibor had a chance to examine the automaton at length. The chess table, or rather cabinet, at which the android sat was four feet long, two and a half feet deep, and three feet high. There were casters on its four feet. It had three doors in front: a single door on the left, a double door on the right. Below these doors a long drawer ran the entire length of the cabinet. Both the drawer and the doors were fitted with locks. There were two doors with locks at the back of the cabinet too, one to the right and one to the left of the chess player, both of them noticeably smaller than the doors in front. The stool on which the android sat was firmly attached to the chess cabinet. The frame of the cabinet was walnut, and the doors had a decorative grained veneer. The tabletop slid over the cabinet itself and could be pulled back only in front, away from the android. There was a square recess in the middle of the tabletop, into which the chessboard now lying on one of the workbenches would soon be fitted.

When Jakob and Kempelen carefully slid the top off the cabinet and opened all five doors, Tibor could see the internal organization of the machine. Its base was entirely covered by green baize. Like the doors on the front of the cabinet, the interior was divided into two compartments, the left-hand one occupying a third of the space and the right-hand one the other two-thirds. The two compartments were completely cut off from each other by a wooden partition. The one on the right was empty except for two curved pieces of brass that looked like parts of a sextant.

The clockwork of the automaton was in the smaller, left-hand compartment. At the bottom of the mechanism lay a cylinder with pins sticking out of it at irregular intervals. A comb with eleven metal teeth was fitted above the cylinder. Tibor supposed that the pins were to strike or move these teeth in different sequences, like the strings of a clavichord or harpsichord. He had seen something similar before, but on a much smaller scale, in a musical box: if you turned a handle the little cylinder went around, and pins struck metal tongues of different lengths, producing notes that joined together to play a tune.

Kempelen told Jakob to wind the clockwork up. The assistant put a crank into a hole in the left-hand side of the table and turned it several times. The cylinder began revolving, and the intricate collection of cogwheels and springs of different sizes behind the cylinder and the comb moved too. Tibor watched the clockwork closely, expecting something to happen, but he saw only the continuous movement of the wheels.

"What does that clockwork do?" asked Tibor, when he had watched it long enough for the demands of civility.

"It makes a noise, that's all," replied the assistant, before Kempelen could reply.

"Jakob's right," Kempelen confirmed. "The idea is to make it look and sound like a complicated bit of clockwork. You'll be doing the real work, so the machinery is purely ornamental. Just an extra."

"Just an illusion," Jakob corrected him.

Tibor was surprised by the liberties the assistant took, but once again Kempelen didn't seem to mind. "Or an illusion, if you like."

Tibor looked at the chess machine again. He was small, but not so small that he could fit into the cabinet—let alone move inside it. The large right-hand compartment might perhaps have been large enough but for the curved pieces of brass inside it.

Kempelen anticipated Tibor's question. "So now the magic begins."

Jakob put his hand inside the table and pushed aside the partition between the two compartments—for it was not just a single partition but a partition in two halves, and now the two compartments suddenly became one. Nor was that all: Jakob folded back a hinged, baize-covered wooden flap on the floor of the right-hand compartment. Finally, the last illusion was the drawer under the three doors, for it was only half as deep as the cabinet, so that once the false base was removed, there was about ten inches more room inside.

Jakob brought Tibor a stool, and as the other two supported him, he climbed into the machine, sat down on the left behind the clockwork, and stretched his legs out into the space left behind the half-drawer. There was enough room. He wasn't touching anything, not even the clockwork next to his right shoulder. Wolfgang von Kempelen might have made the automaton especially to fit his measurements. The pride on the inventor's face was obvious.

"But how am I supposed to play chess in here?" asked Tibor. "I can hardly move."

There was a board in the side of the cabinet to Tibor's left, where the android was sitting. Kempelen released a latch, and the board folded down on Tibor's lap. Through the opening it had left, Tibor could see into the wooden figure's internal arrangements. Kempelen pulled a brass rod out of the android's stomach, guided it to the board on Tibor's lap, and moved it several times. The Turk's left arm moved simultaneously.

"This is called a pantograph," he explained. "Every movement you make with it down here will be made on a larger scale by the Turk up above. So far it can only move its arm, but soon it will have a hand too, and then it will be able be able to pick up the chessmen."

"But how will I be able to see the chessboard?"

Kempelen drew his breath in sharply. "Well, that's a problem we still have to solve. But I already have several ideas."

"And the chessmen—how can I . . ."

"We still have four months to go, Tibor. Within that time we'll have the answer to all your questions." Kempelen and Jakob picked up the table-top that they had removed. "Now we're going to leave you in the dark."

The two of them slid the tabletop back into place. Jakob closed all the doors. For a moment Tibor felt as if he were sitting at the bottom of a square well, for some light still fell in through the recess in the middle of the tabletop—but then Kempelen fitted the chessboard into it, and everything was pitch-dark. Sounds from outside were audible but muted. However, the loudest noise that Tibor heard was his own breathing.

"Now for a game of blindman's buff," he heard Jakob saying outside, and then the cabinet moved. Jakob was turning it on its own axis on the casters.

The swaying motion suddenly brought back Tibor's memories of those two days floating along the river Elbe, shut up in a wooden barrel without any hope of rescue. His hands instinctively clenched into fists. His heart was in his mouth, and every time it beat, he felt as if his head were swelling and then deflating again. The roar of his bloodstream in his ears was like the rushing of the river. The side of the cabinet to his left and the clockwork on his right suddenly seemed to be moving, as if they wanted to crush him between them, as if the sharp teeth of the cog-wheels were going to tear him to pieces. The air was stuffy, with a heavy smell of wood and oil. Tibor was going to ask them politely to slide the tabletop off again, but as soon as he opened his mouth, he found that he was screaming, screaming for help first in German, then in Italian. He had seen the boards used to make the chess cabinet, and he knew they were so thick that he could never get out on his own. If no one outside helped him, he was nailed up alive in a coffin. He'd be battering the walls until he suffocated, died of thirst, or went out of his mind.

When Jakob and Kempelen had removed the tabletop and hauled Tibor out of the machine by his arms, he was drenched with sweat and as pale as the android's incomplete face. Kempelen brought him a glass of water; Jakob handed him a towel. The dwarf felt even smaller as he sat on a chair drying the sweat from his face, while Kempelen and his assistant looked down on him.

"Is there anything you haven't told me?" asked Wolfgang von Kempelen finally, when Tibor had emptied his glass of water.

"No, it was the darkness."

"You'll have a candle."

"I'll get used to it. I promise."

Kempelen nodded but did not take his eyes off Tibor. Jakob was already beginning to grin again. "A dwarf afraid of the dark! Wonders will never cease! I thought it was dark as pitch down in those mines of yours, right?"

That was the end of the day's work for Tibor, and he returned to his room. Kempelen gave him a small chessboard to take with him, and all the books about chess that he possessed—Silenus's *Chess; or, The Game of*

Kings, Rabbi Ibn Ezra's *The Art of Playing Chess,* Stamma's *Essai sur le jeu des échecs,* a copy of his *Secrets of the Game of Chess;* also, of course, Philidor's famous *The Art of Becoming a Master at Chess,* and, finally, fresh off the press in Venice, *Il giuoco incomparabile degli scacchi*— telling him to study them in the next few weeks in order to perfect his game. Tibor knew of these books but had never actually seen any of them. And now he had all six in his hands. He put the rabbi's book at the bottom of the pile and opened Stamma first, but to his disappointment it was a French edition, not a German translation. He tried deciphering the contents with the aid of his Italian mother tongue, but it was hard work, and he finally lost his powers of concentration entirely as he imagined Kempelen and his ill-natured assistant wondering whether he, Tibor, was really the right man for the chess machine's first appearance before Her Majesty the Empress. His own doubts of the whole project had not changed in any essentials, but he didn't like to think that others might doubt his abilities too.

That afternoon Tibor was invited down to the first floor to meet Kempelen's wife, Anna Maria, and his daughter, Mária Teréz, in the drawing room. Anna Maria von Kempelen was slender, brown-haired, and attractive, but a constantly suspicious expression marred her features. She held the child all the time, even when she was asleep, and Tibor felt that she was doing it just so that she wouldn't have to give him her hand. Kempelen had provided coffee and cakes, so Tibor sat there eating gingerbread and drinking coffee with cream out of fine porcelain, while Kempelen allowed not so much as a moment's awkward silence: he talked without stopping, trying to interest Anna Maria in Tibor and vice versa—he spoke of Tibor's adventures and the time Anna Maria had spent as companion to Countess Erdödy—but his cheerful conversation was of no avail. Anna Maria responded in monosyllables to her husband's remarks. When Tibor boldly ventured to praise the delicious Advent gingerbread, she replied briefly and without looking at him that Katarina the cook had made it, not she herself. The most difficult moment of all came when Kempelen left the room to fetch more gingerbread. The two of them were silent for a whole minute, which Tibor spent examining a portrait of the Empress, listening to the sleeping child's breathing and the ticking of the grandfather clock and hoping Kempelen would soon be back from the kitchen. Kempelen brought this coffee party to an end after half an hour, saying, "Well, we still have work to do," and Tibor hoped he would never have to see Anna Maria again. If it had been up to her, he was sure he never *would* see her again. He didn't know if it was he himself that she disliked so much, or just the part he was playing in the fraudulent affair of the chess automaton. Probably a little of both.

IN THE DAYS leading up to Christmas, the three men tried to find a way for Tibor to see the chessboard. They experimented with a semitransparent board and a periscope inside the torso of the Turk, but neither idea really worked. The workshop couldn't be adequately heated, so the three of them worked in topcoats and wore gloves. When they stopped for a break, Tibor sat by one of the windows to look down at Donaugasse and the people of Pressburg walking through the snow, farmers and fishermen on their way to market, the nobility on horseback or in coaches, charcoal burners with sleighs laden with coal and firewood, tradesmen and servants: all of them people whom Tibor would never meet. He could see them, but they didn't see him. He liked that.

Wolfgang von Kempelen was often out. Although the Empress had given him leave of absence from his duties, many tasks still required his presence. He had to go to the Royal Hungarian Chamber several times a week. At these times Tibor would rather have withdrawn to his room to read the books Kempelen had given him and play the championship chess games noted down in them—but work on the chess machine came first, so he had to help Jakob, whose company he found as uncongenial as Anna Maria's.

While they practiced the use of the pantograph, Jakob, as so often, sang one of his scurrilous songs.

His Grace the Pope lives very well from pardons that his churchmen sell.
He drinks the finest of choice wine, I wish the Pope's good life were mine.

But no, poor soul: no girl's sweet kiss transports him to the realms of bliss.
For warmth in bed he cannot hope; I wouldn't want to be the Pope.

The Sultan lives in splendid style, you'd think that he would
    always smile.
With lovely virgins he may play, I'd be the Sultan any day.
But no, the rules of his Koran forbid him liquor, the poor man.
He may not drink a drop of wine—the Sultan's life will not be mine.

I wouldn't want to live their lives—no liquor or no merry wives?
Put them together, though, let's see . . . yes, happily I'd either be.
Come here, my love, give me a kiss, the Sultan's joys I'd hate to miss.
And pour some wine, my pious brothers, here's to the Pope and all
    you others!

"You know something?" said Jakob, having finished his song. "It's a funny thing, but you'll never, not in a hundred years, get to be that towering figure in the world of chess, a grandmaster."

"Why not?"

"Well, look at you," said Jakob, starting to laugh already. "A *grand-master*? A towering figure? I mean, it's physically impossible!"

Jakob roared with laughter, and Tibor felt so angry that he made the Turk's arm hit Jakob in the face just as he was bending over it. The assistant's spectacles fell off and into the machine, and he put a hand to his nose. When he took it away again, there was blood on it. Incredulously, Jakob wiped the blood from his nostrils and looked at it on his hand.

"Did you see that?" he indignantly asked Tibor.

Tibor prepared for Kempelen's assistant to attack him. He might be small, but he was strong, and he had dealt with much more formidable opponents before.

But Jakob didn't move from the spot. "It hit me!" He turned to the android and shouted, "I'm your creator, you ungrateful thing! What's the idea, attacking your father like that? If it happens again, you'll be firewood." Then he burst into his usual hearty laughter.

This was the last reaction that Tibor had expected. Jakob smacked the Turk on the back of its head, wiped the blood from his face, and then went on working as if nothing had happened.

That day a second chessboard was fitted to the flap that lay on Tibor's lap when he was inside the machine, so that he could duplicate the game being played on the tabletop of the cabinet. Wolfgang von Kempelen had the idea of using the same chessboard as a scale for determining the position of the automaton's hand: he adjusted the pantograph so that when Tibor held its end above a square, the chess-playing Turk's hand hovered above the corresponding square on the upper level. As the pantograph now had a grip fitted for moving the Turk's fingers, Tibor was able to pick up and move chessmen on the board above. The one disadvantage of this solution to the problem was that he had to look sideways at the chessboard in front of him, for as the chessmen stood on the android's board above, they were to his own right and left. At first Tibor found it difficult to think around an angle of ninety degrees, and although he still won every game, adjusting his ideas was a laborious process and gave him a headache.

THE SNOWFALLS of the last few days gave way to hazy, still, cold weather, and on 22 December the chess automaton was covered with its linen cloth again. "We've done enough for the time being. Let's give ourselves and the automaton a week off."

When Kempelen was in his study, Jakob said goodbye to Tibor. "Happy Christmas. You'll be bored to death. I hope at least those books will keep you company."

"Are you celebrating Christmas with your family?"

"No and no. My parents are either in Prague or dead, or both. And I don't celebrate Christmas anyway."

"Why not?"

"Because of my religion."

Tibor frowned. "You're not a Lutheran, are you?"

Jakob raised his hands in reassurance. "God forbid, no! I'm Jewish."

Tibor was dumbfounded. The assistant relished the sight and clapped him on the shoulder. "We'll see each other in the New Year. Meanwhile I'd be happy to ask you out for a glass of mulled wine, but we both know you're not allowed to leave these hallowed precincts."

When Jakob had left, Tibor addressed Kempelen. "Is he really a Jew?"

"Yes."

"But he's fair-haired."

"Not all Jews have black hair, humps on their backs, and hooked noses, my dear fellow."

"Why didn't you tell me?"

"What difference would it have made?" Before Tibor could think of an answer, Kempelen was going on. "His religion doesn't matter to me. He could be a Mussulman or a Brahmin or a worshipper of the Great Manitou, and it wouldn't make a jot of difference to the fact that he's an excellent carver and joiner. Anyway, you have the Jews to thank for it that you can make a living from chess. But for them we'd still be playing the game with dice today, or maybe not at all."

Jakob surprised Tibor not just by being a Jew but with a present that Kempelen handed him on Christmas Eve. It was a chessman that Jakob had carved for him—a white horse with a dwarf whose face resembled Tibor's sitting on its back. The figure was not particularly finely worked, but Jakob must have spent a couple of hours on it. Tibor looked closely at the horse and its rider, but he could see no mockery in it, nor anything specifically Jewish.

Kempelen's present was far more valuable: it was the traveling chessboard on which they had played their first game together—complete with the red queen whom Kempelen had kept back at the time.

Kempelen invited Tibor to celebrate with him and his family, but he declined with thanks, not wishing to put any more of a strain on marital relations between Kempelen and Anna Maria. On Christmas Eve Kempelen and his family left the house to go to Mass at St. Martin's Cathedral. Tibor would have liked to go there with them. It was a month since he had set foot in a church, made confession, or received the Holy Sacraments. He stayed in the house by himself, praying before his plain crucifix, until the bells pealed out at midnight through the city streets.

THE JEW'S PROPHECY proved accurate. Tibor was bored and longed for any kind of company—even Jakob would have been better than isolation. He did not read much, and he played no chess at all, since he didn't want to think about the board lying at the wrong angle in front of him, at least for a few days. Instead he slept more than he needed to.

Three days after Christmas a child's scream woke him from his afternoon nap. Tibor sat up on his bed and waited for the noise to come again. It wasn't really screaming, more a kind of crowing, an animal sound that varied neither in pitch nor in volume. As if someone were torturing a child who automatically screamed but felt no real pain. It could only be Teréz. Tibor leaped up, left his room, and followed the screams, which obviously came from Kempelen's study. Tibor crossed the workshop and opened the unlocked study door without knocking.

Kempelen's study was distinctly smaller than the workshop, with cupboards to right and left and a desk in the middle of the room, placed where daylight would fall in over the back of anyone who sat there writing. Beside the door hung a map of Europe and a painting of Maria Theresia at her coronation. A dress sword in an ornamental scabbard leaned against the wall. On the desk, surrounded by tools, stood a painted plaster bust showing a section through a human head. It looked as if a sword-stroke had cut it cleanly in half, exposing the interior of the head; you could see the skull, the brain, the teeth, and the nasal and oral cavities, two large caverns ending in a narrow pharynx that went down the throat. The tongue was not long and flat but a fleshy lump. Horrible as the sight was, however, it was not this model that had uttered the screams, but a small object held in Wolfgang von Kempelen's hands, consisting of two shell-shaped pieces one above the other like a half-opened walnut, with a pair of bellows that he was working to blow air into them.

There must be a tongue somewhere inside the shells, and the air passing in made it produce that penetrating sound. Kempelen seemed amused by Tibor's astonishment.

"Good morning," he said, seeing the drowsiness still on Tibor's face.

"What's that?" asked Tibor.

"My speaking machine. Or at least the beginnings of it. The *a* sound. I didn't want to neglect it entirely. I told you about it in Venice, don't you remember? This is only one sound," said Kempelen, making the scream emerge again, "but one day I'll have a whole set of them, sounds and syllables arranged like organ notes, and if you play them in a certain order, the machine will talk to you. A speaking machine."

"But what for?"

"What for? I'm afraid you share that narrow-minded attitude with a great many of our contemporaries. A speaking machine, my dear fellow, is far more useful than a machine that plays chess. Imagine if the mute could suddenly talk again! The speechless would have their voices back! What a great thing that would be!"

On realizing that Tibor did not share his opinion, however, Kempelen dismissed the subject. "Well, how are you? Do you have enough to read? Just help yourself, my library is large. And you're on holiday now, so why not read a book that has nothing at all to do with chess?"

"I can't read anymore. The letters are already dancing in front of my eyes."

"Ah. So what can I do that you'd like?"

"I'd like to go out of doors."

"Hm. I see." Kempelen turned to the window and looked out into the inner courtyard of the building, as if he might find the reason why Tibor wanted to leave the house there. It was early afternoon. A gray mist hung in the air, and soon it would be dark. Kempelen drummed his fingers on the top of his desk. Then he took a key from the drawer on his right, put it in his coat pocket, and stood up.

"Let's go. Put something warm on; I saw an ice floe drifting down the Danube yesterday with two freezing ducks for passengers."

They went into the inner courtyard and through the carriage entrance to the street. Kempelen put a hood that almost entirely hid Tibor's face over his head, and asked him to take his hand.

"Do you think I'll run away?" inquired Tibor indignantly.

Kempelen smiled. "No, I just want it to look as if I'm taking a child for a walk. I've told you once already: no one in Pressburg must know that Wolfgang von Kempelen has a dwarf in his house."

Hand in hand, the two of them turned right into Donaugasse, going away from the city. Kempelen's anxieties were groundless; there were few people out and about in the bitter cold, and those who had ventured into the streets were too intent upon getting home quickly and into the warm to speak to the odd couple. To the right, in the gaps between buildings, Tibor saw the Danube flowing sluggishly on, and when he turned, he saw the city wall, the church spires, and the mighty castle beyond them. There was so little wind that the many plumes of smoke rose vertically to the gray sky, and the cawing of the crows circling slowly among them could be heard clearly.

Then they reached their destination: the large cemetery of St. Andrew's, where the dead had no company but their own on a day like this. Kempelen saw that they were alone and let go of Tibor's hand. Tibor was a little disappointed to find that his first and probably only outing was to be to a graveyard. He would have preferred a marketplace, or some kind of festivity, or a walk through the inner city. But he greedily drew in breaths of cold air, looked at the shrubs and trees, their branches bare in winter, and read the inscriptions on the gravestones and the slabs. The cemetery still lay blanketed in the snow that crunched under their boots. The two men did not talk.

As Tibor was reading the name *von Kempelen,* his companion stopped. Kempelen had brought Tibor to his family vault, a little mausoleum built in the style of a temple and surrounded by ivy. A few ivy leaves stuck through the snow here and there. On the pediment stood an angel with hands outspread, its white marble blackened by water and the years. The two unglazed windows, like the door, were barred. Kempelen took the key out of his coat pocket and opened the barred door. In silence, he stood back to let Tibor go first.

It was cramped inside the vault, and sounds were as muted as they were inside the chess machine when it was closed. In the dim light Tibor read the names and dates of birth and death carved into the stone and gilded. Kempelen had taken off his tricorne and was picking up the dead leaves blown in over the floor of the vault by the wind. Tibor read the name *Andreas Johann Christoph von Kempelen*.

"Your father?"

"No, my father's Engelbert, over here. Andreas was my eldest brother. He died when I was eighteen. He'd just been appointed tutor to the young Emperor when consumption took him from us."

Kempelen took a step to the right, where the gilded letters were brighter and more recent: *Franzciska von Kempelen, née Piani, died 1757*.

"Franzciska. My first wife. She died less than two months after our wedding—think of that. It was the smallpox."

"I'm sorry." Tibor felt all the sorrier because he instantly imagined Franzciska as much more appealing than the present Frau von Kempelen.

"You may often have grieved for having few friends and being thrown out by your own family," said Kempelen, "but never forget, those who have no dear ones can't lose them."

Kempelen knelt down as if to pray, for the last three names were quite close to the floor: *Julianna, Marie-Anna,* and *Andreas Christian von Kempelen*. All of them had died in the year when they were born; their dates of birth and death alike were *1763, 1764, 1766*. With his free hand Kempelen brushed dust from the letters.

"Little Andreas. Called after his dead uncle. Perhaps it was a bad omen. He was born on Christmas Eve, struggled for breath for three days, and died as soon as Christmas was over. He'd be five now."

Tibor wanted to say something as wise and comforting as Kempelen had said to him just now, but he could think of nothing. Kempelen was silent, his gaze no longer fixed on the lettering but on some point far beyond it. The dead leaves rustled in his hand.

"I know!" he said after quite a long time. Tibor looked at him. "I know a way for you to see the chessmen even from inside the cabinet." He straightened up, threw the leaves out of the doorway, put his three-cornered hat on again, and knocked the dirt off his gloves. "Let's go home. My wife has bought some cocoa—she can make us hot chocolate."

As soon as the New Year had come and Jakob was back, Kempelen explained his idea: there was no need to see the chessboard at all. It would be enough to know which piece had just been moved. So he was going to insert strong magnets into all the pieces, and he would fit something to the underside of the chessboard for the magnets to draw up and then drop again when the chessmen were moved.

"That won't be any help," said Jakob. "Tibor will only see which piece is being moved, not where it's put down again."

"Think about it, idiot. The magnet will act on the device under the new square too. Tibor just has to watch the chessboard carefully."

The break had done the three men good. They were working with more energy than in the Old Year, and even Kempelen was infected by Jakob's jokes. "We'll be following in that French charlatan's footsteps after all when we appear in front of the Empress. Hidden magnets will operate our own machine too."

They drove sixty-four brass nails into the undersides of the squares. A little iron disk with a central hole bored into it was fitted on each nail. Once a magnet was placed on a square, it pulled up the metal disk; when it was taken away again, the metal disk fell back onto the head of the nail.

Kempelen sent his manservant Branislav to Vienna to buy an identical set of magnets. Three days later Branislav brought back a box of bar magnets packed in straw to protect them from being shaken about on the journey, and it was laborious but entertaining work for Jakob and Tibor to separate the magnets, which were now wedged firmly together. The magnet idea worked perfectly, and even if Tibor happened to miss seeing which little metal disk was being raised or dropped at a given moment, he could reconstruct the state of the game with the aid of his own chessboard. In accordance with Philippe Stamma's system, both Tibor's chessboard and the one in front of the android had the horizontal lines of squares marked with the letters *a* to *h,* while the vertical lines were numbered 1 to 8.

So they had cleared all the major hurdles. Now that there was no more need for access to the rods and cables inside the android, Jakob could put flesh on its bones and give its head a face. He began his work by setting the two brown glass eyes that Kempelen had bought from Signore Coppola in Venice into the skull, in a way allowing Tibor to move them by pulling a cable. The effect was startling. As soon as Tibor moved those glass eyes, it really did look as if the android were a living creature closely watching its opponent's moves. Kempelen also thought up an ingenious device enabling Tibor to move the Turk's head forward and back again.

Jakob's second task was to make sixteen red and sixteen white chessmen with the bar magnets inside them. He drafted several designs for the appearance of the chessmen, but to his disappointment Kempelen decided on a classic, rather bulky shape with plenty of room inside for the magnets. "We're not reinventing the game of chess," he had told Jakob, "only the player of the game." So Jakob set to work, rather discontentedly, and carved the thirty-two chessmen.

Meanwhile, under Kempelen's tuition, Tibor was learning to operate the automaton: how to pick up the chessmen with the pantograph, move them, and put them down again; how to recognize his adversary's moves, take the opposing pieces, and make the Turk's eyes roll from time to time. It took a high degree of concentration and sensitive feeling, and Tibor dared not think what it would be like when he had to play a real game of chess at the same time, perhaps against an opponent who was his equal. Although all five doors of the cabinet were left open during rehearsals, and it was a cold January, Tibor was sweating every time he climbed out of the machine.

At the end of the month the doors of the cabinet were closed. From now on Tibor would have to manage by the light of a candle. It was bright enough, but its smoke soon filled the small space, and Tibor began to cough. The cabinet had no chimney. They solved the problem in an unorthodox way: since an opening already led straight from the table into the body of the android, Jakob sawed a hole in the Turk's skull to act as a smoke outlet. The fez they had been planning to give the Turk anyway would not only cover the opening, it would also filter out the smoke of the candle and make it unrecognizable for what it was.

DURING ONE of their rehearsals, when Anna Maria had gone to spend the day with the family of her brother-in-law, Nepomuk von Kempelen, the three men had an unexpected visitor. Before Kempelen's manservant Branislav could prevent her, a woman opened the door of the workshop.

"So this is where you're hiding away," she said, with a Hungarian accent. She had curly black hair that fell to her shoulders, and under a fur coat she wore a wine-red dress trimmed with brocade, laced so tightly that the swell of her breasts lay above the bodice like two waves. In his imagination, this was rather how Tibor had pictured the Venetian merchant's mistress, the woman with whom he had spent the night before his death. Her perfume, like the fragrance of apples, reached Tibor's nostrils even though he was inside the cabinet, and the only open door was the one in front of the clockwork. In the darkness behind it Tibor was invisible to the lady, and to make sure he stayed unseen he quickly blew out the candle. The smoke of the wick as it was extinguished drowned out her perfume.

"Ibolya," said Kempelen unenthusiastically. "What a surprise."

The woman stood her ground, while behind her, Branislav was trying to convey, by means of gesticulations, that he hadn't been able to stop her. Kempelen sent Branislav away after he had taken her coat and muff. Meanwhile the Hungarian lady's eyes went from Jakob—who greeted her as "Baroness"—to the Turk and lingered there.

"Is that it? How beautiful." She approached the chess machine, so that all Tibor could see now was her dress. Before she reached the table,

Kempelen intervened, closing the door in front of Tibor with a casual movement.

"What can I do for you?" asked Kempelen. "I'm afraid that, as I'm sure you can imagine, I'm rather short of time just now."

"I have a surprise for you."

"Let's go into my study."

Tibor heard steps moving away and the sound of the study door closing behind them.

"I can imagine what kind of surprise that'll be," said Jakob.

"A baroness?" asked Tibor.

Jakob opened the back flap of the cabinet next to Tibor and looked in. "Don't get all respectful, Tibor. Baroness Jesenák is living evidence that the nobility obey just the same instincts as any humble peasant."

"What's she doing here?"

"I don't know what she's doing at this precise moment, but I can well imagine why she came. You mark my words, it's certainly no coincidence that Anna Maria happens to be out of the house today."

The Banat

WOLFGANG VON KEMPELEN WAS BORN ON 23 JANUARY 1734, the youngest of three sons. His father, Engelbert Kempelen, a customs officer in the Municipal District Taxation Office, rose in Pressburg society through his marriage to Teréz Spindler, daughter of the Mayor of the time, and Emperor Charles VI bestowed the aristocratic prefix *von* on him for his services to the state.

Kempelen's eldest brother, Andreas, studied philosophy and law, served as secretary to the ambassador to Constantinople, and fought in the Silesian War with the rank of captain. A disorder of the lungs kept him from taking up an appointment as private tutor to Crown Prince Joseph, and even the medicinal sulfur springs of Pozzuoli could not avert his early death.

Nepomuk von Kempelen, Wolfgang's second brother, also served in the army and was promoted to the rank of colonel. The imperial family took him into its immediate circle even more readily than Andreas when he became head of Duke Albert of Sachsen-Teschen's chancellery in Pressburg. His friendship with Duke Albert, the Governor of Hungary, was so close that they joined the local Freemasons' Purity Lodge together.

Wolfgang, the youngest son, also studied philosophy and law, first in Raab and then in Vienna. At the age of twenty-one, after traveling in

Italy, he entered the service of Maria Theresia, and made a spectacular start to his new appointment by translating the Empress's Hungarian civil code from Latin into German within a very short time. This achievement impressed Maria Theresia so much that she personally appointed him to a post in the Royal Hungarian Chamber in Pressburg.

In the summer of 1757 Kempelen was appointed Secretary to the Royal Chamber for his achievements. This rapid professional rise was also reflected in his private life, for in the same summer Kempelen married Franzciska Piani, lady in waiting to Grand Duchess Maria Ludovika. But only two months later Franzciska fell ill with smallpox and died. It took Kempelen a long time to recover from this heavy blow, and he immersed himself entirely in his work.

A year later another woman entered his life: Ibolya Baroness Jesenák, née Baroness Andrássy, who had come to Pressburg from Tyrnau with her brother János to be married to the Royal Chamberlain, Károly Baron Jesenák, a man twice her age. The marriage was harmonious enough but not happy: Ibolya remained childless, and because of his position Károly was away more often that he was at home in Pressburg. Ibolya, only just twenty years old, began to feel bored and found diversion in the many receptions and balls that Pressburg had to offer. In her husband's absence she began an affair, and then a second and a third, the third being with Nepomuk von Kempelen. When Nepomuk tired of her, he introduced his brother to her, and his plan worked: Ibolya fell passionately in love with the clever and elegant widower Wolfgang von Kempelen, who was mourning his wife with such reticence yet so persistently and touchingly; whose noble rank was not a high one but who seemed to have the whole world at his feet. Ibolya told her husband about Kempelen's many talents, and Jesenák passed on her praise of him in Vienna. A little later Kempelen was appointed a royal councilor, and at the next soirée that they both attended Ibolya let him know whom he had to thank for this unexpected promotion. Kempelen took the risk of embarking on an affair with the Baroness, and it did him nothing but good: he finally got over Franzciska's death, the unsuspecting Baron Jesenák became his patron, and those who knew about his liaison with Ibolya felt quiet respect for him and, in line with the customs of the time, kept the secret to themselves. Even Duke Albert, who usually discussed nothing but business with Kempelen, would get him to tell racy stories about the hot-blooded Hungarian Baroness.

But Kempelen knew there was no future in an affair with a married woman, which could be dangerous to him in the long run, and by mutual consent the two ended their private meetings. After five years of mourning Kempelen looked for a new wife, and on the recommendation of Archduchess Christine he married Anna Maria Gobelius, companion to Countess Erdödy. By comparison with Ibolya, most women seemed to Kempelen conventional, and that included Anna Maria; their relationship was one of respect and courtesy but never passion. Nor was his wish for a family granted: the first three children born to her husband by Anna Maria died soon after birth.

In 1765 Kempelen was made responsible for the settlement of the Banat area. In this capacity he and his colleagues from Vienna supervised the colonization of the region between the Maras and Theiss rivers, the Danube and Transylvania, bringing in farmers and miners from Swabia, Bavaria, Hesse, Thuringia, Luxembourg, Lorraine, Alsace, and the Palatinate to exploit the land and its mineral wealth for Austria. Small hamlets filled up with German immigrants, villages grew into small towns, new villages were built. Within five years almost forty thousand people settled in the Banat, not all of them good honest souls: twice a year the "Temeschburg Transport" brought disreputable characters due for ejection from their native lands to the region: tramps, poachers, smugglers, women of ill repute. Kempelen had to settle quarrels, check agreements, and preside over courts of law, and his sensible judgements earned him respect from all sections of the local population. His incorruptibility was something new to this region. The Banat was a wild place, and more than once Kempelen and his companions had to defend themselves against the robbers who were always coming down from their hideouts in the Carpathians to raid the plains for loot. Kempelen prevented bandits from being strung up or shot out of hand, and he personally tended their wounds so that they could be brought before the next court of law in good condition. He regularly sent reports on the problems and achievements of the incoming population to the Royal War Council.

Kempelen also wrote accounts of his travels in the wild Banat region, and they were published in the weekly *Pressburger Zeitung*. He thus established contact with the editor of that journal, Karl Gottlieb Windisch, and later made friends with him. Their friendship was maintained when Windisch rose from being an ordinary town councilor to the post of senator and captain of the town militia and was finally elected Mayor of Pressburg, representing twenty-seven thousand inhabitants of the city, including five hundred aristocrats, seven hundred churchmen, and two thousand Jews. About half the people of Pressburg were German by origin; the other half were divided between Slovakians and Hungarians, most of the nobility being Hungarian.

While the settlement of the Banat was successfully going ahead, and imperial laws were introduced, Kempelen was appointed *Director salinaris*, with responsibility for the Hungarian salt-mining industry. He was in charge of an authority with more than a hundred employees, in which his own father had once worked in a humbler capacity. The Baron used the little free time that this onerous position left him to continue his studies in the field of mechanics and hydraulics. In the first instance he needed this knowledge to understand the machinery used in the salt mines and to improve it if need be. But soon he also began to take an interest in automata, he read works by and about Regiomontanus, Schlottheim, Leibniz, de Vaucanson, and Knaus, and he fitted out a workshop on the top floor of his house. It was when he heard a player of the bagpipes at a village festival making sounds remarkably like a child's voice that he first conceived the idea of building a speaking machine.

Károly Baron Jesenák died in 1768. Ibolya moved in with her brother János Andrássy. She did not mourn her husband for long before she began making fresh advances to Wolfgang von Kempelen. But her efforts were fruitless, for in May 1768 his daughter, Mária Teréz von Kempelen, was born—and lived. Their child's birth bound Wolfgang and Anna Maria von Kempelen together more closely than their wedding ever did.

In September of the following year Kempelen presented a final report in Vienna on the settlement of the Banat. The Empress was pleased with Kempelen's work and asked him, as a kind of reward for his efforts, to stay at court in Vienna for a while. Wolfgang von Kempelen moved into an apartment in the Alser Vorstadt, a Viennese suburb. He was among those present at the Frenchman Jean Pelletier's performance at Schönbrunn Palace, and when Maria Theresia, after the show and the wild applause that it earned, expressed her regret that only foreigners and never Austrians amazed the world with new inventions and experiments, he spoke up. He promised the Empress that within six months he would show her an experiment that cast Pelletier's into the shade. The Viennese courtiers scented scandal in the air, for this man Kempelen, boldly as he spoke, might be high in the ranks of officialdom but was only a low-ranking nobleman. What was more, he came from the provinces, and he had never been renowned as a scientist. But Maria Theresia listened to him, even gave him six months' leave for his task, and promised him a hundred gold sovereigns if he succeeded in surpassing Pelletier's scientific magic.

Kempelen knew that neither his abilities nor the time available would allow him to build a speaking machine. But both were enough for something that would appear to be an automaton. He planned to make a chess machine. He remembered a story told by his friend, the apothecary Georg Stegmüller, who had visited a village tavern in Steinbrück on one of his journeys through the empire. In that tavern he had seen a dwarf winning money at chess from three of the local inhabitants in swift succession. If a small human being, a boy or girl, could be hidden in a machine and win some of its matches, he would be sure of acclaim.

While Kempelen was working on his chess-playing automaton, he realized that it must win not just some but all of its matches. He had to find the itinerant dwarf whom Stegmüller had seen playing chess, poor as the prospects of doing so might appear. So he went to Steinbrück by the shortest route and from there on asked his way. A number of people remembered the dwarf with the traveling chess set, and Kempelen was able to follow Tibor's trail to Venice, where he found him in the *piombi* in November—ripe for the plucking, so to speak.

Wolfgang von Kempelen had shown the Empress that he was an able and loyal civil servant. Now he would show her that his abilities reached further. And for that neither Baron nor Baroness Jesenák was needed.

Pressburg, Donaugasse

KEMPELEN LEANED AGAINST THE EDGE OF HIS DESK AND turned Ibolya's present in his hands: a little book containing a tale in verse by Wieland. The Baroness sat on a chair opposite him, looking at him with shining eyes.

"With all my love on your birthday, Farkas. And I wish you every success with your automaton."

"Thank you. Of course you know it's not my birthday until the day after tomorrow."

Ibolya smiled. "Just as I know that your wife certainly isn't going to invite me here for coffee and cake. I wanted to see you alone. Give your Jakob time off, and we'll spend the rest of the day together."

"It can't be done. I really do have to work."

"You always have to work!"

"I'm sorry."

Ibolya sighed. "Oh, Farkas, I'm so melancholy. Don't you want to do anything about it?"

"It's the weather. Drink a hot Tokay."

"What a horrible man you are. An oaf who doesn't know how to behave! And guess what I had to drink before I got into the coach?"

Ibolya Baroness Jesenák stood up, approached Kempelen, put her face close to his, raised her chin so that her mouth was level with his nose, and breathed out, almost imperceptibly. Her breath did indeed carry a slight aroma of Tokay, as if Kempelen were holding his own nose over a beaker of hot water and wine.

"Delicious" was all he said.

"I shall go to your fat Empress and tell her what a dreadful man you are, and she'll send you off to do forced labor in those salt mines of yours, or at least banish you to the South Seas as ambassador to the cannibals. Yes, that's what I'll do."

"I believe you would, too."

The Hungarian placed a hand on his thigh. "Oh no, I'd never do that. I'll go on telling her what a talented man you are. I'll say that any task, however difficult, is safe in your hands." She began rubbing her fingertips up and down his thigh, then scratched her nails over the fine weave of the fabric of his breeches. When she kissed him, the kiss still smelled of sweet wine. He left his hands where they were on the desk. Ibolya moved away again, wiping her lip rouge from his mouth with her thumb.

"It's all so sad! But I understand. We're star-crossed lovers: first you're married and I'm not, then you're a widower and I'm married, and now it's the other way around. Enough to make anyone weep."

Kempelen just nodded.

"Will it ever be the way it was before?"

"No. Certainly not, but I'll have more time again once the chess machine is finished."

"More time. More time for me too?"

"We'll see each other in Vienna, Ibolya. I'll look forward to that."

Kempelen accompanied her back through the workshop and told Branislav to bring her furs. Ibolya said goodbye to Jakob and looked at the Turk again with unconcealed admiration. At the front door of the house Kempelen took his leave of her, kissing her hand, and then went back to the workshop. Meanwhile Jakob had helped Tibor out of the cabinet, and they were both looking out of the window as the Baroness got into her handsome coach. Kempelen gave the two of them a disapproving glance when he saw them standing there staring. But if what had just happened made him feel at all awkward in front of Tibor and Jakob, he didn't show it.

THE DRESS REHEARSAL, the chess machine's first match, took place a little later, and Dorottya, the Kempelens' Slovakian maidservant, had the honor of being the first person to play against the automaton. Tibor was already inside the cabinet when Kempelen went down to the ground floor to fetch Dorottya. The dwarf could hear Jakob walking around the automaton several times. Then the assistant stopped and called out some incomprehensible words: *"Shem hamephorash! Aemath! "* All of a sudden it didn't sound like Jakob at all.

"What are you doing?" asked Tibor.

"Aemath! Aemath! Come to life!"

"Stop that!"

"Do not interrupt me, mortal man," Jakob warned in husky tones. "If you interrupt the seven life-giving spells, Rabbi Jakob can never bring the man made of wood and linen to life."

"Stop it at once, or I'll come out and make you!"

"You can't come out, remember? You can sing in there, my little bird, but you can't fly," said Jakob in his normal voice. "There, that's done it! The inanimate material has come to life."

"No, it hasn't."

"Yes, it has, you horrible dwarf. Now keep quiet, the maid will be here any moment."

Tibor heard Jakob placing one hand on the tabletop and drumming his fingers on it. "What a phenomenon," he remarked after a while. "A Mohammedan with a Christian brain and a Jewish soul."

"You ought to be locked up."

"No, you're the one who ought to be locked up. I'm a Jew, so they'd burn me instead."

Work on the Turk was finished. Jakob had made the thirty-two red and white chessmen with the magnets inside them, and together they had dressed the Turk. The android wore a collarless silk shirt, turquoise with brown stripes, and a caftan over it with sleeves to the elbow. The red silk caftan was trimmed with white fur on the sleeves and all over the collar, giving the Turk a positively majestic appearance. It wore white gloves on its hands, so that not a scrap of the arms themselves was visible. As the three fingers of the left hand that picked up chessmen formed an unattractive claw shape, even at rest, the Turk had been given an Oriental tobacco pipe with a very long stem, found by Jakob in a Judengasse junk shop, to hold between them. To protect the sensitive mechanism of the fingers, the hand and the pipe it held lay on a red velvet cushion until the automaton began to operate, when the cushion and the pipe were removed. The Turk's baggy trousers were linen dyed blue with indigo, and its wooden feet wore wooden slippers with turned-up toes, bought by Kempelen in Venice, like the glass eyes. On its head the Turk wore a white turban with a red fez on top. The fez had been made of several layers of felt, to filter the smoke from the candle before it came out into the air.

Jakob had devoted most of his time to the Turk's head—papier-mâché over a wooden skull—and various operations had changed the face. Its nose was larger now, its cheeks more angular, its mouth narrower, the ends of the moustache more pointed—as time went on the Turk acquired a sterner, darker expression. Last of all Kempelen told Jakob to turn up the Turk's eyebrows at the outer ends, giving the impression that the android was angry with its opponent. Kempelen was extremely pleased with the result; Jakob kept repeating from time to time that as God was his witness, it would have given him more pleasure to make a pretty woman chess player.

Kempelen came back with Dorottya and Anna Maria. Old Dorottya tripped into the workshop with small steps. The Turk was placed so that it stared straight into her eyes, and Kempelen had to urge her to come right into the room, so intimidating was the look it gave her.

"Mesdames, allow me to introduce you to the chess-playing machine," said Kempelen, very much the master of ceremonies.

The Slovakian maid examined the automaton with mingled curiosity and fear. Kempelen walked around the device and turned the handle on the side next to the clockwork several times. The faint sound of the mechanism was audible through the wood. The Turk's left arm rose and passed over the board until its hand reached the white pawn in front of the king. Here the arm stopped. The thumb, forefinger, and middle finger opened at the same time, and the hand came down over the pawn's head; then the fingers closed, took the pawn by its neck, picked it up, and put it down again two squares farther on. After completing this operation, the arm moved back to its left and came to rest beside the chessboard.

Dorottya had been watching the show with her jaw dropping.

Kempelen nudged her. "Your move now, Dorottya."

Dorottya shook her head. "Oh no, sir. I don't like to."

"Come along, now. Look, he's waiting for you."

"I don't know how to play the game."

"Then it's high time you learned. It's a very stimulating way to pass the time." Kempelen accompanied Dorottya to the chess table and showed her the row of red pawns. "For instance, you can move any of these little figures one or two squares forward."

Finally Dorottya picked up a pawn from the edge of the board and put it down one square farther on, looking carefully at the Turk's hands as if afraid that they might suddenly reach out to seize her. She took a step back, then sniffed the air. "Is there a candle burning somewhere?"

"No" was all that Kempelen said.

The android raised its arm again to move its knight, the one on the right-hand side of the board, but did not pick the piece up properly. The knight fell over as the arm moved on.

"Stop," ordered Kempelen. "You missed it." He stood the knight up again, while Tibor could clearly be heard moving about inside the chess machine.

Anna Maria cleared her throat to draw attention to this faux pas. Dorottya, however, thought that Kempelen was talking to the machine and the machine could understand him. She crossed herself and muttered something in her mother tongue. Tibor failed to get a proper grip on the knight at the second attempt too, whereupon Kempelen brought the game to an end.

"We'll stop now." The Turk laid its arm beside the chessboard again. "You can go, Dorottya, and thank you for your help."

Dorottya nodded and left the workshop, visibly relieved, closing the door behind her.

"Well, she'll have something to talk about over the next few days," said Jakob, smiling. "She'll be the center of attention at market."

"Who do you think you'll fool with this?" asked Anna Maria sternly. "The Empress of Austria, Hungary, and the Austrian Netherlands, with her entire court? I can only wish you luck."

Jakob removed the tabletop from the cabinet and helped Tibor out of the machine.

"It won't work," said the dwarf. "I told you so. I said so before, back in Venice."

"You obviously seem absolutely determined to prove that it will fail," replied Kempelen abruptly. "And if that's your attitude it *will* fail, I entirely agree with you there."

"The dwarf is right," said Anna Maria. "If you won't listen to me, then at least listen to him. Tell the Empress it can't be done. She'll understand. Bury this Turk, and go back to your proper work."

"That's just not acceptable. We still have over three weeks. Jakob, get pen and paper, and we'll list what still has to be done."

Anna Maria, finding her suggestion turned down, snorted audibly. Kempelen turned to her. "Will you excuse us, please?"

She looked for support to Jakob, the only one who had not yet given his opinion, and when he said nothing, she marched out of the room and slammed the door behind her.

Kempelen dictated to Jakob the problems they had to solve: first Tibor's accuracy, second the smell of the burning candle, and third and last the telltale noises inside the cabinet. "Let's try to find suggestions, never mind how outlandish. Tibor, you are warmly invited to take part, unless you're not interested because you think that nothing will make it work. In which case, of course, you are excused."

Tibor obediently shook his head. "No, I'll help."

"Good. Let's start with the candle."

"We could use an oil lamp instead," Jakob suggested.

"That won't smell any less. If anything, the opposite."

"Suppose we left the back flap open?"

"Then we'd have to keep the back of the automaton out of sight the whole time. But I want people to be able to see the Turk from all sides, so that we can turn it whenever we like."

"In that case Tibor will have to play in the dark. And find his way around by feel."

"I can't," confessed Tibor sheepishly.

"Can't do what? Feel?"

"I can't play blind. I've tried, but I can't do it. I have to see the board and the chessmen."

With a sweeping gesture, Kempelen conclusively mimed Tibor's refusal. But Jakob was not going to own himself beaten. "Why don't we scent the automaton? With all the perfumes of Arabia. We'll give our Turk such a strong aroma of musk and sandalwood that no one will smell the candle." And he replied to Kempelen's skeptical expression merely by repeating, "*Never mind how outlandish,* you said."

Tibor felt it was time he contributed something to the discussion. "We'll be playing in the evening. Why don't we just put an extra candlestick on the table? Then people won't wonder why they can smell candle smoke."

Kempelen and Jakob looked at each other. Kempelen smiled, and without a word Jakob crossed *Candle* off the list. Kempelen slapped Tibor on the back. "That's more like it, Tibor. A simple but perfect idea. Somehow we've stopped thinking of such obvious solutions. Carry on."

They turned next to the problem of the sounds inside the cabinet. Jakob said he would line the inside of the automaton with another layer of baize to muffle Tibor's movements, and Kempelen decided to adjust the clockwork that went around, though performing no useful task, so that it would rattle and clatter as soon as it was wound up. That would not only drown out any noise that Tibor made but also reinforce the impression that some powerful mechanism operated the Turk.

"But will it be enough?" asked Kempelen. "We won't be playing to an audience wholly consisting of simpletons who'll be dazzled by the mere sight of the Turk's rolling eyes. There'll be learned men present, scientists, perhaps even engineers. They won't miss any detail, not so much as a sound, however small."

Jakob said that a conjuror he had seen at the fair last year distracted his audience's attention with whichever hand was not at that precise moment making something appear or disappear. For instance, if the conjuror was making a scarf disappear by pressing it into the closed fist of his right hand, he would point dramatically next moment to the empty right hand as he surreptitiously hid the scarf in his left hand behind his back.

"You want me to do a little dance, maybe, to draw attention to myself?" asked Kempelen.

"Well, yes. Or I could wear an interesting costume. Or a fantastic hat. Or no, much better: why not recruit two harem ladies straight from the Orient, scantily clad, faces veiled? We'll have them prowling around the Turk like two cats around a bowl of valerian." Jakob liked this idea so much that he narrowed his eyes and formed his hands into claws.

"That will just make us look even more suspicious. Anyway, I'm not a showman, I'm a scientist. Although I'd have liked to see your hat."

"And I'd have liked to see the harem ladies."

"Well, let's keep those ideas at the back of our minds. Perhaps we can convert them into something . . . less frivolous."

Finally they were left with the question of Tibor's accuracy in working the pantograph. He promised to practice hard over the coming weeks until he was in full control of the Turk's hand, even if it meant working until late into the night. Tibor did not want to let Wolfgang von Kempelen down again. He had momentarily forgotten all that the nobleman had at stake.

Neuchâtel: Afternoon

THE GAME HAD BEGUN EARLY IN THE AFTERNOON, AND
since then over an hour had passed. Twilight was falling outside, and the
light in the hall was growing dim. The candles set on the android's table
were necessary now for anyone to see the state of the game. Now and
then, for instance when Kempelen's assistant moved between the two
chessboards to duplicate the moves on them, or when the windows were
opened briefly to let in some reviving winter air, a gust stirred the Turk's
green silk robes; apart from that it sat as still as Gottfried Neumann.
Kempelen stood in the background, hands clasped behind his back.
However, his eyes were not on the audience, as they had been during the
previous games. He was staring fixedly at the dwarf.

At first it had looked as if the match would be disappointing: Neumann played painfully slowly and took several minutes to think about
even the simplest moves before making them. Yet each move he made
had been a mirror reflection of the Turk's: the moving and taking of the
first pawns and knights, the little castling maneuver, with the rook moving to the square vacated by the king. Only after a dozen moves did his
game take on a character of its own: Neumann was playing no faster, but
with obstinacy and aggression. He threatened the white chessmen with
his bishop, and ten moves later there was a major clash in the course of

which three pawns and four officers were swept from the board. The automaton was still playing more strongly than its human adversary, there was no doubt of that, and the President of the Chess Club kept pointing the fact out to those around him in whispers—but for the first time that day it was on the defensive, and that was sensational enough. The match was becoming dramatic. After every move the people of Neuchâtel craned their necks to see how the game was going. Those who had providently brought chess sets of their own and set them up on their laps, to follow the game on them, counted themselves fortunate.

After the twenty-fourth move the clockwork inside the chess machine stopped again, but this time the assistant did not wind it up. Kempelen stepped forward and said he was sorry, but unfortunately he must stop the game here, for the machine needed a rest, and in the name of the Turk he was willing to offer the volunteer a draw in recognition of his play. There were loud protests. The people of Neuchâtel wanted to see the end of the game, not a tame draw ahead of time. Kempelen raised his hands in a placating gesture. He thanked the audience for their lively interest in his invention, but as he had indicated before the performance, any games that were not finished within an hour would be broken off then at the latest. Moreover, he had to go on to Paris next morning, for he couldn't possibly keep the King and Queen of France waiting. And finally, he added with a smile, his automaton needed to recuperate, for it was "only human."

The people of Neuchâtel were satisfied and calmed down. The first spectators were already rising from their seats when Jean-Frédéric Carmaux, owner of the textiles manufactory, objected, "Herr von Kempelen, with all respect to your automaton and its need for a good night's rest, how are the rest of us to sleep tonight with this unfinished game on our minds? Do wind your Turk up again, and let it play the game to the end, and I'll pay you forty thalers for it."

The spectators applauded, but Kempelen shook his head. "Your offer is too kind, monsieur, but it won't do."

Carmaux was not giving up. He looked in his purse and then said, "Sixty thalers? And a few groschen? With the best will in the world, that's all the money I have on me."

There was laughter. When Kempelen would not accept this offer either, the famous automaton maker Henri-Louis Jaquet-Droz spoke up. "I'll add another forty to make it a hundred."

More applause. People turned to look at young Jaquet-Droz. Carmaux looked from him to Kempelen, who still would not give way. Now a third man and then a fourth and a fifth spoke up; every additional stake was applauded and approved, it was like an auction sale, until finally the sum of a hundred and fifty thalers had been reached—considerably higher than the entire entrance money for the show. Kempelen looked at his assistant, almost as if appealing for aid, but the other man only shrugged his shoulders, at a loss. They whispered a few words to each other. Kempelen seemed about to stand by his decision when Neumann himself—who had been attending to nothing but his chessboard during the whole turbulent auction—raised his hand like a schoolboy and said, "I'd like to go on playing. I'll add fifty thalers."

The noise died down. Kempelen and all the others looked at Neumann. Fifty thalers was a large sum, even for Carmaux. To the little watchmaker, it must represent a fortune.

Two hundred thalers, anyway, were enough to persuade Kempelen to stay. "Very well, messieurs, how can I refuse? I own myself beaten," he said. "But my machine does not and will play on." At a signal from him, his assistant wound up the clockwork again, and silence returned to the hall. "*Merci bien* for your interest, which is greatly appreciated. And may the better player win."

Two servants lit candles in the hall, and Kempelen's assistant exchanged the candles that had burned down in their holder on the chess table. The flames were reflected in the Turk's glass eyes, which looked damp and made the lifeless automaton seem to have genuine life. With three fingers, it reached for its remaining rook.

Schönbrunn

On Tuesday, 6 March 1770, they set off for Vienna with the Turk, which was to be shown at Schönbrunn Palace on the following Friday. The android and its stool were disconnected from the cabinet, and both parts carried separately into the yard. Kempelen's manservant Branislav helped. Tibor had seen the man several times from the little window of his room but had never met him personally. He realized that Kempelen had made a good choice when he hired the sturdy Slovakian, for Branislav was strong, silent, and took so little interest in what was going on that he didn't even give Tibor the dwarf a second glance. That had seldom happened to Tibor before. When the servant and Jakob carried the android downstairs, the idea came into Tibor's head that Branislav himself was like an automaton, doing everything asked of him without answering back or grumbling.

Jakob had organized a carriage and pair in which the chess automaton was packed, well padded to protect it from jolts and bumps along the way, along with their baggage, particularly Kempelen's clothes and wigs. Tibor was to hide away in the carriage too until they were out of Pressburg and on the Vienna road. Branislav would accompany them to Vienna and share the coach box with Jakob, while Kempelen rode beside them on his horse. Katarina the cook had prepared food for their journey:

cold pies, apples, bread, and cheese. Anna Maria was remarkably affectionate as she said goodbye, embracing her husband several times and wishing him luck when he presented the automaton.

Although cold, drizzling rain was falling, Tibor insisted on exchanging his snug place in the carriage for Jakob's seat on the box as soon as they had crossed the Danube. He wrapped himself in rugs and gazed his fill at the unspectacular landscape, the gray sky above the low horizon, the fallow fields and pale red of the moorland heather, with the leafless skeleton of a tree rising from it now and then. On his long and extensive travels from Poland to Venice Tibor had felt sure that he hated such endless country roads, regarding them as a necessary evil between two dry, warm inns, but after three dry, warm months in Kempelen's house he was delighted to be on the open road again.

They reached Vienna in the evening and took up their quarters in Kempelen's apartment at Trinity House in the Alser Vorstadt. Wednesday and Thursday were occupied with more rehearsals. Kempelen came up with an additional trick to surround the chess-playing Turk with even more mystification. He had made a small cherrywood casket, about a hand-span and a half square and two spans tall. Kempelen put the little box on a table beside the chess machine. Tibor and Jakob stared at it.

"What's in that?" asked Tibor.

"I'm not telling you," said Kempelen. "But it will take people's minds off the Turk."

"That's not a harem lady. That's a"—Jakob searched for words—"well, just a box. The opposite of a harem lady, if anything."

"Glitter and brilliance would be much too obvious. But just because this little casket is so inconspicuous, it will attract the eye. And the whole audience will ask itself: what in the world does that mean?"

"Well, what does it mean?" asked Tibor.

"I'm not saying," replied Kempelen, with positively mischievous glee. "But we can tell from Tibor's curiosity that it works! Never mind what the casket contains; it might just as well be empty."

Tibor and Jakob looked at each other. Neither of them was able to share Kempelen's enthusiasm. "*Is* it empty?" asked Tibor.

Kempelen smiled. "One more question out of you, and you're dismissed."

Two of the Empress's adjutants visited Kempelen, first to convey her good wishes for the presentation of the experiment, second to discuss the course it would take and its place in the ceremonial. Afterward Kempelen told his colleagues who was on the guest list and what the protocol was to be. "Four of her Majesty's dragoons will come for us around midday and escort us to Schönbrunn," he reported. "The performance will take place in the Great Gallery, but before it starts we'll be able to put the automaton in a little room next to the gallery where we can be undisturbed. Jakob, we'll need plenty of water for Tibor inside the machine, because it could get hot in there—and a chamber pot so that he can relieve himself."

"Are they going to believe in this?" Tibor asked one last time.

"*Mundus vult decipi,*" said Kempelen, "the world wants to be deceived. They'll believe in it because they'll want to believe in it."

THEY WAITED in the Chinese Cabinet to make their entrance. The murmur of voices in the gallery next door could be heard through the ornately decorated doors, accompanied by a chamber orchestra playing a piece *alla turca* by Haydn. Five footmen had joined Kempelen in the small oval room: two to open and close the doors, two to push the chess machine into the great hall, and one to announce Wolfgang von Kempelen and his invention. While one of them stood at the door to wait for a signal from outside, the other four were talking quietly among themselves and didn't allow the presence of Kempelen and Jakob to inhibit them. One of them was eating dried fruits, another was doing up the row of buttons on his waistcoat, a third was cleaning the leather of his shoes by buffing them on his breeches. Now and then they took a surreptitious look at the chess machine standing in the middle of the black and gold saloon, covered with a linen cloth that ended a few inches from the floor. And under the linen cloth, inside the wood and the baize, sat Tibor, his whole body tense now, trying not to make a single sound. Again and again he checked the position of the chessboard, the operation of the pantograph, and above all the wick of the candle, for if the light went out for any reason at all, he would be lost.

Kempelen was wearing a pale blue coat with satin stripes woven into it. The rest of his clothing, except for his shoes, was white: the cuffs of his sleeves, his collar, his waistcoat and the jabot under it—as if his wardrobe were meant to show that if there was any magic in his performance, it was exclusively of the white variety. On his head Kempelen wore a bob wig. In Tibor's opinion, all he needed was a scepter to make him look like a king. For the first time Tibor realized that he knew only one Kempelen: the Kempelen of his home and his workshop, who dressed casually if never carelessly, in wide ankle-length trousers, his sleeves rolled up over the elbows when he felt hot; the Kempelen who like Tibor himself smelled of sweat at the end of a long day. But this was how Wolfgang von Kempelen obviously looked at court; this was the same man but in different garb, Kempelen the courtier. Tibor had envied him and Jakob their festive costumes. He himself wore only a linen shirt, breeches, and stockings inside the machine; he had even dispensed with shoes so that he could move quickly and silently.

Jakob had felt uncomfortable in his costume from the first. Kempelen had bought him a pale yellow close-fitting coat with a flower pattern for the occasion. Jakob thought the fabric looked "as if someone had pissed on a meadow full of daisies" and protested vehemently but in vain against wearing cosmetics and powder. He kept taking off his queue wig, with its pigtail tied back with black ribbon, to scratch his head—not easy, given that he was wearing gloves.

"Do you do that when you're wearing the kippa?" Kempelen asked him quietly, and after that Jakob kept his wig on.

The music in the next room died away and was followed by polite applause. The footman near the door snapped his fingers, whereupon the other four took up their positions and stood to attention. The Empress could be heard saying a few words. There was more applause. Then two footmen pushed open the double doors, and the little procession entered the Great Gallery: the footman to announce them in front, then Kempelen himself, next the chess machine wheeled in by two servants, and finally Jakob, carrying the little casket with elaborate caution, as if it contained the royal crown of Hungary. A draught of air pressed the cloth against the Turk's face, so that its nose, forehead, and turban could be clearly seen. That detail in itself aroused a soft murmur. The leading footman stopped in front of the Empress, who sat enthroned in the middle of the hall, waited for the men behind him to follow his example, and then announced in a loud voice, "*Votre honorée Majesté, Mesdames et Messieurs:* Johann Wolfgang Chevalier de Kempelen de Pázmánd and his experiment."

Kempelen made a long, deep bow. In the background two footmen were bringing in a small table on which Jakob put the casket, while two others closed the doors of the Chinese Cabinet again. When Kempelen looked up, Maria Theresia was smiling, and he smiled back. The Empress was even stouter than at their last meeting, but that only added to her authority and dignity rather than detracting from it. She was encased in a black gown, in token of her lasting grief for her late husband, with a little white lace at its neck and sleeves. She wore a black onyx necklace, and on the white curls of her wig, in deliberate understatement, she wore a tiny diadem in token of her royalty. When she breathed out, her neckline wrinkled, but when she smiled she looked ageless.

"*Cher* Kempelen," she began, "you stood in this very place six months ago and said that you would succeed in amazing us with your experiment. And now you are here again for us to take you at your word."

"I thank Your Majesty for your confident reception of me, and for the valuable time that you are kind enough to grant me," replied Kempelen in a firm voice. "My experiment, which I now present here *en public* for the first time, is merely a bagatelle, a modest achievement compared with the triumphs of the modern sciences, in particular those of the many excellent scholars who, thanks to Your Majesty's generous support, work here at court, and who amaze the world with their discoveries and inventions." At this point Kempelen turned on his heel and, with a sweeping gesture toward the hall, indicated the faces of Gerhard van Swieten, director of the Vienna School of Medicine; Friedrich Knaus, the Court Mechanician; the Abbé Marcy, director of the Court Physical Cabinet; and Father Maximilian Hell, professor of astronomy. The four men acknowledged his flattering mention with barely perceptible nods of the head. "But if Your Majesty were to be gracious enough to grant me a little applause or a kind word after my *présentation,* then my many months of work, my setbacks and disappointments would all be erased from my mind. Should my experiment contribute the merest iota to increasing the fame of your reign and your empire, then as God is my witness, I shall be a more than happy man."

"And richer by a hundred *souverains d'or* too, if I remember our agreement correctly." Maria Theresia looked around the circle of her guests, and polite laughter rippled through the hall until it reached the windows and the mirrors on the walls.

"Even if it were a thousand sovereigns," said Kempelen, "I long even more for Your Majesty's approval, which is beyond price."

He concluded this tribute with another bow. Maria Theresia nodded in the direction of the automaton.

"Pray do not keep us on the rack any longer, my dear Kempelen. Reveal your secret."

Two footmen prepared to remove the cloth, but Kempelen got in first. Taking it by two of its corners, he swept it off the object it had been covering with a grand and spirited gesture, almost as if he were dancing. At the same time he announced, "The chess automaton!"

For a split second all was still in the hall, and then the spectators took in what Kempelen had revealed. Those present exchanged their first opinions in whispers, and many fans were unfurled to allow their lady owners to refresh themselves with a breath of air. Now those at the back of the company pressed forward too, or stood on tiptoe to see the automaton. A few just looked at one of the mirrors reflecting the image of the Turk.

"An automaton," said the Empress, in a tone that did not make it clear whether she was asking a question or stating a fact.

"An automaton," Kempelen confirmed, after turning back to Her Highness again. "And that sounds as if I were saying 'only an automaton.' For an automaton, to be sure, is nothing new; an automaton is not sufficient to claim Your Majesty's valuable time, or that of the ladies and gentlemen here present." Kempelen kept the cloth in his hand as he spoke. "We know of all kinds of automata: automata that drive or walk, others that play the Turkish crescent, the organ, the flute, the syrinx, the trumpet or drum; turtle automata, automata representing swans, lobsters, and bears, even mechanical pugs—or there's Monsieur de Vaucanson's duck, as delightful as it is true to nature, a bird that eats oats, digests them and—*mes pardons*—excretes them again." Some of the ladies giggled bashfully. "And let us not forget what so far has been the most remarkable specimen among this new breed of beings: an automaton capable of writing, made by Your Majesty's Court Mechanician, Friedrich Knaus."

Friedrich Knaus took a step forward and acknowledged the polite applause with a nod. Although his green coat and his wig were certainly more exquisite in themselves than Kempelen's, the different parts of his costume were so ill suited to one another that he looked shabbier—an impression reinforced by his thin face with its prominent cheekbones. His dark brown eyes looked watchfully at Kempelen, as if he guessed what was coming next.

"Your Wonderful All-Writing Machine, Monsieur Knaus, was a masterpiece of its time. But writing is one thing: what would you say if I had made an automaton that is capable not only of writing"—and here Kempelen raised one forefinger in the air and fixed his gaze on Maria Theresia—"but can think for itself?"

Kempelen heard the whispering that followed this with satisfaction but never took his eyes off the Empress.

"Well, what *would* you say, Knaus?" she asked.

Knaus smiled politely at Kempelen. "Don't take offense, but I would call you a fool. Automata can do many things and will learn many more—but never how to think."

"My machine will prove the opposite. This automaton, thanks to its perfect mechanism, can conquer any human challenger—and beat him at the most taxing of all games, the royal game of chess. The idea came to me after a game that Your Imperial Highness once did me the honor of playing with me."

"Did I play like an automaton, then? Or look like one?" asked the Empress, to the amusement of the whole company.

"By no means. But even if it had been so, when you have seen my automaton play, you would consider that such a verdict merely did you credit. Now, who will be brave enough to face my Mechanical Turk and take up its challenge?"

Kempelen looked around the gallery, but none of those present spoke up or stepped forward. A number of them had come this evening hoping to see Kempelen fail to keep his grand promises of six months ago, and no one now wanted to help him on his way to a triumph. Jakob placed a chair at the chess cabinet opposite the Turk.

"Why don't you play, Knaus?" asked the Empress. "You're a good chess player, I believe, and you know about automata too."

Not only Knaus but Kempelen had started imperceptibly when the Empress's choice fell on the Court Mechanician. Now Knaus bowed to her and said, "It would be too much honor, Your Majesty. My talent for chess is extremely imperfect, and I would not like to weary your guests with my clumsy moves."

"Don't be so coy. This wooden Turk has challenged mankind; now it's up to you to defend the human race."

Friedrich Knaus nodded and sat down at the chessboard on the chair that Kempelen pulled out for him. Then Kempelen went to the handle and turned it vigorously a few times, until it looked as if the springs could be wound up no further. Meanwhile Jakob removed the red velvet cushion and the pipe from the Turk's hand.

"The machine will make the first move," announced Kempelen, and even before the automaton began to stir, he and Jakob stepped back to the second table where the cherrywood casket stood, and there he stayed until the end of the game.

The clockwork began to rattle, and before the astonished eyes of the spectators the Turk's wooden arm rose into the air, hovered above the chessboard, came down on the king's pawn, and moved it two squares forward to the middle of the board. There was no risk in the game yet, and Friedrich Knaus was looking not at the board itself but at the Turk and its movements. Then he moved his red pawn to oppose the Turk's white one. Although this was not an unusual move, the audience's tension was resolved in a brief round of applause for the first complete exchange of moves between man and machine.

The Turk moved a pawn to the right beside the one it had just put down. Knaus looked hard at the pieces, and when he could see no trap set for him, he took the white pawn with his own and removed it from the board. This first successful move against the automaton earned applause too. Friedrich Knaus allowed himself the satisfaction of looking up for a moment and smiling at the spectators. But as he did so, he also saw that his move had not impaired Wolfgang von Kempelen's good temper. He hadn't moved an inch away from his little casket and had even joined in the applause.

Meanwhile the Turk picked up its knight and held it above the ranks of chessmen.

TIBOR HAD TO put his head right back to see the underside of the chessboard. His neck ached already, but he mustn't miss a single move. The metal disk under square g7 fell on the head of the nail with a soft clink; the disk under g5 was drawn up. The Turk's opponent had moved a pawn. Tibor copied the move on the chessboard on his lap. Then he raised the end of the pantograph and pushed it over the chessboard until it was over f1. He compressed the grip to open the Turk's fingers. Then he lowered the pantograph until it would go no farther and loosened the grip. Now he was holding the bishop. He raised the pantograph again, moved it over half the chessboard, and in the same way put the bishop down on c4. The clink of the metal disks above him confirmed that he had picked the bishop up and put it down correctly. He duplicated this move too on his own board. His opponent moved to attack his bishop. Knaus was still playing predictably, and Tibor was not to find out how good he really was until after the first ten or twelve moves.

Kempelen had made the clockwork so loud that it was torture for Tibor at first; he had felt as if he were shut up inside a church belfry. But by now he was used to the noise and even glad that the clockwork almost drowned out the sound of anything going on outside, which would just have distracted him from operating the machine. Only if he put his ear very close to the side of the cabinet could he hear what anyone in the Gallery was saying. A little air came in through the cracks and keyholes in the wood: air that Tibor and the candle were consuming. The candle flame burned steadily, flickering slightly only when Tibor moved. The soot rose; much of the smoke passed through the android's body and into its head, as they had planned; the rest stayed under the tabletop, making patterns of its own there. While Tibor's surroundings smelled of wood, felt, metal, and oil at the beginning of every session, those aromas were soon covered by the smell of the burning candle. After a while he couldn't even smell his own sweat anymore.

Two moves later, Tibor had his first chance to roll the Turk's eyes. He reached into the android's lower body and pulled the two strings moving the artificial eyes several times. The murmuring of the spectators could be heard even through the wood, and Tibor couldn't help smiling secretly at the credulous folk who would fall for such a simple effect. Kempelen had told Tibor to show off everything the automaton could do, and Tibor followed his instructions. When the second red knight moved over to Tibor's side of the board, he performed a small castling move. He was a little disappointed to earn no applause for this trick. Tibor took a sip from the tube containing water that he had stowed in a corner and waited for the metal disks above him to start their dance.

As time went on, the clattering and rattling of the clockwork slowed down and finally stopped altogether. Tibor timed it so that he would be carrying out a move at exactly the moment when the cogwheels came to a halt, stopped the Turk's arm in midair, and moved it no farther—making it look as if the automaton had stopped as a clock does when the springs are no longer wound up. As it was quiet inside the machine now, Tibor could hear the courtiers beginning to talk in subdued voices—obviously wondering whether the invention had been damaged in some way—but then Kempelen told the audience that the automaton had run down, and asked Jakob to wind it up. Jakob turned the handle, and thereupon the wheels went around again, and the rattling began as loud as ever. Tibor completed his move.

At the tenth move Tibor sprang his trap: he exposed his queen, and his opponent took her with his bishop. He heard the spectators' applause as Knaus took the queen off the board and pictured him looking arrogantly around, perhaps raising a hand in acknowledgment of their praise. But if so, he had rejoiced too soon: his red bishop was gone now, and his red king more vulnerable than before. Tibor put the king in check with his knight. Then he reached into the Turk's body again, not to roll its eyes this time but to nod its head. Outside, Kempelen would now explain the meaning of the gesture: a single nod from the Turk meant "check," two nods meant "check to the queen," and, finally, three nods meant "checkmate."

Now the endgame began, not a pleasant experience for Tibor's opponent. Tibor took the red queen and then used his knights and bishops to chase his adversary's king over the board, decimating the red officers along the way, and the Turk nodded its head and rolled its eyes between moves. Soon it was obvious that White was going to win, but Red refused to give up, moving the king from one square to the next and back again in flight from his pursuers until he was finally checkmated. Twenty-one moves. Tibor let go of the pantograph and pulled the string to the Turk's head three times like a bell rope. Then he pressed his ear close to the wall of the cabinet so as not to miss a single clap of the enthusiastic applause that broke out at the end of the game. All his tension was gone, giving way to a blissful feeling like climbing into a tub of warm water. Kempelen stopped the clockwork by inserting a pin near the handle. Now Tibor could hear everything more clearly than ever: the clapping, the shouts of "Bravo!," even the almost expressionless voice of Kempelen thanking the audience.

. . .

WOLFGANG VON KEMPELEN saw how Friedrich Knaus had been sweating; a small trickle flowed over his temples from under his wig, and when he gave Kempelen his hand, it was damp. Knaus would have liked to go straight back to his place among the rows of spectators, but Kempelen would not let go of his hand; only the sight of the first loser completed the picture of the brilliant automaton, and much as they would both have preferred it to be someone else, that first loser was Knaus. When Kempelen finally moved away, he bowed to Knaus and asked the company to applaud the Court Mechanicians who had so boldly taken on the machine—to be defeated in twenty-one swift moves. Knaus smiled back, gritting his teeth. Kempelen scanned the crowd of onlookers to see who were among the witnesses to his triumph. Amid the throng he saw his brother Nepomuk and then the face of Ibolya Jesenák standing next to her brother János and proudly waving to him. A few guests turned away when Kempelen's gaze fell on them, evidently fearing that, like Medusa's head, it could turn them to stone, or rather to a lifeless automaton.

When the applause had died down, the Empress spoke. *"Mon cher* Kempelen, you see us entirely *enthusiasmées.* This clever machine ... this wonderful invention casts even the finest work of the master watchmakers of Neuchâtel into the shade. You have performed all that you promised. What do you think, Knaus?"

"A wonderful invention indeed," agreed Knaus. "One might almost think there was magic at work here. I would dearly love to ... but no, forgive me, I am overcurious."

"Finish what you were going to say."

"Well, Your Majesty, if it does not put that worthy Baron von Kempelen to too much trouble," he said, here looking straight at Kempelen, "I would dearly love to look at the interior of this fabulous automaton, the place where no doubt the mind of the machine that has just beaten me resides."

It was obvious what Knaus was implying. For a brief moment

Kempelen's smile froze. All was quiet in the hall. Kempelen looked at the Empress. "Come along, Kempelen, let him have his wish."

Friedrich Knaus had managed a relaxed smile again. Kempelen went up to the automaton and took a key from his coat pocket. Meanwhile Tibor had extinguished the candle and removed his chessboard and chessmen. Then he had slipped into the larger compartment of the cabinet and closed the sliding partition behind him. When Kempelen opened the left-hand door, Tibor was well out of the way, and there was nothing but the clockwork to be seen.

"This is the mechanism that breathes life and understanding into the automaton," he explained. Then he opened the opposite door at the back of the cabinet, and the light falling in between the cogwheels, springs, and cylinders proved that apart from them, the space was empty. As confirmation, Kempelen took the candle off the table and held it in the space behind the clockwork where Tibor had just been sitting before. The curious spectators bent or knelt down so that they could see into the automaton from both sides.

Now Kempelen closed the door at the back, came around to the front of the cabinet again, and pulled out the drawer as far as it would go. It contained two complete chessboards and sets of chessmen—"as replacements," Kempelen explained. Tibor had used the time it took Kempelen to open the drawer to push the sliding partition aside once more, crawl into the space behind the clockwork, and close the partition again. His legs were under the baize-covered board forming the false base of the cabinet. The front door was still open to show the clockwork, but the space behind it was so dark and the tangle of dummy cogwheels so dense that Tibor could not be seen.

Finally Kempelen opened the double doors and the right-hand door at the back of the cabinet, clearly showing the empty compartment. "I even left a little space free here in case I feel like teaching the Turk to play draughts or tarot."

The courtiers were convinced: the drawer was pulled right out, and four out of five doors were open—no human being could hide in this cabinet, not even a child. Only Friedrich Knaus was still investigating the space between the cabinet and the floor beneath it.

"I see that Herr Knaus is not yet fully persuaded. But I assure you, there is no secret passage leading out of the cabinet." By way of proof, Kempelen and Jakob turned the automaton once on its own axis, and pushed it a little way from where it had stood and then back again.

"And what, if I may ask, is in that box?" asked Knaus, pointing to the cherrywood casket.

"You may ask, Monsieur Knaus, but I fear I must decline to answer. For I would like to keep just a few of my secrets to myself, if you will allow me."

"Kindly allow him," the Empress told her Court Mechanician.

"To be sure, Your Majesty. And yet I am perfectly convinced that automata cannot think, so in that case . . ."

"Now don't be so persistent, my dear Knaus. You have seen that the Turk is a lifeless dummy." The Empress's tone permitted no further contradiction, and Knaus docilely bowed.

At a gesture from the Empress, footmen brought in refreshments for the company—wine and sweetmeats on silver platters—and the chamber orchestra began to play again. Some of the guests crowded around the automaton, which still had its doors open, and the mysterious little casket. Jakob was on guard over both. He answered questions politely, thanking those who praised the device.

Among the first to offer congratulations was Nepomuk von Kempelen. Nepomuk, a man of stronger build than Wolfgang, clad in a stylish brown ensemble with the red, white, and red Austrian sash over it, greeted his younger brother with a clasp of the hand, accompanied by a jovial pinch to the back of his neck. "Whenever people think the Kempelen brothers have done everything in their power, along comes one of us with something new. My heartfelt respects, Wolf. Hey there!"

Detaining one of the footmen by his coattails, Nepomuk took two wineglasses off the man's tray. He handed one to his brother.

"To the von Kempelen family, and may it continue to astonish the world."

"To us!"

"A shame that Father isn't alive to see this."

Nepomuk took a quick sip from his glass and then looked at the automaton. "Anna Maria was complaining of your chess player a month ago, saying it was going to make you look a fool."

"You know Anna Maria. It's not the first time she's prophesied disaster." Throughout this conversation Kempelen's eyes were searching the hall for anyone who wanted to speak to him.

"I think your Turk is brilliant. That grim countenance alone is a great success. Your Jew is a second Phidias. When you get a moment, you really must tell me what kind of bogus magic lies behind it. That fossilized old Swabian Knaus would give his right arm to know."

"You shall have the secret cheaper than that."

"Or no, wait, I don't think I want to know after all; let me die in ignorance. You know how I hate to be disappointed. Ah, hold on to your glass and keep your breeches buttoned up; here comes our nymph."

Ibolya was making her way through the gathering, her pink hooped skirt brushing against the calves of the men she passed apparently by accident, making them turn to look at her. Her pale green bodice had a square, low neckline, so that at every breath she drew, you could see the rise and fall of her breasts. They were whitened with cosmetics, and she wore rouge on her cheeks and a beauty spot just above her red mouth. Her towering wig was adorned with feathers, silk flowers, and ribbons. She carried a fan and a little bag over her wrist. Her smile was enchanting.

"Nepomuk," she greeted the elder brother, and he took her hand, lifted it to his mouth, and dropped a kiss on her lace glove.

"Ibolya. You look like spring itself."

"I feel like spring."

"You smell like it too."

"That will do!" she said, giving Nepomuk, who was bending to smell her shoulder, a little tap with her fan. Then she turned to his brother. "I'm proud of you, Farkas."

Wolfgang von Kempelen kissed her hand too. "Thank you, but please don't call me Farkas here. It's Wolfgang."

"Why?"

"Because we're not in Pressburg, we're in Vienna. They speak German here."

Ibolya pouted, pretending to be injured, and looked at Nepomuk. "So Kempelen Farkas from Pozsony doesn't care to be Hungarian anymore."

Nepomuk laughed and put his hand on Ibolya's waist. "Kempelen Farkas is famous now, Ibolya. The Empress herself has applauded Kempelen Farkas."

Kempelen waved this away. "That's right, have fun at my expense."

Ibolya gulped some wine from Nepomuk's glass, took too large a mouthful, and carefully mopped away the drops running down her chin with the back of her hand. János Baron Andrássy joined the three of them and greeted the Kempelen brothers with a bow. For a brief moment he froze, seeing Nepomuk's hand still on Ibolya's back, whereupon Nepomuk removed it. Andrássy was rather dark-complexioned, like his sister. He was the only one in the Gallery—with the exception of the Turk—to wear whiskers: a black moustache with twirled ends. Andrássy wore the uniform of a lieutenant of hussars: a dark green dolman with yellow buttons, red trousers, and tall boots, his fur cape slung open over his left shoulder. His officer's sword with its regimental scabbard hung from his belt.

"You must promise me," he told Kempelen, "to put me on your list. I absolutely must play a game of chess with this Turk. I'll show him that a hussar isn't routed on the battlefield as easily as Her Majesty's fool of a watchmaker just now."

"I'm sure the automaton would sweat blood and oil if it had to face you, Baron. But I'm afraid there will be no more games. After this evening I plan to dismantle the automaton and devote myself to other projects."

Even as Andrássy was protesting, one of the Empress's adjutants came up to Kempelen and whispered something in his ear. "*Excusez-moi,*" said Kempelen, "but Her Majesty wants a word with me."

"And no one keeps Her Majesty waiting," said Nepomuk. "Off you go."

"Good luck," added Ibolya, and Andrássy nodded to him.

Kempelen relished the envious glances that the courtiers cast at him on his way to the Empress. Friedrich Knaus, mopping his brow with a silk handkerchief, was standing at her side. Kempelen bowed to the Empress and gave Knaus a nod.

"*Mon cher* Kempelen, I was just discussing your amazing invention with Knaus," said Maria Theresia. "We agreed that you have more than earned your hundred gold sovereigns. *N'est-ce pas,* Knaus?"

"Indeed. A thinking machine—who would credit it? I still can't believe it myself."

"Why did you never say what talents lay slumbering within you? All these years I employ you in dull bureaucracy, and then you invent this marvel within such a short time."

"I didn't want to show it until it was perfected, Your Majesty."

"So tell me, what are you thinking of doing next?"

"I shall return to the bosom of dull bureaucracy," replied Kempelen with a smile, "and meanwhile, when my time allows me, I intend to work on other inventions."

"Can you tell us what you have in mind?"

The Empress looked briefly at Knaus, who had been following this exchange with his hands behind his back and a forced smile on his face. "Why, of course he can," he said. "After all, you are the Empress."

"The fact is, I want to make a speaking machine. An apparatus able to use language like any human being of flesh and blood. Any language."

"*C'est drôle,* Knaus. You once planned to make a speaking machine yourself. What became of it?"

"The project had to . . . to be postponed. Too many other duties in the Physical Cabinet, Your Majesty."

"Perhaps the two of you could exchange views sometime and compare your results. Such a project would surely be realized more quickly if you worked together, *n'est-ce pas?*"

The two men dutifully nodded but did not reply.

"Do pray take another look at this famous chess player," the Empress told Knaus.

"There's no need. I was able to observe it quite enough earlier."

"I meant: you are excused."

Friedrich Knaus twitched, understanding his faux pas. Then he bowed to the Empress and Kempelen, but his smile was gone before he had turned entirely away.

"Why is everyone so interested in speaking machines?" asked Maria Theresia. "With due respect, there's more than enough talking done already by the human inhabitants of this world: why should machines learn to speak too? I have sometimes wished for *silent* machines! More thinkers are what we need, thinkers *comme il faut* like your famous Turk." Wolfgang von Kempelen did not reply. "But I am confident that your speaking machine would be a marvel to equal the chess player. Perhaps I am simply not farsighted or young enough to see what points to the future anymore."

"Your Majesty!" Kempelen protested, but her raised hand stopped him.

"No false civilities, Kempelen. That's not your style." Maria Theresia looked across the hall, and her glance fell on Knaus as he stalked around the chess-playing automaton, hands still behind his back and eyes intent, like a heron looking for frogs in a water meadow. "*À propos*, Knaus is not as young as he used to be."

"He has done great things."

"Ten years ago." The Empress beckoned Kempelen closer to her and asked, in a rather lower voice, "Would you perhaps be interested in the post of Court Mechanician? I would like to have you here at court, and Knaus might be glad to be rid of the burden."

"You are too kind, Your Highness."

"Spare me the flattery." The Empress's plump hand took and pressed Kempelen's forearm. "You know your capabilities, and so do I. I also know that the position would please you."

"Your Majesty must not forget that I have other important tasks to perform."

"Settling land and supervising salt mines? Others can do that just as well. You are destined for higher things. Well, think about it at your leisure."

"I will, Your Majesty."

"But this first appearance of the chess machine must on no account be the only one. I want you to introduce this marvel to my Empire and show foreigners what we can do. Go back to Pressburg and exhibit it there. Your other duties may be reduced to a minimum; you have my permission. Your salary will of course remain the same. And then come back to Vienna soon, for my fingers itch to play a game against the Turk myself someday."

"What an honor! And what an event that would be!"

"*En effet.*"

"What about my speaking machine?"

"When no one is interested in your chess automaton anymore . . . then, my dear Kempelen, you may astonish us with your speaking machine." Kempelen bowed. "And now pray rejoin the company. You have talked long enough to an old matron who has lost her charms—off you go to enjoy the praise of the young and pretty." She was no longer looking at Kempelen but was moving her heavy body in her chair, groaning theatrically to heighten the impression of old age.

MEANWHILE Nepomuk von Kempelen had left Ibolya and was talking to other women, and Baron Andrássy was deep in political conversation with a group of his fellow countrymen. Ibolya was wandering aimlessly through the hall, now and then exchanging an empty glass for a full one taken from one of the footmen's trays. She smiled at men when their glances met, and the men returned her smile, but none of them spoke to her. Ibolya ended up in front of one of the many mirrors, inspecting the fit of her bodice and her wig. A silk flower had come loose from the tall framework of hair and was hanging limply down. Ibolya put it back.

Suddenly she sensed someone watching her: someone behind her back. She did not turn but instead looked in the mirror. She scanned the row of white heads behind her, but most of the guests had only the backs of their heads turned her way, and the others were looking elsewhere.

Only when Ibolya looked rather harder did she see the Turk's eyes staring fixedly at her. Then the Court Mechanician's back hid her view.

Ibolya moved away from the mirror and went straight over to the chess machine. There was not quite such a crowd around it now. All the front doors of the cabinet had been left open to allow viewers to see right inside, and the white chessmen on the board still held Knaus's red king checkmated. Ibolya stopped about two paces from the Turk. And yet again it was looking at her with its bright brown eyes. Ibolya returned its glance, examining the face around the eyes: the heavy eyebrows and proud moustache on the upper lip, the stern cheeks, and finally the gleaming brown skin. Now and then a draught stirred the silk shirt where it showed beneath the Turk's broad shoulders, and it looked as if the automaton were breathing. It was strange: the Turk was a machine surrounded by human beings, yet it looked more human than all of them put together. Ibolya had to blink, and it was like a defeat, an acknowledgment of submission, for the Turk kept its eyes steadfastly open.

Only when Baroness Jesenák noticed Jakob watching her was the spell broken. The pressure of her bodice told her that she was breathing faster. Jakob smiled at her, proud of her interest in his work. She smiled back, ashamed of her momentary abstraction in contemplation of a dummy, lowered her lashes, and disappeared into the company to find herself another glass of champagne.

Jakob watched her go. Then he saw that Knaus, who had been inspecting the automaton closely just now, had suddenly disappeared. Jakob looked for him and found him kneeling in front of the open door, one hand already in the clockwork.

"Please, monsieur! No touching!"

Knaus smiled. "If anyone knows about these devices, I do. I won't displace so much as a cog in it."

"All the same, I must ask you . . ."

Knaus nodded, took his hand out of the mechanism, saw that there was a little oil on his fingers, and wiped them clean on his handkerchief. "You're the magician's apprentice?"

"Herr von Kempelen's assistant, yes."

"And responsible for . . . surely not just for guarding this dummy?"

"No, I worked on the joinery."

Knaus passed his now clean hand over the dark walnut wood of the chess table. "Good work too—no, excellent work. You're very talented."

"Thank you."

"You will know that I am in charge of the Court Physical Cabinet. We can always do with capable men here."

"I haven't had any training."

"And is Wolfgang von Kempelen a trained watchmaker? No! All the same, he surprises us all with a work that breaks every known and unknown law of clockwork." Knaus spread both hands, indicating the chess-playing Turk. The irony in his voice was unmistakable.

"I already have a post."

"Yes, I know. In Pressburg. Vienna is a rather more prosperous place than the provinces, my dear fellow."

"Too kind, sir. But I'm perfectly satisfied with my post, so I think I'll stay in Pressburg."

Friedrich Knaus sighed, as if finding it impossible to keep an ignoramus from choosing the wrong path. "Well, that's your decision. However, you can always come to me should you change your mind. Visit me in the Cabinet sometime when you are in Vienna again." Knaus picked up his red king from the chessboard and put it with the other defeated pieces. Then he added, in a low voice, "Listen to me: if there is any deception about this so-called automaton—and I assume there is, for my reason tells me so—I shall be the first to find it out. And then the Empress will hear of it, and God have mercy on those who have dared to trick her and her entire court and bring ridicule on the Empire. The inventor himself will not be the only one to feel the consequences—so will everyone else who had a hand in it. Get that into your head, and for all I care, you can tell your braggart of a master so too." Knaus waited a moment to see his words take effect, then turned away from Jakob and the chess automaton and once again devoted his attention to his companion, a young woman in a turquoise dress.

Softly as Knaus had spoken these last words, Tibor had heard them.

He thought he would ask Kempelen not to leave the door in front of the clockwork open anymore. It had been enjoyable to see a little of what went on after the performance: all those legs and skirts passing his little peephole, all the faces looking into his cave and sometimes right into his eyes without seeing him in the dark, the comings and goings of the company in the hall, so many delicious perfumes worn by ladies and gentlemen alike—and not least to hear the praise heaped on the Turk and its brilliant play by the guests. But when Knaus's thin face appeared in front of the opening Tibor was alarmed, and when the Mechanician actually put his hand into the clockwork, Tibor thought it was all over for them, and Knaus would pull him out as if removing a snail from its shell.

And Tibor had seen Baroness Jesenák again. She was as pretty as the first time, although he had liked the plainer dress she wore then better. He watched her as best he could while she moved through the Gallery with a glass in her hand. When she stopped in front of a mirror, and Tibor saw her face reflected in its gilded frame, it was like looking at a painting. And when she came close to the automaton, he caught her perfume again: the sweet scent of apples.

IT WAS LONG AFTER midnight when the three men returned to Trinity House, in the Alser Gasse, but they were all wide awake. Tibor's sweat had dried some time ago. Jakob had taken off his wig and was now scratching his scalp as much as he pleased. His damp hair stood up in untidy peaks, and the pressure mark of the wig was like a red circlet around his head. He had taken off his close-fitting yellow coat. While he was washing the powder and sweat off his face, Wolfgang von Kempelen came back into the room, his own wig in one hand and a bottle of champagne in the other.

"Let's drink to 'the greatest invention of the century'!" he cried. "I quote Count Cobenzl."

"The century's not over yet by a long chalk," Jakob pointed out. "Who knows what else may be invented in the next thirty years?"

Kempelen handed Jakob the bottle without comment and left the room again to fetch glasses. When Jakob opened the bottle, some of the wine fizzed out onto his hand. He turned to the android.

"I hereby baptize you by the name of"—he looked hopefully at Tibor, but Tibor couldn't think of a name, quite apart from the fact that he was reluctant to lend his support to a Jew baptizing an automaton—"by the name of Pasha." Jakob sprinkled champagne from his fingers onto the Turk's head. "Not very original, I know. But he sits enthroned there at his ease, just like one of those old pashas." Here Jakob nodded at the door and whispered, "He's going to want to extend your contract."

"Who is? Kempelen?"

"Yes. Don't let him do you down. It won't work without you, so don't sell yourself short, do you hear me?"

"How about you?"

"My work's finished. He can do without me if necessary, but not without you."

"But I can't—" Tibor was beginning when Kempelen came back with the glasses, and he fell silent.

Kempelen poured the champagne with such a flourish that it spilled over. He handed first Tibor and then Jakob a glass, raised his own, and looked at the Turk.

"To the chess machine."

Jakob and Tibor repeated the toast, and the three men clinked glasses. Kempelen emptied his in a single draught.

"And that was just the start," he announced. "The Empress has asked me—no, has commanded me, that's more like it—to exhibit the automaton in Pressburg so that everyone can see it play. This machine will be a hit. A *succès fou*." Kempelen poured more champagne for himself and Tibor. "I know I said in Venice that I needed you just for one performance, but that was nonsense. I'd underestimated the effect of the automaton. Can I interest you in continuing to work for me? It was a great experience for you too, wasn't it? Imagine, the Empress herself wants to play against you."

Tibor nodded. Jakob craned his neck as if it felt tense, and Tibor understood his meaning. "But I want more money." He had meant to put it rather less bluntly, and he took another sip of champagne to cover up his embarrassment.

Kempelen raised one eyebrow. "Ah. What sum were you thinking of?"

Out of the corner of his eye, Tibor saw Jakob spreading the thumb and two fingers of his free hand on his thigh, where Kempelen couldn't see them.

"Thirtee—" Tibor began, and when Jakob put more emphasis into his gesture he stopped and changed it to "Thirty. Thirty guilders a month." He didn't trust himself to look Kempelen in the eye. He must seem worse than ungrateful.

But Kempelen nodded. "Let's talk it over when we're home again."

"And there are some things that need changing."

"I entirely agree with you. We won't let anyone else get as close to the machine as Knaus did. We must seat its opponent at . . . yes, at another table. We'll simply say that gives spectators a better view of the Turk. Or we can pretend it's for reasons of safety. How awkward for poor Knaus that the choice fell on him! Such a brilliant mind, but this evening he looked like a village idiot sitting an examination. The sweat must have been pouring off him in torrents. All Vienna will be laughing at him tomorrow." Kempelen grinned, took another sip, and added, "No. All Vienna will be talking of nothing but the chess player. Wolfgang von Kempelen's thinking machine."

"It's not a thinking machine," said Jakob.

"What?"

"I said it's not a thinking machine. All the automaton can do is turn wheels and make a noise. Tibor does the thinking. The entire device is just a brilliant deception."

"But we're the only ones who know."

"I just want to point out that the more often we demonstrate the automaton, the more danger there is that someone will discover the fraud."

Kempelen looked from Jakob to Tibor and back again, then began to laugh. He put a hand on Jakob's shoulder and pressed it briefly. "Our homegrown Cassandra! Old Knaus intimidated you, didn't he? I saw how you two were talking to each other just now. He looked like an angry man to me."

"I don't let anyone intimidate me," replied Jakob with a touch of defiance. "I just think we don't want to tempt our luck too much."

"I entirely understand that over the centuries you Jews have had your confidence most deplorably undermined. But luck, Jakob, luck is *there* to be tempted. I've done it successfully so far, and I intend to go on in the same way. Which naturally doesn't mean that we don't have to be even more cautious than before. I'll be under observation the whole time, and my household too." He turned to Tibor. "So you won't be coming back to Pressburg with me tomorrow. Stay here for two or three days and then hire a carriage. If we do that, then anyone who happens to see you on the way won't link us together."

"I'm to stay here on my own?"

Kempelen looked at Jakob, who nodded. "Very well, Jakob will stay too. But please don't show yourselves out in the street during those three days. Stay indoors."

"Of course," Jakob assured him.

The three of them finished the champagne, discussing the performance; Kempelen told the others the details of his conversation with Maria Theresia, Jakob passed on the praise he had heard from the guests, and finally Tibor described the game against Knaus as it had seemed from inside the cabinet. He said nothing about the incident involving Ibolya Baroness Jesenák, or the fact that, unnoticed, he had overheard the conversation between Knaus and Jakob.

Palais Thun-Hohenstein

ON THE TENTH ANNIVERSARY OF MARIA THERESIA'S AC-
cession to the throne, 20 October 1750, Ludwig VIII, Landgrave of
Hesse-Darmstadt, presented Her Majesty with an automatic clock the
size of a grown man. The Imperial Performing Clock, as it was known,
weighed over two hundred and fifty pounds, and more than half of it was
made of pure silver. Under the clock face there was a small stage, almost
like a toy theater for metal puppets, framed by silver acanthus leaves,
cherubim, nymphs, and the Habsburg eagle. Arcades adorned the back of
the stage, and the backdrop showed the imperial army and Pressburg
Castle.

When the automaton began performing, an extremely complex clockwork device operated the following *tableau animé:* to the solemn notes of
a musical box, the figures of Maria Theresia and Francis I came on stage,
the Emperor from the left and his wife from the right, until they met in
the middle beside a sacrificial altar with flickering flames. Pages accompanied the couple, then knelt before them to present them with their
crowns: Maria Theresia received the royal crowns of Hungary and Bohemia, Francis I the imperial crown of the Holy Roman Empire.

Suddenly a dark cloud passed over the blue sky, and a demon with
features resembling those of Frederick II of Prussia appeared above the

imperial couple. But the Archangel Michael himself, no less, came down from heaven to put the intruder to flight with his flaming sword. Finally the Genius of History took up a pen and wrote on the firmament, in black letters, *Vivant Franciscus et Theresia,* while laurel wreaths descended upon the heads of the royal couple to the sound of fanfares.

Landgrave Ludwig had entrusted the making of this unique gift to his Court Clockmaker, Ludwig Knaus, who worked on it with his younger brother Friedrich. The Viennese court thought so highly of the brothers from Aldingen by the Neckar for their work on this masterpiece that at a later date they both entered the service of the imperial house. Ludwig became engineer to the Austrian army. As for Friedrich Knaus, he came to Vienna after the outbreak of the Seven Years' War and enjoyed a high reputation there as Court Mechanician. He became a member of the Court Physical, Mathematical, and Astronomical Cabinet and made other automata—among them four writing automata, the fourth of which, the Wonderful All-Writing Machine, was presented in the year 1760, again on the anniversary of the coronation. It consisted of a brass statuette that could write up to sixty-eight letters at a time on a moving piece of paper. The Wonderful All-Writing Machine was a sensation and established Friedrich Knaus's reputation as the greatest mechanician of his time.

ON THE WAY HOME Knaus had been looking silently out of the little window of the carriage. The cold, wet weather reflected his own mood. Outside his house he neglected to help his companion out, and she had to call him back to give her his arm. He wielded the knocker vigorously, and as they waited for his manservant to open the door, he used his cane to chase away two pigeons seeking shelter from the rain on a ledge.

"Wouldn't you rather be alone tonight?" asked the lady at his side.

"That would suit you nicely, wouldn't it?" he ungraciously replied. "Who do you think's going to cheer me up if you don't?"

The servant opened the door. Knaus handed him his hat, overcoat, cane, and gloves, ordered a bottle of wine and something to eat, and went ahead up to his bedroom on the first floor. While the lady sat at a little dressing table to remove her wig and clean the powder and rouge off her face, he strode around the room, sometimes with his arms crossed over his chest, sometimes with hands clasped behind his back.

"I could have sworn there was a man hidden in that machine," he said after a long silence. He stopped and looked at her. "Would you be kind enough to contradict me? Or better still, to agree with me. I'm not interested in talking to myself."

She sighed and said, without turning, "But you examined the machine to see if it was really empty. And it was."

"Yes, but a . . . perhaps a monkey? The Sultan of Baghdad is said to have a clever monkey that plays chess. Or yes, a human being . . . without limbs, with no lower body, a veteran who had his whole lower body blown off by a cannonball in the war . . . cutting him in half, as it were . . . for heaven's sake interrupt me, can't you? I'm talking drivel. And what kind of fool would I be to lose against a monkey? I'd rather lose to a machine." Knaus snatched the wig off his head and flung it onto a chair. It fell off. "God, how I hate Kempelen. That arrogant upstart, that provincial lickspittle with his infuriating modesty—vainer than any show of vanity! Why can't he mind his own business? I don't meddle with his paperwork."

"No."

He removed his coat. "The Abbé and Father Hell agreed with me; there has to be something shady about that machine. But of course it makes no difference to them: Kempelen's not poaching on their preserves. Suppose he'd claimed to have discovered a new planet—aha, then Hell would have been up in arms at once!" He slapped powder off the shoulders of his coat with the palm of his hand. "Perhaps it's something to do with magnets. In fact, it must be something to do with magnets. No one's interested in anything these days unless there's a damn magnet in it somewhere. Did you notice the way he stood beside that little casket all through the game? The secret has to be in there. He's controlling the automaton from a distance . . . with the help of magnetic currents. There isn't any thinking machine; Kempelen does the thinking and works the device."

"That would be brilliant."

"Of course it would be brilliant, but it would still be deception. A brilliant deception, and I'm going to uncover it."

By now she had taken out all the pins holding up her blond hair under the wig and was brushing it out. "Why?"

"*Why?* Are you seriously asking me *why?* Because if I don't, I might as well retire from my post, my dear, that's why. I know that Francophile old hag; just let something new come into fashion"—here he altered his voice—"*O ça c'est drôle, c'est magnifique, o je l'aime absolument!*—then everything old has served its purpose. She admires that charlatan, that Hungarian Cagliostro, I could see it very clearly. God knows why, probably because he's of noble rank and I'm not. And Kempelen plans to construct a speaking machine too, would you believe it? That can't be coincidence. He wants to defeat me on my own ground! But I'm not having that. I shall reveal his deception, and that will be the end of him, then he'll be finished, then he can flee to Prussia, or better still to Russia!" With this last remark, Knaus had instinctively raised his forefinger to point east, until he realized what a ridiculous figure he cut and began unbuttoning his waistcoat.

"You're exaggerating," said the lady. "I'm sure he means you no ill. He doesn't even know you. And who can say, perhaps all this fuss over the Turk won't last more than a few weeks."

"I can't wait as long as that. How can I find out the secret?"

As Knaus had no answer to give himself, she replied, "Bribe his assistant."

"What do you think I was trying to do just now? Not everyone can be bought, my dear Galatea."

For a split second she paused, then went on passing a damp cloth over her face.

"I'm sorry," said Knaus, going over to her. He embraced her bare shoulders and kissed her throat. "Truly, I'm sorry. Please forgive me. I don't know if I'm on my head or my heels. I'm so angry that I even turn on what I love best."

She put her hands behind her to undo the eyelets of her corset. Knaus took over for her, kneeling behind her to unhook the corset from top to bottom. Meanwhile he looked at her in the mirror. Her hair was perfect, so was her skin, and so above all were her breasts, but it was her imperfections that he desired: the blue eyes with their inexplicable sprinkling of green, the tiny scar on her forehead, the way the right-hand corner of her mouth was always a little higher than the left-hand corner, the mole above it that made any beauty spot superfluous. As he was kissing her back, inspiration came to him.

"You'll find out!" he said.

"I beg your pardon?"

Friedrich Knaus straightened up, delighted by his idea. "You'll find out how the chess-playing automaton works for me. You can wrap any man around your little finger. You'll win Kempelen over too. No man can resist you! What a brilliant notion! I'm a genius!"

"I won't do it. How do you imagine I could succeed? And I'm not an informer."

"Of course you can't just ask him. You'll have to engineer it more cunningly than that. But you'll find a way. You're a clever little thing. How exactly you do it is all one to me."

"No."

"You can do it! It's not a difficult task. And you have all the time in the world."

"No. Put the idea right out of your head."

She had taken off her clothes now, rose, and let her petticoat slip down her body. Naked, she went over to the bed.

Knaus clicked his tongue. "You *must* do it, Galatea. Because once your pregnancy becomes obvious, you'll have no more clients here at court."

She had dropped the sheet she was holding, and turned. "How did you know?"

"I didn't until this moment. I merely suspected. But your dismay speaks volumes." He smiled. "Don't forget, I may not be a doctor of medicine, but at least I'm a scientist, and we scientists have a keen eye for what goes on around us." She slipped under the sheet, her face turned away from him, and he watched the linen slowly draping itself over her curves with pleasure. "Are you going to get rid of it?"

"No."

"Then you'll have to leave Vienna. News travels fast at court, and once everyone knows about it, you won't be able to practice your profession anymore after the birth. Whose is it, by the way? Mine? Or has Joseph's prick, forgive the expression, found relief in there, leaving a little emperor growing inside you?"

He put his hand gently on her belly, but she pushed it away. Instead, he whispered in her ear, "Galatea, leave Vienna, go and work for me in Pressburg. I'll pay you handsomely, you know that. So handsomely that afterward you'll never need to be anyone's mistress again, not even the Emperor's."

She did not react. He undressed entirely, put out the candles, pressed his body against her warm back, and buried his face in her hair. "And now, my love, I am going to reward myself for my wonderful idea."

ON THE SECOND EVENING after Wolfgang von Kempelen's departure Jakob came in with Tibor's coat. He himself was wearing the close-fitting yellow coat again and had combed his hair neatly back.

"I thought you were never going to wear that again."

"When I go out in the capital city of the Empire, I don't want to look like a common drover. I want to look like the noble cavalier I am at heart."

"You're going out?" inquired Tibor, rather disappointed.

"No, *we're* going out."

"What? Where?"

"No idea. I don't know this city particularly well, but there's sure to be somewhere they'll serve us a decent jug of wine."

Tibor lowered his voice as if someone were listening at the door. "But Kempelen said we weren't to!"

"You sound like the seven little kids," said Jakob, shaking his head, adding in a falsetto, *"Our mother said we weren't to, oh no, we mustn't, we're afraid of the big bad wolf!"*

"I don't know the story."

"Tibor: how many times have you been in Vienna before?"

"Never."

"Well, there you are. Do you seriously intend to spend the whole of your first visit to the pearl of the Habsburg Empire in cramped suburban lodgings, listening to the woodworms eating their dinner? And you ought to be well enough acquainted with me by now to know that I couldn't care less about orders. The fact is, perverse creature that I am, I regard them as a challenge."

Tibor slipped into the jacket that Jakob was holding for him.

"How does the story end?" he asked.

"What story?"

"The one about the seven little kids."

"Oh, that. The kids let the wolf into the house, and he eats them all up." Tibor stared at Jakob, wide-eyed. The Jew roared with laughter and pinched the dwarf's neck. "Never fear! The smallest one survives— hidden in the clock."

It was raining, and had been raining hard all day, so that the two of them had to jump over deep puddles and small trickles that were trying to run into the stream of the Alser Bach. Tibor's stockings were soon wet through, and he doubted whether he was going to enjoy this forbidden outing very much, for he could hardly see much of the city in the twilight. They passed the Invalidenhaus and the church of the Trinitarians, walked down the street between the barracks and the law courts, then crossed the parade ground outside the walls of the inner city, made their way to the Schottentor, past the Schottenkirche, and to the Hoher Markt, until finally they reached a tangle of narrow alleyways that reminded Tibor of Venice. Jakob had the strength of mind to pass one tavern near St. Ruprecht and another in Griechengasse, when a glance through their windows told him that he didn't like the look of either.

At last they found an inn that appeared more inviting than the first two. There was a table vacant near the stove, and they sat down there.

Jakob ordered something hot from the landlord, never mind what, he said, something to warm them up. The landlord brought them two glasses of hot water with arrack and plenty of sugar, "sweet as sin and hot as hell." After that they settled down to sample the local wines. Tibor was warm again now, his boots were standing by the stove to dry, and while Jakob drank yet again, in tones of all-embracing ridicule, to the court at Schönbrunn, Tibor looked in silence at the guests: simple but decently dressed people. Jakob was the only one to catch the eye with his costume and the performance he was putting on: he was making himself out very much the nobleman, speaking haughtily to the landlord, crooking his little finger as he drank, and dabbing the corners of his mouth with his handkerchief every time he took a sip. There were not many women there, but they had all looked at Jakob at least once, and Tibor felt sure that he was well aware of it.

An hour and a half after their arrival a real nobleman entered the inn, his wet tricorne in one hand and a cane with a silver knob in the other. With a broad smile he went up to the bar, looking as if he had just heard a good joke, and asked the landlord what kind of sparkling wine he had in stock. Then he ordered eight bottles of it and asked to have them packed in crates padded with straw for him to take away. While the landlord set to work, the nobleman's eye fell on Jakob and Tibor. He nodded at them, and Jakob politely nodded back, still playing his part. "Monsieur."

"That's an odd servant you have there, monsieur," opined the nobleman, looking at Tibor.

"Appearances are deceptive," replied Jakob. "He's not my servant. If anything, I am his."

The stranger looked at the garments the two of them were wearing.

"Don't let our clothes deceive you," said Jakob. "We're traveling incognito."

"And will you tell me who you are?"

"It would be a poor sort of incognito if we did." Jakob looked at Tibor, who didn't know what to say, then turned back to the nobleman. "Can you keep a secret?"

"Suppose I can't?"

"Oh, then we'll just have to do away with you."

Tibor jumped but did not join in the conversation. Kempelen would be furious if he knew what they were doing, but the alcohol was numbing Tibor's conscience, and he wanted to see what Jakob did next. The stranger's curiosity had finally been aroused. He grinned, took a vacant chair, and sat down with them, leaning well forward over the table. "I'm all ears."

Jakob asked Tibor's permission by inquiring, "Sire?" Tibor nodded. The Jew continued in a whisper. "I'm sure, sir, that you have heard of the famous Marquise de Pompadour, the King of France's mistress?" The nobleman was quick to nod and gestured to Jakob to go on. "Well, La Pompadour became pregnant by His Majesty the King in the year 1745. But as she was not the Queen, the child would have been a bastard, so Louis himself intervened—in a brutal fashion most unworthy of a king, by striking Madame de Pompadour in the belly with his fist."

"*Sacré!*" exclaimed the nobleman.

"Only it didn't lead to a miscarriage. But the pregnancy was cut short by two whole months, and the child—the child came into the world unfinished." Slowly, very slowly Jakob turned his head in Tibor's direction. Openmouthed, the nobleman followed his gaze.

"Monsieur, you see before you the Dauphin, Louis the Sixteenth, by rights successor to the throne of France." Jakob paused for his words to take effect, and then added, "Since his birth we have been in flight from His Majesty's secret police. At present we're on our way to London, where King George will grant us asylum."

The nobleman looked from Jakob to Tibor and back again, then burst out laughing. "I don't believe a word of it!"

"That's all one to us."

The landlord put the two crates of sparkling wine on the counter. The stranger stood up, getting out his purse. Then he brought his hand down on the table. "I'm invited to a soirée that will probably be very tedious, even though wine will flow. Won't you come with me? You would be guests of honor, and I'm sure you'd contribute to our amusement."

"Your Highness?" Jakob asked Tibor, kicking him hard under the table.

"My carriage is outside, with two lovely ladies in it," said the nobleman.

"We'll accept," said Tibor.

He put on his boots, which were dry and warm now from standing by the stove, and to maintain the fiction of his role, Jakob deferentially helped him into his coat. Meanwhile the nobleman settled up for his sparkling wine and paid the two companions' bill into the bargain.

The man's carriage was standing just outside the inn, and the three of them got in with the crates of wine. Tibor went last, to increase the ladies' surprise. The nobleman had not exaggerated; they were indeed lovely, and handsomely dressed, although the rain had left the hems of their skirts as dirty as the men's silk stockings. They giggled a great deal, and when Jakob was made to tell his story all over again, they kept interrupting with questions. The younger of the two actually seemed to believe Jakob's tall tale.

"What's the matter with you?" she crossly asked the others. "Such things do happen!"

After a quarter of an hour the carriage stopped outside a small mansion. They waited for servants to arrive with umbrellas. Finally one did come out, in the company of a man who put his head in through the carriage window and greeted the passengers. "*Bonsoir mesdames, bonsoir Rodolphe*. Don't go in there," he warned them. "It's less fun than a Calvinist Sunday service. We're off to see Thun-Hohenstein. He's invited us to a meeting of a Magnetic Société."

The nobleman addressed as Rudolph told his coachman to drive on to Count von Thun-Hohenstein's palace, and not until the carriage was on its way again did he request the permission of "Your Highness the Dauphin." The drive and a cold draught in the carriage sobered Tibor up, and he realized that what they were doing was terribly wrong. He was about to ask Jakob to let them get out, but as if he sensed it, the nobleman took a bottle of sparkling wine out of the crate, removed the cork, and

offered Tibor the first sip. The wine was delicious. Wine solved everything: Tibor just had to keep on drinking, and he would get through the
evening without any pangs of conscience.

The carriage stopped under a roofed forecourt. Jakob helped the
younger lady up the steps to the house they had reached, and Rudolph
the nobleman escorted her companion. Tibor was going to carry the
wine, but the nobleman stopped him; there was always plenty to drink at
the Count's, he said, and anyway such work was unworthy of a Dauphin.
In the magnificent front hall, they once again met the man who had spoken to them before and his companions. Footmen took their coats, scarves,
and hats, leaving Tibor conspicuous now not just for his small size but
for his inappropriate wardrobe: Jakob and he were the only men there
who did not wear wigs or powdered white hair. All the same, no one
questioned their right to be present, and the servants treated them as
respectfully as everyone else.

A servant stood at the foot of the steps leading to the floor above,
beside a table holding masks like those that Tibor remembered from
Carnival time in Venice. Rudolph's friend explained that it was obliga-
tory for everyone to wear a mask, so as to remove any inhibitions that
might be felt in the course of the evening. None of the guests need fear
to express his innermost nature, he said, if they were all made unrecognizable by masks. Tibor and Jakob took theirs, which were adorned
with feathers and colored stones and hid everything but the mouth and
chin, and let the ladies tie them on. Jakob winked at Tibor through the
eyehole of his mask.

On the upper floor they went first through an empty salon and then
into another, where a buffet stood ready. Some forty guests stood here in
small groups, more women than men. They were all fashionably dressed
and wore masks. The windows were closed, the curtains drawn; it was
warm and stuffy. Candle wax dripped to the floor from two large chande-
liers, and the air was heavy with the smell of wine. Tibor heard a woman
singing not very melodiously in one of the nearby rooms.

Half a dozen guests were assembled around the buffet itself. A toy
made of brass was moving around on the table, a small ship with Bacchus

holding the mast and a little tin barrel standing on deck. The ship stopped in front of one of the guests, who picked up the little barrel, smiling, and drained the wine in it at a single draught. Then he poured more wine into the barrel, and with this cargo on board the clockwork of the ship was wound up, and it was sent on its travels again.

When the doors closed behind the new arrivals, their host approached them. He warmly welcomed their group and, when Rudolph's friend was about to introduce himself, silenced him with a wave of his hand. "No, no, my young friend, let's have none of that. We're all anonymous in this *société*, or rather, we bear other names, as fine as the masks on our faces! I am no less than Neptune tonight—so take some refreshment, make the acquaintance of other nymphs and heroes, for we're all one great family on Mount Olympus here, and the show will soon begin." He looked down at Tibor. "Your trouble is plain to see, my friend; excellent! If you're bold enough, I am sure there are still places free around the *baquet*. One should never give up hope."

Neptune moved on, and the group dispersed. Jakob, Tibor, and the younger of the ladies in their company stayed where they were. "I'll call myself Chloris," said the girl.

"Since you obviously know your way around Hellas," replied Jakob, "be so kind as to think of names for the two of us."

"Then you, brother, are—are Acis for tonight, and you," she said, inspecting Tibor, "of course we'll call you Pan." And she chuckled with delight.

Jakob kissed Chloris's hand, looking into her eyes. "Be assured of the thanks of Acis, O fair one."

Tibor waited for Chloris to move away, then said, "This is madness!"

"Yes, isn't it?" replied Jakob, grinning.

"I mean *madness* in the sense that we'd better get away from here fast, Jakob."

"If you want to leave, then do, but I wouldn't miss this for the world. I'm wearing a mask, and anyway my name is Acis, if you don't mind."

"No mask can hide my height."

Jakob did not reply but let his eyes wander over the company. "That

Chloris is a pretty thing," he said abstractedly, and then—without another word to Tibor—went into the next room, where Chloris herself had gone.

Suppressing his impulse to follow, as well as his anger at Jakob's dereliction of duty and his own fear of being discovered, he helped himself to something to eat from the buffet and a glass of wine, while the clockwork ship bearing Bacchus sailed past him. Then he sat down on a chaise longue, for his deficiencies were less obvious when he was sitting. He didn't know just what he was eating, but it was delicious; he couldn't remember ever having eaten anything so good in his life. A man sat down beside him but paid him no attention. He was breathing heavily, and the skin beneath his mask was pale. His upper body was swaying back and forth with small circular movements.

Tibor heard a nearby group talking about Kempelen. One of the women had obviously been at Schönbrunn Palace to see the presentation of the chess automaton, and now she was describing this memorable experience to the others. She was tipsy, and to Tibor's delight exaggerated wildly; as she told the story, the automaton worked as fast as a steam engine, and the wooden Turk moved with far more agility than was actually possible. When one man expressed doubts—was the Turk really an automaton?—the woman swore, her voice rising, that no one could possibly have fitted into it, not even a child, no, not so much as a baby. She recommended everyone to go to see the Hungarian Baron von Kempelen's chess-playing Turk if they were in Pressburg. Tibor felt light-headed with pride.

By now other guests had noticed him, and were giggling behind their fans or pointing at the dwarf. And he know he must be a comical sight, sitting beside the drunk on the chaise longue with his legs not even reaching the floor. Tibor emptied his glass and went into the salon next door.

This room was considerably smaller. In the middle of it stood the *baquet,* an oval tub about four feet long and one foot deep. It was full of water, and dark iron filings floated on the surface. A dozen wine bottles were arranged in the water, radiating out, their necks toward the side of the tub. The singer, who was standing on a small platform in one corner of the room, was still performing, as if she were a musical box that would never tire. Tibor looked for Jakob, but there was no sign of him. Many doors led out of this room, like the last, with guests passing in and out now and then, and Tibor supposed that the Jew had gone through one of them. He couldn't see Chloris, Rudolph, and the others either.

Now two men entered wearing black clothes and plain masks. They put a lid on the tub, closing it off. There were holes in the lid exactly over the places where the bottles lay. Next the men ran iron rods through the holes and into the bottles, so that the ends of the rods stuck out.

The host entered the salon, accompanied by two ladies, and several more guests followed him. He clapped his hands, whereupon the singer fell silent and the two men in black arranged twelve chairs around the tub. Neptune explained that the magnetization was now about to begin, and anyone seeking a cure for some disorder should sit by the *baquet*. Several ladies took chairs at once, followed by Neptune and the ladies with him, and then some more of the guests. Others deliberately stepped back; they just wanted to watch the show, not to be part of it. There were still two seats left empty opposite the host.

"Come along, come along, little man!" he called to Tibor. "Magnetism works wonders, and it's never hurt anyone yet!"

Tibor politely shook his head, but suddenly someone took his hand—a young woman in a pink dress with gold flounces, her face covered by a mask adorned with peacock feathers—and drew him over to the *baquet*, laughing. She sat down, and as she did not let go of his hand, and all eyes in the salon were now bent on him, he followed her example. Neptune applauded.

While the two assistants asked all the spectators to leave the salon and close the doors behind them, Tibor's neighbor leaned down to him. "I'm Callisto," she whispered.

"I'm Pan," replied Tibor, feeling like a liar.

She laughed briefly, and her laughter was clear as a bell. "Don't be afraid, Pan. It's like beautiful magic. I've heard that magnetism has even restored a blind woman's sight."

The whispering suddenly stopped, and when Tibor turned around he saw why: a man in a purple robe had entered the salon. He had shoulder-length hair and a piercing gaze and held a white bar magnet in his hand. Walking solemnly through the hall, he looked hard at each of the volunteers, including Tibor, and then announced, "A fluid fills the universe, linking together all that it contains: the planets, the moon, and the earth, and also natural things: stones, plants, animals, and men, and the different parts of the body. The fluid flows through our limbs, our bones, our muscles, and our organs. It links the head to the feet and one hand to the other. But should this fluid fall into imbalance, then disorders arise, diseases, colics, ill humor, and anxiety. I am here to restore the balance again and free you from your sufferings, and for that purpose I use the divine power of animal magnetism." At this point he held his magnet up in the air in front of him as if it were the philosopher's stone. "The fluid will flow through your bodies, will break down your complaints and the blockades inside you like crumbling dams, sweeping them away now and forever."

"Ah," sighed a woman softly, "ah."

The master signed to his assistants to put out all the candles but one. "Now we will bring on dark night, so that you can concentrate entirely on what is deep within you, with no distracting sights. During the healing process you will feel sensations that are strange to you, and do things that you do not intend to do, but have no fear: you can suffer no harm, it is only the fluid taking possession of you, and I shall be here all the time to watch over you. Now take hold of the iron rods."

Almost blindly, Tibor reached for the rod. The iron quickly warmed up in his fingers, but he felt nothing else. "Next press your knees firmly against the knees of your neighbors. It is essential for the flow that you should all be linked, with none breaking the chain!"

Tibor heard skirts rustling on both sides of him, and then his neighbors' knees touched his. He spread his legs a little wider in order to return the pressure. The singer began again, but this time her song was even more disjointed than before; no words could be made out, single notes were interrupted by long pauses, and she changed abruptly from the top to the bottom of the scale and back again—it was like a madwoman's song. Tibor couldn't hear any noise in the other rooms now. The master was speaking calmly to a woman patient, repeating himself for the most part, talking about the flow of the fluid, balance, the power of animal magnetism, the stars, and the planets. Sobbing could be heard. Looking up, Tibor saw that it came from one of the women next to Neptune. The master was standing behind her and doing something with his magnet, Tibor couldn't see what, and his two assistants were also at work behind other guests. The sobbing grew louder. Other sounds were added; laughter, then a giggle that sounded deranged, a lustful moan, animal-like growling, breathless whimpering, and suddenly a scream. However hard Tibor tried to peer through the dark, he couldn't make anything out. The magnetizer talked on, unperturbed, but his voice, like the singer's, grew louder to drown out the wild sounds made by his patients. Callisto's knee suddenly began to twitch and wouldn't stop; Tibor had to move farther forward on his chair and stretch his leg out if he was not to lose contact with her. A woman was weeping and seemed to be calling out for her mother.

Suddenly Tibor felt pressure on the nape of his neck; one of the assistants or perhaps the magnetizer himself was standing behind him, running a magnet over the back of his head, down his spine, and over his arms. Tibor felt warmth where the magnet had touched his skin, a warmth that lingered long after the magnet had moved on. An electric shock ran through the hand holding the rod and passed through his whole body. He was breathing faster, much faster, and he knew that if this went on, he would soon lose consciousness. Now the warmth was moving from his belly to his loins. Tibor felt ashamed of himself. For a brief moment it shot through his mind that what he was doing was a sin, a dance of ecstasy around a golden calf, but he abandoned himself to it. Callisto groaned, with the assistant behind her, and Tibor placed his free hand on her knee, to hold it close to his and stop her groaning, but most of all to feel her. Instead of rejecting this indecent intimacy, Callisto put her hand on his and pressed it. A chair fell over, and someone toppled to the floor. That broke the circle, but the sense of warmth lasted. The magnetizer reassured the circle, but there was no need for reassurance anymore; the participants were beside themselves. One man kept kicking the side of the tub, a woman leaped up screaming and tearing her hair, another man was tugging at his limbs as if to free himself from his own body, like Heracles trying to tear off the poisoned shirt; many fell unconscious to the floor, others flung themselves down. Callisto guided Tibor's hand up her thigh until his fingers met her private parts, which he could feel even through her clothes. Now she pressed her legs together as if to crush Tibor's hand between her thighs. The singer stopped performing, unable to compete with the noise in the salon anymore.

Suddenly Callisto leaped up so violently that her chair fell over backward, and she pulled Tibor out of the salon by his hand, calling "Erato!" as she went. The woman thus addressed rose too and followed them. Beyond the side door they came to a corridor, and Callisto led them to the right, the floorboards creaking under her shoes. Then she pushed a door open, and only when she, Tibor, and the other woman were in the room beyond it, and the door was closed, did Callisto let go of Tibor's hand. Erato had brought a candelabrum from the corridor to light the room.

They had found their way—whether by chance or not, Tibor didn't know—to a small bedchamber furnished only with a dressing table, two armchairs, and a four-poster bed. Callisto was still breathing heavily. The hair and clothing of all three were in disarray.

"He's so wonderful," said Erato, glancing at Tibor. She had been shedding tears, as the smudged makeup below her mask showed, but whatever the reason for her grief, it all seemed to be gone now. Callisto was about to remove her mask, but the other woman stopped her with a gesture.

"There, Pan," said Callisto, "now let's see if you live up to your name."

The women smiled at each other. Tibor did not react.

"Undress," said Callisto in a neutral voice.

"I'm not Pan," said Tibor defensively, although his excitement had not died down.

"Then we must arouse the Pan in you," replied Erato. Tibor held his breath. The two women took each other's hands and brought their faces together in a long kiss. They had to turn their heads to keep the feather-decked masks from clashing. In the flickering candlelight they looked like two birds performing a strange courtship display. Tibor's back was touching the wall; unconsciously, he must have taken a step back. Without entirely moving away from each other, the women looked at Tibor again, pleased with the impression their kiss had made on him. Then they began undressing each other, their eyes on Tibor almost all the time, well aware of the magic of what they were doing. Tibor felt dizzy, and with every garment that the two of them dropped carelessly to the floor, his desire grew greater. They climbed into the bed and undid each other's corsages, crying out with glee and moaning lustfully, and Tibor took a step now forward and now back, unable to think clearly at all.

Of course he had seen naked women before and had slept with two. It had amused his dragoons back in Silesia to pay a soldiers' whore to make a man of the fifteen-year-old, but his comrades had enjoyed it more than he did. Later, on his travels and two days' journey from Gran, he had an affair with a peasant girl who had a pretty face but a clubfoot. Tibor thought it sad that here were two ugly people making love to each other, a man and a woman to whom no other lover would ever yield, but he stayed for several days, until her father got on the trail of their affair and Tibor had to flee. He hadn't loved her, and of course he hadn't loved her leg, but the rest of her body had been wonderful, and he often thought back to it with longing. Now he suddenly found himself under the canopy of the four-poster bed with soft sheets and pillows below him, caressing all the skin he could get his hands on, the skin of the two girls who now wore nothing but their silk stockings and the masks, and they laughed triumphantly to see that they had indeed succeeded in turning him into Pan. Touching those soft white thighs and arms would have been enough for him, but they guided his hands greedily to other parts of themselves, their bellies, throats, breasts, and last of all between their legs. Meanwhile they were undressing him from top to bottom, but he too insisted on keeping his mask on. He knew that his prick was no larger than other men's, it was just that he himself was much smaller than those others, and as he had secretly hoped, the sight of his erection didn't fail to impress them. The women giggled; Erato touched and held his penis but didn't venture to kiss it. Now Tibor was groaning too. He clung to the sheets. Soon Erato was leaning back against pillows heaped at the head of the bed, with Callisto's back drawn close to her tender places, caressing her friend's breasts from behind and licking the side of her throat. Callisto spread her legs wide, Erato beckoned to Pan, and he approached, supported himself on the bed with both hands, and thrust into Callisto. Since the legs of the two girls were lying on top of each other, he could touch four thighs at once. He let his head fall between Callisto's breasts, which Erato was holding against his cheeks.

Soon, only too soon, the pleasure of the senses was over. Pan suppressed his orgasmic cry as best he could, and as if a bucket of cold water had been emptied over his head, he suddenly saw his situation in the sober light of day: here he was, entwined with a fabulous creature that had two feathered heads and four legs and was now beginning to laugh from a single beak at the sight of the dwarf who had spent himself in its twin gardens of delight. He felt his amulet of Our Lady cold on his chest. Sweat stood out on his brow, particularly under the mask.

"Your magnet released me from my suffering, Pan," said Callisto, who was as breathless as he was, and they both laughed again. Tibor was already looking for his clothes where they lay in the bed and scattered on the floor.

TIBOR WENT BACK to the large salon where the buffet stood. The room was empty except for a couple talking quietly, who ignored him, and two drunks sleeping it off—one of them the man who had been sitting on the chaise longue beside Tibor. He lay snoring on the carpet next to a pool of vomit. Tibor wondered why he couldn't have crawled a little farther, to throw up on the floorboards instead of the expensive carpet, but probably it didn't matter to these people. Tibor would have liked to know what the room next door with the *baquet* in it was like now, but he didn't want to go and look, for he was reluctant to meet the strange magnetizer in the purple robe. He wasn't anxious to see Callisto and Erato again either. Instead, he helped himself to some of the remaining food and drank another glass of wine. The clockwork ship commanded by Captain Bacchus had run aground in a soufflé and lay there listing heavily.

Jakob reappeared only a quarter of an hour later. He was wearing a different mask now and apologized profusely for making Tibor wait so long. Then he picked up two unopened bottles, and they left the salon. They put their masks back on the table where they had received them. Down below only two tired footmen were on duty. The footmen brought their coats, said not a word about the bottles of wine they were taking away, and wished "the noble gentlemen" goodnight.

Outside, the rain had stopped. Jakob took a deep breath. Passing the carriages of those few guests who were still inside the rooms and salons of the Palais, Jakob and Tibor left on foot. On their way home through the sleeping city, they drank the contents of one of the two wine bottles, and Jakob gave a detailed description of his encounter with Chloris, who had allowed him to kiss not just her hand and her mouth but her throat too and later on even her porcelainlike feet. Tibor kept quiet.

Neuchâtel: Evening

WHETHER CARMAUX, JAQUET-DROZ, AND THE REST HAD paid to see Kempelen's chess machine beaten by the dwarf, or just to watch a fascinating game between the two of them, what they got was mainly the latter. Neumann drove White back into the Turk's half of the board and chased the white queen from square to square. He even succeeded in bringing off the rare trick of a pawn promotion: the pawn on c7 had made its way right to the other side of the board and became a queen on e1. Neumann earned applause, although in the course of the following moves all three queens were taken.

After the thirty-sixth move the Turk's arm stopped again. The chessmen on the board had very obviously thinned out. Night had now fallen, and this time no one opposed Kempelen when he interrupted the game, saying that all concerned needed to rest. The chessboard would be left untouched overnight, he said, and they could finish the game next day. He added that he hoped to see as many as possible of those now present again, particularly the chess automaton's opponent. Neumann stood up without a word and mingled with the spectators who were leaving, many of whom praised his play, shook hands with him, or clapped him appreciatively on the shoulder. He left the inn on the marketplace in the company of his colleague Henri-Louis Jaquet-Droz; the latter's father, Pierre; and several others. At the same time Wolfgang von Kempelen and his assistant were wheeling the chess cabinet and the Turk into the next room.

Once the audience had left the hall, and the doors were closed and the curtains drawn, they opened the cabinet to let out the player hidden there. He was a little taller than Kempelen, young and thin, and he looked pale and sweaty after all that time inside the device. Groaning, he stretched his arms and legs, rubbed the nape of his neck, and turned his head this way and that on his shoulder. It made an audible cracking sound.

"Anton, fetch Johann a towel. And water," Kempelen told his assistant.

The chess player drank a little first, then rubbed the sweat from his brow. "God in heaven," he said, "I thought you were going to leave me to perish in there, and I'd look like a dried prune before you let me out."

"But you heard that about the money, didn't you?" said Anton.

"Oh yes."

Kempelen put his hands down on the table to the left and right of the chessboard. "I'm an idiot to have let myself in for this bargain."

Anton rubbed his hands. "What, with two hundred thalers bet on it? I'd play against Old Nick himself for that money."

"We're going to lose," said Kempelen, glancing at the chessboard.

"You'll keep the money anyway. The condition was only that the game should be finished. There was nothing about the Turk winning."

"And anyway," Johann interrupted, "we won't lose." He joined Kempelen beside the chessboard and pointed to the position of the pieces. "He has two fewer pawns. And he's playing an old-fashioned game. He's ventured too far out with his attack, and now I'll get him. I've never lost yet."

"Then it will be your first time tomorrow. We'll lose, never mind what it looks like to you now. Believe me, we'll lose," said Kempelen, and Johann dared not contradict him.

Anton shrugged. "Never mind if we do: two hundred thalers! You didn't make that much in Regensburg and Augsburg put together."

"They'll be avenged. Because if we lose, our reputation is ruined, and money can't compensate for the damage." Kempelen began pacing up and down the room.

"You should have seen him," Anton told Johann. He placed his hand at waist height. "A dwarf, no taller than this. When he sat on the chair, his little feet didn't even reach the floor."

"Another watchmaker?"

"Sure to be. They all are here. A dwarf watchmaker, think of that! Odd. There was once a dwarf watchmaker like that in Amsterdam. He was only a head taller than the clocks he made."

"Quiet," said Kempelen. "I have to think."

His two employees fell silent and went about their work—Anton checked the cabinet, Johann put on a clean shirt—until Kempelen spoke again.

"Johann, go and find out where he lives, or where he's staying the night."

Johann and Anton looked at each other.

"What are you going to do?" asked Anton.

"You leave that to me."

"Can't Anton go instead?" asked Johann, looking injured. "I'm dead tired."

Kempelen shook his head. "They know him from the performance, but no one here has seen you. You won't have any trouble finding him— he's a dwarf. And ask if his wife is with him."

"A she-dwarf?"

"No, you fool, a normal human being . . . pretty, too."

When Johann had gone, Anton said, "A dwarf who plays chess as well as that! He wouldn't have to hunch up inside the machine. You should have hired him instead of Johann."

Kempelen did not reply.

Pressburg, Judengasse

THEY CLEARED OUT THE ROOM NEXT TO THE WORKSHOP. Jakob called it "the creator's spare-parts store," for this was where Kempelen kept all the items that had been made during the building of the chess automaton but in the end were not used because they were imperfect, including a number of artificial body parts such as hands, fingers, and heads, as well as wigs, all put away in cupboards and crates or just hanging from the ceiling. Another android could easily have been assembled from them, but the end product would have been an absurdly botched job: a female head on a male body, with arms of different lengths ending in one white and one black hand. Tibor found a velvet-lined box in which two more Venetian glass eyes lay. When they had emptied the room, Branislav took out the rubbish in a crate. Wooden legs and spread hands stuck out of it, looking as if they belonged to drowning men trying to find safety and something to clutch. This room was now to house the Mechanical Turk itself. It could be safely stored here between performances. Kempelen had a lock fitted to the door, and the window of the room was walled up completely.

Meanwhile the workshop was turned into a theater for the Turk's performances: the workbenches and tools went, the sketches and construction drawings were taken down from the walls. They put up two more tables next to the cabinet: the mysterious casket was to stand on the smaller of them. The other table would also have a chessboard on it: this was where the Turk's opponents would sit, for no one was ever again to be allowed as close to the automaton as Knaus had come. Finally, chairs were brought in; twenty seats with an aisle down the middle.

As Kempelen had hoped, the fame of the sensational chess-playing machine had accompanied him from Vienna back to Pressburg, and even during the preparations he was frequently asked when the automaton was going to play its first game in Pressburg. Letters and notes came from aristocrats and ordinary citizens alike. Two weeks after the premiere at Schönbrunn, Kempelen had to go to Ofen on business to do with the salt mines, so the chess-playing Turk would not give its first performance here until he was back. Kempelen invited prominent citizens of Pressburg to the show: city councilors, rich merchants, Freemasons, and those who might be expected to give the Turk instant and extensive publicity. From then on the provisional arrangement was for the automaton to play twice a week; Kempelen settled on Wednesdays and Saturdays, even though it meant that Jakob had to work on the Sabbath.

Kempelen and Tibor came to an agreement: as requested, Tibor would get thirty guilders a month. In return, he pledged himself to spend at least three hours a day reading books about chess or practicing the game himself. His usual opponent was Jakob, who neither improved his own game nor showed any inclination to do so. As Kempelen himself had very little free time, he asked his wife to play chess with Tibor. He made it clear to Anna Maria that the success of the chess machine, and of the Kempelen family with it, depended on Tibor's playing a perfect game, and without practice his skills were bound to decline.

So the two of them met again. They spoke not a word to each other during the games and even at the end of them said only what was absolutely essential. Tibor's brilliant performance in front of the Empress did not seem to have made any difference to Anna Maria's attitude. To his surprise, however, she played chess well, even better than her husband. As before, Tibor won every game, but she put up a stout defense, and soon Tibor was aware of something like a passion in her: a passion to resist him, to avoid defeat for as long as possible and take as many of his white chessmen as she could before losing her own king. It was not an attractive passion, but at least it showed some kind of emotion. Tibor actually felt sorry for her persistent attempts to defy his unbeatable talent. Once he was going to let her win and took his king down a blind alley from which he would have been unable to escape, but she wasn't taking charity; she refused to accept the move, telling him to think harder about it—and afterward it looked as if she hated him all the more.

In spite of the daily games of chess, Tibor soon began to feel bored again, and as Jakob was bored too now that his own work on the automaton was finished, the Jew offered to teach Tibor joinery and watchmaking. Kempelen let them use his tools and materials for the purpose, and under Jakob's instructions the dwarf practiced those skills in the workshop or in his own room. In return, Tibor wanted to teach Jakob more about the art of playing chess, but although Jakob thanked him, he turned the offer down.

"I can think of more interesting ways of wasting my time," he said. "In fact, maybe it's about time I moved on."

"What do you mean?" asked Tibor.

"Time for me to leave Pressburg. Try something new. I don't want to let myself turn into some moss-grown Philistine."

"Oh no!"

Jakob smiled. "Don't worry, I'm not an idiot. For one thing, I don't want to miss seeing the Turk's triumph, and for another Kempelen is paying me as well as he pays you. And do you know why he's paying me so much?"

"Because you did such a good job."

"Good God, no! All that's behind us now. He's paying me not to leave him. Or give away the secret of his Turk."

"You wouldn't do that."

"I don't mind if he thinks I would," said Jakob, slapping his trouser pocket so that the coins jingled inside it.

But on one point Kempelen was not to be moved: he would not let Tibor go to church to make confession. Tibor hadn't confessed for three months, and it was more than he could bear. He was particularly anxious to confide in some servant of God about his experiences in Vienna, which now that he looked back on them seemed to him like a dream of ecstasy. But Kempelen wouldn't let Tibor set foot outside the door.

When Jakob heard of Tibor's wish, he flung a length of cloth over his shoulders like a priest's stole and asked in a deep voice what sins he was thinking of confessing. Then he picked up a nail in each hand and said, "Upon my soul, I'm as good a man as your Jesus: I'm a Jew too, I'm a carpenter, I have nails in these hands, and my father never troubled his head about me either."

Tibor didn't feel like laughing. It irked him to think that he had used those three days of freedom and anonymity in Vienna just for fleeting pleasure instead of seeking out a church at long last.

If he couldn't have absolution in the confessional, he wished he could at least enjoy the blessing of saying the rosary. But he had no rosary, and he didn't want to ask either a Jew or a freethinker like Kempelen to get him one. So he found another way around the problem: he used his chessboard as a rosary. The squares of the board would be a substitute for the rosary beads. Tibor assigned a prayer to each of the sixty-four squares, and as he moved the queen from square to square instead of slipping beads through his fingers, he could work out which prayer he had to say when, and which prayers were still ahead of him. After that Tibor said the rosary every day, and soon he had become so used to thinking of the chessboard as a chain of numbers that the mere sight of it gave him a certain amount of comfort and peace of mind.

TOTALLY UNEXPECTEDLY, Dorottya gave the Kempelens notice that she was leaving. Anna Maria and Wolfgang tried to persuade their maidservant to change her mind, but in vain: she had to go back to her home village of Prievidza as soon as possible, she said, because her sister there wasn't well, and she must look after her sister and her family. But as Dorottya didn't want to leave the Kempelens in the lurch, she added, she had already thought of a replacement, and by a stroke of great good luck her cousin's daughter from Ödenburg happened to be looking for a maid's post at this very moment. She was a pretty if rather naïve girl, said Dorottya, she had excellent references, she'd been brought up in a convent school and was knowledgeable in all branches of housekeeping, and she could start work at once.

Next day the Kempelens received Dorottya and the young woman in the large kitchen on the ground floor of the house. The girl wore plain linen clothing in shades of green and brown, with a white scarf over her blond hair. She looked around the kitchen respectfully when Dorottya brought her in, as if it were an imposing throne room.

"This is Elise Burgstaller," Dorottya introduced her.

Elise bobbed the Kempelens a curtsy. Then she took two neatly folded pieces of paper out of the basket she had brought with her and handed them to Anna Maria. They were character references describing her as an industrious and virtuous servant; both had been written in Ödenburg, one was signed by a wig-maker and the other by a Hungarian baron. Hesitantly, and in a soft voice, Elise described her career from the convent school in Ödenburg to her previous posts and now her move to Pressburg. When Kempelen asked why she wasn't married yet at the age of twenty-two, she blushed and explained that neither she nor her guardian had yet found the right man. Dorottya kept nodding to everything Elise said. Then Teréz woke up and called for her mother. When Anna Maria brought her into the kitchen, Elise clapped her hands to her mouth in her delight at seeing the "little angel." "You must be very proud," she told Anna Maria.

The Kempelens sent Dorottya and Elise out into the courtyard so that they could discuss the matter privately in the kitchen.

"She seems just right," said Anna Maria.

"She appears to be a little—forgive me—a little stupid, or am I wrong?"

"Dorottya is far from clever herself, but she was a good maidservant."

"So you don't want to look any further?"

"No, why should I? Do you want me to wait until you make me a mechanical maid?"

So Elise Burgstaller started work in the Kempelen house. Dorottya spent two days acquainting Elise with the house and its routine, and then she left Pressburg with a generous financial bonus from the Kempelens, a guilty conscience—and a bag containing fifty guilders, the bribe given to her by Galatea, the Viennese courtesan, whose money, simple clothes, forged references, and fictional life story had gained her access to Wolfgang von Kempelen's house, where she now took up service as a maid called Elise.

"WHEN THE CAT'S AWAY, the mice will play," Jakob had said, and it was true that the atmosphere in the house was a little more free and easy once Kempelen had ridden off to Ofen. The Turk was locked in its room. Anna Maria sent Tibor a message by way of Jakob that she wouldn't be playing any practice games against him until further notice, and Tibor turned to reading literary works instead of the notation of chess matches, for Kempelen's selection of volumes of poetry was impressive. Now and then he practiced his dexterity in filing metal.

While he was assembling a clockwork mechanism four days after Kempelen's departure, Jakob came into his room without knocking and with two old frock coats of Kempelen's over his arm, one green, the other dark blue. He had found them during the clearance of the room next to the workshop. "Which color do you fancy?"

Tibor looked up from his work and replied, "White."

Jakob burst into abrupt laughter. "Very funny, you crazy gnome. You can have one more try, but for heaven's sake don't say black."

"Green?"

"That'll do."

"What are you planning?"

"That's a secret." Jakob looked at Tibor's work over his shoulder. "You want to file that pin down a little shorter. It has to fit into the socket just so . . . and speaking of pins fitting into sockets, have you seen our new maid yet?"

Tibor shook his head.

Jakob pointed to the little window of Tibor's room. "She's hanging out the washing in the yard. Take a look—your own little pin will thank you for it," he said, going out.

Tibor moved his stool under the window, climbed up on it, and looked down into the courtyard. Washing lines were stretched from wall to wall, and the maid, who had brought out a large basket, was hanging white cloths, sheets, and coverlets on it so that the dark paving of the yard was crisscrossed with white lines like a chessboard. From above, Tibor couldn't see her face, but he had a good view of her breasts, particularly when she bent to take more washing out of the basket. Once she stretched her back, hands on her hips, and looked up at the window. Tibor immediately withdrew his head and waited a few seconds before looking again. Now Jakob came out into the yard carrying the green frock coat and the box in which scissors, needles, thread, and buttons were kept. He greeted her cheerfully, handed her the pegs she needed to hang out the last sheet, and then showed her the frock coat. They sat down on the bench together, and Jakob moved a little closer to her so as to explain something about its fabric. Finally she began to mend and shorten the coat, while Jakob watched her, both arms stretched out along the back of the bench. Then he put his head back, looked up at Tibor, showed his teeth, and licked his lips lasciviously with his tongue—until the maid spoke to him and he returned his attention to her. Tibor got off the stool and, without much enthusiasm, went back to his clockwork. He thought it strange that the new maid had a beauty spot above her mouth, for such things, Tibor had thought since Vienna, were exclusively for the nobility.

Next day Jakob helped him into the green frock coat that Elise had mended. It fitted perfectly—apart from its length, for the skirts of the coat touched the floor. Tibor looked inquiringly at Jakob, who thereupon presented him with a pair of shoes: shoes with such enormously high heels that they were almost stilts. They fitted Tibor, even if he wobbled a little standing up in them, and made him almost ten inches taller—still much shorter than Jakob, but not a dwarf anymore.

"If we put wide-legged pantaloons over the shoes, no one will notice the difference," said Jakob. "Congratulations on your birthday."

"But it's not my birthday. Not until October."

"I can't wait that long."

"What's all this in aid of?"

"It's so that you won't attract attention when we go into town. This isn't like Vienna; there are people here who know me."

This time Tibor did not object that Kempelen had forbidden it. Their outing in Vienna had been fabulous, and now he wanted to see Pressburg. Furthermore, out of doors spring was coming, while he was shut up in his room day after day. He couldn't remember when he had last felt the warmth of the sun on his skin. Anna Maria von Kempelen had gone out to a salon and wouldn't be home until evening.

They slipped past the servants and out of the house. It was early afternoon, and the streets of the city were full. That made the two of them less conspicuous in the crowd. Tibor was now wearing an old wig and a tricorne and carrying a walking stick. The last item was necessary to help him stay on his feet, for walking was difficult in the shoes that Jakob had made him, particularly on cobblestones. More than once he lost his balance and began to fall, but he always managed to stay upright with the help of his stick, or Jakob's hand to support him, or the wall of a nearby house. No one paid any particular attention to Tibor. Glances fell on him and moved on again. Jakob's disguise had made the dwarf one of the crowd.

They crossed a wooden bridge over the city moat and entered Pressburg through the Lorenz Gate—for the first time Tibor was within the city walls, which so far he had seen only from the outside. Jakob took him straight to the main square outside the Town Hall. They stopped by the Roland Fountain there. Tibor plunged both hands into the cool water up to his cuffs and watched the countless reflections of the sun on the quivering surface until his eyes hurt. He felt like a hermit who has rolled away the rock at the mouth of his cave after years and steps out into the world, curious to see what it looks like. He was delighted with everything: the other people, the sun, and the clouds above the city rooftops, the first green of the trees, the smell of horse dung and the noise in the streets. Jakob didn't talk. Tibor couldn't remember that he'd ever been silent for so long before.

Tibor raised his eyes from the fountain when the clock on the Town Hall tower struck four. He looked at the bell tower and the Town Hall with its colored tiles until the sound had died away entirely.

"The Mayor's complaining, we'll have to move on," said Jakob.

"The Mayor . . . ?"

"That's what they call the bell, because he died in it," explained Jakob.

"In the bell?"

"The Mayor of the time commissioned Master Fabian, the best bell founder in town, to cast the bell for the Town Hall tower. While it was in the making, the Mayor often came to visit Master Fabian in his workshop, and there he fell in love with the bell founder's beautiful wife. And she fell for the rich Mayor too, with his honeyed compliments and valuable presents. But Master Fabian found out about their affair, and on the day when he was heating the metal for the bell in the smelting furnace, he asked the Mayor to explain himself. The Mayor acted innocent and denied his love affair to the last. And when he proudly boasted of "his" bell, saying that he and the bell would always be as one, the furious bell founder could no longer stand it. He pushed the Mayor into the molten iron. The liquid fire swallowed the unfortunate man up so fast that he couldn't even scream. 'You will indeed always be as one with your bell!' cried Master Fabian. That very evening he poured the metal into the mold, and before the bell had cooled entirely, he had left the city and was never seen again. Nor was the Mayor, of course. But when they hauled the magnificent bell high up into the Town Hall tower on strong ropes, and it rang for the first time, the Mayor's wife cried out that the bell was calling her, she could hear her husband's voice in it! Everyone thought she was deranged, but she climbed up to the bell tower, and in the side of the bell she discovered a speck of green in the yellow metal. That, she said, was the Mayor's emerald ring—the very same emerald that she had given her husband on their wedding day, and the furnace hadn't been able to melt it down. Now it was glowing green in the side of the bell. Ever since then that bell has been called *the Mayor*, and they say that if you don't have a clear conscience, the sound of the bell will strike terror into you."

Then Jakob showed Tibor the place where Kempelen did his real work: the Royal Hungarian Chamber in Michaelergasse. Passing along Venturgasse, they reached Herrengasse and the grand palaces of the nobles of Pressburg. But Tibor had eyes only for the tower of St. Martin's, which rose above all the other buildings, its top crowned with a likeness of the crown of Hungary. A few minutes later they were standing outside the massive gray stone cathedral, and Tibor was looking at it like a man dying of thirst who sees a fresh spring.

Jakob wrinkled his nose. "Our God lives in better places than this."

Tibor cast him such a venomous look that Jakob raised his hands to placate him. "Calm down," he said. "How long will you need for—for lighting your candles, or whatever it is you have to do?"

While Tibor was still thinking about it, Jakob added, "I'll come back for you in an hour's time. And perhaps you'd better not kneel down. Who knows if you'd ever get up again with those shoes on?" With these words he turned and strolled off, hands in his trouser pockets, going back the way they had come.

Tibor did in fact have difficulty in getting up after he had knelt down in front of the Pietà. He had to haul himself up by a grating before he could stand upright in his shoes again. Taking holy water from the bronze font, he touched it to his forehead. Then he put several guilders in the church collecting box. It was the first time he had spent any of the money that he had earned. Finally he lit a candle and prayed for the soul of the Venetian merchant.

Tibor looked around the cathedral nave until a woman left the confessional and he could take her place. Kneeling down, he drew the purple curtain, took a deep breath of the fragrance of the old wood, and waited for the floorboards under his knees to stop creaking. "Father, forgive me, for I have sinned in thought and deed. I wish to confess in humility and repentance." How good it was to say those words again. "It has been . . . almost three and a half months since I last made confession."

"That is a long time," said the priest on the other side of the grating.

"I'm sorry. I wanted to come sooner, but I couldn't."

"What have you done?" In the brief pause in their conversation, Tibor could hear the faint whistling in the air as the priest breathed in through his nose.

"I have broken the Third Commandment. I have often failed to come to Holy Mass."

"You know that that is a mortal sin?"

"Yes. But I was prevented. You could say I was forbidden."

"Anyone who forbids you to attend Holy Mass is a godless evildoer, and you should break with him."

"Yes."

"What else have you done?"

"I have . . . offended against the Sixth Commandment. I have had unchaste thoughts. I have desired women. I have desired many women."

"We are often led into temptation, and it is sometimes difficult to resist it."

"Yes. I have slept with a woman."

The priest nodded. "What else?"

Tibor was still thinking what to confess next—having drunk immoderately in Jakob's company, or having made friends with a Jew?—when the curtain was suddenly drawn aside. There stood Jakob. Tibor started with alarm, while Jakob pointed to the way out with his finger. The expression on his face showed that he meant it seriously. Tibor shook his head vehemently, and when Jakob tugged his sleeve, he shook his hand off.

"My son?" asked the priest.

"That was all, Father." Tibor signed to Jakob to close the curtain again. Rolling his eyes, Jakob took a few steps away from the confessional.

"Good. As penance you will say three Our Fathers and eight Ave Marias. And try to mend your ways. When the flesh tempts you, seek comfort in prayer. And don't wait so long before your next confession, do you hear?"

"Yes, Father."

"Deinde ego te absolvo a peccatis tuis in nomine patris et filii et spiritus sancti."

"Amen." With difficulty, Tibor got to his feet again and reached for his stick.

A little way off Jakob was scrutinizing the statue of St. Martin as if nothing had happened just now. "Don't you spend enough time in wooden boxes anyway? What makes you want to get into another in your free time?"

Tibor did not reply and walked past him without a word. Only when they had left the church did he turn to Jakob. He was breathing heavily, and his face was flushed.

"You interrupted me in the middle of my confession!"

"Yes, but it was important."

"What . . . what can be so important that you have to disturb my confession?"

"I wanted to prevent you from telling that cleric about the chess automaton."

For a moment Tibor was left speechless. "What? What is there to confess about that?"

Jakob grinned. "Well, we're fooling people on a grand scale. Isn't that forbidden among you Christians? It is with us."

Tibor hadn't thought about it, but now he remembered what he had said to Kempelen in the leaden chambers, the *piombi* of Venice. *Thou shalt not bear false witness.* Jakob was right: strictly speaking, what they were doing with the chess automaton was a sin, an offense against the Ninth Commandment.

Jakob saw Tibor's mind working away. "But if you weren't going to confess it anyway, all the better."

"There's such a thing as the secrecy of the confessional," hissed Tibor.

"Yes, exactly. And there's such a thing as a chess-playing machine. You don't seriously think a priest would keep a story like that to himself, do you? In a couple of days' time it would be all over town that the automaton's brain had been to confession."

"How can you talk like that? Holy confession—these are things you Jews just don't understand at all."

"And why not?"

"Because you're not bothered about the salvation of your souls, you're not interested in anything but yourselves and the present day, you just grab more and more property all the time—and you don't spare a thought for the people you're sucking dry like leeches in a swamp, and if your conscience does happen to trouble you now and then, you off-load it all on a goat and chase it out into the wilderness, or you slaughter a chicken and wave it in the air, and all your sins are forgotten, or so you think at least—but one day you'll be judged too, you Jews, of all people, will be judged, and then may God have mercy on you!"

Jakob scratched the back of his neck. "So that's what you think of us?"

Tibor, still enraged, nodded vehemently. At that Jakob suddenly lunged forward and knocked him down. Tibor fell to the ground on his back, striking one elbow painfully on the paving stones. He looked blankly up at Jakob.

"I've put up with this kind of thing long enough, Tibor," he said with unaccustomed severity. "But that's the end of it. I may not set much store by my religion, but if you think you have a license to insult my people, you're much mistaken. I don't know why all of you think none of it can hurt us. I mean, no one has a right to condemn you just for being a dwarf, right? Don't look at the jug, look at what's in it. And if I haven't yet managed to change the idea you have of us, then keep your opinions to yourself in future, because otherwise you're going to spend several very, very lonely months here."

A few people near the cathedral had stopped and were looking at the two of them, but that didn't bother Jakob. Tibor rubbed his smarting elbow.

"Now I'm going into the Jewish quarter, where I live," said Jakob, rather more calmly, "and you're warmly invited to come with me. But if the presence of so many bloodsuckers and chicken-slaughterers all together disgusts you, then go anywhere else you like."

Tibor nodded, and Jakob offered his hand, pulled him to his feet, gave him his stick and hat, and knocked the dirt out of the skirts of his coat.

"Are you all right?"

"My arm hurts." Tibor could feel his shirt sticking to his elbow under the frock coat. Obviously the skin had split.

"Well, you almost broke my nose a couple of months ago, so now we're quits. And I didn't even complain at the time."

In silence, they left the city center by the Weidritz Gate, passed the synagogue, and entered the Jewish quarter. It lay in a dip between the city wall on one side and Castle Mount on the other. Jakob had a room in a house in Judengasse. To get there, they first had to enter a dark, tiny courtyard and then climb a series of steep staircases, sometimes inside the building and sometimes outside, to Jakob's lodgings right under the roof. Whether he lived on the third or fourth floor Tibor couldn't say, for it seemed as if there were not just separate stories but a number of mezzanine floors too, and no one apartment was on the same level as any other. Similarly, the rooftops, rafters, and bay windows were so closely interlinked that Tibor couldn't make out which belonged to Jakob's building and which to the building next door. Pigeons sat in their own droppings on every windowsill and ledge, and the courtyard echoed to their cooing. Outside one door Jakob raised a loose tile from the roof, a key tumbled out, and he opened the door with it. They entered a small corridor with two doors leading off it. The door belonging to Jakob's room wasn't locked.

It was about twice the size of Tibor's room in Kempelen's house and contained furniture that might once, decades ago, have been valuable. Disorder reigned; sketches lay about on the table and the floor, along with blocks of wood, some carved and some still virgin, and tools. A dirty seven-branched Jewish candelabrum stood beside the bed; its metal was tarnished and covered with candle wax like a stalactite. The seven candles were burned down to stumps, and three of the wicks had already drowned in molten wax. There was a window and a pointless narrow door leading nowhere. If you opened it, you saw the open sky beyond and the roof ridge of the building next door just a step lower down. There was a view of red-tiled roofs and black chimneys sprinkled with bird droppings, with the city wall and church towers beyond. Jakob pointed to a hole in the carpet of rooftops; the little cemetery of the Jewish community was down there. Tibor saw the tower of St. Michael's, which had a clock on three of its sides but not on the fourth, the one facing the Jewish quarter. That, Jakob explained, was because the Jews hadn't contributed a single thaler to the tower when it was being built.

A few buildings farther on, a junk dealer had his shop on the ground floor—the very same shop where Jakob had bought the Turk's pipe. Some of the wares were on display outside; as the street was only just wide enough for a horse and cart here, the objects were crammed close to the wall of the house. Some hung from nails in the wall, others from an iron shop sign bearing the inscription *Aaron Krakauer, Ironmongery*—there were pots and pans, crockery, clothes, furniture, and all kinds of oddments, none of it in the kind of state that would have tempted Tibor to want it.

When Tibor and Jakob emerged into the street again, a Jew with gray hair and beard, a black caftan, and a round cap was just carrying out a little table. The table had a chessboard set into it, inlaid with squares of light and dark wood.

"Shalom, Jakob," he said with a gap-toothed smile.

"Good day, Aaron."

"Fancy a *borovicka*?"

"Is the Danube wet?" Jakob asked.

Grinning, the old Jew disappeared into his shop again. Jakob took two chairs off a pile and put them at the table along with the junk dealer's own armchair. Krakauer came back with a clay bottle and a little decorated box and put both on the table. He was surrounded by the smell of old paper. Reaching behind him into a basket, he took out three small glasses and wiped the dust out of them with the hem of his coat before pouring out the schnapps.

Meanwhile Jakob introduced Tibor. "This is my friend . . . er . . . Gottfried Fürchtegott Neumann, from Passau. He's a bell founder's journeyman on his travels."

Fürchtegott—"Fear God." At least Jakob hadn't lost his sense of mischief. The three men clinked glasses and drank. The juniper spirit burned Tibor's throat and lips and tasted horrible. Blinking, he picked a hair that had been in the glass off his tongue. He wished he had a glass of water to wash the spirit down, or better still milk.

"So what's the news, Aaron?" inquired Jakob.

"Don't be so modest!" the junk dealer reproved him, pouring more schnapps. "Needless to say, the Mechanical Turk built by your Herr Kempelen is the talk of the town! Congratulations."

"Thank you."

"I want to see that automaton sometime. Even better, I'd like to play against it myself. Rabbi Meier Barba says he's going to write to Herr Kempelen to ask if he'll display his homunculus here in the ghetto one day. Do you play chess, Herr Neumann?"

Before Tibor could say anything, Jakob answered for him. "No, Gottfried thinks chess is only to help wastrels pass the time and dreamers forget the world."

Krakauer looked keenly at Tibor, who just shrugged and said, "Well, yes. Isn't that so?"

"Oh, by no means, Herr Neumann! Not at all! You must know that chess can work wonders. It once saved the people of the Jewish quarter here from starving. That was in the days when Siegmund was King of Hungary. He was a bad king and an even worse businessman, and of course he borrowed the money for his pleasures and the building of Pressburg Castle from the Jews—and never paid any of it back. The community's coffers were growing emptier and emptier. One day, when he demanded a thousand guilders for one of his wars and the Jews couldn't scrape the money together, the tyrant was very angry; he had them all driven into the ghetto, the gates were closed and barred, and he posted guards outside them. The Jews were to be locked in until they stumped up that thousand guilders. But the poor souls didn't have the cash! In their need, the rabbi sent a letter to the provost of the cathedral asking for his help. And despite all their differences, the provost agreed. He and the King sometimes played a game of chess together, and when they were sitting at the chessboard next day, the provost said that if he won the match, he'd like to ask a favor. After two hours he had beaten the King, and he asked him to open the ghetto again before the people inside starved or died of diseases. Then King Siegmund did in fact rescind his order, and the Jews were free. Next Sunday, when the provost had invited some high-ranking clerics and city councilors to dinner, a young Jew brought him a roast goose with the rabbi's best compliments. And when the provost carved the magnificent bird, it was stuffed not with apples or onions . . . but with gold pieces."

"Such religious harmony," said Jakob, with a sidelong glance at Tibor.

"Amen to that," said Krakauer, raising his glass again, "and *Allah'u akbar* and *Adonai echad* too!"

After a third *borovicka* and then a fourth, the Jew invited them to look around his shop for something they might like. It was dark and stuffy among the shelves, some of them piled so high with all kinds of junk that an avalanche would probably have fallen on Tibor if he had removed one of the inextricably wedged objects. On an old desk stood a stuffed animal such as he had never seen before: a desiccated yellow fish or amphibian with a smiling mouth, two black glass eyes above it, and a long tail. But the really curious feature was that it stood upright on two chicken's claws, and it had a little pair of antlers on its head. When Jakob spotted this creature, which resembled a basilisk, he said he was surprised that no watchmaker had ever thought of stuffing dead animals with clockwork to revive them. "A kitten mechanically lifting its paw, or a dog always wagging its tail once it was wound up, even though it died long ago—why, their grieving owners would pay a fortune for that."

Tibor found a shabby Italian edition of the *Decameron* and wanted to buy it, but Krakauer insisted on giving it to him as a present. "I don't want money, Herr Neumann. Fate will ensure that I profit from our meeting in some other way one day," he said. The *Decameron* was one of the books that had been banned in the monastery at Obra on pain of severe penalties, and now Tibor found out why. The stories were certainly very spicy. He particularly liked the tale of the lovers Egano and Beatrice, who met over a game of chess. Tibor had never stopped to think that his own playing might open a woman's heart, and in his dreams he slipped into the role of Egano.

. . .

THE CHESS-PLAYING TURK defeated the brewery owner Michael Spech in the humiliatingly short space of sixteen moves. Spech took his defeat with good humor, and claimed to know so little of the game of chess that, so he said, even a weaver's loom could probably have defeated him. The second match, against no less than the Mayor of Pressburg, Kempelen's friend Karl Gottlieb Windisch, publisher of the *Pressburger Zeitung*, lasted considerably longer and went to forty moves, so that the applause when checkmate was reached was more for Windisch than for the automaton. All the two dozen guests invited had come, and Kempelen's brother Nepomuk had asked to attend again too. Anna Maria was the perfect hostess. Acquaintances of the Kempelen family agreed that they had seldom seen her so cheerful. After the performance she told Katarina and Elise to hand around drinks and food while the guests talked to one another. Listening to the noise of the many conversations in progress, Tibor could hear Windisch suggesting to Kempelen that he might place an announcement of future performances by the Turk in the *Pressburger Zeitung*. The publisher seemed more interested than any of the other guests in the way the automaton worked, and he showered Kempelen with questions.

They had agreed to open the doors of the cabinet before instead of after performances in future. The advantage of that was that at the end of the game Tibor no longer had to clear his own chessmen out of sight, retract the pantograph, and fold his chessboard away, all within a very short space. But there was plenty of time for him to set it all up between the closing of the doors and the beginning of the first match. After Kempelen had closed the front doors, he opened the back door on the right-hand side of the android again, on the pretext of having to make an adjustment, and when he introduced his candle into the automaton, Tibor could light his own from it. If Tibor's candle ever went out in the course of the match, then Kempelen could light it once more, again saying that he had to adjust the clockwork.

When Tibor was standing bare-chested over a basin of water after this performance, washing the sweat away, there was a knock on the door and Kempelen came in—with his brother. He proudly indicated Tibor and said, "There he is."

Nepomuk frowned and rubbed his chin. "I see."

"Don't you like him?" asked Kempelen. The two of them were acting as if Tibor, who had now picked up a towel, couldn't hear them.

"Yes, of course. What is there to dislike? He played well." Tibor acknowledged this commendation with a nod. "No, it's more . . . well, the idea of the whole thing."

The brothers left Tibor's room again and continued their conversation outside. Tibor rubbed himself dry. It irked him to find someone expressing anything but enthusiasm for the chess automaton.

He spent the afternoon practicing the mechanician's craft again. He had filed down a number of increasingly faultless cogwheels, and then, as there was no use for them, they had to be thrown on the scrap metal heap. Now he was making something that he intended to be useful to him personally: a key to the Kempelen house. Only Kempelen himself and his wife had keys, one for the front door and one for the workshop, from which, in turn, Tibor's room was reached. One day he summoned up his courage and kneaded the stump of a wax candle in his pocket until it was soft. Then, when Kempelen briefly disappeared into his study, leaving his bunch of keys in the workshop, Tibor pressed the wards of the two keys into the wax. After that he found iron bars thick enough for the purpose, sawed them up, and filed away at them until they fitted exactly into the depressions in the wax. He hid the two finished keys under a loose floorboard, and he felt freer knowing that in future he could leave the house whenever he liked.

Weidritz

WHEN WOLFGANG AND ANNA MARIA VON KEMPELEN WERE
invited to Fertöd to attend a ball given by Nikolaus, Prince Esterházy,
Tibor and Jakob made their second forbidden expedition into the city.
They waited until it was dark, then skirted the city wall on their way to
the fishermen's settlement of Weidritz, where the Golden Rose tavern,
which Jakob frequented from time to time, stood on Fischplatz.

Tibor was wearing his built-up shoes again. His legs and above all his
feet had hurt for a long time after their first outing, and now the pressure
points felt sore again, but it was worth it for this brief spell of freedom.

The Golden Rose was in a building with beams that now sloped under the weight of time and the force of gravity. Soot from the candles
and the smoke of many tobacco pipes clung to the low ceiling. In spite of
the acrid air, the yellow glass windows were all closed. The guests in the
tavern were Germans and Slovakians; Tibor could see as few Hungarians
as there were women present—with the exception of the two barmaids,
who tripped with practiced ease past the chairs and tables, avoiding the
lewd touching and pinching of the customers and smiling all the time.
They carried large beer tankards and wooden boards with hollows where
tin schnapps cups were lined up. There was dicing at one table, tarot cards

at another, a game of tocatille at a third. You got used to the noise, just as you did to the stink of tobacco, alcohol, sweat, and fish. From his place behind the bar, where he was drawing beer and filling schnapps glasses, the bald-headed landlord greeted Jakob with a friendly wave.

They found a free table in a niche, and Jakob sat where he could see as much as possible of the interior of the tavern. It was a relief to Tibor to be sitting again, able to take the weight off his feet. He stretched his legs but dared not take off the built-up shoes. Jakob handed him a couple of cushions to put on his chair.

One of the two barmaids came over and wiped the table with a cloth, distributing little puddles of beer and breadcrumbs around the surface rather than cleaning it. The girl had sandy hair that hung over her ears in little curls, and she was pretty, even though the bad air inside the tavern had muddied her pale skin and her nose was slightly crooked, as if it had once been broken. Jakob openly stared hard at her, and although she kept her own gaze just as firmly fixed on the table, she was smiling.

"Constanze, you're beautiful," said Jakob. "And mind you, I say so even though I'm not drunk yet."

"You say so when you are too," she replied.

"One of these days you must model for me—promise, will you? I'll make your beauty immortal. You will be my Aphrodite, my Beatrice. My Helen of Troy."

Constanze was still smiling, although she tried not to. "What would you gentlemen care for? Beer?"

"Anything you like—it will all taste like nectar if it comes from your hands, fair Constanze!"

The barmaid flicked her cloth at Jakob and turned away. The two men watched her go. Then Jakob winked at Tibor. "She's a sweetheart. And she drinks so much herself that kissing her is like licking out an empty wineglass."

Tibor was overcome by a brief but violent moment of desire when he looked at Constanze again. He wanted to feel what he had felt in Vienna once more, only this time without masks and without being magnetized first. He felt the blood rise to his face, and his ears turned warm before he managed to quell his inner turmoil. He had sinned once already, and repeating a sin was even worse than committing it the first time.

"She'll keep me company until the time's ripe for Elise," said Jakob.

"Our Elise?"

"Oh yes. Elise is amazingly lovely once you take her cap off. And so naïve you wouldn't believe it! Even more pious than you too. That's why I'm taking my time."

"Kempelen will throw you out!"

"No need to snap at me, Rumpelstiltskin, he won't. I've already told you why he *can't* throw me out."

Tibor felt like forbidding Jakob to have anything to do with Elise, but by what authority could he say so, and above all, on what grounds? He imagined Jakob kissing her, and it made him feel uncomfortable. Jakob was a man with no morals and always would be.

"Are there any other Jews here?" asked Tibor, looking around the room.

"No. There aren't any Jews here at all. I'm not a Jew here either, understand?" And on meeting Tibor's questioning gaze, he explained, "They don't have to know everything about me. I want to be able to drink my beer in this tavern in peace. They don't give you a drop of it at the Jewish Cultural Institute, where folk spend the whole evening with little bits of wood tied to their foreheads arguing about the Talmud. Not my idea of fun."

Constanze brought the beer, and Jakob raised his glass to her charms. After the first sip he drank another health, this time to Tibor.

Over the second beer, Jakob called for dice. He explained the alarmingly simple rules to Tibor, who asked twice whether there really wasn't something he had missed. After a few games to get Tibor used to it, they played, at Jakob's suggestion, for a stake of two kreuzers a time. Jakob won almost all their games, but that didn't matter to Tibor. After all, the wages that Kempelen was paying meant that he had more money at his disposal than ever before in his life. The game of dice itself struck him as tedious, since he had no influence on the numbers that were thrown—however much Jakob assured him that spitting on the dice first, a long throw, and throwing with the left hand, because it was the hand nearest the heart, would have a positive effect on the outcome. They played until the first guests were staggering wearily out of the tavern, talk died down, and the barmaids could stop for a rest.

In the middle of a game Tibor caught the word "Kempelen." Someone was babbling it at the next table, which was separated from theirs by a wooden partition half the height of the room. He stopped playing and signed to Jakob to keep quiet. The assistant moved to his side, and together they listened to the conversation being conducted in a hodgepodge of Slovakian and German.

Its subject was the fact that Kempelen had bricked up the windows of his house—not to keep out the curious or intruders but to keep someone in: the Turk. "If he's got the gumption to win a game of chess against the Mayor, he'll be able to open an ordinary door and run away, no problem. That's why the bricked-up windows," said one of the three men who were talking.

Jakob put a hand in front of his mouth to hide his mirth.

"What makes you think he wants to escape?" asked the second man.

"I heard him screaming. I happened to be walking past the house one morning, and I heard him screaming up above. An inhuman sound, it was, like an animal being slaughtered."

"Maybe it *was* an animal," said the third man.

"Or a real human being," said the second again. "I mean, an automaton can't scream—can it?"

"Suppose he's tormenting human beings—that's even worse," replied the first. "Mary Mother of God be with us! Peter told me his v ife saw that simple servant of Kempelen's, you know, the one with the great long arms, well, she saw him carrying a basket full of body parts away one day, arms and legs in it, there were, and she saw hair too, says Peter. It was all burned outside the city walls."

"That'd account for the screams, then."

"And his maidservant, she left town soon after the Turk was born—well, either that or Kempelen drove her away—but whichever it was, no one heard from her anymore. Could be she knew too much."

The three of them fell silent for a moment. Tibor heard them lifting their beer mugs to their mouths and putting them down again several times. Jakob made a beckoning gesture, as if to entice more out of them through the partition, and sure enough, the first man soon spoke up again. "He's in the Lodge."

"What?"

"Kempelen. He's in the Lodge. He's a Freemason, may the devil take the lot of them. They're probably getting him to make them clever slaves, and the Empress—God save her—lets this godless blasphemy dazzle her. Bishop Batthyány ought to put a stop to it, so he ought. If I was facing that Turk, no question, I'd get me a club and smash his brainbox in. Not because he's a Mussulman—he can't help that, poor soul!—but to put him out of his misery."

Here they dropped the subject of Kempelen but continued talking about Turks and the Empress Catherine of Russia's triumph on the Black Sea in the Turkish war.

JAKOB WAS STANDING at the bar with Constanze when Tibor came back from the privy about midnight; he was talking to her, and she was smiling as she had smiled before. Tibor sat down and watched Jakob take Constanze's hand, run his fingertips over her fingers, trace the lines on her palm with his nail, and stroke the skin there where the fingers met it. The landlord didn't seem to mind, and Constanze did not withdraw her hand from Jakob's. She pushed a strand of curly red hair back behind her ear. Then she said something briefly to the landlord, and meanwhile Jakob looked at Tibor and formed his mouth into a kissing shape. After that he devoted himself to Constanze again. Tibor realized that this was the end of their evening out together. He finished his beer, put enough coins on the table to pay the bill for them both, and left the tavern. Jakob just nodded to him; he couldn't wave because both his hands were now holding the barmaid.

The moon was rising over the city, casting a sharp shadow like the shadow of a sundial behind the Plague Column in the middle of the

Fischplatz. Beyond the fishermen's settlement the Danube rushed by, or was that rushing sound the roaring in his ears? Tibor clung to the door frame with one hand until he was accustomed to the fresh air in his lungs.

He started home through the Weidritz quarter. He would have liked to take off those shoes and go barefoot. He had seen two constables in the Fischplatz on their nocturnal rounds, but now the streets were empty, and the sound of his shoes and his walking stick on the paving stones echoed back from the walls of the houses. So he jumped with alarm when a woman's voice addressed him. "Where are you off to then, handsome?"

Tibor turned slowly. To his left, a small covered alley turned off the road—in the dark he couldn't see where it led—and the woman was leaning against the wall of the building at its entrance. She wore a pale dress and had a scarf over her shoulders. Her hair was long and dark, and she had painted her mouth red. In a way she was not unlike Baroness Jesenák. Her accent showed that she was Slovakian. Tibor just looked at her and said nothing.

"Fancy a little love?" So saying, she picked up her skirt to show her calves, encased in white stockings. When Tibor shook his head so slowly that it could be misunderstood to mean he was thinking about it, she pulled the skirt further up, until Tibor saw the flash of a garter around her thigh.

"No," said Tibor.

"I'll give you a special price, a fine gentleman like you."

"No."

The woman smiled, put a finger on her lips, and said, "Five groschen." Then she pointed between her legs with the same finger and said, "Ten groschen."

She moved away from the wall of the building, for Tibor had not made his escape fast enough, and took his free hand in hers. Then she bent down and kissed him. Although Tibor pressed his lips together, her tongue found its way past them. It tasted deliciously of fresh herbs, of mint and lemon and cinnamon, so intense a flavor that it burned cold on Tibor's lips. Tibor remembered one of the dragoons saying that whores had foul breath because every man they kissed left his bad taste behind, and those hundreds of unpleasant flavors united into a single unbearable one, worse than Lucifer's bum—so girls who took a pride in themselves chewed pleasantly flavored herbs to avoid scaring their customers off.

As she was kissing him, she put a hand to his crotch and took hold of that part of him that had automatically risen during the kiss. Opening his eyes, Tibor saw that she had not closed hers. She ended the kiss and drew him by his hand into the dark alley. He had stopped resisting.

The alley was unpaved, and the trodden earth was so softened by rain that Tibor had to take great care how he walked. It soon curved and came to a dead end. A small piece of carpet was lying unrolled on a flight of steps, and the whore sat down on it and pulled up her dress.

Once again Tibor said, "No"—he was in no condition to say anything else—whereupon the whore stood up again.

"I see what it is. You want to be true to your little lady at home. Very noble of you." She stood up again, picked up the piece of carpet, pushed Tibor back against the wall of the building, spread the carpet out at his feet, and knelt down in front of him. With practiced gestures, she opened his trousers, took out his prick, and kissed it, holding it with one hand. A few seconds later she interrupted what she was doing and looked up at Tibor.

"I'll have six groschen off of you."

Tibor swallowed before he spoke. "You said five just now."

"That was before, fine sir. Want me to stop?"

Tibor gave her the money with trembling hands. Smiling, she put the coins away in a hidden pocket and went on. But Tibor couldn't come to a climax: Jakob's shoes hurt even more when he was standing than when he walked in them. He had to hold the wall so as not to fall over, and he couldn't decide whether to look at the opposite wall or at her head, bobbing up and down so grotesquely between his legs like a mechanical toy. He didn't want to be there anymore. His intoxication, so great just now, seemed to have vanished. He closed his eyes, but even in complete darkness he couldn't summon up images of prettier women and more attractive settings.

Voices could be heard out in the street: a woman and several men. Tibor opened his eyes again. He couldn't escape from this blind alley. But the voices were not coming closer, just getting louder. The whore went on with what she was doing. Then the woman in the street screamed. Tibor pushed the whore's head away. A woman had screamed, and what was more, he knew her voice. The whore did not protest when Tibor left her. As he went, he buttoned up his trousers, stumbled, and fell headlong into the wet mud. With the aid of his walking stick he got to his feet again; the woman was still screaming, and the men's voices were distinctly louder now too.

As he emerged from the blind alley, one man was holding Elise firmly from behind while another tried to undo her bodice—in vain, for the Kempelens' maid kept kicking out at him. She had already lost one shoe. When she struck her attacker in the stomach with the heel of the other, he was so angry that he slapped her face. The blow was so powerful that her head jerked aside.

None of the three saw Tibor coming. The dwarf struck Elise's assailant behind the knees with his stick, bringing the man down to the paving stones at Tibor's own level. Tibor struck him a blow on the forehead with his fist, and when the man's chin fell on his chest, he brought the walking stick down so violently on the back of his neck that the wood broke. Then the dwarf turned to the other man, who had now let go of Elise. She struck him wildly in the belly with her elbow, but he hardly seemed to feel it, for he was even larger and tipsier than his friend, and in addition he wore a leather apron. Tibor flung himself on the man and got him down on the ground, where they rolled over the paving stones. Tibor seized his opponent's throat and squeezed it as best he could with his small hands, trying to ignore the pain of the blows falling on his face and body. Gradually they lost force, his victim was struggling for air, and he pushed Tibor's head away from him with large, coarse hands. His arms were longer than Tibor's. Tibor braced his neck to withstand them. His muscles were quivering in protest.

The first man had now recovered from his fright and the blows and picked up an empty wooden crate that he had found against one wall. He came up on Tibor from behind with it, but he had forgotten Elise. She stuck out a leg, he tripped over it, and before he could stand up she had kicked him in the head. She hit his temple, and he sank to the paving stones without a sound.

Tibor's grip on the other man's throat gave way, his fingers slipped off the sweaty skin, and finally the man pushed him off. Tibor fell backward and felt the chain around his neck break. His opponent's hand had caught in it. Tibor rolled over on his belly and got to his feet again, but the man had run for it. Tibor watched him go. Something warm was flowing into his right eye; his brow must have split open. Putting his hand to the open wound, he realized that his whole face was covered with mud. Shutters were being opened in the nearby houses now, and lights appeared.

A hand was laid on his shoulder. Tibor spun around, but it was only Elise, who was breathing as heavily as he was. The other man lay at her feet. She was looking at Tibor, and he looked back with his one good eye. Her hair was in disorder, her skin gleamed with sweat, and her bodice was torn open down to her breasts and dirty from her attackers' hands. Although her eyes were wide with fright, and her mouth was open, for a moment Tibor thought that he had never seen anything so beautiful.

Steps were approaching now from the way the man in the leather apron had gone. The constables were on their way. Tibor looked down at the ground, but his amulet was nowhere to be seen. He looked at Elise again, then ran off in the opposite direction. She tried to detain him, calling, "Wait!" But there was no holding him now. He ran away as fast as his artificial legs would carry him.

Back in the Fischplatz, he slowed down. When he turned, he saw someone running after him. It was one of the two constables, and he was waving his musket as he ran. Tibor hurried on, disoriented for a moment; he could go back to the Golden Rose, where Jakob was, but what good would that do him now? To his right lay the city wall with the Weidritz Gate, now closed, and to his left was the Danube, so all he could do was run straight ahead in the direction of the castle. The constable called to him to stop, first in German, then in Slovakian.

Tibor stumbled and fell. He thought one of the artificial legs was broken. Stripping them both off as well as he could, he ran barefoot, impeded by his trousers, which were much too long for him now. The constable came closer and, when he saw that the fugitive wasn't going to stop, spared himself the trouble of shouting after him anymore.

Tibor reached the Zuckermandel settlement, between the Danube and the slope of Castle Mount, a cramped suburb of single-story houses with one unlit street running through it. The place smelled not only of fish but also of blood, fish oil, and acid from the tanners' workshops. Tibor's strength was failing. When Zuckermandelstrasse went around a slight bend, and he was out of his pursuer's sight for a moment, Tibor climbed the nearest wall into the yard of a house on the river side of the street. He dropped incautiously onto the other side and made a painful landing on stones, lumps of metal, and dead leaves in a small niche between the wall and a shed. Crouching there, he heard the constable run past in the street.

Tibor swallowed with difficulty. Gradually his breathing calmed down, and the pain in his lungs and the stitch in his side disappeared. He rolled up his torn trousers. One of his stockings was red at the heel where Jakob's shoe had rubbed the skin. Tibor wanted to massage his sore feet, but any pressure on them hurt. The fine green frock coat that Jakob had had altered for him was smeared with mud, just like his face. The wound over his brow had stopped bleeding, but the brow itself was swollen, so that a dark shadow obscured the vision in his right eye from above. His oozing eyelids made a faint smacking sound when he blinked. He had ruined his clothes, lost his shoes, and spent six groschen on a few lewd caresses that brought no relief. In retrospect he disgusted himself. So it was no coincidence that his amulet of the Virgin was gone: why would the Mother of God stand by him after he had abandoned her again? Instinctively, he reached for his neck, where his beloved picture of the Madonna no longer hung from its chain. It was a gesture that had given him a sense of security every day from the battle of Kunersdorf until now, when his fingers grasped empty air. He said a toneless Ave Maria, remembering the night when he came by the medallion.

ON 12 AUGUST 1759, the Prussians were caught between Russian and Austrian troops in the Kunersdorf Hills near Frankfurt. The Prussian cuirassiers who were supposed to fall on the enemy's flanks from the right had difficulty in crossing the impassable moorland. The stream known as the Hühnerfliess that flowed between the fronts was only a wretched little trickle, but its bed was marshy, the Prussian cannon sank in it, and the one bridge across the stream was so narrow that the gun carriages could hardly get across. Two horses were shot under Frederick II, and a third took a bullet in its jugular vein just as he was putting his boot in the stirrup to mount. A Russian bullet hit the King himself but was miraculously turned aside by the golden tobacco box in his waistcoat pocket. Shattered by the defeat, the King did his best to die with his men on the battlefield; he called out for an enemy bullet to take his life, but his adjutants seized his horse's reins and galloped to safety with their commander in chief. Instead of pursuing Frederick without stopping to draw breath, as the Austrian general Ernst von Laudon wanted, the exhausted Russians under General Pyotr Saltykov stayed at the scene of their victory to celebrate all through that night—and Laudon, whose troops amounted to only a quarter of the Russian numbers, had to do as they did willy-nilly.

Tibor was thankful when the lieutenant told him and his comrades that the battle was over, and they were not going to pursue the Prussians across the river Oder, where the sun was now setting. A cask of water went the rounds, and they drank greedily, for it had been a still, cloudless day, perhaps the hottest day of the year, and the water supplies in their canteens had been quickly exhausted. The dragoons peeled off their uniforms, which were dusty on the outside and wet with sweat on the inside, and rubbed the dirt off their faces. No one spoke. There were groans, but no wailing, for their regiment had lost only a handful of men, not one of them from Tibor's own column. From the hill where they sat they could see the Oder with Frankfurt on the other side, and around them countless plumes of smoke rose from fires still unextinguished; small pillars of smoke above the battlefield, great clouds of it hanging over Kunersdorf, Trettin, Reipzig, and Schwetig, the Frankfurt Council villages that the Cossacks had burned more for the pleasure of destroying them than for any tactical reasons. Only the stone church of Kunersdorf had withstood the flames.

After half an hour the lieutenant made them go on again; they were to set off for Reipzig to look for any retreating Prussians in the ruins of the village. They took their horses by the reins and walked down through the dry grass to Reipzig, reaching it in the dark. Here and there a few flames still lit up the night, but the rest of the houses were embers and ashes. Some men stayed with the horses at the entrance to the village—including young Tibor—watering them at the local stream, the Eilang. The others, with loaded rifles and fixed bayonets, went down the incandescent streets, which were even hotter than they had been by day in the full sunlight. When a charred beam fell, sparks flew up to mingle with the stars in the sky.

After they had checked the abandoned village, the column divided up into groups around Reipzig. Tibor, Josef, Wenzel, Emanuel, Walther, and their corporal, Adam, made camp between the outskirts of the village and the Reipzig paper mill, the only building spared by the Russians. Josef was given the first watch. The others rolled up their blankets to make pillows and fell asleep at once.

Tibor awoke in the night, drenched with sweat. He lay there, stared up at the sky, and listened to the crickets, the murmur of the Eilang, the clatter of the millwheel, and the breathing of the men as they slept. Wenzel, who was now on watch, had gone to sleep leaning against a tree trunk. Tibor rose and went barefoot through the grass to the stream, drank a little of its tepid water from the hollow of his hand, and washed the sweat off his face. As he undid his trousers to relieve himself, the clattering of the mill that he had heard in the background since their arrival abruptly stopped. The waterwheel had not been particularly loud before, but now it was completely silent. Tibor tried to see what was going on in the dark, but he could make out only vague shapes. He looked back at his comrades. They were all fast asleep.

Tibor went downstream along the sandy bank to the mill. While he was on his way, the clattering started again. Perhaps it was just that a branch had caught in the paddles of the wheel. All the same Tibor kept going. The door to the mill was closed, but there was a window open. Tibor looked in. In the darkness he could make out a number of the wheels and belts that connected the stamping mill to the millwheel, then a large cauldron, a pile of rags and firewood, and finally large sheets of paper hung up to dry in the rafters like square clouds, illuminating the mill with a faint light of their own. The door to the next room was closed.

Beside the stamping mill a figure lay on the floor: a woman with her head on a sheepskin. She was asleep. Her hands and feet were tied with leather straps, and a large piece of fabric gagged her mouth.

Tibor made sure that he had his little knife with him, then climbed in. His footsteps were drowned out by the clatter of the mill. As he approached the woman, he saw that she was not lying on a sheepskin after all but on a whole lamb, dead with a bullet hole in its forehead. But the woman was alive. She awoke with a start as Tibor attempted to loosen her gag, and tried to scream. Tibor signed to her to keep quiet, but it was too late; she had been heard. The door to the next room opened, and a soldier stood in the doorway. Tibor breathed a sigh of relief: he was not a Prussian but a Russian. A Russian officer. Tibor immediately came out with the few Russian words they had been taught, saying "Austrian" and "friend." The Russian answered in his mother tongue, grinned, and never stopped talking as he approached Tibor. Tibor nodded, although he didn't understand a word of it. Then the Russian pointed to himself, Tibor, and the woman and made a graphic gesture. Tibor did not react, but when the Russian repeated the gesture rather more elaborately, he shook his head. He was a boy of dwarfish stature, facing a full-grown Russian soldier. He had to get back to camp in a hurry and fetch help.

"Fritz," said the Russian, pointing to the woman again.

"I know," replied Tibor. "All the same, I don't want to. Thank you. Goodbye."

The gagged woman wailed as Tibor made for the door. Apparently guessing his intentions, the Russian seized him from behind by the head. Walther had told him about that grip. It was the way you broke a man's neck. So instead of resisting the pull on his head to turn it around, Tibor went with the sudden jerk of the Russian's hands. He took the knife from his belt and drove it into the officer's thigh. With a surprised groan, the Russian let go of him, and Tibor ran for cover behind the stamping mill. The Russian removed the blade from his flesh and threw the knife carelessly away. He was grinning again and began talking to Tibor as he came closer to him. When he reached the stamping mill, he worked a large lever linking the paddle wheel to the mill itself. The cogwheels and belts began moving with a crunching sound, and the arms of the machine pounded down into the empty basin. The Russian was obviously trying to prevent Tibor from ducking underneath the machinery and getting away. Tibor did it all the same: as the Russian came around the side of the machinery to catch hold of him, he jumped over one of the belts and climbed across a bevel wheel lying flat. However, the officer caught his bare foot and held him tight. Tibor's ankle and the Russian's hand slipped between two bevels on the wheel, and as it turned, their joints were caught and squeezed in the teeth of the wheel next to it. Tibor screamed, the Russian grinned. The mechanism of the mill stopped. Tibor and his assailant were inextricably linked, and Tibor had no idea how to free himself. Any movement between the wheels made the pain worse, and the pressure exerted by the mechanism was as strong as ever. It would have taken several strong men to turn the wheel back again.

With his free left hand, the Russian reached down into his boot and took out a narrow dagger. Tibor was lying over the wheel before him as if on a sacrificial altar. The Russian said something, then drew back his arm to strike. A shot rang out. As if stung by a wasp, the Russian screamed, dropped his dagger, and writhed in pain. There was a gaping hole in his side. The Russian cursed, felt the wound with his free hand, scratched the hole as if it were an itching insect bite, moved up and down on the spot a little undecidedly, and then died. Before he slumped beside the wheel, his fingers closed even more tightly around Tibor's foot.

Walther, standing in the doorway, lowered his rifle. "*Parbleu!* Like General Ziethen coming out of the bushes!" he said. "He's a Russki too, Big Man. The Russkis are on our side."

Three of them had come: Walther, Emanuel, and Corporal Adam. They freed Tibor from the mechanism of the mill. His foot was suffused with red and blue, but no bones were broken. Then they untied the woman, who lived in Reipzig and hadn't made her escape soon enough. Grinning, Emanuel suggested doing what the Russian hadn't got around to with her, but the corporal sternly called him to order. The woman thanked each of the four men with a kiss on the cheek, and she handed Tibor the chain from her neck, with a little medallion of the Virgin on it, saying that she hoped it would always protect him. Then she burst into tears. Walther tried to comfort her, but Adam snapped at him, told him that consoling Prussian women wasn't their job, and sent her away.

Meanwhile Emanuel got the corporal's permission at least to burn the mill down. The dry rags burned like tinder. The soldiers stayed inside the mill until it was too hot, for the sight of the burning paper in the roof rafters was as pretty as a fireworks display. They left the Russian officer to burn with the building, his right leg automatically twitching to the last like a dead insect's, but they took the lamb back to camp with them—Walther carrying Tibor on his back—and consumed their midnight banquet by the light of the burning paper mill.

EVER SINCE THEN, ever since his fifteenth year, Tibor had worn the medallion and kept it on him, and now it was gone, trodden into the mud of a Pressburg alley.

Tibor heard the footsteps pass the wall. Presumably his pursuer was going back to the Fischplatz, the other constable, and the fallen man—and Elise. Elise: what in God's name had she been doing there in the fishermen's settlement at midnight? As far as Tibor knew, she was living in Dorottya's former room in Spitalgasse, not far from the Kempelens' house, and a considerable distance away. And who had the two men been? He was proud of having been able to help her, even if she didn't know who he was. Although they had been so close to each other when he was inside the chess-playing Turk and she was serving Kempelen's guests, they would probably never meet, and that brief contact just now—her attempt to stop him—would not be repeated.

He rose to his feet. He was so much shorter again! He had been small all his life, but after a few hours in Jakob's disguise, he had become accustomed to his new height. The wall was too high on this side for him to climb it; he would have to find some other way out.

He moved out of the niche between the wall and the shed, into a walled courtyard beside a house. For a moment Tibor was frightened, see-

ing many faces staring at him in the moonlight, but those faces were dark
and did not move, and they ended just below the neck: he had landed in
a collection of statues or perhaps a sculptor's studio. A good two dozen
metal busts were assembled in this yard, some mounted on wooden or
stone plinths but most standing or lying on the ground; some stared up at
the stars, some straight down at the stone slabs beneath them; a few
looked right across the yard, others at a wall. A couple of busts were
gazing at each other with eyes so wide that it looked as if they were com-
peting to discover which would blink its leaden lids first. There were so
many faces here that one pair of eyes at least was always examining
Tibor. Never mind where he stood, he always felt their gaze upon him.
And what faces they were too! Not the kind you usually saw cast in metal,
not the faces of kings and emperors, generals or priests, with clear-cut
features, proud eyes, and perfect wigs—but the heads of men who had no
hair, whose throats and breasts were exposed, allowing you to concentrate
entirely on their ugly grimaces. Each countenance expressed a different
feeling, one grief, another amazement; anger here, idiocy there, weariness on one face, revulsion on another. They showed merriment, lust, bad
temper, and nausea more graphically than living faces. With the different
lines of the folds around their eyes, mouths, and throats, their foreheads
and their noses, all human emotions were caught forever in copper and
lead in this cabinet of curiosities. And now Tibor realized that they were
not in fact different faces; he was seeing the same face over and over again
in a large number of different versions.

Tibor heard a sound from the nearby house. Someone seemed to be
groaning in pain, and only now did he notice that a light was burning
indoors. A gate led from the walled courtyard into the street, but it was
locked. He slipped up to the lighted window and looked in. A man of
powerful build was sitting there by the light of several oil lamps, with his
back to Tibor, at a table on which stood a mirror and a small, damp clay
bust on which the artist was working with his fingers and a set of wooden
spatulas. His torso was naked, but on his head he had a *baranica*, the fur
cap worn by the local peasants. The man shaped the clay, then stopped,

put his left hand to the ribs on his right side, and pinched himself so hard that his flesh seemed to soften under his fingers. He tried to suppress a groan but managed to bear the painful grip for over half a minute, while he studied his twisted expression in the mirror. It was easy to guess that the clay face in front of him was being modeled to show the same features as those on the many busts in the yard—and the features of the man in the mirror, for when Tibor looked, he could see them reflected there; his face was the living original of the lifeless duplicates outside. Furthermore, the man's eyes were looking straight at Tibor in the mirror. Tibor hoped that he might not have been spotted in the dark, but in vain: the man immediately jumped to his feet.

Tibor took a step back. He was trapped in this yard, an intruder here; he could only hope that the sculptor would give him a hearing and let him go unscathed. But when the door opened and a cone of light from one of the oil lamps fell out into the courtyard, Tibor saw that the man was holding a pistol. "Go away, go away!" he shouted. "You won't get me!"

Tibor opened his mouth to speak, but what could he say in reply to this startling announcement? He ran to the gate, although it was locked. Hearing his footsteps, the sculptor spun around and aimed the pistol at him.

"*Vade retro!*" he cried, pressing the trigger. A white flame shot from the gun.

If Tibor had been a man of normal size the bullet would have gone through his head. As it was, it hit the bust in front of which he was standing—the yawning likeness of the artist himself—straight in its open mouth. The leaden bullet struck the leaden gums and was swallowed with a dull sound. The sculptor dropped his pistol and went toward Tibor.

"I can put you in chains! I'll catch you before you catch me!" he cried. Tibor ran for the open door, the only place where he could go, but his assailant barred the way to the studio. The two of them chased each other around the busts like children playing catch in the woods. The sculptor was faster and nimbler than Tibor, and when the dwarf leaped for the door, his attacker grabbed his legs from behind and brought him down. As he laughed triumphantly, he turned Tibor on his back. His laughter immediately died away. The light from the workshop fell on Tibor's face, and now at the latest it was obvious that the sculptor had taken him for someone else. Amazement spread over the man's face. He let go of Tibor, and when the dwarf made no move to stand up, he helped him to his feet.

"I'm really very sorry," he said, his voice suddenly gentle. "What a monster I am! What have I done to you?" He put out his hand to Tibor's brow but stopped just before touching the wound. "Come along, let's see to that."

Tibor followed him into the studio. The artist pulled out a chair for Tibor and brought a basin of water and a towel. First he washed the dried clay off his own fingers, then he cleaned the mud and blood from Tibor's face. Meanwhile he kept apologizing to Tibor for the wounds that he was convinced he himself had inflicted, assuring him that he had foolishly confused him with someone else entirely. Taking a blanket from his bed, he put it over Tibor's shoulders. Then he went into his kitchen two rooms away, and Tibor could hear him doing something with pans and water.

The dwarf took this opportunity of looking around the little studio, which also seemed to be the artist's living quarters. It contained his bed, a large table to work on, and several chairs, as well as various dishes and jugs, his tools, and books with such titles as *Microcosmic Preludes to the New Heaven and the New Earth, Accounts of the Visible Flaming Fire of Ancient Wisdom,* and *The Seven Sacred Pillars of Time and Eternity.* Several alabaster medallions were propped against one wall. The portraits on them were ordinary, not distorted by grotesque expressions. Tibor recognized one of those faces: it was that of the magnetizer, the robed healer who had treated Tibor and the others assembled around the *baquet* by the power of animal magnetism.

Tibor looked at the clay head on which the sculptor had just been working. Its eyes were wide, its mouth open, its lower jaw hung slack, the whole head was tilted slightly backward, and the muscles in the throat were tense. There was no doubt what that grimace expressed; it was dread, horror before something unknown, repellent, frightful, and monstrous. Tibor had seen such an expression not long before, not on the sculptor's face but on Elise's. Kempelen's maid had looked at him, Tibor, in just the same way, even as he himself was marveling at her beauty:

immaculate beauty that not even her look of revulsion could disfigure. Tibor's eyes went from the clay bust to the mirror, and his own face looked back—the battered chin cut off by the lower edge of the mirror because his body stood no taller—a face with black, lackluster hair and brown eyes set much too deep in their sockets, lurking there like craven rats; stupidly girlish cheeks, with dimples and bumps everywhere like dough that hasn't risen properly in the oven—and all that on the deformed, potato-shaped body of a gnome. What had he expected? Had he thought Elise would fling her arms around her rescuer in delight? The women in Vienna had given way to unbridled passion under the influence of magnetism, and he had been wearing that beautiful mask too; the whore just now and the whore in his youth had been paid for their caresses, and the girl in Gran had given herself to him only because she was ugly too. Now Tibor's features took another turn for the worse: he narrowed his eyes, the corners of his mouth drooped, and his chin quivered as he began to weep. He watched himself weeping: the grotesque shaking of his grotesque body when he sobbed. He followed the path of his tears making their way into the crooked furrows of his face, he watched the snot running from his nose—and the more he wept, the uglier he was, and the uglier he was, the more he had to weep for it.

"Why are you weeping?" the sculptor asked, without any audible note of pity in his voice.

Tibor had not heard the man come back. He put a teapot and two Chinese porcelain cups down on the table and poured out a whitish, hot beverage. Tibor mopped the tears off his face, first with the blanket around his shoulders, then with the sleeve of his coat.

"Why do you think?" said Tibor. "Because I'm ugly."

The sculptor handed him a cup. Neither of them spoke for a while. Tibor clasped his cup in both hands and breathed in the steam rising from it. It was hot water with milk.

"Look at me," said the sculptor, "and tell me if you think I'm ugly too."

Tibor looked at the man opposite, whose face was as regular in shape as his naked torso. He shook his head. He would have given anything for a figure like the sculptor's.

"What about the faces out there in the yard?"

"Yes. They're ugly."

"But it's me out there, over and over again, cast in copper, lead, and tin, and the grimaces I'm making are ordinary. So ugliness is relative. Just as a handsome man can look ugly, an ugly man can look handsome. We all have everything within us."

While Tibor was thinking about that, the sculptor closed the door into the yard again and shot two bolts across it.

"Who were you expecting just now?" Tibor asked him.

"The Spirit of Proportion," replied the man, looking out of the window through which he had seen Tibor.

When the artist did not explain any further, Tibor asked again, "Who?"

"The Spirit of Proportion. It comes by night and sometimes by day to pester me while I work. It doesn't want me to discover the secret of proportion."

"I don't understand."

"The whole world is subject to the laws of proportion. Everything in the world stands in a certain proportion to everything else, just as our faces are in proportion to the rest of the body. If I feel pain in a given part of my body, my face distorts in a certain way." He pinched himself hard in the right-hand side of his ribs again, making the same face as the little clay bust that he was making. "In all, there are sixty-four such grimaces. Many of them are already out there in the yard, finished. But I won't rest until I have cast all sixty-four in metal."

"Why?"

"Because then I shall have deciphered the system of proportion, and he who rules that system is also master of the Spirit of Proportion!"

Tibor had obviously ended up in the house of a raving lunatic, and he could count himself lucky that the sculptor hadn't gone after him with several pistols at once. He sipped his drink, wondering how he could get out of this madman's company unscathed.

"What may I call you, Spirit?" asked the sculptor.

"What . . . ?"

"For you are a spirit, aren't you? Of course you are a spirit."

Tibor nodded. "Yes. Yes, I'm a spirit. No one can see me . . . except for you."

"I know," said the sculptor, smiling.

"And you mustn't tell anyone about me."

"Why not?"

Tibor was momentarily at a loss but then pronounced sternly, "Because if you do, I'll haunt you too."

This idea seriously seemed to trouble the man. He raised his hands beseechingly. "Forgive me. I didn't mean to anger you. No one will ever hear about you."

"Good."

"And what may I call you?"

Tibor's glance fell on the medallion showing the magnetizer. "I am the Spirit of Magnetism."

The sculptor started and humbly bent his head. "You honor me with your visit, Spirit of Magnetism. Forgive me for my attack on you."

"You passed the test in refraining from further violence and treating me well." The artist nodded. As he apparently believed everything Tibor was thinking up on the spur of the moment, he added, "But now I must be gone. I must . . . er, must fly back to my temple. Open the doors for me, and in future I will . . . my magnetic powers will come to your aid in your search and your struggle."

"Will you come back?"

Tibor tried to guess what answer the deranged man wanted, then said, "Yes. For you have found favor in my sight, O faithful servant." He made a gesture like a blessing.

Out on the road from Zuckermandel back to the city, Tibor wanted to laugh at the experience he had just had, but somehow the laughter wouldn't come. Instead, he just kept shaking his head in silence. He would have to tell Jakob this story. On the way home he avoided the Fischplatz and the street where he had rescued Elise, and reached the Kempelen house just as the sky over the vineyards was turning blue again in the east.

FURTHER performances by the chess-playing Turk took place throughout April, and they were all sold out. Tibor was enjoying playing inside the Turk more and more; he hadn't had so much fun playing chess since he had first learned the game. His matches were like the sonatas that Kempelen played when he was in a good mood—the delicate sound of the harpsichord even made its way through the floorboards and into Tibor's room, and then the dwarf would put his work down, lie on his bed, stare at the ceiling or close his eyes, and listen to his employer's faultless playing.

Every game opened with an *allegro,* a fast, formal series of moves with the first pieces—the king's and bishop's pawns, the knight fighting for the four central squares, the alternate taking and sacrificing of unimportant pieces—almost without thought or tactical consideration, an opening tried thousands of times before, the logical, quasi-mathematical series of moves set out in countless chess books. Then came the *andante.* The game slowed down, went on and on, the opponents were now trying to put their strategy into practice; every move demanded much thought, for a mistake could end the game prematurely. Pieces were still taken, but now their loss was painful; valuable officers were removed from the board, sometimes the queen herself was lost; in move and countermove you always had to wonder whether your own knight was really worth less than your opponent's rook. Was it worth sacrificing two officers in order to take the opposing queen? Then either Tibor's tactics worked out, or his opponent made a fatal mistake, and now came the *presto,* the king was trapped and checkmated by an officer in a logical series of endgame moves that the opponent, if he understood them, could halt only by surrendering ahead of time. Alternatively there might be a *scherzo,* in which the red king was chased across the board by white officers, and the faithful few who were supposed to halt his pursuers were mowed down. At last came the final chord vibrating through the chessboard, when the red king was set aside, checkmated.

Meanwhile Tibor's opponents were getting progressively stronger. Knaus, Spech, and Windisch had been men who brought their names and reputations to the table rather than their talent for the royal game. But now really good players came to pit themselves against the Turk, members of chess clubs who had read their Philidor and their Modena masters. People began making notes of the Turk's matches in order to compare them, to understand the system behind its play, and to devise an attacking strategy. The games went on for longer and longer, and Kempelen began to think of using sand-glasses to time the moves and make the guests play faster.

Finally, on 11 April, Tibor had to accept a draw for the first time, after forty-four moves. In recognition of the achievement of this first opponent whom the automaton had not been able to beat—an old, almost blind elementary-school teacher—Kempelen waived the man's entrance money. Afterward Tibor apologized to Kempelen, but he took it calmly. In fact, as Kempelen had suspected, this draw only added to the Mechanical Turk's fame: for one thing, its fallibility made it seem more human to the people of Pressburg, and for another, the result spurred on its next opponents to try for a draw against the machine too, or even to be the first man to defeat it.

Soon loud complaints were heard to the effect that the chess-playing automaton was not a machine at all but was guided by a human hand—after all, a machine would always have won. Kempelen invited his accusers to performances to see for themselves that the cabinet with the chessboard on top was empty, and so was the Turkish dummy; no mirrors were fitted inside it, and there were no invisible wires either under or above the tabletop working Pasha's hand like the wires operating a marionette. Magnetism was at work, they cried, until Kempelen allowed one skeptic to put a strong magnet beside the chessboard or the mysterious casket, as he liked, and it made no difference whatsoever to the Turk's play. He also complied with a request to remove himself from the vicinity of the cabinet and the casket, and amid the laughter of the guests he once left the room entirely and went to get himself some refreshment, while the automaton played on even in its creator's absence.

Jakob caught a young fellow trying to blow Spanish snuff into one of the Turk's nostrils in order to make the supposed man inside sneeze and thus give himself away. With Branislav's assistance, Jakob turned this young spark unceremoniously out. Another time Tibor ate something that disagreed with him and gave him wind, and after his farts had entirely enveloped him inside the machine, they made their way out, so that the spectators in the front rows noticed the smell and asked whether the Turk had been overindulging in the caraway of its native land.

Ibolya Baroness Jesenák came to two of the performances. Tibor knew she was there before she could be heard or seen from inside the cabinet, merely by the delicious fragrance of her perfume. After she came for the second time, Anna Maria informed Kempelen that he must forbid the widow Jesenák to enter the house and tell her to stop flirting with him, whereupon husband and wife fought a brief but bitter battle from which Anna Maria emerged victorious. Wolfgang von Kempelen sent a note to Ibolya Jesenák in which, with regret, he asked her to refrain from further visits.

HIRING ELISE turned out to have been a good idea. Her cheerful if rather quiet nature made her presence about the house much more agreeable than Dorottya's. Anna Maria gave her the job of tidying up the workshop after performances—though only when the Turk was locked in its room, or under the supervision of Jakob, who found it a welcome assignment.

After the last performance before Easter, while she was sweeping up around the empty chess machine, he sat at the window sketching a portrait of her in charcoal, so that he had an excuse to keep looking at her.

"How does it work?" she asked suddenly.

Jakob looked up from his sketch.

"How does the machine work?" she repeated.

"By a complicated mechanism," replied Jakob.

"How can any mechanism play chess?"

"It's a very, very, very complex mechanism."

"I don't believe it."

"What do you know about these things?"

"Nothing. But I just can't imagine it."

"It's so, all the same."

"It's not," Elise insisted.

"Yes, it is."

"No."

"Yes."

"No."

Jakob put his paper and charcoal down. "Very well, you win. It's not."

"So?"

"So I mustn't tell you how it works, and you know that too."

Elise put her broom down and took a couple of steps toward him. She glanced at the drawing. "That's lovely."

"Not half as lovely as the model."

Elise blushed and looked down. When she had composed herself, she said, "Do tell me. Please."

"Kempelen would wring both our necks."

"I won't tell anyone else, I promise I won't. Cross my heart."

Jakob sighed.

"Please, Jakob."

"Not for nothing."

"What do you want?"

With his finger on his lips, Jakob told her. "A kiss."

"To think you . . . the devil I will!" replied the indignant Elise. She picked up her broom and went on sweeping. Jakob shrugged and returned to his sketch. Elise swept the floor for a while, watching Jakob out of the corner of her eye, then abruptly dropped the broom, went up to him, and brushed his cheek in a quick kiss. After that she wiped her mouth with the back of her hand. "There you are."

"Are you trying to fool me?" asked Jakob. "When I say a kiss, I mean a kiss. Not a goodnight peck."

Elise looked sulky and once again came closer for the kiss. When their lips touched, Jakob reached out to hold her by her shoulders. At first the maid resisted; then, for a sweet moment, she gave way; but finally she pushed him back again.

"There, did that hurt?" asked Jakob, smiling.

"So now, how does the Turk function?"

Jakob signed to her to sit down, and she went to sit by the window with him. He moved a little closer to her and lowered his voice. "Do you know that some people say there's a human being hidden inside the cabinet?"

Elise quickly nodded.

"Well, they're not altogether wrong."

And then Jakob gave her his version of the truth about the chess-playing automaton: the Turk, he said, wasn't really a wooden dummy but a real human being, a genuine, stuffed, and glossily painted Turk, a dead Ottoman chess grandmaster whom he and Kempelen had stolen one night from a mausoleum in Constantinople and who had been brought back to life by the rituals of a priest of Pantheism from the Caribbean Islands. They had cut out his brain first and filled the cavity with saw-dust, all but those of its meanderings that were necessary for playing chess, so now the living corpse could do nothing else. The Turk, he said, could be awakened from sleep by means of a simple magic spell, and vice versa—but by now Elise had stopped listening and cuffed Jakob's head for his impertinence in stealing a kiss and then dishing up such a tall tale. She left the workshop in a state of high indignation. Jakob was still laughing long after the door had closed behind her.

EASTER CAME, and on Good Friday Tibor slipped out of the house with help of the key he had made. Jakob had replaced the stiltlike shoes that Tibor had abandoned in the Zuckermandel district and mended the torn coat. This disguise worked even in daylight, and no one paid any attention to the dwarf, who now, with a three-cornered hat on his head to keep off the rain, made pilgrimage from Donaugasse to St. Savior's Church in Franziskanergasse.

A one-legged beggar was sitting on the church steps, close to the wall for shelter from the rain, his crutches on his lap and a bowl for alms in front of him. His right temple was crisscrossed with ugly scars. Tibor was searching for coins in his pocket—the beggar was looking another way—when a memory came back to him. He knew this man. Tibor hastily walked on with his face averted before the beggar could turn, and disappeared into the church. He stopped in the porch. The man had been none other than Walther, his comrade in the dragoons, the man who had saved his life in the Kunersdorf Hills and whom, like the rest of his column, he had last seen at Torgau. Walther had had two legs and a handsome face then. A grenade must have left the poor devil like this. How long ago it all was! He would happily have given Walther something, but he didn't want his old comrade to know that he was here.

St. Savior's was very much smaller than the cathedral, although the exterior was in the same massive style, but the interior was whitewashed and had gilded leaves and angels adorning many nooks and crannies, so that in spite of the gloomy light the church glowed. Tibor mopped the rain off his shoulders and went in. An organ was playing. He looked around. He had really meant to pray to the Madonna first and then make confession, but when the door in the side aisle opened again, Anna Maria von Kempelen came into the church with Teréz, while Elise shook out their umbrella just outside the door. They mustn't see him. Tibor fled into the nearby confessional. He could see out through its coarse wickerwork side without being seen. He'd wait here until the three of them had left the church again. The priest spoke to him, and Tibor began his confession.

When Elise and Teréz appeared right outside the confessional, he was startled, stammered, and fell silent. Surely Kempelen's maid wasn't going to confess? If she was, then she'd wait until he had finished and she would be bound to see him! No, she was helping Teréz sit down in a pew, then knelt beside the child to pray. Tibor breathed a sigh of relief and went on with his confession. As he did so, he watched Elise, and the sight made him keep stumbling over his words. He had guessed that she was a God-fearing girl, and here was the proof of it. At least the women in Kempelen's household hadn't abjured their religion. And how vulnerable she looked with her eyes closed, and her delicate mouth shaping silent prayers! As she did so, she was holding—here Tibor narrowed his eyes to see better—his amulet of the Madonna. Without a doubt it was the chain from Reipzig that he had lost during the scuffle in the Weidritz streets. She must have found it in the road: the sole memento of the unknown and ugly man who had come to her aid in her hour of need. Tibor wasn't listening to the priest anymore. A wave of warmth passed through his body. He didn't emerge from his ecstatic state until Anna Maria joined the other two, and Teréz squealed loud enough to be heard all over the church. Then the two women moved away with the child between them.

Tibor watched until they were out of sight, then finally answered the priest's question. "No, Father, that's all."

He received his penance and absolution, made sure that Elise and the others had gone, and then went over to the Madonna. Elise had found his amulet, and now she was presumably wearing it around her neck, over her breasts. Tibor was happy. He knelt down in front of the statue of the Virgin Mary and thanked her for this dispensation of Providence. Then he prayed.

The strong colors of the statue of the Madonna stood out from the white background of the church: the brown of her hair, the red of her dress, and the dark blue of her gold-lined cloak. In her left arm she was carrying the infant Jesus, who held a bright red apple in his hands. Her head was devoutly bent as always, so that she looked into the eyes only of someone who was either kneeling in front of her or as small as Tibor. Her hair was parted neatly in the middle and covered with a white veil only at the back of her head, so that it fell loose over her shoulders like frozen waves. The hair was carved from wood and painted, but Tibor imagined it as fragrant and silky soft. Her hands had no wrinkles or marks on them, and her fingers were so slender that every one of them was a work of art. Her free right hand rested on the cloak—how wonderful it must be to feel that hand stroking you, to clasp those fingers with your own as they twined together like two perfect cogwheels, and then, with the back of your hand, to caress her regular brow, her cheeks flushing under that touch, her red lips opening slightly, sending out warm, moist breath, your touch moving over her throat and the hollow of her shoulders, the slight curve of her collarbone, and finally going on down to the neck of the dress, draped into folds everywhere except over the breasts, which stood out under it as distinctly as her thighs. Her feet, peeping out from under the hem of her dress, were bare, so why not her thighs too? One movement of his hand, and the blue cloak would be removed; another would loosen the red dress; its material would slip soundlessly down to the floor, caressing all those wonderful curves, just as his hands and his lips would soon caress them too . . .

Tibor gasped for breath as if he had stayed under water too long. He felt the arousal in his crotch, warm, pleasant, demanding—and so unspeakably low and vulgar, so unlike his real self. He staggered out of the church with his tricorne pulled far down over his face to hide his shame. Even the rain couldn't quench Tibor's lust. It went away only when he had vomited beside the wall of a building. Tibor hurried back to his room, not caring whether Elise or anyone else saw him, tore off his coat and his shirt, and wondered how he could atone for such perversity—for prayer was no solution. Who was going to hear his prayer now? He even turned his rosary the chessboard upside down and took the crucifix off the wall. Then his glance fell on the watchmaking tools on his table, the little files, saws, and pincers, miniature copies of the instruments of torture in Hell, and Tibor used them now with a view to escaping Hell hereafter. He drove them into his body where no one would see the marks later, cut and tore his skin until he was bleeding and his eyes were swimming with tears, and when he couldn't go on any longer, he implored God again and again to forgive him for his degenerate desires. He halfheartedly bound up his wounds and fell into a feverish sleep—on the hard floor, so as not to alleviate his pain, and to make sure he would leave no blood on the sheets.

The Palais Grassalkovich

ON THE OCCASION OF THE WEDDING AT VERSAILLES OF
Princess Maria Antonia, or Marie Antoinette as she was known in France,
to the Dauphin Louis XVI, Prince Anton Grassalkovich, head of the Royal
Hungarian Chamber, invited the Hungarian and German nobility to a
ball at his summer palace on the Kohlenmarkt. Among the guests would
be Duke Albert of Sachsen-Teschen and his wife, Archduchess Christine,
as well as Prince-Bishop Batthyány; the Primate; Prince Esterházy; Counts
Pálffy, Erdödy, Apponyi, Vitzay, Csáky, Zapary, Kutscherfeld, and Aspre-
mont; Field Marshal Nádasdy-Fogáras; and many more. There would be
a dinner, a ball, and finally a fireworks display. In between the dinner and
the ball the Prince wished to surprise his illustrious guests with an exhibition of the chess automaton, and he and Wolfgang von Kempelen had
agreed at the Royal Chamber that the Turk would perform.

Grassalkovich's surprise was a great success, and the applause for Kempelen and his chess machine in the Conference Hall of the palace was more
than enthusiastic. When it came to choosing one of the guests as an opponent for the Turk, Grassalkovich invited Field Marshal Nádasdy-Fogáras
to play in recognition of his military achievements. The gray-haired officer declined with thanks; he was far too old, he said, to challenge such a

modern machine. Instead he passed the honor on to a lieutenant in his regiment who was well known for his great skill at the game of chess: János Baron Andrássy.

Baron Andrássy was the first of the android's opponents who set out not just to avoid defeat but to win, and he played even more aggressively than the Turk itself used to play: disregarding all losses, he commanded his red troops to advance, and the foot soldiers marched through the enemy lines in wedge formation. The red fusiliers fell in great numbers where they were not protected by Andrássy's cavalry, but he had broken through the white lines, and the opposing king was suddenly exposed and could save himself only by castling. Andrássy's general went in pursuit, the officers crossed the field of battle and kept escaping the attacks of White, and the Turk's soldiers and officers were forced to the sides of the board. Andrássy seemed sure of victory, but he could no longer reach the white king, who had entrenched himself behind his guns, where even the cavalry could not reach him.

And now White prepared to strike back, and the battle swung the other way. The few remaining red infantrymen were mowed down, their officers were surrounded in the center of the board. Andrássy now paid the heavy price for sacrificing all his fusiliers in the attack: even the least of the white soldiers overcame the red officers, while the Turk's cavalry gave them cover, often in ranks of two or three, thus thwarting all possible attempts at revenge. Finally only Andrássy's general was defending his king, but the battlefield was now open to the force of his guns, and they shot down everything in their way. Avoiding the line of fire, a white cavalryman approached the last cannon and finally took it but a little later fell himself, cut down by the general. At the end of the skirmish, the casualties of both armies lay to right and left, red with blood and white as death, and the two kings and their generals stood on the battlefield minus their followers, lurking in opposite corners and negotiating a truce with gritted teeth, infuriated by each other's good fortune in war. For company they had only two lost infantrymen, one white and one red, who seemed unable to realize that they had escaped the fray unscathed while all their comrades lay around them.

The game ended in a draw and two losers—or rather two winners, for the applause for János Baron Andrássy and Wolfgang von Kempelen's chess-playing Turk was deafening. Even those who were unfamiliar with the rules of the game had instinctively understood which moves were bad for their favorite and which good, and the whole hall had applauded when Andrássy removed a white piece from the board and groaned when the Turk took its revenge. Some of the ladies even left the hall during the game to spare their nerves; others escaped to the balcony. And what a bloody battle it had been! A piece was taken on one side or the other at every second move. Visually, Andrássy had made a brave opponent for the Turk as well. Although he was sitting at a separate table, as soon as the hussar made a move he looked into the android's false eyes, and a smile kept playing around his lips beneath his black moustache, expressing either arrogance or appreciation.

"Austria against the Turks," murmured Nádasdy-Fogáras to no one in particular. "The Emperor against the Sultan—a second battle of Mohács."

The applause was still going on when Andrássy rose and went over to the Turk's table. Before Kempelen could stop him, he seized the Turk's sensitive left hand and shook it with both his own. "We shall meet again, my good friend," he said. "This will not be the last duel between the two of us."

Meanwhile Prince Grassalkovich thanked Kempelen for this sensational performance and for adjusting the cylinders inside his automaton so that it would play only for a draw and not defeat Andrássy.

Then the Prince turned to address his guests. "*Mesdames et messieurs,* Duke Albert, Duchess Christine, my dear guests! It seems as if this evening has given us two new stars in the firmament: Baron Andrássy, who has succeeded in wresting a more than meritorious draw from the invincible chess machine and has held us spellbound for a whole hour by his courageous play." Andrássy raised his hand to acknowledge the applause. "And of course the man who made it possible in the first place for a collection of cogwheels and cylinders to bring the perspiration to our brows, making us wonder if we are really the crown of creation or whether the automaton may not dispute that title with us: Baron Wolfgang von Kempelen, the most skillful mechanician in our Empire—no, what am I saying? In the whole world! He can rest easy in the knowledge that his name will be immortal!"

Andrássy crowned his applause with a loud cry of "Bravo!"

"And I may add," continued Grassalkovich when the applause had died down, "he is a man who, to this day, has been an exemplary official of my Hungarian Chamber. How was I to know that you were destined for higher things, when you never told me of it?"

"Forgive me, my prince," replied Kempelen, smiling and sketching a bow.

Prince Grassalkovich waved away this petition. "You are forgiven, my dear Kempelen, if you will promise to continue providing us with such efficient machines. For I am firmly convinced that this machine is only the first of many. Leibniz gave us a machine that can calculate, Kempelen a machine that thinks! Far too few, in my opinion, have understood what that means for the world: playing chess is only a rehearsal! Imagine how many different possibilities still exist for the use of thinking machines: in administration . . . in finance . . . in manufacturing, and yes, why not in agriculture or indeed in war? I say: build us hundreds of mechanical soldiers, Herr von Kempelen, and send them into battle instead of our sons, for they will need no sleep and no provisions, they will know no fear and make no mistakes, and will bleed only oil! Let us make an army of automata, and with it we will drive Prussian Fritz out of Silesia again and send the Turk back over the Bosporus once and for all!" Here Grassalkovich turned to the Mechanical Turk and added, to general amusement, "But you, of course, may stay."

During the chess machine's performance, the servants had cleared all the tables and chairs in the Hall of Angels, where the banquet had been held, and now a chamber orchestra struck up music for the dancing. Anton Prince Grassalkovich invited his guests to go down there, and the Conference Hall slowly emptied. Kempelen wanted to begin dismantling and removing the automaton, but Grassalkovich urged him to come down to the Hall of Angels with the others.

As he left, Kempelen instructed Jakob to keep watch over the Turk and the casket until he was back. Jakob gathered up the chessmen from the board and put them away in the drawer at the bottom of the cabinet.

Princess Judit, Grassalkovich's young wife, lingered in the Conference Hall with two of her women friends until the last minute, looking at the Turk more closely until Jakob covered it with a cloth.

"Poor Pasha," said one of the Princess's friends. "Now he's all alone until you wake him again."

"Oh, I'm sure he has sweet dreams," Jakob assured her.

"What does an automaton dream of?" asked Judit. "Automatic sheep?"

Jakob shrugged his shoulders. "Perhaps. Or a harem with mechanical concubines."

"And what do *they* look like?"

"You can wind them up, they never rust, and they're as beautiful as the day. Though not quite as beautiful as Your Excellencies, of course."

The three young women giggled, and Judit offered Jakob her arm. "Do pray escort us down. You must tell us all about the Turk's love life."

"I would be delighted, but I fear I can't. I have to watch over his sleep."

"I'll tell the servants to put out the candles, close the doors, and admit not a soul. No one will disturb his slumbers."

Jakob did not reply. Judit offered him her arm again and said, "Surely you won't refuse the request of a Princess Grassalkovich?"

"I would never dare do such a thing." Jakob took the arm she offered him, found that one of her friends had immediately taken his other arm, and went down the stairs talking to the three young women, following the sound of the orchestra, while the servants closed the doors of the darkened Conference Hall where the shrouded Turk slept.

IBOLYA BARONESS JESENÁK was wearing a dress as costly as it was daring that evening, pale green with an excessive quantity of embroidered brocade, flounces, and silk roses and a large pink bow over her breasts. It attracted the men's eyes and aroused mingled envy and derision among the women. The two people in whose honor these festivities were being held, Princess Marie Antoinette and Prince Louis, were long forgotten; Wolfgang von Kempelen and János Andrássy were the center of attention, and those who were not dancing gathered around one or other of them—the statesmen around Kempelen, the officers around Andrássy. The Baron's assistant was answering the questions of Judit Grassalkovich and the young countesses and baronesses. The fact that the two men receiving such acclamation were her brother and her lover did Ibolya herself no good. No one in the hall was taking any interest in her; they all seemed to have forgotten her links with the heroes of the evening entirely. Once again she felt alone. So she allowed Count Csáky to ask her to dance a gavotte, put up with his avid glances and his bad breath, and then realized that she had already drunk too much to dance.

She joined the company around Kempelen's assistant, who was just telling them that he and Kempelen planned to explore the possibility of automatic reproduction, so that automata wouldn't be made by human hands but engendered by other automata. Jakob whispered to the ladies, in confidence, that the Turk was extremely skillful not just at chess but in the game of love. Ibolya wanted to join the conversation, for after all she had known the Turk longer and better than any of the other women here, but the assistant wouldn't let her get a word in. When Jakob demonstrated the winding-up of a mechanical *demoiselle*, champagne spilled from his glass onto Ibolya's manteau, leaving an ugly mark. She noticed two girls whispering and giggling as they looked at her dress. Baroness Jesenák moved away from the little company with a merry laugh, saying untruthfully that she had promised to talk to other guests.

Her brother was surrounded by hussars and was giving an account of his strategy in the fight against the Turk, repeatedly interrupted by the Field Marshal's praise. The Hungarians greeted Ibolya politely but then went on with their conversation. "You must forgive us uncouth soldiers, Baroness," Nádasdy-Fogáras had said, "but the only time we men don't talk of war is when we're on the battlefield itself."

Ibolya was soon bored by the men's discussion. She moved away from the hussars. There was still more than half an hour to go before the big fireworks display. Ibolya looked at the golden angels in the stuccowork above the mirrors. A man she didn't know asked her to dance; she declined with thanks. Then she saw Kempelen coming into the hall and taking two glasses of champagne from the buffet. Smiling, she stood in his way and relieved him of one of the glasses, thanking him warmly.

"So long as Prince Anton doesn't mind your drinking his champagne," said Kempelen.

"I'm sure you'll find him another glass. Your good health, Farkas." Ibolya clinked her glass against Kempelen's, but while she drank, he left his wine untouched and looked at the group of men around Prince Grassalkovich, who were waiting for him to return to them.

"Yours too, Ibolya. Will you excuse me? I have an important conversation to conduct."

"That doesn't surprise me. You're always conducting important conversations."

"I'm afraid that my speaking machine isn't yet far enough advanced to relieve me of that burden." Kempelen took a step forward, but Ibolya detained him by putting a hand on his chest.

"I received your note," she said.

"Yes."

"Did your wife write it?"

"As far as I remember, it had my signature to it."

"Then is it your wife's doing, yet again, that you don't want to see me anymore?" Ibolya let her hand slip down his waistcoat. "Or have you built yourself a little automaton for the game of love? Your Jew tells us that automata are great lovers."

Kempelen rolled his eyes. "Ibolya, please. You read my letter. I'm married, you're a woman with a reputation to protect, we should leave it at that. You said yourself that we're like two star-crossed lovers."

Ibolya looked hard at him, then said, "It looks very much as if you are dropping me."

"No such thing."

"Oh yes, you're dropping me. You don't need me anymore, and you don't even think it necessary to thank me. I and Károly furthered your career, you're famous now, you eat at the lord's table, and you kick away the rungs of the ladder you once climbed to get where you are."

"Ibolya . . ."

"I'll tell you one thing, Farkas: if it weren't for me, you wouldn't be here today, talking to Grassalkovich and the rest of them. But for me you'd still be sitting scribbling in your office like any other clerk."

Ibolya's voice had risen, and Kempelen glanced around in embarrassment. "Please calm yourself."

"I'm perfectly calm. I'm just warning you to be careful. I raised you to where you are—I can just as easily bring you down again."

"Kindly listen: that's not true." Kempelen's own voice was sharper now, although he kept it low and was still smiling. "None of it is true. I am here because I have made a machine that plays chess. And you can't do anything to bring me down—no matter why you might want to."

"Are you challenging me?"

"If so, what will you do about it?"

"I'm warning you, Farkas."

Kempelen saw Grassalkovich waving impatiently to him. "Warn away, but please allow me to enjoy a more profitable conversation." He handed her his glass of champagne, since she had almost finished her own. "Let this keep you company instead of me."

She watched him return to the circle around Grassalkovich with assumed cheerfulness, no doubt apologizing for his delay with a joke at the tipsy widow's expense. Ibolya emptied both glasses of champagne and left the Hall of Angels with another. She didn't want anyone to witness her misery—least of all Wolfgang von Kempelen.

She went back to the Conference Hall, which was neither guarded nor locked, opened the door, and closed it quietly behind her. The only light in the room came from the torches in the park outside. Ibolya crossed the hall, passing the table with the mysterious casket on it, walked once all around the shrouded android, and then pulled back the cloth from the cabinet and the Turk—carefully, so as not to wake the sleeping automaton.

But the Turk was awake already, staring at her with its eyes open, just as it had stared at her in Vienna, almost as if it were expecting her. However, it did not move. This was the first man her brother had failed to defeat at chess. Everyone was talking about him, but ultimately no one really knew him, not even his creator.

"Good evening," whispered Ibolya, letting the cloth drop to the floor. She took another sip of champagne, looking at him. "Are you lonely too?" Emptying the glass, she put it down on the chess cabinet. Then she cautiously caressed the Turk's left hand as it rested on the velvet cushion. She removed the cushion, put it on the floor, and wound up the clockwork of the machine. Then she took off the latch. The mechanism began to turn, rattling. But the Turk did not stir.

"You must move now, my dear," Ibolya said.

At that the automaton obediently raised its hand, passed it over the chessboard, and came down where a white pawn ought to have been. But the chessmen had all been cleared away. Instead of a pawn, the android grasped two of Ibolya's fingers, which had been lying under its hand. It raised them and put them carefully down at the side of the board. She sighed. She went around the cabinet, stood behind the android, and caressed its neck.

"You're so cold, but all hot inside," she said. "That's what makes us different from those dreadful human automata down there, all the hypocrites hiding their real selves under clothes made of wires and heavy cosmetics, don't you agree?"

The Turk nodded. So it had understood what she said. And even more than that—it turned its eyes slightly toward the Baroness, so that they were looking at each other. At first Ibolya was alarmed. Then she giggled.

"Why not?" she said. "After all, it worked for Pygmalion."

She clasped the Turk's head in both her hands and kissed its wooden mouth, leaving traces of her lip rouge. She was breathing more heavily now. The Turk's eyes were positively hypnotic; the mechanism hummed a beguiling melody. From that point on she said no more. She folded the android's right arm back, as she had once seen Kempelen do, gathered up her dress, and sat astride its lap. Then she lowered its arm again, so that she was in its embrace. There was an edge somewhere in the automaton's lap, but the soft caftan padded it as it pressed into her crotch. She stroked the white fur trimmings first with her hands, then with her cheeks, and groaned aloud. She kissed the Turk again, kissed its forehead and its brows, and finally its exposed throat as she held the back of its neck, meanwhile using her other hand to stroke her own legs, moving up and up to her bare thighs. Her pelvis circled on the Turk's lap. Now she took one breast out of the low neckline of her dress and rubbed her nipple against the fur of the Turk's caftan. Leaning against the edge of the cabinet, she threw her head back. With her right hand, she held the Turk's upper arm until the caftan was stretched over it. The fingers of her left hand had found their way into her petticoat and were caressing her lower lips, and the Turk seemed to be helping her: its hand moved up her thigh, pressing her there, and with the touch it became warm. Enraptured, Ibolya took the Turk's hand and was going to draw it toward her crotch, but when she touched it the fingers were soft and short and eluded her grasp. Looking down to her left, Ibolya saw a small arm disappearing into the opening in the cabinet, pulling the door to and closing it from the inside.

She screamed and tried to rise from the Turk's lap before more hands reached for her from inside the machine, but the Turk's two arms held her fast. She struggled and hit out at the rapist, ducked under its left arm, losing her wig, fell to the floor, and crawled rapidly away from the automaton, impeded by her petticoat, which was coming down. Something tore. Only when she had put a little distance between her and the android did she turn and look at it, breathing heavily. However, although the clockwork was still running, the Turk didn't move and just stared straight ahead.

A door was opened. Wolfgang von Kempelen had to accustom his eyes to the darkness in the Conference Hall before he saw Ibolya sitting on the floor and looking at him wide-eyed. Her hair was untidy, her lip rouge smudged, her stockings and her petticoat were at half-mast, and one breast was swelling above her corsage. Kempelen closed the door and stopped the automaton's clockwork. All was quiet now except for Ibolya's breathing. He crouched down beside her.

"Are you all right?" He sounded genuinely concerned.

Ibolya pointed a trembling finger at the chess cabinet, sought for words, and finally burst out with "There's someone in there!"

"Ssh. Keep calm, now." Kempelen put a hand on her arm, but she shook it off.

"Don't you say *keep calm, now*! There was someone in that cabinet."

"You're imagining things. There's only the Turk here. You've had a little too much to drink, Ibolya."

He helped her get up. She pushed her breast back inside her bodice. "Your chess automaton only works because there's someone inside it. You've been deceiving us all." Kempelen tried to hand her the wig that had fallen off, but she didn't take it. "You're a . . . a fraud! You're cheating all of Pressburg . . . all of Europe with what you call a machine!"

Ibolya went over to the cabinet and knocked on one of the doors at the front. "Open up in there!" When no answer came, she tried to open the door, but it was locked.

"Please, Ibolya. There's no point in that."

She spun around to him. "Open it. I want to see who was touching me!"

Kempelen sighed but saw that the Baroness wouldn't take no for an answer. He took a bunch of keys from the pocket of his close-fitting coat but did not hand it to her. "I don't have to open it. You know there's some-one in there—that's enough."

"So you admit it?"

"Yes."

Ibolya laughed briefly and shook her head. "It's incredible."

"Let me offer you my warm congratulations, my dear," said Kempelen, distinctly more cheerful than before. "You are now one of the very few to know the secret of the chess-playing Turk."

"Well, there'll soon be a great many more."

Kempelen stopped short. "You're not going to tell anyone else?"

"Oh no? And why not?"

"Ibolya, let's be reasonable: you will keep quiet about this . . . and in return, I won't tell anyone just what you were . . . well, doing in here." He picked her wig up, as if it were evidence.

"I'm not afraid of that. I can't wait to hear what your fat Empress will say when her favorite genius turns out to be just a conjuror! And I shall enjoying watching Grassalkovich trying to extricate himself from the hymn in praise of automata that he was singing just now."

"For God's sake, what do you hope to achieve by that?"

"Isn't it obvious? I want to pay you back for eating me up and then spitting me out again."

"I beg you, Ibolya: don't do this. My whole existence depends on it. If you want to frighten me, well, you've done it." He took her hands. "I implore you. You can ask what you like of me. Please don't do it. In memory of what we once shared . . . and might soon share again."

"You mean . . . our tender liaison?"

"Yes. Forget what I said just now."

Ibolya smiled and waited for what came next.

"I can't conceal it—I still adore you and desire you, body and soul."

Kempelen had come closer to her, whispering his last words. He was not prepared for the slap in the face she gave him. Incredulous, he put a hand to his cheek.

"Oh, how disgraceful of you to come crawling back, not a quarter of an hour after my presence was so distasteful to you! You want to deceive me just as you deceive everyone else! But I'm cleverer than they are. If you had at least been honest—well, then I might have thought about it. You have no guts, Farkas, you aren't a Hungarian anymore, just an ordinary German, and no Wolfgang deserves my pity."

She snatched the bunch of keys from him and opened the doors at the front of the cabinet, while he watched as if paralyzed. The Turk's left arm on the table twitched.

"So where's the spirit in this machine of yours?"

Ibolya went around the cabinet and unlocked the right-hand door at the back, but she couldn't open it because it was being held in place on the inside. However, Ibolya was stronger; she wrenched the door open. Something rumbled about inside the cabinet. Suddenly, as part of the pantograph broke with a grinding noise, the Turk's arm shot across the tabletop and struck Ibolya on the forehead. Ibolya took a step away, caught one foot in her petticoat, which she still hadn't hoisted up properly, stumbled, and fell backward. The back of her head hit the table with Kempelen's casket on it—it made a sound like a nail being driven into wood—and then she dropped to the floor. The last thing about her to move was the folds of her dress as they gradually settled around her.

For what seemed an eternity, Kempelen and Tibor were left as silent and motionless as the Turk and the Baroness. Then Tibor tried to make his escape from the cabinet through the double doors at the front. His clumsy movements broke the pantograph right off. Kempelen had picked up the keys again. He knelt down in front of the double doors and barred Tibor's way.

"You stay in there," he said uncompromisingly.

"*Madre di Dio,* what's happened?"

"Nothing too bad. She fell. I'll see to her at once, but you must stay in hiding, Tibor."

Kempelen waited for Tibor to nod, then closed the double doors and all the others. He laid Ibolya on top of the cabinet. She wasn't bleeding. Cautiously, he placed two unsteady fingers on her throat, where the pulse of her artery should be beating.

"What's the matter with her?" asked Tibor from inside the cabinet. Kempelen did not reply. "Signore Kempelen! What's the matter with her?"

"She's dead," said Kempelen.

"No," cried Tibor, and when Kempelen did not reply he added, "She can't be!"

"Tibor, her heart has stopped beating. She's dead."

"*O dolce Vergine,*" wailed Tibor. "*O dolce Vergine, dolce Vergine, perdona, ti prego!*" Suddenly he screamed, "I want to get out of here! I want to get out! Let me out!" He hammered on the walls with his hands and feet, so that the cabinet itself throbbed like a pulse under Kempelen's hands. "I want to get out!"

Kempelen crouched down beside the cabinet. "Tibor, listen to me carefully. The only way you'll get out of here safe and sound is inside the automaton. That's why you must stay in there. I'll see to everything."

"No! *Prego*, I want to get out!"

Kempelen slammed the flat of his hand down on the wood. "Tibor, they'll execute you for this. You'll die, *capisce*? You'll die if you leave the automaton now."

Tibor had begun to weep.

"Have I ever let you down?" asked Kempelen. "Have I ever let you down yet, Tibor? Answer me!"

"No, signore," replied Tibor, in tears.

"Exactly. And I won't let you down now either. Everything will be all right if you just do as I say."

"Sì, signore."

Kempelen stood up again. Tibor was begging the Mother of God for mercy. *"Ave Maria, gratia plena, Dominus tecum, benedicta tu in mulieribus . . ."*

"Be quiet!" snapped Kempelen. "I have to concentrate."

Tibor went on praying in silence. Now and then a sob could be heard.

With his eyes closed, Kempelen massaged his temples. Then he put Ibolya's wig back on her head. Picking up her body, he took hold of her champagne glass too and carried her to the balcony. He made sure that the grounds outside were still empty before stepping out onto it.

It was a mild night, almost like summer. Kempelen put the wineglass down on the balustrade of the balcony. He took a deep breath. Breathing hurt him. The light of the torches blurred before his eyes. He looked at Ibolya's face one last time, then raised her above the balustrade and let her fall.

Her body hit the paving of the terrace below headfirst. It would not be discovered until the guests went out to see the fireworks, and Bengal lights bathed the open-eyed corpse in green, red, and blue light by turn. By then Wolfgang von Kempelen would long ago have rejoined the other guests for a lively discussion of the progress at present being made in the development of mechanical looms in England.

Mount Olympus

SHE HAD BEEN BAPTIZED TWENTY-TWO YEARS AGO BY THE name of Elise and adopted the euphonious pseudonym Galatea only because no woman in her profession used her real name. So it was no great change for her to be called Elise again in Kempelen's house. All she had to do was think of a surname. The means employed for her task had worked, yet more than two months after making her bargain with Friedrich Knaus she still hadn't achieved her end.

She had successfully presented a different Elise to every member of the household. To Anna Maria von Kempelen she was the naïve servant who admired the mistress of the house, shared her religious feelings, and envied her the life she led. At the same time she always had an ear ready when Anna Maria wanted to confide her troubles, and she assured her that she was right on every imaginable subject. In Anna Maria's presence she looked as unprepossessing as possible, pulled her cap well down over her face, and walked with her back slightly bent.

If she was alone with Jakob, however, she turned on all her charm: a shy fluttering of her eyelashes, a lock of hair coming loose from her cap, a move to bend over the laundry basket at just the right time to let him see the top of her breasts. For Jakob's benefit she acted the pious virgin flirting coyly but secretly just waiting for someone like him; a girl who wants to be conquered but not all at once, very gradually, and by the arts of seduction that were his alone.

Finally, she was always helpful to the other servant, Katarina, never questioning the cook's rank above her in the domestic hierarchy and an avid listener to gossip about their masters' lives.

Only with Kempelen himself did all her strategies seem to fail. Friedrich Knaus had been wrong about him: he was vain, yes, but not vain enough to fall for pretended admiration. And yes, he was a man, but too self-controlled to give way to her sensual allurements. He was the last person from whom she was likely to learn the secret of the chess-playing Turk.

Yet there was a secret; that was obvious. The ban on going up to the top floor, her orders not to talk to anyone about her work in the house, the bars, the bricked-up windows, Kempelen's caution before, during, and after performances—all of it suggested that he was bent on hiding something at any price. Whether it was just the construction of a perfect piece of clockwork that he wanted to keep secret from spies, or a clever deception simulating some such device, Elise couldn't say. In spite of the months she had spent with Knaus, anything mechanical was still as incomprehensible and ultimately uninteresting to her as chess itself had always been.

Her advances to Jakob had earned her only his tall tale, although they had not been entirely fruitless: for one thing, she knew now that the assistant was not as talkative as she had hoped, and for another, with luck that kiss had given him a taste for more. But if he wanted more from her, he would have to give her more himself.

Apart from that, all she had to show for her efforts was her knowledge of the existence of Jakob's mysterious companion. She had seen the two of them by chance on her way home from the post office one evening: the small, stocky figure with a walking stick had gone to the Golden Rose with the Jew. Unnoticed, Elise had followed the twosome, waited for several hours in the cold, and when the man finally left the tavern without Jakob, she had followed him. She had lost track of him in the dark alleys of the Weidritz settlement, and then two drunks had taken her for a whore and pestered her. And the very man she had been following had leaped to her rescue, apparently out of nowhere, attacked the two crafts-men like a berserker, then hobbled away. A man who avoided the constabulary, even though he had done a heroic deed, most certainly had something to hide. She had picked up the chain torn from his neck and bearing a scratched, worthless medallion of the Virgin Mary, the kind of thing you might give children. She had memorized his misshapen face, but she had never seen him in the city streets again no matter how often she shadowed Jakob, following him right into the Jewish quarter.

Knaus had promised her plenty of time, but now the Swabian was getting impatient. Fresh reports of the Turk's triumphs and the unabated demand for a sight of the marvelous automaton reached him daily in Vienna, but never news from Galatea saying that she was any closer to discovering the secret. Knaus had sent two letters to the post office for her, and in her replies she had assured him that she was on the right track; it was only a matter of time, she said. However, Knaus was in no mood to wait any longer, and her own time was running out; she must be in her third month of pregnancy, and she couldn't hide her swelling belly under her working clothes forever. Her mission must be completed by the time it showed. Then she would go into the country with the fee that Knaus had promised and bear her baby there. Her plans went no further. She had no idea yet what she would do with the child and herself afterward, and when she thought about it at quiet moments, it made her throat feel tight.

Just as Elise was planning new tactics, Ibolya Baroness Jesenák, Kempelen's former lover, died in a fall from a balcony after a performance by the Turk at the Palais Grassalkovich, and events began moving of their own accord, without any need for Elise to intervene.

MOST OF THE PEOPLE of Pressburg saw the widow Jesenák's death as a scandal but not a riddle: the Baroness had always been a moody character, even more given to melancholy than the rest of her melancholic country-men. The number of Ibolya's friends had been limited: men were divided into those who had been involved in a liaison with her and wanted to keep it secret, and those who had rejected her advances, and both groups avoided contact with her. Women had feared her as a rival and punished her with contempt. Only her brother, János Baron Andrássy, was still close to her at the end; malicious tongues even spread rumors that brother and sister had loved each other with more than just their minds—a rumor as unfounded, incidentally, as it was dangerous, considering the propensity of the lieutenant of hussars for fighting duels.

It was certain that since her husband's death Ibolya Jesenák had been merry only when she was drunk. Her farewell was that empty champagne glass on the balustrade. She had thought of the sorrows of her lonely life that night and killed herself in a drunken daze.

The alternative theory was put forward by only a few, but those few stuck to it with particular tenacity: in their view the chess-playing Turk had pushed the Baroness off the balcony to her death. This group did not bother about the undoubted difficulty of explaining just how the crime had been committed—for after all, the automaton was nailed to its cabinet and could move only its head, its eyes, and one arm. Instead, the proponents of the theory dwelled on the strong motives it had for murder. *Primo*, the automaton was a Turk and the Baroness a Hungarian, and all Turks wished to see all Hungarians dead. *Secundo*, Andrássy had wrested a draw from the Turk, so the automaton avenged itself for the affront by taking from Andrássy what he held most dear, his sister. *Tertio* and last, the widow Jesenák's affair with Wolfgang von Kempelen was an open secret among the nobility of Pressburg. Furthermore, the two of them had been seen quarreling in the Hall of Angels not half an hour before Ibolya's death—*ergo*, Kempelen had commanded his creature to rid him of the rejected mistress of whom he had tired.

In support of the theory that the Turk was a murderer was news that soon arrived from Marienthal: the old teacher who had also drawn a game against the chess-playing Turk a few weeks earlier had now died too—of smallpox, to be sure, not by violence, but that didn't seem to make any difference. In any case, several people concluded from this event that the Turk would punish any opponent who dared to defy it with death, or with the death of a beloved relation. There was talk of "the Curse of the Turk," and many who had felt mortified immediately after their defeat by the chess machine now congratulated themselves on the lack of talent that had preserved them from the Turk's fatal curse. A winegrower from Ratzersdorf who had played against it in April now bore witness that he had heard the android's voice inside his head during the game. The Turk had threatened to strike his children and grandchildren down with cholera and dry up his vineyards if the match ended in his favor.

But these fantasists were in the minority. They were the same people who would swear to have seen the Black Woman of the Tower of St. Michael's, or White Lady Luzie, or the ghosts of the twelve murdered city councilors; people who regarded Frederick II as an incarnation of Old Nick and Empress Catherine II as a cannibal with a special liking for babies, and who held Jews responsible for causing the plague. After Karl Gottlieb von Windisch had received a number of letters asking him to write about the Curse of the Turk, he printed a sharp editorial reprimand in his *Pressburger Zeitung*, recommending these muttonheads "either to keep their mouths closed and save their ink or to emigrate forthwith," because the superstition of a few simpleminded folk, said Windisch, put the whole city to shame.

Then the word *heresy* was uttered for the first time in connection with Wolfgang von Kempelen and his machine, and the Church pricked up its ears. Under the chairmanship of the Primate, Prince-Bishop Batthyány, the theologians of Pressburg discussed what stance the Church ought to adopt toward the Baron's machine, and whether he should be instructed to bring the Turk's performances to an end.

It was not least because of this discussion that Wolfgang von Kempelen received the full support of his Masonic brothers in the Purity Lodge, led by its Privy Secretary, Windisch himself, who in conversation dubbed his friend "the Pressburg Prometheus." Kempelen should continue exhibiting his chess machine to one and all, said the Freemasons, particularly now that the Baroness's suicide had shown how the torch of the Enlightenment illuminating their era still hadn't managed to set light to the damp straw in the heads of many of their fellow men. Leaving that marvel of technology to gather dust in a lumber room, they said, would be as if Columbus had turned back halfway across the ocean, as if Leonardo da Vinci had done nothing but paint pictures all his life, as if Klopstock had remained an ordinary teacher.

After this meeting of the Lodge, Nepomuk von Kempelen had a word with his brother. "I hear that you left Grassalkovich's festivities for some time. Forgive me, please, but I have to know whether you had anything to do with Ibolya's death. You or your dwarf."

Kempelen did not answer at once, so Nepomuk apologized again. "I'm sorry that I have to ask."

"No," said Kempelen. "The answer is no. I don't know how Ibolya died, and nor does Tibor. He was inside the cabinet and covered with a cloth too. He couldn't hear anything. It's right for you to ask me. I might well do the same in your place."

Nepomuk nodded. "Poor soul. Perhaps we laughed at her once too often."

"We did nothing to drive her to her death, Nepomuk. At the very most, we could have done more to keep her from making that decision."

"Peace be to her soul. And may her heaven be full of handsome male angels, fountains bubbling with champagne, and a wardrobe the size of Versailles."

Kempelen smiled. "Why wasn't Duke Albert at today's meeting? Is it anything to do with me?"

"It could well be. At the moment he stands between you, or rather the Lodge, and Batthyány if the clergy want to take steps against you. He has to go very cautiously just now."

"Will he come down on Batthyány's side?"

"I don't think so. You're still a favorite of his mother's, he's a sensible man, I work closely with him . . . and yes, of course, I'll put in a good word for you."

Kempelen gratefully pressed his brother's arm.

"Can your dwarf be relied on?" inquired Nepomuk.

"Why do you ask?"

"Because I don't like him. Because I can't shake off the feeling that he's a sly little devil, a spawn of Hell who'll show his true colors one day, and then he'll be dangerous to you. A man who's lived the life of a dwarf, bearing so much malice from the world, is bound to turn malicious himself someday. And now that I come to think of it, the same applies to your Jew. It's an odd team of outsiders you've assembled. But at least it's easy to understand the Jew."

"Jakob has no reason at all to stab me in the back. And Tibor is more loyal to me now than ever. Why, I have more to fear even from my own wife," Kempelen assured his brother. "And for Heaven's sake stop just calling Jakob *the Jew* all the time. He has a name."

THE DAY AFTER Tibor's hand touched the Baroness's thigh it still smelled of her perfume. He had soaped it and scrubbed it until it was sore to dispel the fragrance that reminded him of the woman he had killed. But even after that he still had the sweet scent of apples in his nostrils. Just as Lady Macbeth once imagined that she couldn't wash the murdered king's blood off her hand, Tibor could not rid himself of the ghost of that pleasant aroma. He had slept very little in the nights that followed, and when he did sleep, he was haunted by feverish dreams in which he saw the Baroness's crushed head, her beautiful face smashed to a mush of blood, bones, and brain—however much Kempelen assured him that she had died quickly and painlessly, shedding no blood, and had received her unsightly injuries only in the fall from the window. Now he discovered the truth of Jakob's story about the bell in the Town Hall tower, when he said that its sound struck terror into anyone with a guilty conscience. Every hour the bell reminded him of his crime, and its two notes seemed to keep calling *Mur-der, Mur-der*.

Like the Venetian's death, Ibolya's had of course been an accident. But in the case of the Venetian, Tibor had just wanted to retrieve his property, whereas with the Baroness his own lust had led to the catastrophe. If he had exercised self-control and kept his hand inside the cabinet—or perhaps touched himself, even if it was a sin; after all, the Baroness had done it too—then he could have described the incident to Jakob the next day amid hearty laughter.

Nor was that all: not only had he killed a woman, he had also disappointed Wolfgang von Kempelen, the man who had freed him from prison, who paid him, fed him, sheltered him, and had even given him a friend to keep him company, the man who had revealed to him, inside the body of his wonderful invention, a whole world that would otherwise have been closed to him forever. The man whose prompt action had saved him by making the Baroness's death look like suicide. Tibor would atone for the murder of Baroness Jesenák in the next world, but he was ready to do as much in this one for his ingratitude to his benefactor. Five days after the death at the Palais Grassalkovich he offered to resign from Kempelen's service, claiming none of his pay, and leave the house just as he had entered Venice, with only the clothes on his back, his sole possession a traveling chess set. He would either leave the Empire or hand himself over to the authorities, whichever Kempelen wanted.

"I don't want anything of the kind," said Kempelen. They were sitting opposite each other in his study with the speaking machine between them. Kempelen had had less and less time to work on it during the last few weeks. "You'll stay in Pressburg, you'll remain in my service, and you will go on being the brain of my chess machine."

Tibor shook his head. He felt cold. "No."

"What do you mean, no? I say yes."

"Why are you so good to me? I don't deserve it."

"I'm not being good to you. First and foremost I'm being good to myself," replied Kempelen. "Think about it for a moment: if you go now, I can never present the chess automaton again. And then there really will be questions asked about what happened that night at the Palais. If I can't exhibit the automaton anymore, people will get on my trail. They'll remember that I wasn't in the hall at the time. And if you're not here, I'll have no witness to testify that Ibolya was already dead when I dropped her off the balcony. I'll be accused of murder. Ibolya was a baroness, her late husband was an influential statesman . . . the sentence will not be light. And no one will believe me if I say it was all a dwarf's fault."

"I'll give myself up. I'll take my rightful punishment."

"Thus revealing that the automaton was only a conjuring trick. And the von Kempelen family can say goodbye to Pressburg and the Habsburg Empire forever."

Tibor slumped even further down in his chair.

"We have to go on exhibiting the Turk as if nothing had happened," said Kempelen. "Ibolya killed herself because she wasn't happy in this world, and it's pure chance that the automaton happened to be in the same room at the same time. The talk of those fantasists who are trying to claim that the Turk did it will soon die down."

"My pay . . ."

"You'll get it. I don't want to exploit you by capitalizing on your predicament."

Kempelen looked at Tibor. The dwarf had begun shedding tears. Kempelen sighed, stood up, and came around the table until he was standing beside Tibor. "It was an accident, Tibor. An accident, the result of her deranged behavior. You're not a murderer, Tibor. You're a good man, weak perhaps, but aren't we all? And although my connections with God are only very . . . well, slight, I feel sure that he will forgive you."

Tibor was ashamed of his tears, but even more ashamed of so much else. Kempelen overcame a certain internal reluctance, knelt down, and embraced Tibor. The dwarf clung to him.

"There, there," said Kempelen. Then he moved away from Tibor, gave him his handkerchief, and averted his eyes.

"Is there anything I can do for you?" he asked.

"I want to make confession."

"No. I'm sorry, but that's out of the question. Now more than ever."

"I have to make confession."

"Impossible. In both our interests," said Kempelen, shaking his head. "The Church, above all . . . they're just waiting for an opportunity to damage my reputation."

"*Signore* . . . it's so important. I can't sleep, I can't eat . . . I need the relief of it or I shall die." Kempelen did not respond. "I can't play chess. *Scusa*, but I can't get into that machine again before I've made confession of what I did with it."

Kempelen made a face. "You obviously leave me no choice. Very well, I'll see what I can do. We'll find you a priest."

He led Tibor out of the study. In the workshop Jakob was busy mending the Turk's torn caftan. He gave them a forced smile.

"All problems solved?" he asked.

"Problems, I might add," replied Kempelen, suddenly caustic, "that we wouldn't be facing if you'd done your duty as we agreed. If you hadn't carelessly left the automaton to indulge in the company of young baronesses, Ibolya Jesenák would be alive today . . . and Tibor would be free of guilt, and none of us would have any problems."

Jakob opened his mouth, closed it again, and then said, "Judit Grassalkovich more or less made me."

"Our hearts bleed for you."

"She told me the doors would be closed and guarded!" Jakob insisted. He sounded like a schoolboy being brought to book for some prank.

"That makes no difference. I told you to stay with the automaton. On the flimsiest of grounds, you failed to comply. You left Tibor in the lurch, Jakob. That's not the way for a colleague to behave, and most certainly not for a friend."

Jakob sought in vain for a rejoinder. "I really am sorry," he said at last.

Without a word Kempelen went back to his study and closed the door quietly behind him. Jakob turned to Tibor with a smile.

"My word, what lectures the old witchmaster delivers," he whispered. "Hand me the scissors, would you?"

Tibor looked Jakob in the eye for a moment and did nothing. Then he went to his room and left the assistant with no one but the machine for company. Kempelen gave Jakob the next three days off.

IN THE MORNING Kempelen brought a monk wearing a gray-brown habit belted with a white cord to the house. Tibor, watching from the window, saw them coming along Donaugasse. He couldn't make out the monk's face, because his hood was pulled well down over his forehead. Kempelen asked Tibor to sit on the bed in his room and then put a screen in front of him, first to create conditions like those of the confessional, but second and mainly so that the priest would not see Tibor. Kempelen seemed to have as little faith as Jakob in the secrecy of the confessional. He brought the priest in and introduced him as a monk from the Franciscan house on the Brotmarkt, but gave no name. Then he left the two men alone.

For a long time Tibor said nothing. He was trembling all over and freezing cold.

"Whatever you have done," said the monk, "know this: God forgives all sinners if they will only repent."

He couldn't have found better words. Tibor immediately calmed down, his trembling stopped, and the chill in his limbs went away. "Forgive me, Father, for I have sinned," he began. "I wish to confess in humility and repentance. It has been a month and one week since I last made confession."

"Tell me which of God's commandments you have broken."

And Tibor confessed to committing murder. If the priest was shocked by what Tibor told him, he hid it admirably well. When Tibor had finished, the priest explained that his was not a sin to be atoned for with a few prayers. He told Tibor to speak daily to God and the Mother of God, to resist all the lusts of the flesh, and to hope for support from those who were close to him.

Then the priest left, and Tibor sighed with relief. Of the three confessions he had made in Pressburg, this had been by far the hardest but at the same time the most salutary. The choice of the Franciscan showed, yet again, that he could rely on Wolfgang von Kempelen's decisions.

When he heard the two men on the stairs, he went into the workshop and watched from the window as they left the house. Obviously Kempelen was going to escort the monk back to his monastery. They didn't talk. Tibor was just going to step back from the window when Elise came out into the street, looked around, and then followed the men toward the Lorenz Gate, hastily throwing a shawl over her shoulders. Tibor frowned. Had Kempelen or the monk left something behind, and she was taking it to them? Tibor watched until she was out of sight.

ONCE THEY WERE THROUGH the city gate and had turned into Hutterergasse, Kempelen's companion put the hood back from his head. The man was clean-shaven and pale, his cheeks and nose covered with freckles that made him look younger than he really was. His hair was dark red. It was not noticeable that he was rather taller than Kempelen, because he kept his head bent forward as he walked on.

"No, don't take that off," said Kempelen. His companion looked at him, and Kempelen explained, "We don't want anyone to recognize you dressed up as a monk."

"It's damn hot in this habit. I'm in dire need of a drink," said the red-haired man, but he complied with Kempelen's request.

"He'll obey you," the supposed monk added a little later. "After what I said to him, anyway. He's so tormented by feelings of guilt that he'll do anything you tell him."

Kempelen just nodded. He didn't want to have this conversation in the street.

"You managed that brilliantly. Making it look like suicide although she was already dead, and with half of Pressburg just two rooms away as well . . ."

"Please," said Kempelen, raising his hand to silence his companion.

The man nodded. "I only mean . . . he might well ask for me again. You only have to say. I'll be happy to help you if I'm not on my travels again. I really think I ought to consider turning monk."

"Thank you."

"That crazy Jesenák woman, peace be to her soul. Dallying with an automaton! I don't go kissing my calculating machine or making love to my wife's loom." He laughed. "When do you think you'll be able to approach the Master and suggest admitting me to the Lodge as an apprentice?"

"As soon as enough grass has grown over my present problems. As soon as anyone can hear a new petition from me without thinking instantly of the chess machine. I'm afraid that could take several months. But you can depend on me."

"There's no great hurry."

They turned into Schlossergasse and passed the coopers' and stonemasons' workshops, where the shutters had been opened because of the fine weather, showing the men inside at work. The constant striking of steel on stone echoed back from the walls of the buildings, uniting into an arrhythmical ensemble like drops of rain falling from a ledge. At this very moment, thought Kempelen, the name *Ibolya Jesenák* was now being chiseled on a gravestone in one of these workshops.

"Will the brothers mind that I've bought myself the title of nobility and I'm not Stegmüller anymore but von Rotenstein?" asked the red-haired man.

"Well, you'd certainly have found acceptance simpler as genuine Georg Stegmüller than the bogus Honorable Gottfried von Rotenstein."

"Grassalkovich was just a plain civil servant himself once, and no one questions his noble title today. Perhaps you don't find it easy to understand, being born with the noble *von* yourself."

They had reached the apothecary's shop at the Sign of the Red Crab in the shadow of the tower of St. Michael's, but did not go through its main entrance. Instead they entered the shop by way of a narrow passage between buildings. In a back room Stegmüller changed his clothes, putting on an apothecary's coat instead of the monk's habit. Kempelen let Stegmüller offer him a glass of wine, although he didn't want one and had more important things to do. After that Stegmüller gave him a medicinal infusion that he said would be good for his daughter's cough. Three days before Teréz had reached the age of two, but they had hardly been able to celebrate her birthday properly because of her sickness and everything else that was going on.

"Do you own any weapons?" Kempelen asked abruptly as he was leaving.

Stegmüller seemed taken aback for a moment, then replied, "A Suhl-made flintlock, for when I'm on my travels. I can get you something better if you want."

Kempelen shook his head. "I only wondered."

He left the apothecary's shop and took a different route back to Donaugasse.

ON ASCENSION DAY, which was cloudless and as hot as summer, Ibolya Baroness Jesenák, née Baroness Andrássy, aged thirty, was buried in St. John's Cemetery. The mourners consisted mainly of the guests from Grassalkovich's ball, with a number of hussars from Andrássy's regiment. All her former lovers were there, it was rumored, including the Kempelen brothers and their wives. Wolfgang von Kempelen was sweating in his black garments. He kept his gaze bent on the ground so as to give no one an opportunity to address him. Attending this funeral was a duty, and the less he was the center of interest the better. But it did not escape his notice that the mourners were whispering about him and his automaton.

At the gate of the cemetery, when Kempelen had already brushed the ashes off his hands and thought himself safe, it happened after all: Corporal Dessewffy, a comrade of Andrássy's, and his wife asked Kempelen if they could attend the chess-playing Turk's next performance, and the three were immediately surrounded by other interested parties. Hard as Kempelen tried to keep the mood somber, the first jokes about the automaton were already being cracked. There was a change in the atmosphere only when János Andrássy himself joined the group and asked Wolfgang von Kempelen for a word. At once all was still again.

Kempelen and Andrássy walked a little way before Kempelen finally spoke. "Baron, I would like to offer you my deepest sympathy once more. As you know, since our first meeting I was closely linked to your sister. So if there is anything I can do for you . . ."

Andrássy smiled and waved the remark away, as if to let Kempelen know that it was unnecessary to mention these things. "Just answer one question, that's all I want."

"By all means."

"Where were you when my sister fell from the balcony?"

"I was tidying myself up."

"All that time? You were gone for quite a long while."

"It was a very hot evening, if you remember."

Andrássy nodded. "And did you see my sister during that time?"

"No. She was in the Conference Hall, I was in the privies."

"Her dress was disarranged, her lip rouge and the rouge on her cheeks smudged. And her wig was crooked on her head, as if someone had removed it earlier."

"By all that's holy, Baron, I don't see how I can be held responsible for that."

Andrássy laid a hand on Kempelen's arm to reassure him. "No, don't misunderstand me. I didn't suspect you."

"But?"

"Your Turk."

Kempelen was taken aback. "Baron . . . I hope you won't listen to the tales of those fools who say the automaton killed your sister."

"One of the footmen says he found rouge around the Turk's mouth. And my sister's clothes, as I said, were disarranged."

"So what do you conclude from that?"

"I conclude that my sister didn't commit suicide. That instead she was improperly molested by your machine, and it then pushed her to her death."

Kempelen was about to answer back but stopped himself at once, then said, "That's absurd, if I may say so. As you have just correctly remarked, the Turk is a machine. Machines are incapable of—of molesting or murdering human beings."

"Just as they are incapable of playing chess?" Andrássy had raised an eyebrow and once more was smiling as amiably as he had when facing the Mechanical Turk.

It took a moment for Kempelen to find words again. "Very well, Baron. You believe that my automaton did these things to your sister. I can only assure you once again that it is completely impossible. How are we to settle this unfortunate dispute?"

"By the book," replied Andrássy, "in the military way. I'm asking you to destroy the Turk."

"I understand you." Kempelen took a deep breath and then exhaled again. "I'm sorry, I cannot and will not do it. The chess machine has become a large part of my life, and to take it from me would be like taking your horse and your sword from you. Quite apart from the fact that there'd be an outcry all over the Empire."

"You must do it all the same, or I'll get what I want in some other way." Andrássy's smile had disappeared now.

"How are you going to do that? Do you mean to break into my house with an ax and chop the machine up into matchwood?"

"I would happily do so, but I have other means. For instance, I am going to ask more questions to find out if you were really tidying yourself up all that time. And what you were discussing with my sister, for I'm sure that some of the guests were attending to your conversation. It won't have escaped you that in recent years a certain bitterness toward you had crept into Ibolya's light-minded affections. You had your reasons to wish for her death; you had a liaison with my sister, and after it was over she threatened to make things difficult for you."

"Half Pressburg had a liaison with your sister. If that's all you—"

Without warning, Andrássy struck him in the face so hard that Kempelen was knocked to the ground. Even before he fully realized what had happened, the Baron had snatched off his fur cap, drawn his sword, and was pointing the blade at Kempelen.

"I'll carve you to pieces for that, you bastard. You may be the Empress's favorite toy a thousand times over, but you'll pay for those words spoken at my sister's graveside. Get up!"

But Wolfgang von Kempelen stayed where he was. Andrássy wouldn't hurt a man when he was down. Blood was running from the corner of his mouth where the blow had split it. Several men had seen their altercation and hurried up. Kempelen heard a woman scream but couldn't make out whether it was his wife. How odd, the thought shot through his head, that Ibolya had struck him on the same cheek less than a week before.

"Get up!" shouted Andrássy again, but then he was surrounded by his hussars, while Nepomuk and another man hurried to Kempelen's side. Nepomuk wanted to help his brother up, but Kempelen lay there until the hussars had made their lieutenant see reason, and he put his sword back into its scabbard as forcefully as he would have liked to thrust it into Kempelen's body.

Kempelen rose to his feet. His legs felt curiously weak, and Nepomuk had to support him. Andrássy came up to him again, shaking off the hands that tried to hold him back. He stopped just in front of Kempelen, breathing fast through his nose, his eyes narrowed, and he took off his right glove, keeping his gaze fixed on the other man. He struck Kempelen in the face with the glove and then threw it at his feet. There was blood on the white fabric.

"It's your choice, von Kempelen: destroy your Turk or cross swords with me." Then Andrássy made his way back through the hussars around him and went straight to his carriage, without picking up his *kalpak* or exchanging another word with anyone.

JAKOB TURNED the bloodstained glove in his hands and passed it on to Tibor, shaking his head.

"*Destroy your Turk or cross swords with me,*" Kempelen quoted. "What an antediluvian relic! He probably spends his spare time hunting dragons or the Holy Grail."

"A duel?" asked Jakob. "He'll . . . well, he'll defeat you."

"He'll kill me. Why not say it straight out? Of course he will, whatever weapon I choose. He's been fighting since he was a child. But I'm not going to accept the challenge." The other two looked at him, a question in their eyes. "He'll calm down. Or his many adjutants will make him calm down. I'm counting on his thinking better of this soon. The blood on that glove will be the only blood shed in this business."

"I'm sorry, *signore*," said Tibor.

"I know you are. You don't have to keep repeating it."

"Shall we rest the Turk for longer than we planned?" asked Jakob.

"No. We've rested it long enough to show respect. We'll exhibit it again after Easter. Now of all times people will be clamoring at our door from curiosity about the Curse of the Turk. These days mothers tell their children that the Turk will come for them if they're naughty." Kempelen turned to Jakob, smiling. "Speaking of curses, it's not just the Turk that superstitious folk fear, they've started talking about a golem said to be going about his nefarious business in our streets. I heard that at the Royal Chamber. But this Pressburg golem is only half the size of the Prague original, and he wears a fine frock coat over his clay body. Apparently he almost killed two leather workers in the Weidritz district, but the constabulary intervened just in time. The constable who followed the golem said he shrank as he ran, and then dissolved into the mud entirely. Better ask your rabbi if he had anything to do with that."

Tibor said nothing, but when Kempelen had gone he asked Jakob, "What's a golem?"

"Once upon a time Rabbi Löw of Prague, who was very powerful, made a man out of clay just as God made Adam, and breathed life into it with spells from the Kabala. The golem was created to protect the people of the Jewish quarter from hostile Christians. For instance, it was common to dump corpses secretly in the Jewish part of town and then accuse the Jews of murder, so the golem was to patrol the streets by night. A golem is mute and simpleminded, but he understands and carries out all the orders he is given. The word *aemaeth* is written on his forehead, meaning 'truth,' and if his master removes the first letters, that leaves the word *maeth*, meaning 'death,' and the golem crumbles to dust again. But it's not just that golems are useful: the dangerous thing about them is their tremendous strength, and the way the clay flowing into their bodies from the ground makes them larger by the day. A rabbi once had a golem which grew so tall that he couldn't reach its forehead anymore to delete the letters and destroy it. So he thought of a trick: he told the golem to help him off with his boots, and when the colossus bent down, the rabbi tore the letters off its brow. Then the golem was *maeth* and turned back to lifeless clay. Only it was such a huge lump of clay that it fell on the rabbi and its weight crushed him. So what do we learn from that?"

Tibor shrugged.

"Don't play about with ghosts or you'll be their victim someday," said Jakob. "At least that's what it says in the Kabala."

Tibor remembered that night in the fishermen's settlement. It amused him to think that his fall into a muddy puddle had earned him the reputation of being a legendary Jewish golem.

THE CLERGY of Pressburg had agreed to urge Kempelen to retire his chess-playing Turk, which represented presumption in the face of God's creation, so the Pressburg Prometheus was summoned to see the Pressburg Zeus, to wit Joseph Count von Batthyány, Primate of Hungary and Archbishop of Gran.

Prometheus climbs Mount Olympus, receives a friendly welcome from Zeus, and while the two of them exchange civilities and make small talk, each is sizing up his opponent. Zeus intends to impress his visitor with his title and all the pomp and circumstance that go with it, and to pronounce a verdict that will sound mild but will be firm as a rock all the same, spoken in a tone that brooks no contradiction. Prometheus, on the other hand, is planning to flatter the powerful god with assumed humility but to resist his intentions come what may and parry the crumbling arguments of religion with logic and perhaps some sophistry too.

"Is real mankind not good enough for you, so that you have to make artificial men?" Zeus begins the skirmish, with a smile.

"My Turk is only a machine like any other that serves humanity, and like any other machine its purpose is to relieve mankind of labor and make life easier," replies Prometheus.

"Relieve mankind of labor? What labor do you mean? The labor of playing chess?" This shot fired by Zeus does not miss its mark. "Your machine is neither of any significance nor pleasing in the eyes of God."

"What makes one machine more pleasing in the eyes of God than another? Is a loom a better machine only because it makes something? Or is it the shape of my machine that troubles you: a Turk, an unbeliever? Would you reject a loom in the same way if it came shaped like a Mussulman making a carpet? I'll happily change my automaton's face and have it baptized if you like, although I fear that then it may go rusty."

Zeus allows himself a small smile at this image but shakes his head. "I dislike not the form of your machine but its function: to think. Thought is the quality that God reserved for man alone in His great Creation. Thought, the thinking soul alone, distinguishes us from brute beasts. A mechanical man who can think—even more, who can surpass mankind himself in his own unique gift of thought—this must not be. You are setting yourself above God and His works."

"By no means," says Prometheus, bowing his head a little to show humility. "I am a mortal man like any other."

"And for that very reason your intelligent machine must not be."

"But it is, and the fact that it is does not expose God's creation as incomplete but on the contrary does it all the more credit!"

Zeus leans back and rests his chin on his hand. "You'll have to explain that to me."

"I am a man made by God, and with my God-given talents I was able to construct a thinking machine. Man thinks, but God guides his thinking: I am only one of his tools."

"A blind alley," says Zeus, dismissing this argument. "By your crooked logic in saying that God guides mankind, you would ultimately lay every deed done by man at God's door, however godless it may be, for instance lying, robbery, and murder. But the responsibility for your works lies with yourself, not God." Prometheus starts to protest, but Zeus silences him with a gesture. "And do you mean to change my mind with theological arguments—you, who have as little to do with the Church as your creature does? When did you last attend Holy Mass? When did you last make confession? When did you last converse with the One whose arguments you pretend to be citing now? At least be honest enough to stand by your godlessness and the ideals of your Freemasonry, stand by what you call Enlightenment, although I say, once and for all, that it clouds the true light."

And Zeus reaches for heavy chains, iron rings, and a hammer, seizes Prometheus, and with a few strong blows fastens him to the rock. "You too have a liver, Baron Wolfgang von Kempelen," says Zeus, calling down an eagle to peck it out. "Your man-machine is grist to the mill of such heretical philosophers as Descartes, who try to fool the world into thinking that machines would be an improvement on men. And that man is only an imperfect machine and merely thinks he has a soul. Have you ever wondered what lies at the end of all these materialistic theories? Uncertainty and chaos, murder and mayhem."

Prometheus struggles against his chains, but it seems impossible for him to break free by his own power alone. "Even Descartes said that human beings have a God-given soul."

"Because he was afraid of the Church. That was nothing but lip service paid by a coward. In fact he was a man of your kind. They say he had an automaton himself, a copy of his daughter who died young. When he was sailing to Sweden, God raised a storm, and the pious sailors did well to throw the automaton overboard, as Jonah was once cast away, to calm the waves and sink that work of black magic to the bottom of the sea. A copy of his dead daughter! What heresy! Only to One was resurrection from the dead granted."

For a brief moment the sun flickers, and when Prometheus looks up, he sees the eagle that is to punish him circling there, black against the blue sky.

"Don't forget that your great scholar Albertus Magnus himself had an automaton," Prometheus objects.

"Which the even greater Thomas Aquinas very rightly destroyed with an angry kick," says Zeus, dismissing the objection, "and thus proved that sins are sometimes punished even on this earth. La Mettrie, that ill-starred materialist who wished to be even more provocative than Descartes, and babbled to all the world that mankind was a machine, choked to death before his time on a pasty garnished with truffles. I can think of no more fitting end for a materialist. May God be merciful to his immortal soul and forgive me my derision."

Time is running out for Prometheus. No Heracles will come to save him. The eagle utters a cry, and Zeus prepares to leave.

"I am not the first man to have built automata, and I shall certainly not be the last!" Prometheus calls after him. "Never mind what you command me to do—you won't be able to halt progress, just as you couldn't stop the Lutherans, or suppress knowledge about the place of the earth in the universe, or indeed stop the materialists, not that their doctrines mean anything to me. You couldn't stop it any more than Christ could once be stopped."

"If what you say is indeed true, then I shall be content to have fought well and to have won at least this battle. And kindly refrain from the incredible impertinence of comparing yourself with the Savior, unless you want to make me seriously angry."

The eagle prepares to fall on the body of Prometheus, but with a gesture Zeus keeps it at a distance. He approaches Prometheus one last time, his tone confidential. "I value clever men like you and mean them no harm. Be thankful that you have only me as an opponent. In Spain builders of automata like yours are still persecuted and burned by the Holy Inquisition. If the fires of Hell do not deter you—"

"Spain is a long way from Pressburg. So are the Middle Ages. Would you threaten a Galileo with the pyre today?"

Prometheus tenses his muscles, his features are distorted, the back of his neck quivers. Sweat stands out on his brow. His chains grind with the effort he is making. Zeus has no reply to that. He beckons the eagle down.

"The Church is by no means as powerless as you may wish," says Zeus as he leaves. "For instance, the Empress, who has made me the Church's chief servant in this country, is a very devout woman."

"The Empress," replies Prometheus with a sudden smile, "is my greatest patroness."

His chains are torn from the rock in a cloud of dust and stones, and

Prometheus is free before the eagle ever reaches him. He leaps away down the mountainside. A few pieces of rock still dangle from the ends of his chains, but they do not impede his escape back to the world of mankind and mechanical men.

In a personal letter to Prince-Bishop Batthyány, Duke Albert of Sachsen-Teschen replied to his request for a ban on the presentation of Wolfgang von Kempelen's chess automaton. The Governor of Hungary did not, he said, share the Bishop's religious fears, and even if he wanted to comply with the request, he had no legal means of preventing Kempelen from the exhibition of his machine. In addition, it began at the express wish of the Empress. Duke Albert concluded by hoping that this unfortunate quarrel between science and the Church would soon be set aside.

Prometheus Kempelen thereupon called for a bottle of champagne, and in the absence of other company he clinked glasses with his creation, drinking to his victory against Zeus Batthyány, to Duke Albert's support and his own growing fame. And to the prospect, which had never before occurred to him, of seeing his work inspire not mechanicians and mathematicians alone but philosophers too.

A DAY AFTER the successful resumption of the Turk's performances, the maidservant Katarina walked out of her job as the Kempelens' cook without giving notice. She left the house without asking for the wages she was still owed or a reference, and she wouldn't let Anna Maria even begin to try changing her mind. Thereupon Kempelen summoned Elise to his study to speak to her. Elise had brought a jug of cool water with her, welcome refreshment for Kempelen, whose room was overheated in the July sun. As she entered, he was at work on his speaking machine. He asked her to sit down, and after a sip of water he asked if she was happy with her job and her wages, or if there was anything on her mind. Elise silently shook her head.

"Then do you know why Katarina has left? Was she by any chance afraid of my machines?"

"I don't think so." Elise scratched her head through her cap. "It's very hot in here."

"You may take that cap off. Please do."

Elise hesitated. Then she pulled off her cap and put her hands to her hair to rearrange it. After that she folded her hands in her lap again. "Well, there *is* something," she said, "but I don't know if it's anything to do with Katarina."

"And that is?"

"After Mass last Sunday . . . one of the sextons asked me to stay behind after the service because the priest wanted to speak to me. It was at St. Savior's Church."

"Yes, I know it."

"He was very friendly. But he said things happen in this house that are not in accord with the Christian faith . . . the machine and so on. And I think he was suggesting that I ought not to go on working here. And saying they could find me another, better job anytime. Maybe they said the same to Katarina."

Kempelen looked at some indeterminate point behind Elise and thought about it. "Yes, of course they did," he said. "So why are you still here?"

"Because I can't believe that you are blaspheming against God in this house. And I like it here."

"That's good. Elise, I'm raising your wages."

"You're too kind, sir."

"I want to reward your loyalty—and you'll have to work harder until we find someone to replace Katarina. What's more, that won't be the only time you're exposed to hostility. Perhaps you should attend Mass at a different church in future."

Elise nodded.

"There's a little coterie of people opposed to progress," explained Kempelen, "and I most fervently hope they will soon calm down. But there are other opinions too: look, one of our guests has written an article about the automaton and me. Fresh from London!"

Kempelen reached for an open journal and handed it across the table to Elise.

"This is in English?" Elise asked after a glance.

"Oh, of course. Forgive me." Kempelen took the journal back. "In any case, the writer has nothing but praise for the Turk." He skimmed the lines. "Here we are: *It seems impossible to attain to a more perfect knowledge of Mechanicks, than this gentleman hath done.... At least, no artist has yet been able to produce a machine so wonderful in its kind, as what he constructed.* And he concludes by saying: *Indeed one may expect every thing from his knowledge and skill, which are exceedingly enhanced by his uncommon modesty.*"

Taking a deep breath, Kempelen pored over the lines. Then he looked back at Elise, who was smiling at him, bright-eyed, and caught himself out in his own arrogance. "Yes, well, not so very modest of me, I suppose!"

They both laughed, sharing the joke.

"Excellent," said Kempelen. "That will be all, then."

As Elise rose to go, he bent to put the English journal down on the table and ricked his neck as he straightened up again. He closed his eyes and put his hand to the back of it, where it hurt.

"Ever since I went to see Batthyány, my neck has been in a bad way," he explained. "It feels as if I'd been carrying rocks."

"May I . . . ?" asked Elise. "I know what to do in such cases; a kind nun at my school taught me."

Before Kempelen could reply, she had gone around the table to stand behind him. She placed one hand on his neck and began to press down. Kempelen remained tense until the other hand touched him too.

"The pain will go away after a few minutes," she said in a rather softer voice.

She massaged his neck for a moment and only then seemed to realize that she was taking a liberty. Her fingers slowed down, finally stopped moving entirely, and she raised them from his skin.

"I'm so sorry," she said shyly. "I wasn't thinking." He could almost hear her blushing.

"No, no. Do go on. It's pleasant."

With this permission, Elise began again. Like a tired man fighting sleep, Kempelen felt his eyes trying to close as the pressure of her fingers agreeably relaxed his aching muscles, but he kept opening his lids again.

"How's your aunt in Bystrica?" he asked.

"Prievidza," Elise corrected him. "She's well, thank you."

Only now did Kempelen close his eyes. He breathed in her fragrance, which he had never noticed before. And in spite of the housework, her hands were still soft. He imagined her putting back a strand of hair behind her ear with one of them. Otherwise he thought of nothing at all.

More particularly, he did not hear Anna Maria approaching the study. He saw her only when she was standing in the doorway, wide-eyed as she took in the scene before her.

Elise did not withdraw her hands until it was too late, putting her arms behind her back as if to hide two delinquents. For a few seconds everything froze just as it was. All was perfectly still apart from a wasp that had lost its way and kept flying into the windowpanes.

"You can go, Elise," said Kempelen.

Without a word, Elise picked up her cap and left the room under Anna Maria's stern gaze.

"Would you care to explain that to me?" asked Anna Maria.

"Would you care to close the door first, please?"

Anna Maria complied with his request but still stood there looking pale, with her arms crossed over her breast.

"My neck hurt; it's been painful for the last few days. She offered to treat it. I was glad to accept the offer. That's all, no more and no less."

"You'll put her out on the street."

"Calm down. She was only massaging my neck."

"She's not your wife."

"No. It's a long time since my wife offered to do any such thing."

"We're giving her notice at once."

"No, we're not, because then we won't have a maid at all," Kempelen pointed out. "If you want to be angry with someone, take it out on me. She's as meek as a lamb—it's not her fault."

"Is she to be your new Jesenák?"

"Anna Maria, please. That's not funny. I've always done what you asked, but there must be some limit to your jealousy. I'll agree to anything else you like, but Elise stays."

"Anything else?"

"Yes."

"Then part with your Turk."

Kempelen put one hand behind his ear as if he had failed to understand what she said. "Why in the world would I do that? The Turk is making us rich—bringing in wealth that, by the way, you haven't scrupled to spend these last few weeks. It opens all doors to us, it makes us the talk of the town—"

"I've had quite enough of being the talk of the town. People are saying that the automaton killed Ibolya Jesenák."

"Only fools say so, and as you're not a fool, you know it's not true."

"It frightens me to think who has her death on his conscience if it wasn't the automaton."

"For the hundredth time, she killed herself!"

"Katarina left for fear of the Turk."

"No, Katarina left for fear of the priests. There's a difference."

"That doesn't make it any more tolerable." Anna Maria sat down on the chair that Elise had been occupying just now and drew it up to the table. "I want to be back with the man I married. You had a good position, you were sure of your pension, and you had excellent prospects of rising further. But now you put all your money and your time into inventions, or rather conjuring tricks, you hire a godless Jew and a monster, you risk being exposed in front of the Empress, excommunicated by the Bishop, and killed by the Baron, and all that for fame, for the hope that one day, long after you're dead, a bronze statue of you will stand in some square in this city."

"Can you be envious of what I'm doing?"

"No. Never. I want only the best for you. For us. I love you."

Kempelen snorted. "Then don't tell me how to live my life."

"Dismiss Elise."

"What are you afraid of? Surely you don't think I'll fall in love with her? You know better. You're afraid she might take over your marital duties."

"Stop that—"

"You're afraid she might be the woman who can give me children . . ."

"Please!"

". . . who don't die as soon as they're born . . ."

Anna Maria covered her eyes with both hands and screamed, "Wolfgang!"

". . . like Julianna, Andreas, and Marie."

Anna Maria began to weep, and Kempelen fell silent. He had gone too far. Only now did he notice, to his discomfort, that he had counted out the dead children on his fingers. He said nothing, looked at her as she sat there looking increasingly bowed, and felt like taking a hammer to the laboriously constructed parts of his speaking machine.

Then he left his study without touching Anna Maria and went down to the kitchen. He found Elise in tears too, gave her that day and the next day off, and told Branislav that in the morning he was to take Anna Maria and Teréz to Gomba, the Kempelens' country estate a short day's journey to the east of Pressburg. Mother and child were to spend the summer there with Branislav in attendance. Kempelen asked Branislav to take particular care of his wife, who, he said, had suffered a little breakdown, probably as a result of the oppressive heat.

TIBOR HAD MET Elise by night in the Weidritz quarter, and he had seen her following Kempelen and the Franciscan. She wasn't simply curious; she was a spy. This suspicion was confirmed when they were alone for a little while after a performance: he inside the chess machine, she trying to open Kempelen's mysterious casket with a skeleton key when she was supposed to be sweeping the floor. Of course she thought herself unobserved and didn't put the skeleton key away again until she heard steps on the staircase. Inside the darkness of the machine, Tibor had trained his hearing to be acute, so although he had not seen any of this, he had listened, holding his breath. Now that Anna Maria, Teréz, and Branislav had left the house for a while, Elise was at more liberty to pry. Kempelen and above all Jakob had relaxed their vigilance. One day, when Tibor was sitting at his own table working on an endgame problem, a piece of metal was suddenly inserted in the lock of his door, scratching about and trying to force it. However, Tibor had double-locked the door, as he always did after the surprise visit from Kempelen and his brother. He did nothing, he couldn't do anything, he just stared at the lock and tried not to make a sound. It was obvious that Elise wasn't very good at manipulating a skeleton key, and she failed with his door too: after about ten minutes she gave up, with a sigh of exasperation. Tibor sat still for a long time after that. For he knew that sometime soon she would manage to open the door and discover the secret of the Mechanical Turk.

Why didn't he tell Kempelen? One word from him, and Elise would be out on the street, the chess-playing Turk would be safe, and with it Tibor, who could expect to go to the gallows for the Baroness's murder. Perhaps it was pride—a sense of superiority over Kempelen and Jakob—pride in knowing something that they didn't know. They probably both thought Elise too stupid to be capable of anything of this kind. Only Tibor knew what she was really like. He had watched Jakob falling for her flirtatiousness time and again, he had heard Jakob's boastful claims that he was going to turn Elise's head—and if he had been jealous at first, now it amused him to see Jakob imagining that she adored him, when all she wanted from him was the secret of the Mechanical Turk.

Elise was walking through a labyrinth, and Tibor was there at its heart, waiting for her. He was the prize, the treasure chest, the maiden in the tower, and the idea pleased him. All her efforts were directed at him, although she didn't yet know it. They would meet again. Of course everything might then move very fast, and Tibor could die, but that seemed to him unlikely. He had watched Elise long enough, Jakob had told him her life history, he had seen her in church, she wore his amulet of the Virgin over her heart—she was not the kind of woman who would give him away. And if he was mistaken in her, well, it was God's will.

In July a courier brought Kempelen an invitation from Maria Theresia to the Viennese court. After all the stories she had heard about the fabulous machine, said the dictated letter, the Empress could no longer resist the temptation of playing a match against it herself, and at that game, in the middle of August, she wished to speak to Kempelen about his other projects and her support for them. Moreover, *"mon cher fils Joseph,"* who had been away on other duties at the time of the machine's first presentation, had expressed an interest in seeing the Turk face to face. Kempelen felt all the more justified in his decision to send Anna Maria off to Gomba, for now he could prepare undisturbed for what might be the most important performance of all in his chess machine's career.

He hoped that the invitation to Vienna would also bring Tibor out of his persistent state of depression. "Everything will be better after Vienna," he said, without explaining exactly what would change then, and how. Perhaps the Turk's appearances would gradually become fewer, so that Kempelen could devote himself entirely to the speaking machine. Perhaps Kempelen had tired of his quarrels with Baron Andrássy and the Church and now with his wife as well. Then Tibor could go back to his old life, which to be sure he had never particularly enjoyed, but at least he had been free of guilt there and to some small extent pleasing in the eyes of God.

KEMPELEN AND JAKOB had gone out, and the automaton was standing in the workshop, not in its storeroom—there could have been no more tempting bait for Elise. She opened the workshop door easily now, then examined the chess machine. The Turk looked sternly at her, as if it knew that she had come to expose it, but while its clockwork wasn't wound up, there was nothing it could do to prevent her.

She sat down on the floor to the right of the android to work on the back door that revealed its mechanism. Even as she was looking for the right skeleton key on her bunch, the door was pushed open from inside, with improbable silence because the hinges were so well oiled. Open-mouthed, Elise looked at the cabinet and then into the darkness behind the door. She saw a face smiling sadly at her. For a moment it seemed to be bodiless, and she thought it might be an optical illusion—the mechanism here was arranged in just such a way that it could resemble a face in the shadows: two cogwheels for the eyes, a spring for the nose, a cylinder for the mouth—but when the face moved, she saw a torso too, and an arm. She blinked.

"Good day," he said, and as she was a long time in replying, he added, "I'm the secret of the chess machine."

She breathed in deeply, preparing to say something, but then her breath failed her and not a word would emerge. Audibly, she breathed out again.

"That's what you were looking for, isn't it?" he asked quietly, so as not to alarm her.

"Yes," said Elise.

"I was expecting you. I knew you'd come."

She narrowed her eyes. "I know you . . . you were the man who . . ."

"Yes," said Tibor, looking at the chain around her neck. The medallion itself was inside her bodice.

And once again they were both silent, Elise because she didn't know what he intended to do, Tibor because he didn't know what to say.

"Look, this is how I move the Turk's hand," he explained at last.

Elise moved closer to the cabinet, and Tibor showed her, not without pride, how he guided the android's arm with the pantograph, and how he moved its eyes and head. He explained that the sole function of the mechanism in the cabinet was to make a noise, and how it was possible for him to stay hidden from the audience even though all the doors were opened. Only then did he leave the cabinet through the double doors, and since she was still sitting down, he was on about the same level as her.

"You're . . ." *Smaller,* she had been going to say, but she didn't finish the sentence.

Tibor did it for her. "Small. Yes. I was wearing shoes with built-up heels then." He sat down opposite her, as if to do away with their difference of height. "Is there anything else you'd like to know?"

"What's your name?"

"Tibor."

"Mine is Elise."

"I know."

"Why are you telling me all this, Tibor?"

"You'd have found it out for yourself sooner or later. I've been watching you."

"I don't understand . . . why didn't you tell Kempelen?"

"Because I didn't want him to dismiss you. Because I think what you're doing matters to you. Jakob told me your parents are dead. I know what it's like to be alone. And in spite of everything, I don't think you mean any harm. Did someone offer you a reward to find out about the Turk?"

Elise nodded, and she was prepared for the next question.

"Friedrich Knaus?"

"Who?"

"You don't know Knaus?"

She shook her head. "The Bishop asked me . . . well, not the Bishop himself. A priest asked me for him." The priest had indeed spoken to her, but only to try to persuade her to give notice, as she had told Kempelen. "He asked me . . . no, he said it was my Christian duty. After what happened at the Palais Grassalkovich."

Only now did Elise realize that Tibor had been in the same room as Ibolya Jesenák before her suicide, might even have been the last person to see the Baroness alive. Then it dawned on her that the death couldn't have been suicide; the dwarf had killed a woman who knew his secret. This logical chain of reasoning led to the conclusion that he was about to kill her too, and his sympathy for her orphaned status was as much of a fake as her own claim to it. She carried a knife in her petticoat, but she'd never be able to get it out quickly enough. And she had seen how he dealt with two grown men. She was lost.

Tibor saw how pale she had turned. "It was an accident," he said quickly. "A mishap. She fell unluckily. Then he threw her off the balcony to make it look like suicide. No one wanted it to happen."

"I believe you," she said, although she didn't.

They sat there in silence until Tibor began again. "What will you do now?"

"I don't know. What ought I to do?"

"Don't give us away. I killed the Baroness. If that comes out, I'll be pursued and captured, and Kempelen says I'll be executed. It makes no difference whether it was an accident or not. Is the Church paying you something?"

"No, nothing. We never discussed it."

Tibor nodded. "That just shows how honorable you are. Because if it was a question of money, Kempelen would certainly pay you more. Or I would."

Tibor wiped a little dust off the feet of the cabinet with one finger. He wished he could sit here with her forever, no matter how awkward the subject of their conversation was.

"I'd like to ask you a favor," said Tibor, "if only because I helped you that time in the fishermen's settlement. I'd like you to tell me in advance when you're going to give us away. Let me have a few days to get out of Pressburg. I need a bit of a start. And Kempelen . . . Kempelen is a good man. He deserves a start too. In return I won't say anything about this meeting until then."

Such a bargain could only be useful to her. She herself could decide whether to keep her side of it. She agreed.

"By the Mother of God?" he asked.

"By the Mother of God," she replied, feeling a little pity for his innocent trust.

"Let us go to Vienna first," he asked earnestly. "Just a week can't make any difference to you. It may be our last performance, and then it will all be over, and it won't matter to the Bishop either, so you'll be able to face both him and Kempelen with a clear conscience."

She remembered that she was still wearing his chain and pulled it out of her bodice as if to return it to him.

"No," he said, raising his hand. "Please keep it. As a pledge. Let me have it back when you're going to give us away. Not before."

Elise looked at the scratched picture of the Virgin Mary and nodded. At that moment she decided that she wasn't going to tell Knaus anything just yet. There could certainly be no greater triumph imaginable for the Swabian than to unmask the chess automaton as a fraud during its game against the Empress, and he would undoubtedly have rewarded her richly for the chance—but she didn't want him to have a triumph like that. If Knaus was to defeat Kempelen, then let him do it quietly.

And why should she give up the life she was living at the moment? She was being paid by both sides. Why should she slaughter the two geese who laid such golden eggs just yet? The later the revelation came, the greater would be her reward. Perhaps she could use Knaus's enduring resentment of Kempelen's success to put up her price even further. She had duped men, had exploited both their male lusts and their childlike faith in a word of honor once given, and perhaps for the first time in this difficult year she felt strong again.

Only that evening did it dawn on her just what kind of person she had met: a misshapen Venetian dwarf, a sensitive and deeply God-fearing murderer, a chess-playing genius, and one who operated the greatest invention—or rather the greatest confidence trick—of the century from inside. How improbable it was! A monkey or a human being who was only a torso, as Knaus had suspected, could not have surprised her more.

Vienna

FOR SAFETY'S SAKE, TIBOR TRAVELED INSIDE THE CHESS
machine. Jakob had protested that it was an inhumane way to transport
anyone, but Kempelen reminded him that Tibor was safe only as long as
the secret of the Turk was safe too. The dwarf resigned himself to his
fate, asking only for plenty of water to help him survive the journey in
the midsummer heat. The air above the plain of the river March was still,
the March itself and the Danube had dried up to mere trickles of warm
water, moving so slowly in their beds that you might have thought they
were flowing against the current. In Branislav's absence, Kempelen had
hired two men to escort them to Vienna and back again—both of them
mounted, like Kempelen, while Jakob once again sat on the box of the
carriage and pair. The chess machine stood behind him. It was not covered, so that the Turk seemed to be looking down the road over Jakob's
shoulder.

There was a milky haze over the sky. The diffuse light of the sun took
away any sense of depth, and as there was not a breath of wind to stir the
grass and leaves, the landscape looked like a dusty painting.

They were an hour out of Pressburg when horsemen riding at a gallop
caught up with them: János Baron Andrássy on his Arab, his corporal Béla
Dessewffy on one side of him, on the other György Karacsay, a lieutenant

in Andrássy's regiment. The three hussars rode past Kempelen's party, then turned their horses so that Andrássy and Kempelen were face to face.

"Baron," Kempelen greeted Andrássy.

"Baron," replied Andrássy. "Are you fleeing the city?"

"Why, no," said Kempelen. His two men had ridden around the carriage and taken up their position next to him, on their guard. "I'm accepting an invitation from Her Majesty."

The Baron raised an eyebrow to express his appreciation. "However, I'm not letting you go any further before you pay your debts."

Opening his saddlebag, Andrássy took out a flat case, which he opened. Two pistols lay inside it, wrapped in green baize.

Andrássy looked around: the road ran through meadows with a few trees standing here and there. "I can't think of a more suitable place. Careful, it's already loaded." He handed Kempelen one of the pistols, handle first.

Kempelen did not take the pistol offered him. He kept his hands on his saddle. His two men were getting nervous, and as if their horses sensed their uneasiness, they too began to prance about. Lieutenant Karacsay rode up to them and said something, whereupon the men—after a sideways glance at Kempelen—trotted back the way they had come. Stunned, Jakob watched them go.

"Or would you prefer the sword?" asked Andrássy. "Béla will be my second, and I'll be happy to accept your assistant as yours."

"I'm not coming to blows with you, Baron. I value both our lives too much. By God and all the saints, I have nothing to do with your sister's death."

"But your machine does."

"Not my machine either, although if it learns to hold a pistol or wield a sword someday, I'll let you know, and then you can fight a duel with it. But until that time, let me ask you to make way and allow us to pass."

The Baron shook his head and took the second pistol out of the case.

"Baron, I'm on my way to the Empress," Kempelen warned him, "and even you are not above the law."

"I'll let you pass for her sake," said Andrássy, cocking the hammers of both pistols, "but my demand holds good, and let me lend it emphasis. You took what I loved from me. I'll do the same for you."

Andrássy took aim at the Turk with the pistol in his left hand, but Jakob, who by now had leaped to his feet on the box of the carriage, had raised his hands, shouting, "No!" to prevent the Baron from firing it.

Andrássy lowered the weapon for a moment and smiled. "A Jew as protection? Do you seriously think that will keep me from shooting?" He aimed again and fired. Jakob jumped down from the box just in time and fell to the ground. The bullet went through the Turk's hollow chest. Andrássy raised the second pistol, closed his left eye, and pressed the trigger.

The bullet passed through the varnish and wood and baize of the cabinet, brushed past a metal tongue in the clockwork and made it ring, went on its way through the tangle of cogwheels, smashed one of them, knocked another out of place, ricocheted off a cylinder, and changed course, now effortlessly penetrating linen and skin and burying itself in the flesh beneath them, scorching hair, tearing veins and muscles, until it hit a rib, and there at last its force was spent. Along with some splinters of bone, it stuck fast in a torn muscle and the blood flowing from the veins it had severed, while the narrow passage it had made in passing through closed up behind it.

Andrássy did not take the trouble to put his pistols back in their case but simply tossed them loose into his saddlebag.

"Baron, you are a loathsome fossil," said Kempelen with composure.

"I won't bear you a grudge for that insult, uttered in the heat of the moment, since I expressed myself just as inelegantly in the cemetery," replied Andrássy, picking up his reins. "I'll expect you back in Pressburg. And don't keep me waiting too long, or more than wood and iron will be damaged."

He spurred his horse on, and Dessewffy and Karacsay followed him, raising their hands to salute Kempelen as they left. The hussars ignored Jakob. The assistant had to step back to avoid the horses, stumbled, and fell into the small ditch beside the road. When the hussars had gone about forty paces, Jakob sprang up, suddenly full of energy, and ran a little way after them through the churned-up dust, swearing as he ran. "Come back, you cowardly bastards! Come back, Andrássy, you scum! You filth! You lousy . . . bewhiskered . . . Hungarian . . . bagful of maggots!" He felt like throwing stones at them, but as he couldn't find any, he reached in blind fury for sand and tore up tufts of grass to fling.

"That will do, Jakob," called Kempelen, who had unsaddled his horse by now and climbed up into the carriage.

Coming to his senses, Jakob hurried to join Kempelen, who was just opening the double doors of the cabinet. They pulled Tibor out by his arms. A few chessmen tumbled out of the cabinet with him. There was a round, red mark on his white shirt, spreading over his chest.

"Have they gone?" asked the dwarf, his jaws clenched.

"Yes."

Even now Tibor did not let himself cry out but merely suppressed a groan. They carried him back into the space behind the automaton in the carriage and tore his shirt open. The entry wound to the right of his chest was small, but from time to time bright red blood came gushing out of it. They turned Tibor on his side, and Kempelen frowned as he saw that on Tibor's back his shirt was wet with sweat but not blood. "The bullet's still inside him."

Jakob looked questioningly at him, not realizing what that meant.

"Get water and cloth."

Meanwhile Kempelen took off his coat and rolled up his sleeves. He opened the lid of the cherrywood casket. It contained his tools. He took out all the pincers and spread them on the floor of the carriage beside Tibor. When Jakob brought the water, he poured some of it over two pairs of pincers and then rubbed them dry. He handed a particularly long pair to Jakob.

"You must hold his wound open with those."

"What?"

"Stick them into the flesh and then push them apart. Otherwise I won't be able to get at the bullet."

"I can't do that!"

"Pull yourself together, man!"

Jakob took the pincers. He had begun to tremble, he was perspiring and ashen gray. Kempelen picked up a second pair of pincers.

"Let's get it over with."

Jakob knelt down beside Tibor's head. He was still looking at the pincers as if he had never seen anything like them before.

"Herr von Kempelen?" a voice called in the road.

Kempelen stood up and climbed up on the box. Their two errant companions were back.

"We're here again," said one of the two men, unnecessarily. "The officers said we could go back." Then he saw a bloodstain on Kempelen's shirt. "Is everything all right? Can we help?"

"You can clear out, the pair of you," replied Kempelen. "I have no use for cowards of your sort."

"What about our money?" asked the man after a pause, sounding subdued.

Kempelen took a couple of coins out of his purse and tossed them to the men. "That's all you're getting. Now go to the devil."

He waited until they had ridden away and then turned back to Jakob and Tibor. "Very well, here we go."

Hesitantly, Jakob came closer to the wound. Then, taking a deep breath, he pushed the pincers into the flesh. Tibor screamed in pain, flinging up his arms and legs. Jakob immediately withdrew the pincers and dropped them in sheer fright.

Kempelen picked up one of the chessmen lying scattered around them. "Open your mouth," he ordered.

He put the chessman between Tibor's teeth, and Tibor bit down on it. Kempelen sat on him, holding Tibor's arms down to the right and left of his body with his own knees.

"Hold his head," he told Jakob, who put Tibor's head between his thighs and held it jammed there. Now Tibor could move nothing but his legs.

Kempelen looked at Jakob. The Jew inserted the pincers into the wound again. Tibor alternately opened his eyes wide and kept them tightly closed. He was writhing with pain, but the other two held him down. Jakob's pincers reached Tibor's ribs, and the touch of something solid horrified him more than ever. Kempelen nodded, and very slowly, with his tongue between his lips, Jakob opened the pincers. Blood shot out. The chessman crunched in Tibor's teeth.

"There it is," said Kempelen. "Open them wider. Courage."

Jakob did as he was told and then held the pincers open. The blood-stained muscles settled around the two prongs. Kempelen got to work with his own tool. Tibor groaned.

"Stop complaining. You killed his sister," said Kempelen.

His pincers slipped once, but then it went very fast, and he withdrew them again, holding the distorted bullet in their bloodstained tips. Thankfully, Jakob followed his example, and Tibor's muscles relaxed. He pushed the chessman out of his mouth with his tongue. What had once been a white rook was now a piece of crushed wood, soggy with saliva. Paint that had come off it still stuck to Tibor's lips.

"Bandage him up," Kempelen told Jakob. "As tightly as possible."

Then he got off Tibor, let the bullet drop carelessly, and cleaned the blood from his hands and his tool with a cloth. He put the pincers down on the chess cabinet. All three men were sweating heavily. Jakob tore some cloth into strips and began clumsily bandaging Tibor's arm and shoulder with it. Kempelen took several sips of water and watched him. Then his gaze wandered to the Turk. The shot through its chest had not done it any harm; he could hardly make out the holes even on the silk shirt and the caftan. Andrássy's second shot had been more serious for the machine as well as for Tibor. Kempelen opened the door to the mechanism and at first glance saw the displaced cogwheel. Reaching for the pincers, he tried to repair the damage but soon realized that he would need more time.

Meanwhile Jakob was bandaging Tibor up, as he did so letting fly a furious tirade against Baron Andrássy, obviously more to help him let off steam than to comfort Tibor.

An hour and a half after the attack, they continued their journey to Vienna.

THEY LAID TIBOR on Kempelen's bed. When Jakob had changed his bandages and Kempelen had brought him something to eat, he fell asleep at once, although it was only late afternoon. The other two set about repairing the damage to the chess automaton, laborious work because they had few tools and no spare parts with them. They said little and above all avoided discussing whether the match could go ahead as planned in two days' time.

Next morning Kempelen rode to Schönbrunn to see one of Her Majesty's adjutants and ask whether the performance could be postponed. It could not. The Empress had too many engagements and had kept the day free especially for the Mechanical Turk, so its failure to appear would have amounted to an insult.

Kempelen returned to the Alsergrund drenched in sweat and was glad to find it at least a little cooler in his apartment. He had brought some fruit from the market and sat down beside Tibor's bed with it. The fresh bandage was red again now.

"Can you move your arm?" asked Kempelen.

Tibor raised his right arm, spread the fingers of his hand, and then clenched it into a fist. It was only when he lowered the arm again that the wound hurt.

"Will you be able to play tomorrow?"

"If I have to."

Kempelen nodded. "Good. That's the right attitude. And you do have to. There's no way around this performance, and everything's at stake this time. At the same time I can promise you that it will be over quickly. Maria Theresia is good, but no more. I've played against her and won."

"Won? Against the Empress?"

"I think it was a kind of test. She wanted to know if I'd let her win, as I suppose all her courtiers do. So I beat her—and passed the test."

Kempelen asked if there was anything else Tibor would like, then left him alone. After that he discussed the machine with Jakob. It could all be repaired except for the broken cogwheel, but the clockwork would go around even without it. They wouldn't be able to cover the ugly bullet hole in the cabinet with new veneer until they were back in Pressburg, but Jakob had patched up the felt so that no one could see inside.

When Jakob urged him to fetch a doctor to examine Tibor's wound and perhaps stitch it, Kempelen pointed out that an unknown doctor would endanger them all. Anyway, the wound was small, which was good, and was already bleeding less. If it hadn't begun to heal by the time they were at home in Pressburg, he said, he would try to find a doctor they could trust there. Jakob still wouldn't let the subject drop until Kempelen finally silenced him by indicating that Tibor was trying to sleep in the next room, and he went back to his work.

MARIA THERESIA granted Baron Wolfgang von Kempelen the honor of a walk with her in the grounds of Schönbrunn Castle before she played her match against the chess automaton. Kempelen had given her his arm. A guardsman and a lady-in-waiting followed at a suitable distance. They walked up the rise to the south of the castle, so that they could look down on the view of Schönbrunn, Vienna, and the Vienna Woods behind the city. The sky was cloudless, and parasols were a necessary protection even in the morning. It was going to be another hot day: a day that was bound to end with a thunderstorm.

Maria Theresia, dressed in black even on a day like this, had been breathing hard on the way uphill. Now she put her hands to her back, then dabbed the sweat from her brow with a handkerchief.

"I'm a foolish old woman," she complained. "Am I trying to prove something to you by taking this walk? Or to myself? I'd do better to save my strength for your Turk."

"If it's any comfort, Your Majesty," said Kempelen, "my own wig is positively swimming on my head."

She pointed to the hill. "Hohenberg is going to build me an Arc de Triomphe here. And down there, at our feet, I want a fountain."

Kempelen turned. "Then I suggest—if Hohenberg hasn't planned it that way already—that the reservoir should be placed up here, either in front of your triumphal arch or behind it."

"Don't tell me you know all about fountains too!"

"We've built a great many wells in the Banat."

"In the Banat, yes, of course," said the Empress. "Kempelen, Kempelen, it's never *ennuyeux* where you are. Very well, I'll come back to you when my fountain is to be built, and you shall see to its waterworks."

"It would be an honor, Highness."

They climbed down the hill again and walked past the flower beds back to the castle.

"Speaking of the Banat," said the Empress, "I shall have to send you back there, I'm afraid. If it didn't need the best man we have, I'd send someone else."

"I will happily go."

"For another year at the most, and then you shall have a rest from that *sujet*. I am sure you want to work on your new machine—the one that speaks. How is it getting on?"

"So far it is silent, Majesty. But I'm making good progress. I lack money, certainly, but most of all I lack time."

"I can take a hint, Kempelen. Have no fear—you shall have your money. I feel sure that your Turk will win it from me, or that's how I envisage it. Then you shall have everything you require, and a place in the Court Cabinet too if you like."

The Empress briefly put her parasol to one side to look up at the sky. "*Il fait très beau,*" she said. "We will play out in the garden, your Turk and I. On a fine day like this no one wants to be shut up in the castle, *n'est-ce pas?*"

The chess automaton was carried out of the white and gold room and taken into the garden. As there was not enough room for all the spectators in the shade of the trees, the cabinet was placed in the full midday sun. Its four wheels dug into the gravel, crunching. Very soon the dark tabletop was so hot that no one could touch it, and the air above it was flickering. The wood distorted, making creaking, cracking noises. The heavy fur trimmings on the Turk's caftan looked strangely out of place.

The spectators were fewer than at the premiere but more prominent, including many such statesmen as von Haugwitz, von Kaunitz, Count Cobenzl, and Field Marshals Laudon and Liechtenstein. Some had come out of curiosity, others because the Empress had told them to. They were discussing politics with Emperor Joseph and trying not to look too impressed by the sight of the Mechanical Turk. Like his mother, the young Emperor was a little fleshy about the jowls, but his height prevented him from looking plump. He just had to avoid dropping his chin on his chest. As usual, he wore a plainly cut close-fitting coat, almost Prussian in appearance, dark blue with red lapels, with a yellow waistcoat and yellow trousers, and over his shoulder a sash in the Austrian colors. Like the other men, he had come out into the sun unprotected—Kaunitz, whose complexion was pale and who wore no cosmetics, had already burned his nose—while the women could at least put up parasols for protection and cool themselves with fans. Hands reached out greedily to the trays carried by the footmen bringing water and apple juice into the garden. A Negro in the costume of a chamberlain served grapes and looked at the chessboard with interest, although he gave the Turk a suspicious glance. The Empress's youngest child, Maximilian Franz, was there too, pulling at the Mechanical Turk's garments until his nurse told him to move into the shade. The Empress advised Kempelen to take the chess machine to Paris sometime; her Maria Antonia, she said, loved clockwork dolls.

Friedrich Knaus was lurking among the spectators too, trying not to stand out as the man famous for being the Turk's first victim, but he also wanted to see the chess machine in the hope of finding out at long last how it worked. Jakob noticed him and whispered to Kempelen, whereupon the Hungarian went briskly up to him and gave him a friendly handshake.

"How good that you are delighting us with your presence a second time," said Kempelen. "Or did the Empress command you to be here?"

"Oh no, I'm here of my own free will," replied Knaus, with a sweet smile. "Why would I want to miss an appearance by your chess machine, as you call it? Let us hope that its predictable triumph will not anger the Empress too much."

Meanwhile everything had been set up. When the Empress saw the separate chess table, she protested, "I want to face the Turk, just as Knaus did."

"But Your Majesty, the automaton is not entirely . . ."

"Not entirely safe? Oh, let's have none of that, *c'est ridicule*. You surely don't believe that this good Turk of yours really threw the unfortunate *veuve* Jesenák out of a window recently?"

As usual, the performance began with the display of the empty cabinet. After all the doors had been closed again, Kempelen took a candle and once again looked in at the door where Tibor sat, so that he could light Tibor's candle out of sight of the spectators. Then he closed that door too. Normally Kempelen would have placed his own candle on the chess cabinet, but out here in the blazing sun there was no need for one, so he blew it out.

The Empress sat down at the table. A servant moved her chair in, a second took up his position behind her with a parasol, and a third handed her her spectacles.

"Now let us see if this Mohammedan can defeat a Christian woman!"

Kempelen wound up the clockwork and took off the latch. Then he stationed himself beside the table with the little casket containing his tools. As confidently as ever, the Turk moved his knight forward. Maria Theresia put on her spectacles to examine the move, then moved her own knight. There was applause at this point, mainly from those of the spectators who had not seen the chess automaton in action before, but the Empress immediately looked around and quelled it. "That was no great achievement, I assure you. Or if so, only because of this extraordinary heat."

True enough; Tibor couldn't remember ever having sweated so much in his life. Once the automaton was out in the garden, he had poured some of the water in the cabinet with him over his shirt to cool himself. But he had just been wasting drinking water, for by now he was drenched anyway. His clothes clung to his skin; even the felt and the wood below him were damp. He didn't have enough room to wipe the sweat from his brow with his sleeve and instead had to do it with his hands, trying to rub them dry on his shirt. When he bent over his own chessboard, salty droplets fell on the chessmen. Tibor felt as if he had swollen in the heat, had risen like dough or iron; he was bumping into corners that he had never touched before, and his bent back ached. There were so many wheels going around beside him; why had they never managed to install a wheel with a fan on it, something to blow a cool breeze into the stagnant air inside the automaton? Although perhaps then the candle would have gone out, and the candle was the most important part of his equipment. Its flame didn't seem to Tibor much hotter than the surroundings. He could hardly smell the smoke; his own sweat and even the strong smell of the sun-baked wood overpowered it. Tibor felt as if beetles or ants had got into the machine with him and were crawling over the back of his neck and through his hair, but it was only drops of sweat. The sweat ran into Tibor's mouth without quenching his thirst, it burned his eyes and particularly his wound, for his bandages had been soaked first of all. The hole in his right breast was thudding like a second heart. His entire right arm tingled. It had obviously gone to sleep, and his fingertips were already numb. Tibor couldn't tell whether that was because of his wound or the awkward position he had adopted to spare his injured chest muscle. But moving the pantograph was a laborious business. Tibor had to take care that its grip did not slip from his sweating hand with a move only half-performed. He wanted to use his left hand to take the burden off the right hand, but he had never practiced doing that, and the one move he did manage left-handed was jerky and uncertain. But he wasn't going to complain of his injury: the gunshot wound seemed to him an appropriate, almost welcome punishment for the murder he had committed. After all, on the eye-for-an-eye principle the bullet could have shattered his head. The cylinder that it had touched before burying itself in his body was turning beside Tibor, and the little dent in the brass regularly moved down, disappeared, and reemerged. Then it stopped. The clockwork had run down.

Tibor waited. It was time to wind the springs up again. The game against the Empress would earn him Kempelen's profound respect: playing against the most powerful woman in Europe in these circumstances, with a bullet wound in his chest, and winning easily—without a shadow of doubt, that would be a unique achievement.

"We might think your Turk was feeling the heat too," said Maria Theresia, as Jakob wound up the clockwork again beside her. "Its movements seem strangely sluggish. Yet it should be accustomed to such temperatures in its native land, *n'est-ce pas?*"

"It's possible that the heat has distorted the metal inside it."

"So even machines have human weaknesses?" replied the Empress, smiling, and she returned her attention to the game.

Kempelen glanced at Joseph, who was now devoting more and more time to talking to von Haugwitz and not, as Kempelen suspected, solely about the chess automaton. Moreover, Joseph was not the only one whose attention was elsewhere. Kempelen resolved never again to stage performances by the Turk out of doors.

Meanwhile Maria Theresia had seen the entry hole of the bullet in the door of the cabinet to her left. "What happened there?" she asked. "Do you have mice?" And before Kempelen could embark on an explanation, the Empress put her little finger into the hole. "Or is it an airhole for the clockwork?"

Tibor saw the felt bulging in through the wheels; then the little seam split, and he could see the entire finger—a pink worm wriggling as it explored its new surroundings. In panic, Tibor's hand shot out to shield the light of the candle, an unnecessary precaution, since the finger had no eyes. When his hands came close to the candle, pain stabbed through his injured chest. Tibor's hand jerked and accidentally pressed the candle flame down into the wax, where it was immediately extinguished with a soft hiss. Everything went dark.

"Please, Your Majesty, be careful! Don't catch your finger between the wheels!"

At Kempelen's warning, the Empress took her finger out of the hole again. The torn felt came together behind it.

A man deep in a cave whose only torch has just gone out could not have felt more desperate than Tibor did now. The dwarf forced his panic down: after all, he and Kempelen had worked out a plan for just such an eventuality. If his candle went out, for any reason at all, Tibor had only to make the Turk roll its eyes. That signal would tell Kempelen that he must look inside the mechanism and find some excuse to light Tibor's candle again. In the dark Tibor reached for the wires moving the eyes and pulled them. The Turk rolled its glass eyes until only their whites showed.

A murmur ran through the audience. "Isn't your Mussulman well?" asked the Empress.

Kempelen stepped forward to look at the android. The signal was clear, but he had blown his own candle out. There wasn't an open flame in sight. He had no way of helping Tibor.

"It's only thinking," explained Kempelen. "It will soon play on. Just make your move, Your Imperial Highness."

The Empress made her move. Above him Tibor heard the two magnets being drawn up and dropped again, but he couldn't see them. He raised his right hand to the underside of the board, his chest hurt as he felt for the magnets, but among all the nails and little iron disks he lost his bearings. He touched a cogwheel that pinched his upper arm, and lowered his arm again. Very well, so Kempelen wouldn't be helping him. *It will soon play on.* That was an order to Tibor to bring the game to an end, whatever happened. He closed his eyes—a purely formal gesture, for it was pitch-dark anyway—and recalled the state of the game to his mind. The Empress's bishop had been threatened by one of his pawns, so it followed that she must have moved the bishop back to one of the two safe squares. But which of them? Tibor decided on the one farther back. That was how he would have played. He felt for the chessmen on his own board—cautiously, to avoid another misfortune like the snuffing of the candle flame—picked up the red bishop, and put it on the corresponding square. He couldn't play blind, but he didn't have to, or not completely blind: he would simply feel the pieces and the state of the game. Next he made his own move, aggressively advancing his queen, for if there was one thing he wanted it was to bring this game to a rapid end. He had made a good enough start; the Empress couldn't endanger him now. He operated the pantograph perfectly. His heartbeat slowed down. Was it cooler in the machine without the candle? Whether it was or not, the sounds seemed to him louder now that he couldn't see: the mechanism, the murmuring of the spectators, the gravel crunching under every footstep, even the Empress's quietly wheezing breath where she sat not three feet away from him.

The game went on. After the Empress's next move, and those that followed, he felt for the little metal disks, and this time, keeping calm, he could deduce the state of play from them. He took one of the Empress's unprotected knights. Four moves at the most, and she would be checkmated.

Tibor moved a pawn on his own board forward. But when the Turk carried out the same move, it knocked a piece over. Tibor could hear it quite clearly. There had been a piece on the square that he had thought was empty. The Empress's bishop. So she hadn't moved it back after all. Tibor put his pawn down.

"What's this?" asked the Emperor Joseph. "Is the automaton making mistakes?"

Tibor had to cancel the move, and Kempelen would stand the red bishop up again. He reached for the pantograph and in so doing knocked several of his chessmen over. One rolled off the board and fell to the wooden floor of the cabinet with a sound that seemed to Tibor so loud he thought everyone must hear it. The pantograph couldn't pick up the pawn on the board above. Tibor tried again. At the second attempt he succeeded. He moved the pawn back, but now he had no idea what to do next. He moved a pawn at the side of the board one square forward—a completely pointless move, but at least not incorrect. He sensed the confusion of the audience, but he mustn't let that distract him. He had to reconstruct the state of play as quickly as he could. There was total chaos on his own board. By feel, Tibor could tell that several figures were lying down, sometimes two of them sharing a square, one had disappeared entirely, and even with the help of the metal disks it would be impossible for him to restore the state of the game now. Maria Theresia made her move, and a little metal disk clinked above him in the darkness, but it made no difference anymore. Tibor was lost. All he could do was prevent this defeat from turning into a complete catastrophe, for the clockwork was still going around, rattling, as if the Turk were actively thinking. Tibor had to stop the mechanism. He picked up a chessman and pushed it between two cogwheels. There was a brief crunch, and then the clock-work stopped.

Neither Kempelen nor Jakob realized that it had come to a halt because Tibor had stopped it, not because the mainsprings had run down. Jakob wound it up again. But the chessman stayed put, the wheels stood still.

"What now?" asked the Empress, her voice increasingly stern.

"*Un moment,*" said Kempelen. "I'll look into this."

He opened the door at the back, and the sudden bright light made Tibor blink. Like steam escaping from a pan when the lid is taken off, some of the heat evaporated from the automaton, letting in a breath of cooler air. The two men looked into each other's eyes. Tibor admired Kempelen's ability to remain self-possessed and sure of himself even in this situation. He just shook his head, and Kempelen immediately closed the door again.

"Congratulations, Your Majesty," said Kempelen. "The victory is yours, for unfortunately I fear that my Turk must retire from the game. It has suffered damage on account of the heat, and sad to say, the repairs will take some time."

"We have won?" inquired Maria Theresia.

"Yes, and thus Your Majesty is the first opponent to beat my chess automaton. I could have wished for none worthier. Applause!"

But only a few of the spectators complied with Kempelen's request. There was general confusion.

The Empress expressed the criticism felt by all present. "A victory won too easily against the greatest invention of the century. I would rather have lost than win in such a way."

"Oh, I shall insist on a return match, of course," replied Kempelen, and now his voice was shaking a very little.

"Against a damaged machine?"

"I'll have repaired the damage by tomorrow; it's only a bagatelle, and then we can repeat the game, or resume from the present state of play."

"We are going to Salzburg tomorrow."

"Then I will await your return, and we——"

"No, you will not."

"But for me it's——"

"Perhaps we will visit Pressburg again sometime." The Empress rose from her chair, and she was no longer acting the part of an old woman. "We like Pressburg. Adieu until then, Herr von Kempelen."

Kempelen was going to say something else but thought better of it and bowed, smiling. As he glanced down at the gravel on the ground, he noticed that a slight breeze had risen and was cooling his sweating face. When he looked up again, the Empress had already moved away. The spectators were drawing aside to let her pass. Most of them were looking at Kempelen as he watched the Empress, just as his creation the Turk beside him was watching her. Kempelen turned to Jakob and said something noncommittal, to avoid those glances. He went on smiling as if the performance that had just failed really was no more than a bagatelle that did not trouble him further. Jakob's expression was not so well controlled until Kempelen hissed at him, *"Contenance."*

Clouds came between earth and sky. When Kempelen turned again, most of the audience had dispersed. The majority had followed the Empress into the palace. Joseph and von Haugwitz were continuing their conversation as if the chess automaton had been only an uninteresting and indeed annoying interruption. The footmen were clearing away the chairs and refreshments. No one wanted to talk to Kempelen—except for Friedrich Knaus, who had not moved from the spot and was now facing him, hands clasped behind his back and head slightly bent, the very image of attentive respect. With measured steps, almost at a leisurely stroll, he went up to the cabinet and looked at the Turk with a smile.

"Ah yes, the heat," he said, and tapped his knuckles on the tabletop significantly, as if he knew what was underneath it. "I've noticed that clocks do run a little more slowly in extreme heat. But as for stopping— oh no, they never stop."

"Can I help you in some way?" asked Kempelen.

"Help me? Oh no, my dear sir, I don't need help. But perhaps you do? I have an excellent workshop in the city, and if you should wish to repair your . . . er, machine, you will be very welcome there. I will assist you with my tools and my modest knowledge of mechanics, if you like. Out of friendship, so to speak, friendship between brothers in the same craft."

"Thank you. That won't be necessary."

Knaus nodded to Kempelen, and to Jakob too. He was preparing to go when he turned again, put a finger to his lips, and smiled. Then he allowed Kempelen to share his amusement. "Do you know what His Imperial Majesty said of our automata just now? He said they were relics of a bygone time, dusty toys from the days before the war, and it would be better to put money and energy into more sensible inventions. Think of that: only yesterday still *avant garde*, today *antiquité*. If he weren't the Emperor, I would have argued with him passionately."

He left the garden at a leisurely pace, his feet dragging over the gravel, and on the way he took the time to bend down to a bush of white roses and smell the flowers. Kempelen, Jakob, and the machine were left on their own. Not even Jakob dared to say anything.

THE SKY had quickly grown gray over the city, but the rain kept everyone waiting. They just had time to get back to Kempelen's apartment before the storm broke. When Tibor climbed out of the automaton at last—hungry, thirsty, and stinking of dried sweat—Kempelen was standing at the window with his back to him. Tibor took the glass of water that Jakob handed him only after explaining to Kempelen the series of unfortunate circumstances that had led to his failure.

Kempelen asked no questions, did not nod, looked at Tibor only when he had finished, and then said briefly, "You weren't playing particularly well before it happened either."

Tibor went away to wash, and while he was washing, his sense of guilt changed to annoyance. After all, he had done everything humanly possible to bring the game to a successful conclusion. It had been Kempelen who allowed the Empress to sit at the chess machine itself, and it had been Kempelen who didn't relight his candle as they had agreed. And when Tibor took off the stained bandage that stuck to his skin as if it had grown into it, and saw his wound, now surrounded by an angry red ring, he reminded himself that it was Kempelen who had not prevented Andrássy from firing the shot, who had failed to protect him as he promised he would.

As soon as Jakob had rebandaged Tibor's chest, he went out with a coat over his arm. Kempelen told him to stay, but Jakob said there was no more for him to do here, so he might as well take a look at the city. After all, he said, he had a right to some free time. When Kempelen repeated his command more firmly, Jakob replied, "I'm happy to be persuaded, but I won't be ordered about." He obviously felt that the atmosphere in Kempelen's apartment was intolerable and even preferred to brave the hail that had begun beating down on the Alser Gasse outside. Tibor would have been only too happy to go with him.

Kempelen was still standing at the window when Tibor told him he was going to lie down for a while. Then he added, "Was that the last performance?"

"I don't want to talk about it today."

Tibor nodded. "You shouldn't have put your candle out."

Kempelen spun around, forefinger raised. "I warn you," he said, "don't you dare to blame me for the wretched game you played in the garden. You'd better remember it's not the first time I've had to take responsibility for a mistake of yours."

Tibor should have kept quiet, but he couldn't. "There's no comparison! I wasn't guilty of anything today."

"Not a word out of you," said Kempelen, looking out of the window again. "I don't want to hear another word."

Tibor fell silent and lay down on the bed in the next room. He closed his eyes.

To his surprise, the first picture to appear to him in the dark was not of today's failure or the embittered Kempelen, not of the inflamed ring around the wound in his chest, nor of the dead Baroness whose image had haunted him so long—it was Elise's face. He could have wished that one hour he had spent with her to go on forever. He remembered how they had sat opposite each other in Pasha's company—as if they were old friends, their knees very close, the warmth of her body almost tangible—confessing frankly to each other that he was a fraud and she was a traitor! He remembered how the sun had shone into the workshop, lighting up the hovering motes of dust like pollen in the air, turning her beautiful hair into a golden halo—his holy medallion in her hand, her fragrance in his nostrils. The picture of Elise stayed with him until he fell asleep. An unaccustomed sensation had taken possession of Tibor, a sensation that he had been waiting for all his life.

J. JAKOB WATCHED THE PEN trace the character on the paper. Then the framework holding the paper was pushed a little way to one side, and the pen wrote the next letter: *a.* Once again the paper moved, and *k* and *o* followed. After that the little brass woman dipped her quill into an inkwell to write *b* with fresh ink. Now the paper went back to the beginning but moved a line higher up, so that his family name was written under his first name: *Wachsberger.* The paper was moved after every letter; the pen took new ink on board after every fourth character. The little statuette writing all this down—a Greek goddess with her hair up and a flowing tunica, the pen in her right hand, her left hand supported—sat on a large globe representing the world and borne up on the wings of two bronze eagles, which in their own turn perched on a plinth of richly ornamented black and brown marble. The frame with the paper stretched on it was connected to the machine, which stood as high as a man and was decorated with brass flowers. By comparison with Knaus's Wonderful All-Writing Machine, the appearance of Kempelen's chess automaton was plain and almost paltry.

> *Jakob*
> *Wachsberger*
> *Écrit à Vienne*
> *Le 14ᵉ août MDCCLXX*

It looked as imperishable as the inscription on a gravestone. Friedrich Knaus took the paper out of the frame, carefully blew on the ink to dry it, and handed it to Jakob, with a wink. "But don't show it to your employer, or he'll want one too."

Knaus unbolted the globe. Five sections opened out like the petals of a flower, giving a view of the machinery within. Here again the superiority of his machine showed: the parts were more precise, smaller, and the mechanism more ingenious than the Turk's clockwork. Jakob put his spectacles on to inspect it more closely. Knaus pointed out in particular the cylinder on which the characters could be set, at present adjusted to write Jakob's names, the place, and today's date.

"I'm still proud of it," said Knaus, placing one hand on the marble, "even if it's not the latest thing any longer. Admittedly its usefulness is slight, for any child can write faster. And its abilities are limited: it writes only what one tells it to write, and there can be only sixty-eight characters at a time. It does not correct mistakes, it does not write works of its own, it does not think . . ." Knaus looked at Jakob, who was examining the cylinder so intently that he didn't seem to be listening. "But what it does, it does of its own powers. It is entirely honest. It doesn't pretend to be what it is not."

Now Jakob did look up. "Is this going to be an interrogation? Because if so I'm leaving at once."

Knaus raised his hands in a placatory gesture. "No, no. The chess automaton is of no interest to me."

Jakob raised one eyebrow. "Since when?"

"Since noon today." Knaus sat down at his desk. "I would like to offer you tea or some pastries, but your visit is a little too much of a surprise for that. You were lucky to find me in the Cabinet at all." Jakob folded the paper with his mechanically written name on it and took the chair that Knaus offered. "However, thank you for taking up the invitation I issued so long ago at last. You've seen my machine, I have shown you my workshop. So what more can I do for you?"

"In the spring you made me an offer to come and work for you. Is the offer still open?"

"Why, yes. If you haven't forgotten any of your skill in the meantime."

"How high would the wages be?"

"Shall we say twenty guilders?"

"A month?"

"What did you think? Not a week, surely?"

"That's too little."

"Is it, indeed?" inquired Knaus, smiling. He folded his hands and leaned back.

"It's definitely too little."

"Your ship has sprung a leak today, my dear fellow, and you'd do well not to look askance at the helping hand being held out to you. Or you'll sink with all aboard, more particularly your dashing captain."

"What happened today was only a little setback. A mistake in the system."

"It was not a *little* setback, it was a once-and-for-all setback. I've seen men fall out of the Empress's favor for far less reason."

Jakob took his spectacles off and folded them up. "You only think he's going to fail because that's what you want."

"The one doesn't exclude the other. Did you notice the expression on his face today? Of course you did; you were standing there beside him. A look of despair, rarely seen in him so far, but despair will haunt him more and more often in future. He looked, so to speak, overtaxed. He looked like five soundly whipped galley slaves. He's even thrown his wife out of the house because she overtaxes him so much."

"How do you know that?"

"He's never learned to deal with setbacks. The modern Prometheus has become a modern Icarus. Believe you me: Wolfgang Kempelen is on his way down—and I don't know why you should go the same way with him."

"Out of loyalty."

Knaus laughed. "Yes, to be sure. That's a good one!"

"I want thirty guilders. That's the minimum, or I stay in Pressburg."

"We could agree on twenty-four, or no, let's say twenty-two, but you won't get any more out of me. Remember: other journeymen would pay to work for me in the Court Physical Cabinet."

"And other master craftsmen would give a fortune for what I know."

For a moment Knaus said nothing but drummed his fingers on his desk. "Good. If you will tell me how that ridiculous chess machine works—yes, that offer still stands—then I really would dip deeper into my pocket."

Jakob looked at the floor, then at the goddess sitting on the globe.

"I am afraid I make only clockwork, not time itself, and mine is strictly limited," said Knaus, when no answer came. He rose again and pushed his chair abruptly back. "Think about my offer, but at the same time remember that your price now is likely to fall rather than rise."

And Knaus opened the door of his study to let Jakob out. "Goodbye, then," he said in farewell. "Although I feel sure that we shall soon meet again."

"Is this the way you usually treat your employees?" asked Jakob.

"I never wanted to be liked by my employees, only by the rich and powerful. If that answers your question."

And with these words Knaus closed the door. A broad smile spread over his face once he was alone. With a spring in his step, he went over to his Wonderful All-Writing Machine, and in great high spirits he kissed the writing goddess's pretty bare feet. The taste of brass lingered on his lips for a long time.

Neuchâtel: Night

JOHANN HAD DISCOVERED THAT THE DWARF WAS STAYING at the De l'Aubier Inn, whether in company, and if so whose, he couldn't say. Obviously the wealthy textile manufacturer Carmaux had insisted on paying for overnight accommodation for the Turk's opponent. Gottfried Neumann's exploits were still being celebrated by a number of citizens in the main room of the inn.

Neumann, Johann had found out, had come to Switzerland thirteen years before, allegedly from Passau. He had a small workshop in La Chaux-de-Fonds, with two employees, and he had specialized in *tableaux animés*—paintings with built-in clockwork that, once wound up, presented a picture of real life: blacksmiths hammering, farmers threshing grain, women drawing water, horses galloping, boats sailing past, clouds crossing the sky. Neumann was reported to be a friend of Pierre and Henri-Louis Jaquet-Droz's and had helped them with useful ideas and advice in the creation of their famous trio of automata—three androids, one of them a writer, another a draftsman, and the third a lady musician.

Kempelen waited another hour, telling his wife that he would have to go out again, then set off with Johann. The night was extremely inhospitable; a keen wind from Lake Neuchâtel drove snowflakes down the streets to settle in nooks and crannies and cling to the walls of buildings, either spending the night there or blown on after they had taken a brief rest. The paving stones were covered with hoar-frost. Both snow and ice would melt away next morning in the spring sun, but now it looked as if winter were on its way back. Kempelen kept on the lee side of the lanky Johann.

When Kempelen and Johann had brushed the snow off their coats and entered the warm inn, the landlord immediately came up to tell them that the place was closed. Kempelen pressed a few groschen into the man's hand, which silenced him. Then he ordered two glasses of punch, asking the landlord to close the door and let no one else in.

The main room of the inn was empty except for the landlord himself and, sitting at one of the tables, a solitary figure who now looked up: Neumann. He had a piece of paper covered with writing in front of him, together with a stick of charcoal and a glass. Kempelen went over to him, tugging Johann along by his sleeve. Neumann didn't move from the spot.

"You're alive," said Kempelen.

"So are you."

"Yes," replied Kempelen, and he was smiling again. There was a long moment of silence between them.

Instinctively, Johann made a movement that revealed his uneasiness at this joyless greeting, whereupon Kempelen spoke again. "I ought to introduce you to each other. This is Johann, Johann Allgaier, and this is Tibor—"

"Gottfried. Gottfried Neumann."

"*Gottfried* . . . well, you really have thought of everything."

Tibor and Johann shook hands. "Is he its brain?"

Johann started, but Kempelen put a hand on his arm. "It's all right, Johann. He knows about it."

"You play very well," said Tibor.

"Thank you, sir. Let me return the compliment." Johann's glance fell on the paper on the table. Tibor had been sketching their interrupted game on it.

"They don't have a chessboard anywhere in the house," explained Tibor, "so I've had to draw it."

Johann pointed to the middle of the board. "There's going to be a tough battle between my rook and your bishop there."

"Yes, I think so too."

"Do you think you'll win?"

"I shall try to."

The landlord brought the mulled wine. Kempelen asked if there was anything else Tibor would like, but he shook his head. Then he requested both the landlord and Johann to leave him and Neumann alone. The landlord left the room after adding several logs to the fire. Johann sat down with his punch by the hearth and put his feet up. After he had drunk the punch, he fell asleep, or at least looked as if he were asleep.

Kempelen sat down opposite Tibor, who was examining him intently.

"You're looking well," said Kempelen, after drinking a sip of wine. "A few gray hairs now." Smiling, he ran his hand through his own hair; his forehead was higher these days, his hair not so thick.

Tibor looked at Johann. "He's tall. How does he fit into the cabinet?"

"I altered parts of it. The whole of the back side is empty, and he sits on a sliding board so that he can move more easily."

Tibor nodded. Kempelen looked at the sketch again. "You were saying you want to win?"

"Yes."

"That wouldn't be good for me."

Tibor did not think an answer necessary.

"Johann is a stronger player than you are," said Kempelen.

"Then there's nothing for you to worry about."

Kempelen sighed. "I want you to lose. For the Turk, it's really important. I'm about to travel through the whole of Europe: Paris, London, perhaps Berlin, the Fair in Leipzig. I don't want to begin the tour with a defeat." Kempelen took his coat off. "I'll return you the fifty thalers you were willing to stake."

Tibor said nothing.

"You want more. I might have known it. How much? A hundred? A hundred and fifty? You can have the whole two hundred as far as I'm concerned. I don't want the money."

"Nor do I."

"You can hardly be so rich that such a sum means nothing to you." Kempelen moved a little closer and lowered his voice. "Tibor, I've been corresponding with Philidor—the great Philidor, in a way your own teacher. Even he said he was prepared to play against the Turk—and to lose! There's nothing dishonorable about it."

"I won't lose unless your Johann defeats me. And if you've come here only to bribe me, you can leave again as soon as you've finished your punch."

"You want to get even with me, don't you? You want to humiliate me, and that pleasure's worth your fifty thalers to you."

"If I wanted to get even with you, I'd have broken the doors of the machine open in front of everyone today, saying, 'Look, here's the secret of this mechanical marvel!'"

A log crackled in the fire.

"Why did you rebuild the Turk?" asked Tibor.

"Why do you ask?"

"Because I'd hoped you wouldn't. Because I hoped never to see the Turk again."

"It can't make any difference to you." Kempelen rubbed his eyes. "There are a number of reasons. I'm not making progress with the speaking machine. And money was running short. Teréz has a little brother now, they're traveling with me too, and I have to provide for the children. Emperor Joseph, I can tell you, isn't as generous as his late mother. And he doesn't like me. But a year ago Grand Duke Paul of Russia visited Vienna, and it was his great desire to play a match against the Turk—so Joseph asked me to refurbish the Turk for his distinguished guest. It took me a good deal of time and work to restore the machine to its original condition, as I'm sure you can imagine. The body's entirely new. And the eye color has changed. I took the opportunity to convert and extend the cabinet so that normal . . . taller people like Johann can play in it. And suddenly everyone remembers the machine, and they're all writing about it, Windisch publishes his book, and because my own country knows the Turk already, I'm going farther afield to exhibit it in Europe. Pressburg isn't what it used to be, not since the Empress died and Ofen became the capital of Hungary again."

"Do you seriously expect your tour to be a success?"

"What do you mean? You're not trying to intimidate me, are you?"

"Who's going to come to see machines acting like men? There are plenty of men now who have to live and toil like machines. Men enslaved to real machines. Like the new looms, for instance."

"How profound," said Kempelen, gulping his punch. "The Turk was a great success in Bavaria. I'm afraid you're alone in your dislike of modern progress, Gottfried."

Tibor rose from the table, crumpled up the drawing of his unfinished game, and went over to the fire on the hearth.

"Isn't Baron Andrássy after you anymore?" he asked, without turning around.

"Andrássy died four years ago. Killed in the Bavarian war. I presume that he died as he would have wished."

"The Curse of the Turk."

"Exactly. What a tasteful remark."

Standing beside the sleeping Johann, Tibor threw his sketch on the fire and watched the flames reduce the drawing of the chessboard to ashes. He wouldn't be able to think about it anymore tonight anyway.

At the Sign of the Red Crab

TIBOR OPENED HIS EYES. ELISE WAS STANDING IN FRONT OF him wearing a red dress under a dark blue cloak, with a swaddled baby in the crook of her left arm. She smiled as she took a step toward Tibor. Passing her right hand over his bare chest, she found the hole that the bullet had made. "An airhole for the clockwork?" Tibor was excited. She put her hand inside his breast, fingertips first. It disappeared up to the wrist, as if his flesh were butter. Then she took the hand out again. She was holding his heart. It was red and shiny, like an apple. But when she turned it in her fingers, he saw that it wasn't a heart but a clock. Tibor looked down at the hole. Beneath the skin lay torn battens, wires, pipes. They were embedded in straw and clay. Oil oozed from the pipes. When he looked up again, Elise had gone. His penis was as hard as wood. His limbs really were wood; when he moved his arm, he saw that it was carved from a piece of pale wood, with a large hinge at the elbow holding his upper arm and forearm together. Many other little hinges moved his fingers. Glassy-eyed, Tibor looked in a mirror. Blue-black Hebrew characters spelled out the word *aemaeth* on his forehead. How strange that it didn't look like mirror writing to him. How strange that he could read it at all. He turned away. He must go to a church. They'd help him there.

The church was high-roofed and built of dark stone. Incense wafted among the pews like mist. Tibor went to the altar, where the priest was smoking a pipe. The tobacco smoke was the incense. The priest wore a turban. It was Andrássy, wearing the Turk's caftan. He beckoned Tibor closer with his left hand and smiled. "Defeat me." There was a chessboard on the altar. Tibor began the game. Of course he would win. Andrássy was playing with black instead of red pieces. The chessboard had black and white squares too. Tibor blinked: the chessboard was larger now. It measured nine times nine squares. Now there were a hundred squares in all. Now there were two hundred and fifty-six. Now the whole altar was covered with black and white squares. Tibor was still playing with sixteen pieces, but Andrássy had some new ones. Chessmen such as Tibor had only read about before: a crow, a boat, a cart, a camel, an elephant, a crocodile, a giraffe. They moved in curves. They made great leaps. The bird was removed at one point and then, without warning, took Tibor's knight on a square very far away. Andrássy smiled. How like his sister he looked. Paint was peeling off his cheek. The skin fell to the floor in flakes, and his bones showed behind it. The flesh was crumbling off his body like dry mortar from the wall of a house. Finally he was only a skeleton, his head a hollow skull. But his smile was still there. The skeleton's hands were now moving together. When Tibor made a move, his opponent made two. The white chessmen fell in swaths. In the end the bestiary of black pieces had only the white king to defeat. "*Maeth*," said the skeleton. Tibor took his king off the board to prevent it from being taken. He put the piece in his mouth. It was white, and when he bit it, it bled. He had the warm taste of iron in his mouth. He swallowed both the blood and the chessman. The skeleton reached out for him. Tibor tried to elude it and run away, but there were strings fixed to his head and limbs. His opponent was holding those strings. He drew Tibor toward him. He hauled the wooden Tibor up onto the chessboard. With bony fingers, he tried to remove the characters from his forehead. Tibor screamed. The Turk's free hand closed around his mouth, stifling his scream. Tibor couldn't breathe anymore.

. . .

TIBOR CAME TO HIMSELF with a start. Elise was holding his mouth closed with her hand. Wheezing, he breathed in through his nose. His eyes were wide open. He would have struck away any other hand immediately, but now he stayed motionless. She was sitting on his bed, holding a candle in her other hand. Why was she sitting on his bed? How had she come to Vienna? Where were Kempelen and Jakob?

It took him several moments to return fully from his dream to reality. Of course he wasn't in Vienna now. They'd traveled back to Pressburg two days ago. He was in his room in the Donaugasse house. That still didn't explain what she was doing here, of course—in his room in the middle of the night. He hadn't seen her since their return. It was as if he had fetched her here straight from his dream, although she was wearing her normal garments with a shawl over them, not a red dress and blue mantle. Dream and reality were alike only in that his upper body was sweating and naked except for the bandage, and he could taste blood on his tongue.

"All right?" she asked.

Tibor nodded. She took her hand away from his mouth. There was saliva and blood on her palm. She wiped her hand on the sheet. Tibor had bitten his tongue in his sleep; he licked the blood off his lips and pulled the sheet a little farther up to cover himself.

"I'm sorry, but you were going to scream, and Herr von Kempelen mustn't hear us." She was almost whispering.

Then she put the candle down on the bedside table and removed her shawl. Tibor looked at the face of the clock on his little workbench. It was just after four in the morning and still as hot as midday.

"Why . . . what are you doing here?" asked Tibor. "What's happened?"

"I found a bloodstained bandage thrown away and thought it must be something to do with you. I was worried."

She pointed to his bandage. Tibor looked down at it.

"A shot," he explained. "Andrássy."

"Bad?"

"I don't know. The wound isn't large, but it won't heal up."

"You're feverish."

"Yes."

"May I look?"

Together they removed the bandage. Her fingers touched his, and his arm too, his back and his chest. They moved the fabric aside, and with the candle in her hand Elise leaned very close to his chest. The shot through the thigh that Tibor had suffered years ago in the battle of Torgau had closed up fast and almost painlessly. Andrássy's handiwork, however, refused to heal. The angry ring around the wound had spread and was inflamed. The edge of the wound was firm, but the torn skin had not closed up. The first pus gleamed in the flickering candlelight. Tibor knew already that it was bad, but now the sight of Elise frowning made him feel very uneasy. She sighed.

"You need a doctor."

He could have wished she'd said something else. "We can't call one in."

"On Kempelen's orders?"

"He's right. A doctor would give me away."

"It's already beginning to fester. If no one tends this wound, you may die of gangrene."

"If that's the alternative to being strung up, well, I'm in God's hands."

Elise shook her head. "Has Kempelen done anything about your wound?"

"He doesn't know about these things."

"Fancy that. You mean there's actually one field of study that he doesn't understand?"

Tibor was surprised by her sharp tone. Elise noticed and lowered her eyes. "I can get a doctor for you if you like."

"No. Really."

"All right." She reached for her bag, which she had put down on the floor, and took out a bottle, several white cloths, and scissors, needle, and thread. "Then I'll do it."

Tibor looked at her wide-eyed. "Do *you* know about these things?"

"Not much, but at least it's better than doing nothing and trusting in

God's hands, which are a long way off." She looked at him. "I'm sorry. I didn't mean to blaspheme. I'm just anxious."

Tibor nodded. "I'm sure God understands."

She opened the bottle and handed it to Tibor. "Drink this."

Tibor frowned, but he took a sip. It was *borovicka*. Making a face, he put the bottle down again, nauseated.

"All of it," said Elise.

"What? Why?"

"Because you'll need it," she told him, holding up a needle bent into a curve. "Just leave me a little."

So Tibor drank the juniper spirit. There was nearly half a liter of it. He disliked the taste to the last, but at least it became more tolerable. The alcohol took effect almost immediately: he noticed his vision, movements, and thoughts all slowing down, and the pain in his chest ebbed away. How strange that on two of the three occasions when he had encountered Elise, he'd been drunk. Meanwhile Elise was threading her needle. She soaked one of her cloths in the dregs of the spirits that Tibor had left.

"Can I begin?"

His head heavy, Tibor nodded. Elise wiped his chest with the damp cloth. The bitter smell of the *borovicka* spread through the room. When her cloth touched his wound, it felt as if she held a red-hot poker against it. He groaned out loud while his hands clutched the bed. Tears came to his eyes. Elise withdrew her hand.

"*O santa Madre di Dio,*" he said, when he could speak.

"I'm sorry."

When he had relaxed again, she went on cleaning his chest and the wound but moving with the utmost care. Tibor's hands clenched into fists. He was gritting his teeth.

"Hold on to my dress if it helps," she said.

Tibor moved his hand to her thigh, where her dress was gathered, and clutched a fold of fabric. He could feel her thigh under it when she moved. That didn't seem to bother her. She cleaned her own hands and the needle with the spirit-soaked cloth. Then she began stitching. Tibor had to lie flat on his back. She leaned over him, and only her cap prevented her blond hair from brushing his chest. The prick of the needle hurt less now, though probably only because of the *borovicka*. He watched her at work. She was concentrating and involuntarily bit her lower lip as she stitched.

"Can I talk?" asked Tibor.

"So long as you keep still."

"Where did you learn to do that?"

"My mother taught me a few things. I learned the rest in the convent school. Although I was sewing linen and wool then . . . not flesh and skin."

"Where do your parents live now?"

"In Heaven," said Elise. "They died when I was a child. I grew up with my godparents."

"And you're not married yet?"

"No, I'm still waiting."

"But surely you'd like to have a family of your own soon, wouldn't you?"

Elise sighed. She didn't look up from his wound. After a brief moment's silence she said, "Of course." A little later she asked, "How about you?"

Tibor raised his head slightly and looked at her, but obviously she hadn't been laughing at him when she asked that question. "I can't imagine anything I'd like more."

"How long have you been on the road?"

"Since I was fourteen."

"What made you leave your parents' house?"

"They did," he said with a sad smile. And he told her how although his mother and father had never loved him—after all, his healthy siblings gave them plenty of children to love—they had put up with him until malicious gossip in the village induced them to turn him out of their farm. He described his wanderings in Austria, Bohemia, Silesia, and Prussia, his experiences in the war, his time in the monastery, and the years on the road playing chess after that. Now and then he had to stop when one of her stitches hurt especially badly.

"Why didn't you go into another monastery?" she asked.

"I never felt I had the stature to be a monk."

"You think the abbot would have objected to a small one?"

"I didn't mean my body. I meant my soul."

Elise looked into his eyes. She opened her mouth, but no words would come. Then she returned to her stitching.

"So how is it that you play chess so well?"

"I don't know. I really don't know. But I think . . . I think God has blessed us all with some quality of perfection. We can only hope to find out what our own good quality is someday. Why do I play chess well? Why can Jakob bring dead wood to life? Why are you so beautiful?"

Elise did not reply. She picked up her scissors and cut the thread just above Tibor's skin. Tibor sat up, with difficulty, and looked at his chest. A seam like the points of a star now lay above the entry hole of the bullet, pulling the flesh together. Elise reached for a clean cloth to mop the sweat from her brow.

"You remember what we talked about," said Tibor. "Are you going to tell the Bishop now? Is it time for me to get away?"

Elise shook her head. "You're injured. You can't travel yet. I'll wait."

Tibor smiled. "I'll go to Kempelen tomorrow and ask for my money. He owes me more than two hundred and fifty guilders. I've never had so much money in my life, and I don't need all that. I want you to have a hundred guilders. For what you've done for me, and for your own future."

"I won't take it."

"No, of course. I knew you'd say that."

"You're drunk."

"Yes, but it doesn't make any difference."

Elise picked up a fresh bandage and bound up his chest. "Where will you go?" she asked.

"I don't know. I'll just run."

When Elise had finished, she gathered up her implements and the soiled cloths in silence. Then she sat on the edge of the bed for the last time.

"You'd better leave the candle burning. By morning it will have drowned out the smell of the *borovicka*."

"I love you," said Tibor suddenly. "Mary Mother of God be my witness,

I love you. I love you so much, I want you so much, so much that I'd take a knife and stick it into me, just to feel your hands tending me again."

After that all was quiet. There was nothing to be heard but the faint hiss of the candle. Elise struggled with herself for a long time, and then she had to swallow. Tibor fell back against the wall, exhausted.

"Forgive me," he said. "Please don't say anything. Especially not anything kind. Go away. Go away now, and I'll sleep and carry on dreaming."

Elise rose and picked up her bag. She looked at Tibor. Then she bent down to him, pressed a kiss on his perspiring forehead, and left the room. Softly as she stole away, Tibor could hear every one of her footsteps all the way to the staircase. Outside in the yard, a thrush began to sing.

SHE OUGHT NOT to have kissed him. But she had wanted to kiss him as he lay there, small and weakened, drunk, mortally wounded, immortally enamored. He obviously took her for some kind of saint. He wanted to give her a hundred guilders. What madness! Give half his fortune to her, the woman who had lied to him from first to last and was going to deliver him up to the executioner someday? His innocent trust, his overwhelming piety in the face of all the blows of Fate, positively incensed her. She reached the Lorenz Gate and turned into Spitalgasse. The first birds were singing above the rooftops. Pressburg was only a village. In Vienna there'd have been people out early on the streets at this hour, or still up late. But the cobbled roads of Pressburg were a playground for birds, foxes, hares, and rats. Elise was going to change her clothes in her room and then return to her daily duties in the Kempelen house, as if nothing had happened.

But everything had changed again so quickly. Tibor's revelation before the journey to Vienna had been a triumph for her. All of a sudden she had Kempelen and Knaus in her power—but then the Turk came back from Vienna, and all she could gather from the unusually silent Jakob suggested that the performance before the Empress had been a failure. She had hardly seen Kempelen since then, and when she did, he said only the bare minimum to her. What would Knaus want her to do now? Could she, should she withdraw? She wanted to. A Jakob who had lost his usual cheerfulness, a Kempelen whose arrogance had turned to melancholy: she could do without such company. She wanted to go back to Vienna, take off the coarse-woven clothes of a maidservant, and appear at court again in silk and brocade.

Yet when she thought about it more closely, she didn't care very much for Knaus and his like either. And she didn't want to abandon Tibor. He trusted her, even loved her, and although of course she didn't love him, never would and never could love him, she felt responsible for him, however much she resisted that feeling.

She felt a need to change direction, go downstream along the Danube, lie down in the damp grass, watch the stars fading and the fish leaping in the morning light. She was tired of the life she led. She knew she wouldn't have been any happier with the other life—the life that she had pretended to the dwarf was hers—but now she wished she had led it after all. She'd rather be an unhappy maidservant than an unhappy courtesan, an unhappy informer.

The child moved inside her. She stood there in the empty street, waiting for the feeling to pass.

ELISE RETURNED to the Kempelen house just after six in the morning. She had bought rolls and croissants in the Grüner Markt, along with fresh eggs and milk. When she had put her purchases down in the kitchen, she fetched wood from the interior courtyard. Although the air was mild, she was shivering, and she crouched beside the open range for a little while, letting the fire warm her. Then she put water on for coffee. While it heated, she ground the coffee and put it in the pot. She took butter and honey from the cupboard, placed both on a tray beside the rolls, and then cut ham. When the water began to simmer, she turned back to the range. Wolfgang von Kempelen was standing in the doorway in his shirt, pantaloons, and tall riding boots, arms crossed, one shoulder against the door frame. He was smiling. Elise started and instinctively put a hand to her breast.

"Good morning," he said quietly, as if the house were full of sleepers who mustn't be awakened too early. "I didn't mean to make you jump, but you were so busy that I didn't want to disturb you at work either. Do go on."

Elise took a deep breath. "How long have you been standing there?"

"Oh, forever," replied Kempelen. "The water's boiling."

Elise took the water off the range and poured it over the coffee grounds, which sank to the bottom of the pot, hissing.

"You look tired. Did you sleep badly?"

Elise nodded but didn't take her eyes off the coffeepot. She could have said the same of him, for judging by the dark rings under his eyes, he hadn't slept all night—although there had been no light in his room. She had made sure of that before going in search of Tibor. Nonetheless he seemed cheerful; the despondency she had observed in him the day before had given way to a strange mood of reverie.

"Poor Elise. I ask a lot of you, don't I?"

"That's all right."

"It will get easier for you again. I shall soon be asking my dear Anna Maria to come back from Gomba, bringing Teréz. Then we won't be on our own anymore, and perhaps you'll have less work to do. That coffee smells delicious, by the way."

"Thank you, sir."

"Can I help you?"

"No, thank you, I've nearly finished."

"And you can have this afternoon off."

"Thank you very much, sir." Elise put the coffee on the tray and poured milk into a little jug. "How did it go in Vienna?" she asked.

"Oh, wonderfully well," he replied, and repeated, looking up at the ceiling, "Yes, Vienna went wonderfully well. We'll take you with us next time."

Elise went to the kitchen dresser to get him a cup and saucer. She had to stand on tiptoe.

Kempelen moved away from the door. "Wait." He took the crockery out for her and put it on the tray. Then he looked at her. Touching her chin with the fingers of his right hand, he raised it slightly, then let his hand pass over her cheek to her ear and kissed her. She closed her eyes.

He ran his tongue over her lips. Then he touched her head with his left hand too. They were so close to each other now that her breasts were rubbing against his shirt, and each noticed the other breathing faster. She pulled in her stomach so that he wouldn't notice its swelling curve. She kept her hands in the air, unable either to touch Kempelen or to let them drop back to her sides entirely. Knaus's kisses were greedy and wet, and for all Jakob's boastful talk he had kissed like a schoolboy. But not Kempelen: in other circumstances Elise would have enjoyed that kiss. Now she understood why Baroness Jesenák had desired him.

Then Kempelen moved back, but he still held her head in his hands and went on looking into her eyes. He pressed his lips together as if he were thinking about something. Their firm line dissolved into a smile. He let her go, but with the fingers of his left hand he tucked a strand of hair back behind her ear, nodded, picked up his breakfast tray, and left the kitchen without another word. Elise heard his brisk footsteps as he climbed the stairs to his study. Involuntarily, she licked her moist, cold lips.

THAT AFTERNOON Kempelen knocked on Tibor's door. He did not go in but asked the dwarf to join him in the study as soon as he could find the time. Tibor dressed and went through the empty workshop to Kempelen's room. The speaking machine was lying on the floor in a corner, protected from dust by a cloth. Kempelen had pushed the sectional side of the plaster model up against the wall, so that it looked as if a head were partly walled up there. A number of documents lay on the desk: letters, notes, articles from journals, and a calendar, all very tidily arranged. On a separate table stood a tray with pastries, two cups, and a pot of coffee, its powerful fragrance filling the whole room.

Kempelen had moved his armchair over to the window and crossed his legs. He had a drawing board on his knees, with an unfinished drawing of the open chess automaton pinned to it. He appeared very cheerful. He seemed to have cast off the nervous tension caused by Ibolya's death, his problems with Baron Andrássy and the Church, and above all the fiasco at Schönbrunn, and he looked years younger. What a contrast to

Tibor, who was drained of blood and perspiring, bearing the marks of the pain he had suffered for the last few days! Too much *borovicka* had left him with a headache and nausea. He hadn't eaten anything since morning, although he had drunk large quantities of water.

All the same Kempelen said, "You look as if you're cured." He put the drawing board, his sketch, and his graphite pencil down on the desk and moved his chair closer. "Are you feeling better now?"

"A little."

"I'm glad to hear it. Would you like some coffee? Or perhaps a wine or a liqueur?"

"I'll have a coffee, please."

Kempelen poured coffee for Tibor and handed him the cup. When he had helped himself too and was sitting down again, he said, "I want to discuss the future with you."

Tibor nodded. The coffee was delicious, both invigorating and satis-fying.

"I'd like to ask Mayor Windisch to take another look in person at the chess automaton and then write an article about it. This," he said, tapping the drawing board, "is going to be a copperplate engraving. I'd do it myself, only my time . . . well, the *Pressburger Zeitung* is read far beyond this city, and an account of the Turk would be a good subject for Windisch's journal and a free advertisement for us." Kempelen picked up a copy of the *Mercure de France* that had recently arrived from Paris. "If the automaton's being discussed as far away as the French capital, then it certainly will be here."

Tibor put his coffee cup down, but before he could say anything, Kempelen began again.

"I want to stage another grand appearance like the one at the Palais Grassalkovich, but in front of an audience of ordinary citizens this time. I might hire the Italian Theater. Or we could go to Engerau Island and show the Turk in the very appropriate setting of the Turkish Pavilion. With a cup of mocha and a tobacco pipe for every spectator! Isn't that a famous notion? And of course we'll continue giving weekly performances in this house. Summer will soon be over, it will be cold and dark, people will want *divertissements* again, and the Turk is the very thing for them. An automaton shrouded in mystery, perhaps even carrying a curse, seen by candlelight while the wind whistles down the streets outside—they'll all move a little closer to one another. Anna Maria will soon be back from our summer residence, and then we'll look around for a second maid so that we can entertain the crowds of visitors properly. I'm thinking of getting the automaton to perform the Knight's Tour in future too—you know it, the knight moves to every one of the sixty-four squares without landing twice on any of them. A pretty little trick. And we must go on our travels again! It's time we performed in Vienna for the general public and not just the Empress—although I'll still be pressing her to let us have a return match. And then we'll see where else we might go. Ofen, Marburg . . . Salzburg, Innsbruck, Munich, perhaps Prague . . . I feel sure the Turk will be more than warmly welcomed everywhere. Crowned heads and scholars will flock to our performances. Tibor, I shall sacrifice the most famous men and the best chess players in Europe to you on the altar of the Turk!"

Tibor did not reply.

"What do you say?" asked Kempelen.

"I thought you said . . . you said Vienna would be the automaton's last performance?"

Kempelen was taken aback, or at least looked as if he was. "I never said that. When am I supposed to have said it? And above all, why?"

"I thought . . . because of your enemies. And because you want to make the other machine."

"They're not mutually exclusive. And as for the nuisances pestering us, Batthyány has no authority over Duke Albert, and it's to be hoped that Baron Andrássy let off steam with that unfortunate attack."

"We lost to the Empress."

"Well? Did your other setbacks cause any loss of interest? Not at all! Quite the contrary: as soon as the Turk showed a little weakness for once, spectators came in their hordes! The Empress is a demigoddess to her subjects; it won't surprise anyone that she, of all people, was the one to defeat the Turk. Which doesn't mean," said Kempelen, with a twinkle in his eye, "that you have carte blanche to lose in future."

Tibor appeared to be taking a sip of coffee, although the cup had long since been empty except for the muddy black grounds at the bottom. He had to think.

"Above all, I must convince Joseph," Kempelen went on, "because one day in the not too distant future the Empress will be no more, and then I must be in his favor. The sooner I persuade him that the Turk isn't a useless clockwork toy but a genuinely infallible marvel, the better. Quite apart from the fact that it's time to give that hunchback Knaus a lesson and pay him out for his presumption."

"I can't play," said Tibor.

"Why not?"

"I can't move my arm properly yet. I don't want a repeat of what happened in Vienna."

"It happened because you had to play in the dark, not because of your wound."

"But the danger's there all the same."

Kempelen nodded. "Of course, of course. You're right." He thought for a moment. "I'll get you a doctor as soon as possible. He can tend the wound, stitch it up if necessary, and then you'll heal up faster and be ready to play."

"No," said Tibor, instinctively pulling his shirt collar a little higher, although the dark stitches couldn't be seen through the fresh bandages anyway. "Didn't you say that a doctor—"

"Never fear. I know one I can trust."

"I don't need a doctor."

"Don't be silly, Tibor. Of course you need a doctor. I've resisted the idea for far too long, so don't you suddenly try turning me against it." Kempelen took his quill pen from the inkstand and added a note to a list of some length. "Naturally we won't begin the performances again until the wound is entirely healed." He looked up from his list. "Is there anything else you'd like?"

"Can I have my wages paid?"

Kempelen lowered the pen. "Why? Don't you trust me?"

"Yes, but——"

"If there's anything you need, just tell me or Jakob, and we'll get it for you."

"That's not the point."

"What is the point, then?" Kempelen put the quill back on the inkstand. "If you trust me, there's no reason for your wages to be paid just now. There's nothing for you to spend them on, and they're as safe with me as in any deposit bank. Unless—unless you're planning to leave Pressburg without my knowledge. In that case, I'm damned if I'm giving you the money to do it."

Kempelen looked hard at Tibor, who was fully alert now. His nausea and headache had suddenly disappeared, and even his wound no longer hurt him.

Putting his coffee cup down on the desk in front of him, Tibor said, "Yes, I do want to leave Pressburg. I don't want to serve the Turk anymore. I'm grateful to you for all you've done for me, but I want to leave your service before anything worse happens."

Kempelen did not move for some time, and then he clasped his hands as if in prayer. He kept his gaze bent on Tibor, but he blinked rather frequently, as if something had got into his eyes.

"Do you want higher wages?" he asked at last.

"No. I don't want any more wages at all."

"I understand. So you really do want to give it up." Tibor nodded. "Can you tell me why?"

"I can't stand this life any longer. If I'm not shut up in the machine, I'm shut up in my room. I appreciate your company and Jakob's, but I want to go out again and mix with other people."

"But other people out there mock you and despise you. Have you forgotten?"

"No, but at this moment I'd rather have even their mockery than their absence."

"Perhaps we can find a way to accommodate you somewhere else . . . somewhere you can move about more freely."

"That's not good enough. I don't want to play chess inside that machine either. I can live with operating a device condemned by my Church, I can live with the fear of Andrássy, but I can't live with the guilt of having killed another human being." Tibor looked at Kempelen's sketch of the automaton. "Whenever I see the Turk, even now, it reminds me of the Baroness, and I can't bear it."

For a moment Kempelen looked as if he were going to contradict Tibor, but then he said, "We had an agreement."

"Dock my wages if you think I've broken it," replied Tibor. "Deduct twenty, fifty, a hundred guilders, I don't care. Just leave me enough to keep myself for a week. But I have to go. I'm sorry. I must go. I know I shall be ruined if I stay."

"You'll be ruined if you leave me! I freed you from the leaden chambers in Venice. You were sick, you'd been beaten black and blue, you were on bread and water in a dark cell, in rags that stank of brandy. Do you want to go back there? This house may be a cage, but it's a gilded cage where you lack for nothing."

"I'll never end up again as I did in Venice, God be my witness. And if I do fail, then it will be my last failure in this life."

"Are you feverish?"

"I'd have said all this to you before, if I hadn't been hoping so hard that you'd dismiss me anyway after Vienna."

"You know I can't go on without you."

"Find another chess player. I'll help you look for one, I'll train him. Find someone else like me."

"There isn't anyone else like you. You're unique."

Tibor looked briefly at the desk on which Kempelen's ambitious plans were lying. "I'm sorry. I do have to leave," he insisted.

Kempelen took a deep breath, then leaned back in his chair, arms folded over his chest. "I'm sorry too. Because I have to forbid you to go."

"With respect, *signore,* you can't. I'm a free man."

"You're right, I can't forbid you," Kempelen conceded. "But I could threaten you."

"What with?"

Kempelen smiled sadly. "Oh, Tibor, Tibor. Don't let's get to the point where I have to make threats. For the sake of our friendship."

"What would you threaten me with?"

"Tibor, we don't want to poison our relationship, do we? What a miserable atmosphere there'd be in this house if we were at daggers drawn but still had to work together!"

"What would you threaten me with?" Tibor insisted.

"Very well," sighed Kempelen. "With setting the constabulary on you if you desert, telling them how you first dishonored Ibolya Baroness Jesenák and then murdered her."

"It was an accident!" cried Tibor.

"Not the way I'd tell the story."

Tibor leaped up from his chair. "Then I shall say she wasn't dead yet when you threw her off the balcony!"

"And supposing you were brazen enough to tell such a monstrous lie—which of us would be believed? An Austro-Hungarian baron and royal councilor—or an Italian dwarf whose last known address was a prison cell in the city of Venice?"

Tibor did not reply. He was breathing so heavily that his right lung pressed painfully against the wound.

"You have a choice," said Kempelen, "a choice between me and the gallows. You can go on living comfortably in the automaton—even if you do feel you're a prisoner there—or you can be free. Free and dead."

"Will I get different accommodation, then?"

"No, not anymore. You ought to have accepted that offer when I made it; I've withdrawn it now. I know you want to abscond from Pressburg, so you're staying in this house where I can keep an eye on you. And if you try making plans to escape all the same, I should tell you that the country around Pressburg is densely populated. There are no forests or mountains where you could hide. You'd have no money and no one to help you. And you can't disguise your height. The constables would catch up with you before a day was out."

Tibor felt like going for Kempelen's throat, or better still trampling on the shrouded speaking machine until that unfinished masterpiece lay in splinters. But it would be disastrous to lose physical control of himself. Taking firm hold of the edge of the desk, he managed to contain his fury.

"*Sei il diavolo,*" he hissed.

"*Non è vero,* Tibor. I didn't want to threaten you, I told you I didn't, but you wouldn't listen. You've left me no option. And although you presumably hate me at this moment, you are still very dear to me. The fact that I am getting a doctor for you, despite all the difficulties, ought to prove it."

The two men were silent. Kempelen stood up and passed Tibor, keeping a suitable distance between them, to open the door to the workshop. "Let's bring this unfortunate conversation to an end," he suggested, "before we say even more to damage our friendship."

Tibor left the study, and as soon as Kempelen had closed the door behind him, tears came to his eyes. For a moment he contemplated opening the door to the staircase, leaving Kempelen's house in the clothes he stood up in, and simply walking along beside the Danube until he had left the city behind, just to enjoy the open road and the sky above for a few hours before mounted constables caught up with him, threw him into a dungeon, and then led him to the scaffold. But then he opened the left-hand door after all, the one leading back to his room. To vent his fury, he began tearing up the old bandages. He wished Elise had brought him not one but two bottles of *borovicka* in the night.

CALENDULA OFFICINALIS, *Chamomilla, Salvia officinalis.*

Kempelen glanced fleetingly at the names in careful script labeling the jars of pottery, porcelain, and dark glass. *Verbena hastata, Cannabis sativa, Jasminum officinale, Urtica urens, Rheum, China officinalis.* These medicaments could not be tightly enough sealed inside their containers to keep their aroma from wafting out into the air: dried leaves, flowers, and fruits, powdered roots and bark, pounded minerals and therapeutic earths, tinctures, extracts, potions, oils, and alcohol all mingled in one great, overpowering odor. The dispensary at the Sign of the Red Crab smelled as if a dish consisting entirely of spices had been cooked there. It was not a pleasant aroma. Stegmüller himself had long ago become steeped in the smell of his apothecary's shop, which made people reluctant to share a small space with him. He smelled of medicinal remedies, but because medicinal remedies were used only on the sick, he smelled of sickness too. Stegmüller's attention had been drawn to that fact, but even rosewater and sweet perfumes couldn't drown the odor of the dispensary. They merely added a little more to the cacophony of scents. *Ginseng, Lycopodium clavatum, Camphora, Ammonium carbonicum, Ammonium causticum.* Kempelen opened the jar of liquid ammonia and sniffed it. Its penetrating smell drove his weariness away but struck his sober stomach unpleasantly.

Then Kempelen went around behind the heavy counter to the shelf where minerals were kept: *Zincum metallicum, Mercurius solubilis, Sulphur.* He heard Stegmüller moving on the floor above. It was still early morning. Kempelen had expressly asked the apothecary for a word with him before his employees came to start work at the Red Crab. The shutters were still over the windows, and only two oil lamps lit the dispensary with its black wooden furnishings. *Silicea, Alumina.* The shelf next to the therapeutic earths had a glass front, and the containers on it were much smaller: *Aconitum napellus, Digitalis purpurea, Equisetum arvense, Atropa belladonna.* Kempelen inserted a fingernail under the frame of the glass door and pulled. It wasn't locked, and it opened with a small squeak. There was hardly any smell inside the glass. *Conium maculatum, Hyoscyamus niger.* A floorboard creaked above Kempelen's head. Obviously Stegmüller's search was taking him some time. Kempelen picked up a brown ampoule bearing the inscription *Arsenicum album.* It was closed with a stopper covered with red sealing wax. Kempelen held the little flask up to the light of an oil lamp and tipped the floury powder in it from side to side.

Behind him Stegmüller was running downstairs. With one quick movement Kempelen put the arsenic back on its shelf and closed the glass door. He still had his fingers on the frame as Stegmüller came into the dispensary, and pretended he had merely been wiping some dust off the wood.

"I'd mislaid the powder horn," explained Stegmüller.

The apothecary put the powder horn, a little bag of lead bullets, and his pistol in its case on the counter. Although Stegmüller couldn't possibly smell more strongly of medicaments than his dispensary already did, Kempelen thought that his return had augmented the odor. He took the muzzle loader out of its bag and looked at it.

"It's done me good service," said Stegmüller. "When we were out in the Bohemian Woods once, we were——"

"Can you bring me a lamp? It's so dark here."

"I'll open the shutters. It must be nearly light by now."

"No, I'd rather have the lamp, Georg."

Stegmüller smiled. "Gottfried. Georg was yesterday."

"Of course. Gottfried."

Stegmüller brought two lamps and showed Kempelen how the weapon worked. "You don't have a gun of your own? And yet you've traveled as far as the wilds of Transylvania."

"I have a pistol. Pretty but no practical use to me. Others have done the shooting so far. *Who lives by the sword shall die by the sword.* I'm happy enough to follow that maxim."

"Except that Baron Andrássy obviously lives by maxims very different from ours."

"Yes."

Kempelen cocked the hammer and let it snap back again.

"If you want to practice with it," said the apothecary, "I know a piece of land near Theben area where we'd be undisturbed."

"I still have no intention of fighting a duel with Andrássy. But if he attacks me or mine another time, I don't want to be empty-handed again."

"Keep it until you don't need it anymore."

"Thank you."

"Now, about your dwarf. Where exactly is the wound? And what state is he in?"

While Kempelen replied, Stegmüller was laying out instruments, medicine, and bandages on his counter, then packed them into a bag.

"You ought to have sent for me while you were in Vienna," he said,

when Kempelen had finished. "That kind of thing can have fatal consequences."

Kempelen put the pistol back in its case. "Did you follow Jakob a few
times, as we agreed?"

"Yes, but he's harmless. Always in some tavern or other, but that won't
interest you. He drinks a lot for a Jew, doesn't he? By rights he ought not
to touch wine."

"What about my maid?"

"Pretty Elise? I can't find anything wrong with her. She turns the
young fellows' heads when she goes to market . . . but she's probably waiting for some knight in shining armor to come along." Stegmüller grinned
at Kempelen, who did not react. "She went to the post office once, but she
didn't hand anything in or take anything away."

"She's probably expecting a letter from her aunt. Or her godparents in
Ödenburg."

"Are she and the Jew romantically involved?"

"Definitely not. She's almost as Catholic as Tibor—she'll be doing all
she can to avoid Jakob. Thank you for your help."

Stegmüller put his hand on Kempelen's. "Your friendship is thanks
enough, Wolfgang," he said. "That and my forthcoming admission to the
Purity Lodge as an apprentice."

Stegmüller put his bag over his shoulder while Kempelen picked up
the pistol, the powder horn, and the lead bullets.

"And you remember," said Kempelen, "not a word to anyone—"

"This true apothecary would swallow his own poison sooner!" said
Stegmüller, tapping his knuckles on the glass door behind which the
arsenic and other poisonous drugs were kept.

ELISE IMMEDIATELY recognized the false Franciscan whom she had followed to the apothecary's shop near the tower of St. Michael's. Kempelen
now introduced him to her as Dr. Jungjahr. Jungjahr—or the Honorable
Gottfried von Rotenstein, for she had found out his name—greeted her
by kissing her hand. Kempelen, who was treating Elise as if nothing had

happened between them the day before, asked her to make some coffee. The men took it up to the workshop, and Kempelen told Elise not to disturb them for the next few hours.

Tibor, however, did not recognize Stegmüller as the priest who had once heard his confession. The apothecary asked Kempelen to bring him a stool, and he sat down beside Tibor's bed, while the Baron stood by the table watching everything. Kempelen was acting to Tibor as if nothing had happened between the two of them either, as if their quarrel had never taken place. He spoke to Tibor in tones as friendly as Stegmüller's, taking care to appear cheerful. Stegmüller asked Tibor to remove his shirt. He was surprised to see a little network of black stitching over the wound and looked inquiringly at Kempelen.

"Who put those stitches in?" asked Kempelen.

"I did it myself," replied Tibor, taking care to let no defiance enter his voice.

Stegmüller examined both the wound and the stitches and nodded appreciatively. "That's good work. Primitive, but good. Where did you learn how to do it?"

"In the war."

"The wound was inflamed, but the inflammation is already dying down," said Stegmüller, more to Kempelen than to Tibor. "There's not much left for me to do."

"Why didn't you tell me?" asked Kempelen in a considerably sterner voice.

"I never said I needed a doctor," replied Tibor. "I just told you I can't play chess anymore."

Kempelen nodded to Stegmüller, who cleaned the edges of the wound again, applied some ointment, and put on a new bandage. As he worked, Tibor looked keenly at the supposed doctor, while Kempelen himself was watching Tibor. Neither said anything, and there would have been total silence in the room except that Stegmüller talked to himself as he worked.

At the Sign of the Golden Rose

TIBOR SAW THE BIRDS IN THE SKY FROM HIS LITTLE WINdow. Judging by their cries, they were geese. If he cupped his hands behind his ears and closed his eyes, he could even hear their wing beats. The wedge of the flock in flight was so perfectly shaped that its sides could have been drawn with a ruler. Each bird seemed to preserve the same distance between itself and the bird in front, and when the leader flapped its wings, the wing beat appeared to run on through both ranks like a rippling wave. Perhaps Descartes was right: God was a magnificent engineer, and these creatures were nothing but machines, *perpetua mobilia*, driven by springs and moved by cogwheels—for no human being, not even the best soldier on the parade ground, was capable of such perfection. Man's mind would always prevent him from achieving it. These birds might be as stupid as clockwork, but they were as regular as clockwork too. Tibor thought of the artificial duck created by the French automaton maker, which he had seen in pictures. It could walk, peck up oats, and digest them, but it could not fly, for its plumage was heavy iron instead of lightweight horn. Did Vaucanson's duck regret its inability to fly south in the autumn with its flesh-and-blood counterparts? When Tibor looked up again, the formation of geese was gone, and he saw only the gray sky.

The weather had changed within a day. The sultry heat gave way to damp, cold, rainy weather, as if August had jumped straight to October, forgetting September entirely. Tibor's mood had changed just as quickly: his happiness after his encounter with Elise—the similarity of their stories, her friendly manner, most of all her loving care and that final kiss—had lasted only half a day. In the two days after his quarrel with Kempelen he was overcome by a lethargy he had never known before. He spent his time lying on his bed, idle but not asleep, and if he had to do something—for instance eat, drink, or obey the call of nature—he did it mechanically, just as his wound was healing up of its own accord and without any effort on his part. He didn't want to work at the unfinished clockwork on his table anymore. Now and then he picked up a book, but it was pointless, for he read the lines without paying any attention to them. Even thinking was difficult. He had to force himself to do it.

In the few moments when he was really awake, however, he knew that this paralysis would not last. Presumably his body and mind were gathering energy for something yet to come. What it was Tibor didn't know. He would let it surprise him and everyone else too.

KEMPELEN GAVE Jakob and Tibor the task of renovating the chess automaton thoroughly, repairing the damage caused by Andrássy's attack and Tibor's own chaotic play in the grounds of Schönbrunn Palace. Kempelen himself was in the Royal Chamber all that day and had said he was going to a meeting of his Freemasons' Lodge afterward. Tibor was glad of his absence. By now the dwarf had learned enough about precision engineering to help Jakob with the repairs. After a few hours of work, Jakob fitted a new veneer of grained wood to the part of the door through which the shot had passed, and their work was done.

"You're so quiet," remarked Jakob, although he had been even more silent himself that morning. "It's a long time since the two of us went out on the town. I haven't had a really thick head for ages. Let's go for a drink again tonight—what do you say?"

"Kempelen will be here."

"We'll smuggle you past him somehow. Come along, we'll find our-selves a couple of girls, a Jewish girl and a Catholic girl; a Sarah for me and a Maria for you."

"No," said Tibor. "I don't want to."

"Don't pretend to me. You're not allowed to, that's what it is."

"Jakob, I simply don't feel like it."

"You're afraid of Kempelen," said Jakob, unthinkingly poking him in his bandaged right shoulder. "He's putting pressure on you over that Ibolya business. I might have known it. On the surface it looks as if her death was damaging to him—the questions the clerics asked, that lunatic Hungarian—but the fact is, he's turning it to his advantage. Because your guilt means he can control you as long as he likes."

"What nonsense you talk," said Tibor gruffly, beginning to clear the tools away.

But he wasn't stopping Jakob that way. The Jew went on, raising his voice. "After the Turk's first performance he was in your hands; now it's the other way around. Ibolya's death was very convenient for him. You two are like the Pressburg sisters—did I ever tell you about the Pressburg sisters? Now that's a strange story, if you like!"

"I'm not interested."

"They've been dead twenty years or so. Twins they were, sisters who'd been stuck together since birth by their backs, just as if a can of glue had spilled inside their mother's womb. The Ursuline convent took them in. Scientists came from as far away as Passau to examine the children who'd grown together, but no physician dared to cut them apart. They were in-separably linked forever. So the two of them grew up, and one was larger and stronger than the other. The sisters often quarreled, especially in their youth. And when they couldn't agree on where they were going, the big one just bent her back so that the little one's feet couldn't touch the ground and marched off, taking her scolding sister with her. That's what you and Kempelen are like." Tibor went on clearing the workshop in si-lence, while Jakob stared thoughtfully at the ceiling. "Now, what became of the pair of them? I think . . . I think the little one died, and less than a day later the big one was dead too. Or was it the other way around? A pity, really, or we could take them out tonight. I'd carry you on my back, you could have the little sister and I'd have the big one . . . well, never mind that. Do you see what I'm getting at?"

Tibor was standing by the workbench with his back to Jakob and didn't reply. Jakob picked up a piece of wood left over after the repairs and threw it at Tibor's head.

"Hey, Alberich, talk to me!"

Tibor slowly turned and rubbed the back of his head where the wood had hit it.

"Will you tear yourself away from Kempelen and come to the Rose with me?"

"Everything's always so easy for you," said Tibor. "Everything's just a joke to you. Women and wine and looking good, that's all that you think matters. I could die soon, but it doesn't seem to bother you."

"Not in the least! If you're going to die soon, it's all the more important for you to enjoy life now!" Tibor turned away again, but Jakob was going on. "For heaven's sake, you think so much of tomorrow that you forget about today. You even try to make plans for your life after death. How disappointed you'll be when you do die—which I promise you won't be for a long time yet—and you find out that there isn't any life after death, and you've wasted all that time and trouble."

"One more insult to my faith, and I'm leaving the room."

"Is that supposed to be a threat? *I'm leaving the room!* My word, you terrify me. Oh pray, don't on any account leave the room, I beg you on my bended knees! What have your faith and your glorious Mother of God ever done for you except pester you all your life, and finally they land you in this infernal mess?"

Tibor was as good as his word and prepared to stomp back to his room, but Jakob crossed the workshop and stood in front of the door, barring his way. "Do you know who you remind me of?" Jakob asked him.

"I'm not interested."

"Guess."

"I said I'm not interested. Let me by."

"You remind me of the Tibor I first met in this very place nine months ago: a scared little crosspatch who couldn't take a joke, who hit out with his little Catholic hands and feet at everything that makes life worth living."

"And you remind me of the shallow, selfish Yid who doesn't care a bit for other people's feelings and drives his fellow men frantic with his stupid chatter! Let me into my room."

Jakob stepped aside and let Tibor pass.

"For the last time," he said, "are we going out for a drink tonight?"

"No."

"Then I'll ask Elise."

Tibor had almost closed the door behind him. Now he spun around. "You won't."

Jakob raised an eyebrow, surprised by Tibor's violent reaction. "Oho," he said. "Jealous?"

"Find other girls to play about with," Tibor told him. "There are plenty in town. She deserves better."

"Does she, indeed? And that means—*you*?"

"Not you, anyway."

"Have you been discussing it with her? Are the pair of you by any chance meeting on the sly?"

"No," lied Tibor.

"Then perhaps you ought to sometime. Yes, I know Kempelen's forbidden it. But her company is very, very invigorating." Jakob assumed a knowing expression. "Undoubtedly more invigorating than just staring at her out of your little window when she hangs out the washi ιg. And then you might find out that she doesn't entirely fit the idea you seem to have of her. By the way, she smells delicious."

Tibor said nothing. He reached for the doorknob.

"Will you come if she comes?" Jakob asked for the last time. "Just the three of us. We'll kiss her on the right cheek and the left cheek with the city at our feet, a merry, tipsy cloverleaf. A trio of Little, Pretty, and Jew!"

Jakob managed to snatch his hand away from the door frame just before Tibor slammed the door hard behind him. His mocking smile lingered on his face for some time. When he caught himself grinning like that, although he was alone in the room and did not in fact feel at all like smiling, his features relaxed. The Turk wasn't good enough company for him. He picked up his coat and left the workshop and the house.

Jakob's legs took him to Michaelerstrasse faster than necessary, so that in spite of the cool weather, heat was rising to his face as he stood outside the Palais where the Royal Chamber was housed. He looked up past all three stories to the gable with the Hungarian emblem and the two white statues of Justice and Law above it. Then he went into the building, introducing himself to the porter as a colleague of Councilor von Kempelen's. A clerk with a bob wig was sent up to Kempelen's office. A little later he came back, asking Jakob to follow him. They climbed white marble steps covered with red carpet runners to the third floor. All the men they met greeted them politely and were so finely dressed that Jakob felt ashamed of his plain coat and linen pantaloons. Going down a corridor, the two of them reached Kempelen's office. The clerk knocked on the door, and Kempelen told them to come in.

"Jakob," he said, with an expression of pleasure, rising from his desk. "What a delightful surprise!" He shook his assistant's hand as if he hadn't seen him for weeks. "Bring us some lemonade, Jan. My assistant looks thirsty."

The clerk bowed, left the office walking backward, and closed the door behind him. Only then did Kempelen's smile disappear.

"What's happened? Tibor?"

Jakob shook his head. "I have to talk to you."

"Now? Here?"

"You know me. I'm impetuous. I want to get this off my chest."

Kempelen offered Jakob a chair on the other side of his desk. The room was richly furnished in the French style. The tower of the Town Hall could be seen through the tall windows, and where the walls were not hidden by shelves of files, maps of the Banat and Hungary covered them.

"Well?"

"Perhaps it really is Tibor," admitted Jakob. "He doesn't want to play chess anymore. He's exhausted and he's wounded. We ought to let him go before he dies on us."

"Your sympathy does you credit, but it seems to me that Tibor is well able to speak for himself. And he and I have agreed to continue as before."

The clerk brought in a tray with a jug of lemonade and two glasses.

"I should really be serving champagne," said Kempelen. "It's a year almost to the day since you began working for me. How time flies!"

He undertook to pour the lemonade, and the clerk left them alone. Kempelen handed Jakob a glass. "To the year that's just past and the year to come."

"Is it to be another year we spend together, then?" asked Jakob.

"Why, yes! Why not?"

"Because I'm beginning to get bored. I'm a number of things— carver, automaton builder, watchmaker—but not a showman. I've spent the last few months doing nothing but pushing the chess-playing Turk around, winding up the fake clockwork, and looking portentous as I bring out a casket that contains nothing but tools. Just now, while we were repairing the machine, I realized how much I miss my real work."

"Do you want higher wages?"

"Everyone wants higher wages. But most of all I want new work to do. Let me build another android. Let's have a different figure instead of the Turk. Or let me build a body for your speaking machine."

"No. The speaking machine doesn't need any stupid dummy. It will shine for its abilities, not its looks."

"Well, if you have no work for me . . . then I'll have to go looking for some myself. If only to get away from the graveyard atmosphere in your house these days."

"Where will you go?"

Jakob shrugged. "To Ofen . . . back to Prague . . . Kraków or Munich . . ."

"You left out Vienna."

"Very well: or Vienna."

A gray pigeon landed on a windowsill, began to coo, turned its head, and looked through the glass. It felt silent. With quick little movements of its head, it inspected the two men. Suddenly it flew away again as if something had alarmed it.

"The Viennese makers of clockwork devices," said Kempelen, "and Friedrich Knaus in particular, if you happen to have been thinking of him, will take you on not because you're a gifted craftsman but because you've worked for me. They'll want to worm the secret of the way the Turk operates out of you."

"I won't tell them. I'm loyal."

"They'll offer you a great deal of money."

"I can't be bought."

"Don't pretend to me and yourself. Everyone can be bought. It just depends how much for."

"I'll be loyal to you. Tibor is my friend. I won't give him away. I swear I'll take what I know to the grave with me, but that oath is all I can give you."

Kempelen sighed. He put one arm on the desk, palm upward. "Jakob, I need you."

"But not as a furniture mover. That's no fun anymore."

"The . . . fun you mention disappeared the day you failed to do your duty, and Baroness Jesenák was able to get at the automaton after the performance without anyone to stop her."

Jakob stared at the ceiling. "I suppose you're going to reproach me with that forever."

"Because it leaves me under suspicion forever myself. You bear some of the responsibility for her death. So now that you've made our bed, you must lie on it too."

"Of course. By all means! But not traveling the country with your damn automaton!" cried Jakob, sitting up very straight in his chair.

Kempelen put his forefinger to his lips and then pointed to the door to make Jakob lower his voice.

"Let's stop now and just enjoy our fame!" Jakob went on, more quietly. "It's only a question of time before Tibor's discovered. Someone will hide and watch us dismantling the Turk. Your servants will be bribed. That deranged Hungarian will start firing pistols about the place again and put a bullet through Tibor's head. Say someone shouts *Fire!*— and everyone, Tibor included, runs from the hall to escape . . . there are so many things that could happen, so many loopholes. All this nonsense can't go well in the end."

"I don't agree."

Jakob looked at the Town Hall tower. The bell was striking five, and he waited until it had finished. "Then much as I regret it, I'm leaving Pressburg," he said.

"Are you trying to blackmail me?"

Jakob shook his head. Then he rose to his feet. "The machine is in perfect order again. The show at the Italian Theater is far enough off for you to find a replacement for me, if you really need one. I'll happily train him if you want me to. I'd like the rest of my wages paid up to the end of the week. This last year in your service has been a pleasure, Herr von Kempelen. And thank you for the lemonade."

Kempelen rose too, frowning. "So you're abandoning Tibor? Now that he's injured and has no one but you? Tibor, who's always been able to depend on your friendship and your care of him? Can you reconcile that with your conscience?"

"Only partly. But if that's your final attempt to keep me with you, it makes me even more certain that the only decision I can make is to leave," retorted Jakob. He bowed slightly and left the office.

He walked away from the Royal Chamber, striding fast and making for St. Michael's Gate, which was not the way he meant to go. He just wanted to get out of sight of the Palais as quickly as possible, in case Kempelen was watching him from the window. He turned into Schnee-weissgasse, and only there did he slow down, among all the citizens going home from work or crowding into the inns. Jakob stopped outside Haber-mayer the tobacconist's shop and stared at the window, not because he was interested in the many pipes on display but to think about what he had done and what he was going to do next. He didn't want to be on his own just now, but it was still too early for the tavern.

So he returned to Donaugasse in the hope of finding Elise there.

Someone ought to reward him for his heroism in giving in his notice, and if he really had only a few more days to spend in Pressburg, it was time to share a bed with her again. The first time had been wonderful. She had been much more reticent about it than Constanze, but perhaps that was the really wonderful part. That and the suspicion that he might have been her first man.

Elise wasn't in the Kempelen house anymore. It stood there gray and empty as dusk fell. With its barred and bricked-up windows and closed shutters, it looked like an abandoned citadel. Tibor and the Turk were the only occupants at the moment, each of them as silent as the other. But Jakob didn't want to give up the prospect of Elise now—after all, as he walked back he had been imagining what it would be like to undress her and make love to her—so he turned his steps to Spitalgasse, where she lived.

The eight rooms in the Spitalgasse house were all let to maidservants working for the lower ranks of the nobility and the upper middle class. Jakob had been here once before and had enjoyed it, for most of the maids were even younger than Elise, and Jakob had greeted them warmly and heard them giggling behind his back. The landlady was the widow Gschweng, a real dragon who insisted on order and decorum and would have frowned severely on any male visitors. But Jakob saw it as a challenge to get past her, and he had managed it on that first occasion as easily as he did now. He knocked at Elise's door on the first floor, and she opened it. She looked even more surprised than Kempelen had been—positively distraught, in fact. Jakob smiled.

"What are you doing here?" she snapped. "Go away before the old woman finds you!"

"May I come in?"

"Certainly not!"

"Then I'll plant my posterior on this step," said Jakob, suiting the action to the word. "I'll wait until you do let me in, and I just hope you'll have changed your mind before the terrible widow comes this way." And he began to sing at the top of his voice. It echoed up and down the little stairwell.

Margret's the girl who taps the cask to draw the finest ale in town
And lovely Meg will treat you kindly while you drink it down.
A linden tree stands at the door, that's where the amber ale she'll pour . . .

Elise sighed and opened the door fully. Jakob jumped up and entered the room, and even as Elise was closing the door and turning the key in the lock, he was taking off his coat.

"What's your idea?" she asked. "What do you want?"

"You," he said, "you and none but you, Elise."

"Are you out of your mind?"

"Oh yes, the moment I set eyes on you."

Jakob put a hand to the back of her neck and stroked the downy hairs there. Elise ducked away from his touch. "Please don't do that," she said rather more gently.

"Why not? Don't you like it?"

"I have to work."

"No, you don't. Nor do I. Let's enjoy ourselves this evening."

"You frighten me."

Jakob took a step toward her and kissed her. She could feel his stiff prick through the fabric of her dress. As she didn't return the kiss, Jakob let her go of his own accord.

"Kiss me," he said.

"No. Please go away now, Jakob."

Jakob dropped onto her bed. "You said you'd kiss me if I told you the secret of the chess machine. Now I'm going to tell you, and then you'll kiss me. That's the bargain."

"You've fobbed me off with a tall tale twice, and I'm not interested any longer."

"I'll tell you the truth this time. Look at me."

She didn't look at him. "I don't care about it now, Jakob."

"Look at me!" But her face was still averted. "Inside the chess automaton . . . there's a dwarf! A tiny but very clever little dwarf works the machine from inside. And that's the truth, so help me God. My God and your God. I'll show you the dwarf if you like."

Elise kept still.

"Give me my kiss," said Jakob. He was still smiling, but the smile had disappeared from his voice.

"Will you go if I do?"

"Yes."

She went up to him where he sat on the bed. He raised his face to her. She kissed him, and this time it was the kind of kiss that Jakob wanted. Afterward he held her by the arm.

"Do you want Kempelen for yourself?" he asked.

Elise narrowed her eyes as if she had not understood the question. "You promised to go."

"Let me ask again: do you want Kempelen?"

"No."

"I'm not a fool, Elise. I can see through people. Him. You. You've been trying to make him fall madly in love with you lately. And of course I'm a nuisance."

"Let go of my arm."

"It's nothing new. Heaven knows how many noble gentlemen have affairs with their pretty maidservants because their lawful wedded wives have turned into unattractive battle-axes."

"You're talking nonsense."

"Why did he send Anna Maria off to Gomba? Why hasn't he been to see her there for months? And why do I find you shedding crocodile tears in the kitchen on the day she leaves?"

Jakob pulled her arm roughly, forcing her down on the bed beside him, and before she could stop him, he put a hand on her rounded belly under her full-skirted dress. She felt the warm pressure of his fingers on her abdominal wall and sensed the unborn baby's joints giving way under it. "And whose child are you expecting if it isn't his?"

Elise turned pale. She had stopped defending herself now.

"What do you hope to get out of this?" asked Jakob. "Do you really think he'll leave his wife and you'll be the new Frau von Kempelen? Or are you planning to spend the rest of your days as his lover, his *maîtresse en titre*, the mother of his bastard, hoping that he'll find you desirable for

a few more years yet and pay your rent for you? For your information—
not that I want to alarm you, and not that it has anything to do with
this—his last mistress is feeding the worms in St. John's churchyard
now." Jakob stood up. She still had not said anything. "But I don't suppose you've thought about it at all. You just said to yourself: better a
baron who's a royal councilor than a circumcised woodcarver without any
pedigree. You're very pretty, Elise, but very stupid too."

"Get out," said Elise.

Jakob took his coat off the hook. "Damn it, I wouldn't stay even if you
begged me to!"

Outside, he hunched his head down against the rain until he noticed
that no rain was falling, although it had looked as if it would all day.
Within a few hours he had spoken his mind to Tibor, Kempelen, and
Elise, and he felt both relieved and bad about it. He just had to follow
Spitalgasse, and it would take him straight to the Fischplatz, for it was
high time to go and drink in the Golden Rose until Constanze turned him
out. And if she wanted, and if the state he was in by then permitted, he'd
take her home with him and do to her what he would much rather have
done to Elise. He struck up his song again.

> *Last night I couldn't sleep at all, I felt so sad and wan.*
> *I went off to the linden tree, my sadness was all gone!*
> *The moon shone down so clear and bright, Margret took pity on my*
> > *plight,*
> *Meg of the linden tree!*

NEXT DAY, a Thursday, Jakob did not arrive as he should have done to
rehearse with the chess machine. Kempelen gave Tibor the day off and
said they'd catch up with the rehearsal later. Very likely Jakob had drunk
too freely of the St. George grape yesterday evening. Kempelen himself
seemed tired. He hadn't come home from a Lodge meeting until late at
night.

Jakob didn't come back to the workshop on Friday either. At midday

Tibor knocked on the door of Kempelen's study to discuss his absence. Kempelen was wearing his riding boots. He looked even paler than the day before. A pistol in its case lay on the table, along with bullets and powder. Tibor asked Kempelen to send a messenger to Jakob's room in Judengasse or go there himself, in case Jakob was sick or needed help for any other reason. Kempelen sighed and asked Tibor to sit down.

"I'm afraid he's not there anymore."

"What do you mean?"

"You know he was thinking of leaving Pressburg?"

"But not so suddenly."

"How can one ever tell with a man like Jakob? But I'm surprised myself, because he wanted to collect his wages. On the other hand, it's often said that Jews travel light."

"I don't think he's gone."

"Tibor, I'm sorry too. But we'll both have to get used to the idea. He wanted something new to do. If he doesn't come back within the week, I'll look around for a replacement."

Tibor did not reply. He looked gloomily at a map of the countryside near Pressburg and wished there was a pin in the paper to tell him where Jakob was now.

"I'm going out for a ride," said Kempelen.

"Where to?"

"Nowhere. I just need some fresh air and a few trees and fields around me." And as if by way of explanation, he added, "Autumn is on its way."

He rose to his feet and put the holster of the pistol into his belt. Seeing Tibor's inquiring glance at the gun, he smiled. "If I happen to meet Baron Andrássy, I'll take revenge for his attack on us."

From his room Tibor watched Kempelen saddle his black horse. Then he went to the workshop windows and saw him already galloping down the street leading out of town. Tibor waited for quarter of an hour, then fetched his key and went down to the ground floor. He found Elise in the laundry room. His heart contracted painfully at the sight of her, and the fingers holding his key went damp.

"Tibor." She smiled in relief and let the linen she was holding fall into the laundry basket. For a moment she stood still; then she knelt down and embraced him. He closed his eyes, drew her scent deep into his lungs, and hoped she wouldn't hear how heavily he was breathing. He wanted to return her embrace but left his arms hanging by his sides as if he were paralyzed.

"I'm sorry," she said, when she had moved away from him again, "but I just felt like it."

Tibor nodded. She got to her feet, so that Tibor had to look up at her.

"I'm worried about Jakob," he said. "Do you know anything about him?"

She shook her head. "I last saw him when he left the workshop on Wednesday. Perhaps he's left Pressburg."

"I'm going to look for him."

"Good," she said. "How is your wound doing?"

"It will heal up. You did very careful work on it. I told the doctor I'd stitched the wound myself, and he was full of praise."

"Tibor . . . that wasn't a doctor."

"What?"

"It was the apothecary from the Red Crab, Gottfried von Rotenstein. And it was the same man pretending to be a monk . . . that time after the Baroness died. His habit was the only genuine thing about him."

"How do you know?"

"I've seen him. Kempelen was lying to you."

"Yes," said Tibor quietly. "And who knows how often? Maybe even more frequently than I've lied to him."

They were both silent, until Tibor moved. "I must go out."

"Be careful."

Tibor took his stiltlike shoes and the frock coat from his wardrobe, so as to make himself taller again and attract no notice out in the streets.

TIBOR KNOCKED, but there was no reply. He entered Jakob's room, using the key left under the roof tile as usual. He had hoped either to find him asleep or to step into a room with nothing in it except the furniture. But both hopes were disappointed: the bed was empty and unmade, and the table, chairs, and floor were as untidy as ever, covered with sketches, unfinished carvings, tools, and remains of food—bread, sausage, apples, a bottle of wine. Jakob wasn't there, but he hadn't gone away either. Tibor left the room and put the key back. As he went down the narrow stairs, the built-up shoes pinched his feet painfully again.

The old Jewish junk dealer couldn't help Tibor either. He had last seen Jakob days ago but promised to keep his eyes open. Krakauer invited Tibor into his warm shop for a juniper schnapps, a game of chess, or both, but he declined with thanks.

He remembered that Jakob had meant to visit the Golden Rose, so he went off to the Fischplatz. The tavern wasn't open yet, but the bald landlord let him in. The two barmaids were cleaning the tables. Recognizing Tibor, red-haired Constanze asked the landlord to let her take a short break, and joined him at the corner table that he had shared with Jakob before.

Yes, she said, Jakob had indeed been to the Golden Rose. He had spent several hours drinking there and left the tavern long after midnight— "on his own, in a turban, and rolling drunk."

"In a turban?" asked Tibor.

Constanze smiled. "Oh, he's such a joker! You should just have seen him here!"

Jakob had entered the Golden Rose in a bad temper, Tibor learned, and drank his first two glasses of St. George alone, although the tavern was full of fishermen, soldiers, and craftsmen, some of whom he knew. A hatmaker's journeyman had noticed Jakob and sat down at his table, where he was joined by many other journeymen and apprentices from the south of the city. They wanted Jakob to tell them about the "miraculous Turk," and he went along with them, on condition they would buy the rest of his drinks. Then he told them his stories—tales of the fame of the Turk, its matches against Mayor Windisch and the Empress—and his temper improved with every word he spoke and every sip of wine. A baker's stammering apprentice, whose master had attended one of the performances at Kempelen's house, said that the Turk's glass eyes couldn't be distinguished from real eyes, whereupon Jakob set him right: the eyes weren't glass at all, he said, they *were* real, for even the most ingenious machine couldn't see with eyes made of glass. Last year, he went on, when the angry inhabitants of a hamlet at St. Peter's in the Lower Carpathians strung up two members of a band of murderous robbers on an oak tree at a crossroads, Kempelen and he, Jakob, had removed the hanged men's eyes from their sockets before they were pecked out by hungry crows. Later they had glazed the eyes with sugar to preserve their shape and color, then pressed them into the Turk's skull. This account had frightened and sickened half his hearers but amused the other half, so Jakob went on to describe how he and Kempelen had gone out into graveyards by night with lanterns and shovels, looking for a suitable left hand for the Turk. But they had found nothing except some bones from which they carved their chessmen, painting the red pieces with their own blood. Finally, he said, Kempelen bought the hand they needed from an executioner who had cut it off a thief with a long record of crime. They had animated the eyes and the hand by the power of animal magnetism, but all other parts of the Turk, Jakob assured his audience in conclusion, were carved from ordinary wood.

When the subject of the mysterious death of Baroness Jesenák was broached, Jakob had offered to act out the incident. A coat to serve as a caftan was quickly found. A dishcloth had been wrapped around Jakob's head for a turban, and a moustache was drawn above his mouth with a piece of charcoal from the hearth. Jakob took off his spectacles. His companions had cleared the jugs and glasses from the table in front of him and put a chessboard there instead, adding a cushion and placing a pipe in his hand, so Jakob played the part of the Turk. By now he had attracted the attention of the entire company in the Rose. Constanze, the other barmaid, and the landlord himself had stopped work too, to be entertained by Jakob. He had made a few moves, caricaturing the android's behavior: its rigid bearing, its jerky, mechanical movements, the rolling of its eyes. He had berated the guests in the tavern in a heavy Oriental accent, mangling his grammar, and threatened to eat their children and abduct their wives to enjoy them at leisure in his seraglio, whence their shrill screams of ecstasy would be heard all the way to Austria. The tavern roared with laughter.

Then the artificial Turk had ordered a date schnapps and some figs to fill his automatic belly, and the landlord had brought him some Tokay on the house. Jakob had taken a sip and spat it out at once, right into an apprentice's face, saying no wonder the infidels couldn't fight if they drank such sweetened, perfumed water, like women. Loud protests were heard in the crowd. A hussar said that the Turks had been driven out of Hungary long ago and would soon be expelled from the whole continent with a well-placed kick up the backside. The audience had applauded, but Jakob picked up one of the chess pieces and threw it at the soldier's head—whereupon, to much cheering, he began a positive bombardment of all the guests, until all his thirty-two shots had been fired. Then he called for a sacrifice. The other barmaid had slipped away just in time, to shelter behind the landlord's back, so the Turk's stiff finger pointed at Constanze. She had tried to run away too, but several journeymen caught hold of her and, in defiance of all her shrieking and struggling, carried her to the Turk's sacrificial altar. Jakob had begun groping her, feeling her head, and running his hands over her breasts and thighs, all with the same mechanical movements and stiff mimicry, bringing tears of laughter to the spectators' eyes. Constanze herself giggled and screamed by turn. Then Jakob had kissed her, and for a moment Constanze could relax. The hubbub died down a little, and some of the audience, much moved, sighed, "Oh!" One guest even said, "He's in love." "Baroness taste good," Jakob the Turk had declared, "but now must kill!" And he had put his hands around Constanze's neck to throttle her. She played along, no longer giggling but breathing stertorously, and when Jakob had shouted, "Check to the queen!" she sank down on the table, her limbs hanging limp, her tongue sticking out of the corner of her mouth as she rolled her eyes. Jakob had closed her eyelids, saying, "Baroness checkmate." The applause for this performance had been deafening, and Jakob and Constanze were the hero and heroine of the hour. Afterward Jakob had been plied with far more liquor than he could drink—and certainly more than he could hold.

"He kept that turban on, and he still had the charcoal moustache too when he left," said Constanze. "That was a very drunk Turk who left us late at night."

Tibor thanked the barmaid for her information, not that it got him any further. Constanze promised to tell Jakob that "Herr Neumann" had been looking for him if he turned up in the next few days.

Outside by the Plague Column, Tibor stopped to think for a moment. Even if Jakob had collapsed in a niche among the buildings or a hedge somewhere, dead drunk, he would have slept off his hangover by now. Kempelen would be home from his ride before it was dark, and Tibor ought to be back in Donaugasse by then. But he didn't feel it was enough to have told Krakauer and Constanze to give Jakob news of him, so he decided to go back to Judengasse and leave a note in Jakob's room.

His hope that by now Jakob himself might be home was dashed. Looking for a blank piece of paper so that he could write his note, Tibor found on the floor a charcoal drawing of a woman whom he instantly recognized as Elise. He sat down on a chair for a moment to look at the portrait. Jakob was not a brilliant draftsman; it was the model who was brilliant. He would ask Jakob if he could have the drawing. Then his eye fell on an unfinished bust in pale yew wood, standing near the window. Once again Tibor recognized it as Elise, and Jakob had made the carving so true to life that he hadn't even improved upon her little imperfections—the right-hand corner of her mouth that was a little higher than the other, for instance, or the scar on her forehead. Had Elise modeled for him? Maybe in this very place? Maybe even naked?

Work on her face seemed to be completed, but the hair was still sketchy and unfinished. A carver's knife was rammed into the back of the wooden head. Tibor pulled it out, leaving an ugly hole shaped like a half-moon. Tibor hoped the injury would disappear when Jakob carved the hair properly.

The bust on its plinth was level with Tibor's face. He ran his fingers over the wood, tracing the lines of the face, the mouth, the nose, the eyes, and the brows over them. Then he let his fingertips stray to her lips. He could feel the wood gradually warming up in contact with his skin. He took the face in both hands, closed his eyes, and pressed a kiss on the wooden mouth, firmly enough to feel its warmth but too lightly to feel how hard it was.

The door to the stairwell was opened. In his alarm, Tibor knocked the bust over. He heard steps in the passage outside, and then the door to Jakob's room was opened too. Tibor wondered whether Jakob would still have his turban on, and caught himself up, realizing that this was a ridiculous notion—and sure enough, Jakob was not wearing a turban anymore when he entered the room. But it wasn't Jakob either. It was Kempelen.

The two men looked at each other. Kempelen blinked, for in addition to the surprise of finding Tibor here at all, there was the fact that with his built-up shoes he was at least a head taller than usual. In his free hand Kempelen held a set of skeleton keys, none of which he had used, for Tibor had left the door unlocked. Kempelen's hair was windblown, and the ride had brought some color to his face.

Tibor put the bust back in its place again, but so that Elise's face was turned away from Kempelen.

"Aha," said Kempelen.

"I was worried about Jakob," explained Tibor. "I went looking for him."

"Yes." Kempelen entered the room and closed the door behind him. "Did you find him?"

Tibor shook his head.

"You've grown," remarked Kempelen, pointing to Tibor's elongated legs.

"I don't want to be noticed in the street."

"No. Ingenious."

"I'm only going to write Jakob a note, and then I'll go."

"No, go now," said Kempelen. "I'll write the note. Unless—unless you want to tell him something that I wouldn't."

Tibor looked hard at Kempelen, and then, very slowly, shook his head.

"Good. Walk fast, don't go through the city, and enter the house by the back door. You're putting yourself in danger, but if you're clever about it, no one will ever know." Kempelen observed Tibor's practiced gait in the stilt-like shoes and added, "Impressive. Is this the first time you've been out?"

"Yes," said Tibor.

"We'll discuss it further at home."

Tibor left. Kempelen waited a minute, then pushed the back of a chair under the door latch to keep it closed. He took off his coat, laid it on the chair with the skeleton keys, and then began searching the room from wall to wall. He examined every letter, every sketch, every journal, all Jakob's tools, even his clothes and the menorah with candle wax all over it. After inspecting anything he put it neatly on the bed, so that the room was getting tidier by the minute. He left the clothes inside the wardrobe but searched all the drawers and their undersides.

In the pale yellow close-fitting coat that Jakob had last worn at Schönbrunn, Kempelen found a folded piece of paper. Unfolding it, he read out loud the three lines on it. *"Jakob Wachsberger, écrit à Vienne, le 14ᵉ août 1770."*

Kempelen frowned. *Le 14ᵉ août 1770.* August 14 was the day when they had played against the Empress. He read the words again. The distance between the characters was the same, and the letters resembled one another. Every one of the six letters *e* was identical with its brothers in every respect.

"That's not Jakob's writing," he said to himself. "So measured . . . so mechanical . . ." He looked into the distance and then said expressionlessly, "The writing machine."

Folding the paper again, he put it in his own coat pocket. As he did so, his glance fell on the bust. He turned it around and looked into the dead eyes of white yew.

Not a quarter of an hour later he was tying up his horse in Spitalgasse, outside the house where the widow Gschweng let rooms to maidservants and where Elise lived. The widow stopped him on the stairs and informed him that visitors in general and men in particular were not allowed in her house, but Kempelen explained that he was Elise's employer and said he had to enter her room at once to do something important for her. Although skeptical, the widow led him to Elise's door and unlocked it. She wanted to go in with him, but Kempelen firmly forced her back out into the corridor. She protested until he threatened, in a distinctly sterner tone of voice, to speak to the Mayor about her if she went on scolding like that, and closed the door in her face.

In the same way as Kempelen had searched Jakob's room, he now went right through Elise's, with the difference that he left everything in its original place to hide the fact that he had been there. And at the back of the mirror he finally found what he was looking for. She had hidden three letters there. The handwriting bore some slight similarity to the style of the Wonderful All-Writing Machine but was clearly that of a human being. The letters were not dated; nor did they bear any address or the name of the sender.

Chérie,

I receive news from P., though not from you, about the victorious progress of the machine. Almost three months have now passed. If it is really a machine, then come back, have no fear, and tell me. (But then why would he forbid you to enter his workshop?) If you cannot get in by playing on the lusts of the men in the household, do it by force. And if he should find you, the worst he can do is dismiss you.

But should you be delaying because you like to serve two masters, and you are filling your pockets for the time to come, then let me warn you: I will do as I say, & a word from me will ruin you at court forever.

Kempelen saw, from looking at the paper, that he had begun to tremble, but he read the second letter too.

Ma chère,

I thank you for your note. So you are well established. Keep working on the young fellow. Even at Schönbrunn, he had eyes only for the demoiselles, & if he is as I was at his age (or mine) he'll want to devour you tout à fait. *Then come back to me quickly, & I will give K. a return match that he will never in his life forget.*

Tu me manques, *chérie,* & our débauches & *all other women taste insipid by comparison with you. I kiss your round little rump, dear heart, and lick your sweet apples of Paradise.*

Frédérique

Post Scriptum: best for you to destroy this letter, and all the others . . . if
only because of my smutty allusions!

Kempelen dropped both letters on the little table, and unfolded the third.

G.,

    By now you will have heard about Vienna. Found myself smiling over
him tout le jour. It was delicious. As you have had no success yet, I don't
suppose it will be worth my while for you to stay in P. anymore. Perhaps
my hopes of you were too high. I will pay your salaire *only for the rest of*
this month. But if you should find out about the T. sometime after all, I will
pay you half the premium I promised.

                                    Baisers et cetera

Kempelen took the first of the three letters with him, folded the other
two, and put them back in the frame of the mirror. Outside the widow
was knocking at the door and calling for him.

"Go away! I've nearly finished," he called back, and she did as he said.

He was going to hang the mirror back on its nail, but he was still
trembling and couldn't do it immediately. His own face kept dancing
before his eyes, reflected in the glass: pale, sweating, with tousled hair,
collar inelegantly torn open because of the heat. Wherever he tried putting the mirror, it wouldn't catch on the nail; Kempelen took the mirror
away from the wall entirely, just to make sure there really was a nail in
the wall. Finally he got the hook over the nail and let go of the mirror. A
little medallion hanging by a chain over the top corner of the mirror
clinked against the glass. Kempelen looked at it as it dangled before his
eyes, a double image, the original and its reflection, and then recognized
the scratched picture of the Virgin. It was Tibor's amulet. The amulet
that Tibor always used to wear and hadn't worn for a long time. Because
he didn't have it anymore. Because it was here with Elise.

On the way out Kempelen told the widow that it would be the worse
for her if she ever told Elise he had been in her room, and it would also

be the worse for her if she ever told anyone he had made that threat. As she was preparing to faint away at this, he held not smelling salts but a guilder under her nose, and she came around at once.

"HOLY MARY Mother of God, hear our prayer. Protect Jakob and hold your hand over him wherever he may be, go with him on his travels and bring him safely to his journey's end. And help us to overcome obstacles at this time too, O glorious and blessed Virgin. Lead us to your son, commend us to your son's care, plead for us that we may be worthy of Christ's promise. Amen."

"Amen," repeated Elise.

"Perhaps he's celebrating the Sabbath somewhere," said Tibor, after they had risen to their feet and knocked the dust off their knees.

They had met in the workshop again. Kempelen had ridden to the castle that morning to attend a meeting called by Duke Albert, which he said would end that evening at the earliest.

"Or perhaps he really has left," said Elise. "And I think—I think you should go too."

"Go where?"

"That makes no difference. Just away from Pressburg."

"It would be dangerous."

"Never mind. I'll come with you if you like. I'll look after you and hide you. I know people who can help us. I can't promise you it will succeed, but I wouldn't suggest it if I didn't think it might."

Tibor tilted his head to one side, like a dog. "Why would you want to help me?"

"Because . . . because you need help."

"That's no reason why you should. Is it pity, or what's behind it? Why are you doing all this?"

Even as Elise was trying to find words, the double doors to the workshop were flung open so violently that they crashed against the walls. In the corridor stood Wolfgang von Kempelen, just as he had left the house an hour ago.

"Exactly, Elise," he said. "Why are you doing all this? Out of Christian brotherly love? Or is he to reward you for it?" He strode into the workshop. Tibor couldn't take his eyes off him. "I'm sorry that I have to disturb your little tête-à-tête before you've come really close to each other—and that, I can assure you, Tibor, would only have been a question of time. I can also tell you why she's doing all this." He took a letter out of his coat pocket and held it in front of Tibor's nose. "She's doing it because she's not really a simple maidservant from Ödenburg but a very clever spy from Vienna, sent here by no less than Friedrich Knaus, Court Mechanician to Her Majesty and the chess automaton's greatest enemy! He did tell you to destroy those letters!"

Tibor had not been able to read a word of the letter before Kempelen took it back again and slammed it down on the Turk's cabinet. Tibor's movements had become strangely slow, as if he suddenly had syrup flowing through his veins. Elise had turned pale and was looking surreptitiously at the door, as if thinking of escaping from the workshop.

"Knaus, who encourages his pretty agent to employ any methods she likes but particularly those of a physical nature." Kempelen went up to Elise, who took a step back. "You literally had your hands full with the three of us men here, didn't you. She offered me her breasts and her lips. So what did she let *you* do in her embrace, Tibor? Did she undress for you? Did she find out whether certain parts of your body grow if they're worked on in the right way? Were you able to finish with Elise what you began with Ibolya? And did you give her your little amulet of the Virgin in return?" Kempelen reached for the chain around Elise's neck, but she avoided him. Tibor was speechless. "I don't even like to think what you did to our friend Jakob, who was a ramshackle fellow even before your arrival. I'm sure you kissed him and gave yourself to him. A little advance payment for his treachery, and at this moment he'll be getting the rest from Knaus in cash."

"I don't know where Jakob is," said Elise.

"Do you think I'd believe a word you say?"

"I haven't heard anything from Vienna. By all I hold sacred, I have nothing to do with Jakob's disappearance."

"By all you hold sacred? And what might that be? Money? You can stop acting the part of the God-fearing maid. Beneath your paint you're a common, lying whore, and I'm calling you to account for your underhanded behavior!"

Kempelen seized Elise's forearm, and she screamed, more with shock than with pain. Tibor's left arm immediately shot out, and he was holding Kempelen in just the same way as Kempelen was holding Elise.

"Let her go," said Tibor.

"Are you out of your mind? What are you thinking of?"

"Let her go."

But instead of relaxing his grip, Kempelen strengthened it. Now he was really hurting Elise. She tried prying Kempelen's fingers open with her free hand but in vain. Tibor tightened his grip too. Kempelen was trying to shake him off.

"Are you still trying to defend her?" he shouted. "Can't you see that she's been the downfall of both of us?"

Tibor did not reply. His lips were as tightly closed as his hand. The three of them didn't move; only the floorboards creaked beneath their feet. Finally Kempelen pushed Elise away and freed himself from Tibor's hand. Both of them, Kempelen and Elise alike, rubbed their bruised arms. Kempelen's eyes were wide with astonishment as he looked at Tibor.

"In God's name, what has she done to you, to make you unable to tell friend from foe?"

"We're leaving Pressburg."

"What?"

"We're leaving the city."

"We? Are you bewitched?"

"You'll have to look for someone else to play chess."

"What's come over you? There isn't anyone else. We've discussed this already!"

"Then rebuild the automaton so that someone larger will fit inside it."

"That's impossible."

"Give it up, then. That would be better anyway."

"I can't give it up! What would people say?"

"Tell them you've had enough of it and you must spend your time on other projects."

Kempelen adjusted his coat, which was in disarray after the scuffle. "You just try running for it, Tibor, and we'll see how far you get before you're caught and put in prison."

Tibor pointed to the chess machine. "My cell will be larger than that one."

"Cell?" Kempelen laughed out loud. "Don't nurture any false hopes: you'll be strung up as a common criminal."

"I'll confess first."

"No one will believe you."

"Even if they don't," said Tibor, raising his head, "can you live with the risk? The risk that I may be believed, and you'll be revealed as a fraud who dared to deceive the imperial family and the whole Empire? Your fame will turn to shame and disgrace, you'll be exiled, and you can join the scum of undesirable characters you've been deporting to the Banat. And you can begin again there on a farm or down a mine!"

Kempelen shook his head slowly and said quietly, "Is that what you want, then? Is that the thanks you give me? I took you out of poverty and your dungeon, I paid you, clothed you, patched up your injuries . . . I gave you a new home, even my friendship . . . and now this? You call yourself a Christian, and all the same you want to see me and my family ruined? Little Teréz?"

"If you send me to the scaffold, you'll have deserved it. But if you don't, and we both keep silent, neither of us will come to any harm. You have my word."

"Your word, perhaps—but what about hers?" Kempelen pointed to Elise, who had been following this exchange in silence.

Elise looked from Kempelen to Tibor and back again. She swallowed. "I'll keep quiet too."

Kempelen tapped the letter on top of the cabinet with one finger. "You've spent almost six months working to bring us down. Presumably Knaus is paying you a fortune. Why would you keep quiet? Why should I believe you will? And even if you do, as soon as the two of you are in

Vienna and I stop exhibiting the Turk, Knaus will work it out for himself. One way or the other I'm finished."

"You and no one else called the automaton to life. It was you who promised the Empress you would astonish her," said Tibor.

Kempelen stared at Tibor, but his eyes were empty. It was obvious that his thoughts were already elsewhere. He left the room without a word. Even his footsteps on the stairs sounded discouraged.

"Tibor, that was . . . very good," said Elise. "I don't know what he'd have done to me. I was frightened."

Tibor did not return her smile. He took Knaus's letter off the cabinet and went to his room with it.

When she entered the room, he was sitting on his bed, reading the letter for the third time. Instead of simply moving his eyes, he moved his whole head as he passed from line to line. She closed the door behind her and leaned back against it, arms folded over her breasts.

"Would it have made any difference if I'd told you I was working for him and not the Church?"

He looked up from the letter. "It would be a good idea if you told me everything now."

"You won't want to know it all."

"You were never in a convent."

Elise shook her head.

"Who are you then, Elise?" asked Tibor. "If that's even your real name."

"I was born as Elise. But for several years I've been known as Galatea at court."

"Court? Are you—are you a princess?"

"No. I'm a professional mistress. A courtesan."

Tibor started so violently that he tore the letter, which he was still holding in both hands. He almost apologized for the damage. "Knaus's mistress?" he asked, his eyes wide open.

"Knaus's . . . and other people's. All of them fine gentlemen, though. Knaus wanted me to go to Pressburg, but I didn't do it for the money."

"Then why?"

"He blackmailed me."

"What with?"

"I'm pregnant."

Tibor ran both hands through his hair and kept them on his head, as if to prevent it from breaking apart.

"If he had spread that news abroad, my reputation at court would have been ruined. I could never go back. And I can certainly do with the money for the child."

"So Knaus told you to come here and . . ."

Elise nodded.

"Did you sleep with Jakob?"

With a little hesitation, Elise nodded again.

"And Kempelen?"

"No. We—we only kissed once. Would you like some water . . . ?"

"Who's the child's father? Knaus?"

"I don't know."

"You don't . . . how can you not . . . ? Oh, my God."

"It could be Knaus, but—but it could be the Emperor himself, think of that! The Emperor's child!"

Elise smiled radiantly and laid one hand on her belly. Tibor stared at it. He could in fact have done with a sip of water. Now she moved away from the door and took a step toward him.

"Let's not talk anymore, Tibor." Tibor shook his head, and she misunderstood it as agreement. "You defended me just now. It's time I rewarded you for your heroic courage."

She undid her cap, took it off her head, and let it fall from her hand. Then she shook out her hair, and instantly she was even prettier than before. Without taking her eyes off him, she untied the laces of her bodice and took it off, expertly and without haste. Her breasts drooped just a little. She let the bodice fall beside her cap. Now her upper body was covered only by a white dress. She put her hand to its neck and pulled it off one shoulder. Tibor held his breath. He looked at her bare shoulder, her rounded upper arm, the radiance of her white, immaculate skin, the slight shadow under her collarbone: the perfect landscape of her body with its hills and valleys, its slopes and plains. She was even more beautiful than he had imagined her in his dreams. And now she was going to be his. A shiver ran down his back.

She freed her other arm from the dress too and pulled it down to her hips with both hands, revealing her breasts, the curve of her waist and her belly, which showed her pregnancy now, but that only made it even more beautiful. She took a deep breath and knelt down in front of Tibor. He still hadn't moved. Reaching out her bare arm to him, she took his left hand, stroked it, and carried it to her mouth. With her eyes closed she kissed the back of his hand and then his fingers. He could feel every breath and the warmth of her skin. Then she turned his hand over and kissed the fingers where they joined his palm. She licked his wrist where the pulse lay. Now it was his turn to close his eyes. His whole arm was shaking. When he opened his eyes again, she was looking enticingly at him. Slowly, very slowly, she brought his hand to her breast so that he could feel the erect nipple inside his palm. His trembling died down as his fingers closed around her breast. She closed her eyes in rapture, put her head back, and moaned.

Tibor came to his senses. The moan was as false as all the rest of it: her offer of herself, her pose. It wasn't desire that she felt, it was a staged imitation of desire, perfectly performed by a whore who had already made countless men believe, in just this way, that she enjoyed their caresses and that each of them was special, unique. It wasn't Elise who had kissed Tibor just now but Galatea, a woman whom he didn't know and didn't want to know. Revulsion overcame him. Her warm skin repelled him, and so did her nakedness and her tongue, and he pulled his hand away as if he had touched fire. His excitement died down at once. He felt an urgent need to wash the hand with her nauseating spittle on it.

"What is it?" she asked.

"I'm not the Emperor."

He pointed to the medallion lying between her chin and her breasts. "Give me my medallion back, please."

For some time she did not react but just looked at him incredulously. Then she reached behind her to undo the clasp of the chain. Realizing that she was still naked, she suddenly drew the dress up modestly over her breasts and shoulders again, before taking off the chain and handing it to him. She stayed on her knees.

"It's probably better if we don't see each other again," said Tibor. "So goodbye, Elise. I wish you well, you and your child. And please keep your word to Kempelen. He's done wrong, certainly, and he was harsh to us, but at heart he's a good man who doesn't deserve what threatens him." Tibor rose from the bed, picked up her bodice and her cap, and handed them both to her. "I'm willing to give you money for your silence. I don't know what Knaus is paying you—a great deal more, I expect—but I can give you some forty or perhaps forty-five sovereigns. I'll need the rest for myself."

"No." Her voice was faint and failing. "I don't need any money."

"Because it would bind you more than your word does?"

Tibor waited for an answer, but none came. He opened the door. Understanding the gesture, she rose and looked down at him for the last time. As she left the room, she stumbled over the threshold. Tibor closed the door behind her.

She had gone, but her fragrance remained. So Tibor opened the window to let in the damp, cold autumn air. Then he spread his possessions out on the bed, to pack what mattered most for his journey: his clothes, his traveling chessboard, the carved chessman that Jakob had made him, and the clockmaker's tools he had been given.

Sommerein

A MAN LIES BESIDE THE DANUBE NEAR THE SMALL TOWN of Sommerein, with an arm, a shoulder, and his head on the muddy bank itself and the rest of his body in the ankle-deep water. Little ripples rock him constantly. His mouth and eyes are open. His skin is pale green, bloated, and covered with a fine waxy layer so that you might almost take him for a waxwork. The skin of the hand lying in the water is already coming away from the flesh, all in one piece like the skin shed by a growing snake, as if it were only a transparent glove. His clothes are drenched, and they look weightless in the water. The man's body is populated: flies are laying eggs on the exposed skin, and the first maggots are already hatching out. The maggots in turn are food for larger predators, the ants and beetles that have crawled or flown from land to this human peninsula, and frogs swimming up through the reeds. The creatures that fear these carnivores take refuge in the folds of the man's clothing and hide there, in dark, damp caverns of skin and linen. Under the surface of the water, busy water mites and wriggling worms feed. Little fish surround the body to feast on the fraying skin or on the carrion eaters themselves, and out in the open water larger predatory fish lie in wait to eat the little fish in their own turn. The meeting place for all these creatures, however, what might be called the watering hole of this island both above and below the surface, is a wound slashed right through the man's chest, as broad as a finger is long. A blade has passed through the body here, horizontally and not catching between the ribs. The man's shirt is as ragged as his flesh. But the water of the river has washed the blood out of the fabric long ago. The tender red flesh around the wound here is unprotected and ready to eat, and soon rats, martens, and foxes will be sinking their teeth into it, once they are used to the smell.

A raven that has been circling above the human island for some time now lands on its muddy forehead and spongy skin, which tears under the bird's claws. Beetles crawl to land or fly away, frogs jump into the reeds, fish take refuge under stones or in the deep water. But the raven is after a different kind of feast. With its beak, it lifts the wire frame of the man's spectacles off his nose and drops them heedlessly into the water, where they sink. Then it begins pecking the cold eyes out of their sockets. Although it darts suspicious glances around after every morsel, it is undisturbed until it has finished its meal. Smudged lines of charcoal are still visible on the corpse's upper lip. They depict a moustache in the Turkish style.

ON MONDAY MORNING Kempelen received a note in which Mayor Windisch asked him to come to the Town Hall on urgent business. Kempelen shaved and dressed, and an hour later he was admitted to the Mayor's office. Windisch rose from his desk and sent his secretary out. There was no joy in his smile.

"Wolfgang, my dear friend! You look pale." They shook hands and sat down. "I've had all my engagements postponed until later. I wanted to tell you myself. I'd have come to Donaugasse if I could."

"What's happened?"

Windisch picked up a pair of spectacles from his desk and handed them to Kempelen. "They found your assistant yesterday. Near Sommerein."

"Has he done something stupid? Where is he now?"

"I'm sorry, I didn't express myself very well. He's dead. They took his corpse out of the Danube. The body is lying in the hospital mortuary now, and I've sent word to Rabbi Barba."

Kempelen turned the spectacles in his fingers. They had never been polished to such a shine when he saw Jakob wearing them.

"They're going to bury him tomorrow. The Jewish community will see to it. In their faith burial should take place within three days after death at the latest, but that's not possible now."

"Did he . . . did he drown?"

"No. He was already dead when he was thrown into the water. Or at least, he would soon have died of his wound."

Windisch pushed the report from the constabulary across the desk. A blade had gone through Jakob's upper body from behind, right through the chest, just missing his heart but slashing his lungs. The blow had been so powerful that the blade even ripped the front of his shirt. More-over, the dead man's lip was torn, there was a small lacerated wound under one ear, and he had had a black eye—the results of several power-ful blows. A grisly detail was the absence of both eyes, obviously pecked out by a carrion-eating bird.

"You have my deep sympathy. I know you were fond of him, even if he was sometimes a thorn in your flesh."

"Who—who did it?"

"We don't know, and I doubt if we shall ever find out. He'd been robbed and his purse was missing. It had still been with him in the Golden Rose. But it's equally possible that it fell out of his pocket when he was thrown into the river. And who commits murder to steal money? To rob a man, all you have to do is strike him down, or stick a knife in his back if you want to make sure. You don't have to run him right through. No one must hear about this, or I'll have my hands full trying to refute horror sto-ries about ghosts and golems! Perhaps Jakob fell into bad company while he was drunk. His other injuries would bear that out. And regrettable as it is, he wouldn't be the first Jew to be killed out of vile resentment."

Kempelen pushed the report back, and Windisch put it away in a portfolio.

"Of course you don't have to make up your mind today, but I suppose you'll be canceling the Turk's next performance. Wolfgang?"

Kempelen looked up. He hadn't been listening. "I'm sorry, what did you say?"

"The performance? In the Italian Theater."

"No, no. It will go ahead."

"But . . . your assistant?"

"I'll find a substitute."

Windisch inclined his head, and looked keenly at Kempelen. Then he scratched the back of his neck. "Wolfgang, ought I to be anxious about you?"

"Why?"

"You look as if you haven't slept for days . . . you have no servants anymore, Anna Maria has been in the country for weeks . . . and that crazed Andrássy has even written to the Master of the Lodge asking him to tell you to accept the Baron's challenge to a duel. I've warned Andrássy that I won't let such affairs of honor take place with impunity in my city, but he won't listen."

"He'll calm down."

"I wouldn't like to bet on it. These Magyars! Distinguished as they like to make themselves out, there's still a bloodthirsty Attila in every one of them. And what are you about these days with the newly ennobled Stegmüller? Why would we accept an idiot like him into the Lodge?"

"He's a harmless buffoon, Karl."

"A buffoon, yes, and that's the very reason why you should avoid his company before his buffoonery rubs off on you."

Kempelen nodded and changed the subject. "Are you going to write that book of yours about the chess-playing Turk?"

"As soon as I can find the time."

As they took their leave of each other, the two men embraced. Kempelen took Jakob's spectacles away with him. In the square outside the Town Hall, he put them in his pocket. He did not go back to Donaugasse, but went to Kapitelgasse in the shadow of the cathedral, where his brother lived. He found Nepomuk already about to mount his horse and ride to work at the castle. But when Kempelen told him about the incidents of the last few days, Nepomuk ordered his groom to unsaddle the horse again. Instead, he said, he would walk to Castle Mount, and his brother would go with him.

When they had left the city behind and were climbing the steps to the castle, Nepomuk said gravely, "You're up to your neck in the mire."

"So you don't believe she and Tibor will keep silent?"

"*Merde,* no! Why would they? He's a sly one, I warned you of that before, and she's for sale. They'll both talk the moment the money is right."

"What am I to do?"

"You're asking me? Why on earth do you ask me now? You haven't asked my advice for decades, why start at this point? Why didn't you do it before promising the Empress more than you could perform? Because then I'd have advised you to drop the idea, and we wouldn't be having this conversation at all."

"Do you want to humiliate me? If so, then why aren't you glad? You were always jealous of my success."

"No. No, I'm not glad."

"Well, are you going to give me your advice, or do you just want to haul me over the coals?"

"Oh, come on. I'm not worried about the girl. If she's for sale, you have only to offer her more money than the Swabian does. And hope that the code by which such people live holds good with her. It won't be cheap, of course, because you'll have to give her so much that she won't even think of betraying you a second time. The dwarf is the greater evil."

"Why?"

"Because his clock doesn't tick to the same time as ours, and I don't believe he has any morals worth mentioning."

"He's a Christian. Blindly credulous, in fact."

"Or at least he makes you think so."

"But if I can't silence him with money . . ."

"So who else knows about your Turk?" asked Nepomuk, and began counting them off on his fingers. "You, me, Anna Maria, that fool of an apothecary: we'll all keep our mouths shut anyway. Your cheating maid will be bribed. Your Jew and Ibolya are dead and have taken the secret to the grave with them. The dwarf . . ." Nepomuk concluded his enumeration with an airy gesture and said no more.

Kempelen stopped. "You think I should kill him?"

"I didn't say so."

"I won't do it."

"He's disloyal. He'd deserve it, after all you've done for him."

"No, I can't do that."

"Then you should be prepared for anything."

"I can't kill a man."

"We're only talking about a dwarf, Wolf. A monstrosity, a whim of Nature. Who knows, you might even be doing him a favor if he despairs of the world as much as you say. Perhaps he hasn't put himself out of his misery yet only for fear of the fires of Hell that threaten suicides."

"I won't do it," said Kempelen, shaking his head.

The two brothers walked on in silence. The massive castle rose before them. Kempelen looked down the steep slope on his left to the Zuckermandel settlement: the nets, the fishing boats turned keel upward, the courtyard with the sculptor Messerschmidt's strange busts, the skins on drying frames, and the tanners' open tubs. He couldn't hear the men's cries and the noise their tools made, but the stink of the tanners' acid rose to the brothers.

"Will you help me?" asked Kempelen.

Nepomuk uttered a short, dry laugh. "No. I am head of the Duke's chancellery. You'll have to do without my help, because if you fail, as your brother I'll have a hard time keeping my own hands clean. I'm damned if I'm going to end in the mire myself."

The Kempelen brothers parted company at the Siegmund Gate. Nepomuk went into the castle, Wolfgang turned back to Donaugasse, but on the way he visited his deposit bank and the Red Crab.

A MAP of the central parts of Europe hung in Kempelen's study. From the Atlantic coast of France to the Black Sea, from the kingdom of Denmark to Rome, the states were marked off from one another with precise black lines and painted in with different watercolors. Tibor wondered who had decided which color was right for which country. Why was Prussia always blue on all the maps he had ever seen? Why was France purple and England yellow? Why was the Habsburg Empire light red, not dark red? Was the Republic of Venice green because of its meadows or because of the Adriatic Sea? Was the Ottoman Empire brown because the Turks had dark skins or because they indulged in coffee and tobacco? The map had been folded twice, and Vienna lay on the exact point where the two folds intersected, with Pressburg to its right. Wherever Tibor went, if he wanted to leave Austria, the nearest border was at least five days' journey away on horseback, or twice as many on foot. The nearest border was the border with Silesia, and he certainly didn't want to go back to Prussia.

He had seen Saxony and hadn't enjoyed the experience. Poland lay between Prussia, Russia, and Austria, and that made it less than inviting. Should he go to Bavaria? Or back to the Venetian Republic, hoping it would be third time lucky for him there? Or should he escape the coming winter by going south, to Tuscany, to Sicily, to the Papal States? He had been happy enough in Obra; perhaps he should ask for shelter in a monastery again. What else was left to him? Germany and the divided Netherlands were colorful as a patchwork rug on the map, a motley collection of dukedoms, principalities, and electoral states, counties and landgraviates, bishoprics and archbishoprics, and free cities, some of them so tiny that there wasn't room for their names on the map. They ought all to be lined up in squares and made into a colorful chess set. Tibor didn't want to go to Germany. He had no desire to spend the rest of his life with bells on his ankles, court fool to some insignificant landgrave. France, on the other hand, was a single homogeneous area, all connected up, with Paris in the middle like a fat black spider in its web. France meant Paris. He would inevitably end up in Paris, he knew that, much as he hated big cities. As soon as he set foot in France, he would be drawn to Paris as if he were going down a funnel, and he'd end up either a bell ringer or in the gutter. The map on the wall ended at the border between Poland and Russia, but if the Tsarina ate children, he too might end up on her table someday, roasted with an apple in his mouth. In Spain they had burned all the Jews, and people capable of such horrors couldn't possibly be hospitable to a dwarf. He spoke no English, and the mere idea of crossing the Channel put him off the idea of going to England. The same applied to the British colonies, and then there was war the whole time there, and they kept Negroes dragged away from Africa as slaves. He had heard that there were Negro tribes in Africa who grew no more than five feet tall. But that was still considerably taller than Tibor himself. Jakob had told him about the memoirs of an Irish priest who was once shipwrecked on an island called Lilliput, where the people were no bigger than a hand's span in height. Perhaps he ought to overcome his fear of the water, put to sea, and look for that island—where he would be king of the little people, like a one-eyed man among the blind.

Tibor's glance had moved from the map across the wall to the door, where the Pacific Ocean and its islands would be if the map had gone on to embrace the whole world. The door opened, and Kempelen came in.

They sat down. Kempelen seemed—well, it would have been too much to say happy, but at least jovial and not at all hostile to Tibor. He was carrying a leather purse and emptied the contents out on the desk: two hundred and sixty guilders, Tibor's wages with some small expenses deducted, divided into forty gold sovereigns and twenty guilders. Opening the drawer of his desk, Kempelen took out a piece of paper on which he had itemized everything, so that Tibor could see it was all in order. When Tibor put all that money back into the purse and weighed it in his hand, he felt like a robber. But the money was rightfully his.

Tibor asked about Elise. Kempelen had been to see her too and paid her her wages—in addition to a more than generous sum of hush money.

"She won't talk," said Tibor, without really believing it.

"I should hope not. Because if she does, I shall pursue her and call her to account, and so I let her understand. She asked about you."

"What did you say?"

"I said she had betrayed you too, and I can't imagine that you would ever want to see her again. Was I right?"

"Yes," said Tibor. "I hate her."

"Very understandable," said Kempelen. "Where are you planning to go?"

"North," lied Tibor.

Kempelen nodded and drummed his fingers on the desk. "There's something else I have to tell you before you say goodbye. I'm not good at these things, so I'll keep it short, hoping you can stand the shock. Jakob is dead."

Jakob is dead. Of course Jakob was dead. As Kempelen told him where and in what condition Jakob's body had been found, Tibor realized how faint had been his hope of ever seeing Jakob alive again.

The Jew had not said goodbye, he hadn't asked for his wages, and he had taken no baggage, not even the belt where he kept his tools. Jakob was dead, and Tibor's prayers had done nothing to change it. As always, Kempelen's dress sword was leaning against the wall. Tibor would have liked to draw it from its scabbard to see if there was any dried blood on the blade, and if there was, he would have struck Kempelen's head off with it. He nodded when Kempelen asked if he was planning to leave at once.

"I can understand that," said Kempelen. "It's a pity that you won't be at Jakob's funeral. I'm sure he would have liked that. I am going, of course. I expect I shall be the only Gentile there. He's being buried in the Judengasse cemetery."

Tibor thought about it.

"You're welcome to spend this last night here," Kempelen offered. "Or you can take a room at an inn if you don't want the Turk's company or mine anymore. But I won't prevent you. That's all over. You're free."

THIS WAS WHAT loneliness felt like. It had accompanied Tibor all his life and had never troubled him much. But now that he had enjoyed the pleasures of company, now that his hunger for them was aroused, now that he had made friends with three people—one had been his oppressor, another had exploited and betrayed him, and the third had been murdered—now loneliness made him suffer. He went out into the street without the stiltlike shoes, just with his "little Catholic hands and feet," as Jakob had called them. He took smaller steps without the stilts, but he walked faster. Whether people stared or not didn't interest him. He had to find a church where he could pray for Jakob's immortal soul. That was urgent. The last time he saw Jakob, he had abused him and his religion and shut the door in his face, yet Jakob had told him only the truth. And a few hours later he had bled to death and was thrown into the cold, dirty Danube like rubbish. Tibor couldn't help thinking of the Venetian. Was there a curse on him—like the Curse of the Turk, which was the talk of Pressburg— meaning that everyone he had anything to do with must die? Was his mere touch enough to bring death? Would it overtake Elise too someday?

Purposefully, he went up the steps of St. Savior's and made straight for the font of holy water. When he dipped his fingers in the cool water, it struck him that something in this church had changed. Tibor looked around, his hand still in the font, but he couldn't make out what it was. The furnishings and the white walls decorated in gold were just as they had been on Tibor's last visit. A few people were sitting in the pews and waiting outside the confessional. Only then did Tibor realize that it wasn't the church that had changed but himself. He looked at the Virgin Mary with her child, but she no longer seemed to him inviting. She was just a figure. The queen in a game of chess. A lifeless doll like the Turk. How pitiful the rosary that he had prayed day after day on his chessboard seemed all of a sudden. His prayers hadn't prevented him from falling in love with a pregnant whore who tricked him. Mary hadn't protected Jakob. This was not the right place to pray for his soul.

As he left the church, someone called out, "Big Man!"

Tibor stopped. There sat Walther on the steps in the shadow of the porch, just as he had before when Tibor came to confess at Easter, with his bowl for alms in front of him. When he arrived, Tibor hadn't noticed him.

"Hey, Big Man!" called Walther again.

Tibor could ignore him and walk on, or go back into the church, but his old comrade in arms had recognized him. So Tibor approached him.

"Good day, Walther," he said.

"*Sapristi*, are you a ghost? I thought they'd slaughtered you at Torgau!" Walther took Tibor's arm and pressed it, to make sure.

"That's what I thought about you."

Walther laughed and struck the stump of his leg. "So they'd have liked to, those greasy Prussians. Had to make do with my leg—it's manuring the fields of Saxony now. And what d'you say to my ugly mug? I use it to scare the children who cock snooks at me." Walther presented his scarred face, grimaced, and laughed. "But what brings you to this dump? *Sapperment*, just look at you!" he said, plucking at Tibor's green frock coat. "What a fine fellow you are now! The coat, the hat—I'd give something to be walking the streets à la mode like that!"

Tibor told Walther what had happened to him since the battle of Torgau and thought of a reason to explain his presence in Pressburg. "But I'm leaving soon."

"Very nice too. Don't you have a few groschen for an old friend and faithful comrade?" asked Walther, giving his begging bowl a little push to make the coins in it jingle. "Business is worse than bad today, and winter's knocking at the door."

Tibor nodded and reached for his full purse. The sooner he could part from Walther, the better. But as he was undoing the leather string of his purse, an idea came to him.

"Listen, Walther, would you like to earn a few guilders too?"

Walther straightened up. "Let's hear about it."

"I need a horse for my journey. You're good with horses. Do you know where to get one?"

"To be sure! *Dragoons aren't man or beast but worse, they're infantry upon a horse.*"

"Then buy me a horse, a saddle, and saddlebags. And provisions for a week. I need it tomorrow evening."

"A horse and all the rest of it! That won't come cheap, Big Man."

"It doesn't matter. Do you know the little church of St. Nicholas, between Castle Mount and the Jewish quarter? We'll meet in the church-yard there two hours after sunset. I'll give you two sovereigns for your help, and more if you drive a good bargain for me. What do you say?"

"Sounds shady to me—but who cares for that? I'm your man, dam-

mit! I'll be in the churchyard of St. Nicholas tomorrow, Wednesday, with
the reins of the fastest steed since Bucephalos in my hand!"

Tibor took a large quantity of coins out of his purse. "Can I trust you,
Walther?"

"You shouldn't have to ask, but I give you my word as a soldier and a
comrade." Walther winked with the eye on the right-hand, burned side
of his face, though the flesh was so distorted there that he could hardly
close it. "If a dragoon's honor isn't enough, look at this: I've only one leg,
or maybe three," he said, patting the two crutches lying beside him on
the steps, "but all the same you'd catch up with me before the rooster
could crow three times."

Tibor handed the money to Walther, who swiftly stowed it away in
his coat. "God bless you, little one," he said. "You're helping an old crock
back on his legs again. Or back on one leg anyway, devil take it!"

The two comrades shook hands. Tibor had to force himself not to look
back again before setting off for the main square.

TIBOR WAS SURPRISED to find how much the synagogue resembled a
church: like a church, it had a nave and two side aisles. Pillars supported
a gallery with round arches and dark rows of pews like those in the nave.
There was no pulpit. Instead, a platform with an empty lectern on it
stood in the middle of the room. A low balustrade surrounded it, and
steps led up to it on two sides. A heavy chandelier hung over the platform.
The pews were placed so that you could see the platform from all four
sides. There was no altar and no cross in the apse on the eastern wall of
the synagogue, but a shrine with a red velvet curtain to hide whatever
was inside. Two golden lions stood on top of the shrine, holding a kind of
coat of arms in their paws. The shrine too was surrounded by a balustrade
and a circle of candlesticks. To the left was a seven-branched candle-
holder like those that Tibor had seen in Jakob's room and Krakauer's
shop, though theirs were a good deal smaller. The windows of the synagogue were not stained glass like church windows, but the inside of the

room was painted blue and gold, with a great many patterns and friezes, and over and over again the Star of David. There weren't any pictures or statues; apart from the two lions, Tibor could see no depiction of any living creature. Didn't the Jews have saints? Where were Abraham, Isaac, Moses, and the rest of them?

Tibor took off his three-cornered hat and smoothed down his hair. There was a basin of water beside him at the entrance. He was going to dip his fingers into it but then stopped. Did he seriously mean to anoint his forehead with Jewish holy water? But perhaps it wasn't holy water at all? He wished Jakob were here to explain all this.

He went up the nave, listening to the echo of his footsteps, passed the gallery, and went up to the shrouded shrine. Only now did he see that there was a depiction of two stone tablets with the Ten Commandments on the curtain. But the writing was in Hebrew. Tibor placed his hands on the balustrade and knelt down. He prayed. His prayer wasn't to anyone in particular, neither the Christian God nor the Jewish God; he did not resort to any of the set phrases he had repeated all his life. This was just a prayer for Jakob. He was glad that there was no organ playing and no worshippers present, so that he could concentrate on his prayer. Soon the first tears were falling on his clasped hands and the stone floor, and after a while he understood that he was no longer weeping with grief for Jakob but for himself, now that he had lost his friend and so much else besides.

IT WAS ALREADY DARK when Tibor reached the Zuckermandel settlement. He had his money, and Walther was going to get him a horse and provisions. Now all he needed was a gun. Andrássy had shot him. Kempelen had acquired a pistol. Jakob might still be alive if he'd had one. If someone were to follow him, Tibor meant to sell his skin dearly.

There was a light burning in the sculptor's house. Tibor knocked at the little door, although perhaps this was rather too modest a way for a Spirit of Magnetism to materialize.

"Messerschmidt is not at home!" called a voice from inside. But it had clearly been the sculptor speaking.

Tibor didn't knock again. Instead, he put his hands around his mouth like a speaking trumpet and called in a deep voice, "Woe, woe! I am the Spirit of Magnetism!"

All sounds inside the house ceased, and a little later several bolts were shot back. Messerschmidt opened the door and looked down at Tibor, who tried to look as stern as possible.

"Forgive me, Spirit," he said. "I wasn't expecting you."

The sculptor invited Tibor in. Tibor had thought out the gist of his message carefully, and Messerschmidt meekly listened. He, Tibor, the Spirit of Magnetism, had faced the Spirit of Proportion in battle several times in the last few weeks, he said, but the Spirit of Proportion had always managed to run away. Now he needed a pistol so that he could simply hunt down that evil spirit and shoot it with powder and lead. Messerschmidt kept on nodding, and when Tibor had finished, the deranged sculptor immediately produced a pistol, bullets, and a powder horn from the next room. While he was gone, Tibor looked around him. Nothing much had changed in the studio. At the moment the artist was working on a crucifix. Something about the figure of Jesus seemed strange to Tibor, and when he looked more closely, he saw that the Savior was wearing a felt cap and Hungarian national costume. When Messerschmidt came back, he explained that a farmer had ordered a "Hungarian Christ" from him, and he was going to have what he asked for with all its accoutrements.

Tibor wanted to pay cash for the pistol, but Messerschmidt looked so surprised when the supposed spirit reached for his purse that he refrained. As he left, Messerschmidt wished him good luck in his hunt.

In the Belly of the Turk

W HEN T IBOR GOT BACK TO THE D ONAUGASSE HOUSE THAT
night, all the lights were out. Kempelen had left him some supper on a
tray outside his door: bread, sausage, onions, and a jug of red Malmsey. As
Tibor ate, he familiarized himself with Messerschmidt's pistol, and when
he had finished, he loaded it: he tipped a little black powder from the
powder horn into the pan and the muzzle, tamped it down with the ramrod, added the bullet, and rammed that firmly into place too. He did not
cock the hammer but put the pistol down by his bed. He meant to check
once again that his packing was all done—he planned to rise early next
morning and not to come back to the Kempelen house after Jakob's
funeral—but he was suddenly overcome by such leaden weariness that
he dropped onto the bed without undressing or extinguishing the candle
and fell into a deep, dreamless sleep.

When he awoke, it was still dark outside. His head was thudding, his
limbs felt heavy, and he had the greatest difficulty in keeping his eyes
open. There was something scratching at the door; an animal, or was it
still part of his dream? Tibor groaned. A little later the door that Tibor
had locked was opened, and two figures entered his room by the light of
the candle. *"Padre?"* asked Tibor, although he knew quite well that he
was looking not at a priest or a doctor but at an apothecary. The other

man was Kempelen. Tibor wanted to get up and run for it, but when he rose from the bed, his limbs were so heavy that he fell to the floor. Together they turned him over to tie his hands behind his back. They were talking to each other, but Tibor didn't understand what they were saying. Their touch finally roused him from his lethargy. He pulled his hands back and struck the apothecary in the face, he kicked out at Kempelen and resisted their second assault too, then hauled himself up beside the bed and got to his feet, swaying. The wall behind him helped him to stand. The crucified Christ fell off its nail and crashed to the floor. Tibor threw a jug at his attackers; they ducked, and it broke against the wall. He tried to seize the pistol lying beside his bed, but all he could catch hold of were sheets. The apothecary stepped back and took something out of his pocket, while Kempelen approached Tibor with one hand outstretched, saying something, but Tibor, like a dog, could make out nothing but his name, repeated over and over again. That was all he understood. The apothecary turned again. Now he was holding a cloth in his hand and another in front of his mouth. Kempelen lunged to seize Tibor. Tibor didn't react fast enough, and they fell to the floor together. Tibor pushed Kempelen away, but Kempelen brought his fist down on Tibor's chest on the very place where he had been shot, and Tibor writhed in pain. A moment later the apothecary was pressing the damp cloth down on his face. Instinctively, Tibor closed his mouth and breathed through his nose. There was a smell of urine. He went on struggling and saw Kempelen turn his own face away and bury his nose in the crook of his elbow. Then Tibor took another breath and the pain went away. His limbs relaxed, he felt pleasantly warm, and he fell asleep again.

STEGMÜLLER THREW the cloth into Tibor's washbasin and poured water over it and over his own hand. Kempelen opened the window.

"How long will he sleep?" he asked.

"Not for long," said Stegmüller. "He may be small, but he's very tough." He picked up the empty wineglass. "Look at this: he drank a whole glass of it, and still he came around. I made it a very strong dose too."

"Let's go where there's more fresh air."

They carried the unconscious dwarf into the workshop. Once there Kempelen tied Tibor's feet and hands together with hemp cords behind his back and gagged him. He looked at the clock on the wall. It was just after four.

"Now what?" asked Stegmüller, glancing at the bound and motionless body.

"Now," said Kempelen, letting the word linger in the air for a long time, "now we bring his life to an end."

Stegmüller, startled, shook his head incredulously. "No!"

"What did you think I was going to do?"

"I thought—I thought you wanted to punish him somehow . . . or get him out of the country . . ."

"Did you bring the arsenic?"

"Yes."

"Well then. Why would anyone want to use arsenic if not to kill?"

"I don't know about . . ."

"The sooner we get to work the easier it will be." Kempelen stretched his hand out.

Stegmüller slowly took the little brown flask out of the inside pocket of his topcoat and placed it on Kempelen's palm.

"How's it administered?" asked Kempelen.

"Either orally—but then you have to give a very large dose, and it will take a few hours—or you introduce it directly into the bloodstream by scraping the skin or cutting a vein open."

"And then it's fast?"

"As lightning."

"That's what we'll do, then. Do you have a scalpel with you?"

Stegmüller shook his head. Kempelen went to his workbench and found a carver's small knife. He handed it to the apothecary.

"What am I supposed to do with this?" asked Stegmüller.

"What you just described."

"Me?"

"You know much more about it than I do."

"No . . ."

"Look, you cured him!"

"That's a very long way from—no. I'm sorry, I can't do it."

"No one will know."

"That's not the point. I . . ." Stegmüller sought for words, looking at the knife.

"Georg, please pull yourself together."

"Gottfried."

"Georg, Gottfried, who cares? Go on and do it!"

Stegmüller looked Kempelen in the eye. "No. In God's name, no, no, and no again. I will not do it. You can have the poison and my advice on using it, and do it yourself if you're not afraid to, but I won't kill a man."

"The Lodge—"

Stegmüller raised his hands. "No Lodge or anything else in the world is worth it. Not if they were to make me a duke. The salvation of my soul matters more to me." He put the knife down again. "I'm going now."

"No, wait!"

Stegmüller had already taken several steps away. "No. I don't want to witness this act of violence."

"Stay here, you coward!"

"Call me a coward if you like. I won't hold it against you. But I'd sooner be a coward than a murderer any day."

Stegmüller turned and disappeared into the stairwell. Kempelen heard him stumbling as he hurried downstairs. Then all was still in the house again.

Kempelen opened his closed fist, and the little flask came into view. He reached for the carver's knife again and knelt down beside Tibor with it and the poison. The dwarf's bound hands were crossed behind his back, with the right hand on top. Kempelen pushed the cord a little way up his arm to expose his wrist. There were three blue veins under the skin. Kempelen broke the seal that kept the cork in the little bottle and removed it. He put the open flask down. Then he picked up the knife again and put the blade first to one vein, then to all three. He took it away once more, placing two fingers on the veins, and although he was trembling, he could feel Tibor's warm pulse. And now he also noticed the way Tibor's back rose and fell as he breathed. Once again he held the blade of the knife to Tibor's wrist. He pressed it down and then drew it toward him. No blood appeared. The knife hadn't even scratched the skin. There was just a fine white line left on Tibor's wrist by its pressure. Either Kempelen hadn't cut hard enough, or the knife was too blunt. He looked at the hand again. The hand that Tibor had used to move the Mechanical Turk's arm. The white line had disappeared. Kempelen covered his face with his hands and sighed.

He opened the lumber room where the automaton was kept, then opened the cabinet of the automaton and placed Tibor inside, still tied up, in the place where he had been sitting for the last six months. Then he closed all the doors of the cabinet, pushed the front of the automaton up to the wall, facing it, and latched the casters in place. When he closed the lumber-room door, all was dark around the Turk. Kempelen bolted the door and finally placed a stout piece of wood across it and the frame. He put the knife back where he had found it, placed the untouched arsenic in his desk, extinguished the candle, and closed the window in Tibor's room. Then he went into the kitchen to make himself some coffee, taking the bowl containing the narcotic-soaked cloth with him. Outside, rain had begun to fall.

EVERYTHING WAS BLACK, black and silent, black and absolutely still when Tibor came back to his senses. At first he feared that the poison he had inhaled had destroyed his vision and hearing, but then he realized that he was in a place where there was no light and no sound. He still had a damp cloth in front of his mouth, but it was only a gag and smelled of nothing but his saliva. His mouth was dry. He was so thirsty that swallowing hurt. He felt fabric beneath him and behind his head, and the way that his groans echoed back from the nearby walls told him that he was in some kind of box. A coffin. He'd been buried alive. For a moment extreme fear overcame him, but then he smelled metal and oil, a familiar smell, and he knew that he wasn't in a coffin after all. Instead, he was in the baize-lined interior of the chess automaton.

His hands were bound and numb, and so were his feet. He could hardly move. Last time he had been awake, he had been eating supper. What happened after that seemed like a dream. The only thing he knew for sure was that Kempelen, with the apothecary's help, had attacked him and left him unconscious. Tibor had no idea what the time was. It might be an hour after the attack on him, it might be a day. He began shouting as well as he could with the gag in his mouth, and he kicked his bound feet against the opposite wall, but the air inside the cabinet was running short, it was hot in there, and his thirst was even worse. If the Turk was still in the lumber room, which seemed likely, no one outside would hear him anyway.

First Tibor had to free himself from his bonds. He twisted his hands, trying to pull them out of the cords, but it was useless: they were tied too tightly, and he couldn't reach the knots. Only a knife would work on them. He moved his numb, cold fingers and thought. What did he have that could help him? Nothing. His pockets were empty. What was there here inside the automaton? A candle, but nothing to light it with. A chess set, and the clockwork. The clockwork with its cogwheels. He remembered that last performance at Schönbrunn when the sharp tooth of one of the wheels had hurt his arm. Perhaps he could use a cogwheel to cut his bonds. He turned his head to the right, where the mechanism lay in the dark. Since he knew the order in which the little wheels were arranged, he could remember which was the lowest down. Turning his back to the apparatus, he felt with his fingers for the wheel he was looking for and placed his bonds against it. The he moved his hands back and forth. He didn't feel that the wheel had even begun cutting into the cords. Instead, he slipped several times and caught his hands and upper arms on the clockwork. The teeth cut his skin till it bled. When he had got used to his awkward position and developed a certain technique, however, he began making progress; the metal went through the hemp like a saw.

Soon one strand was cut, then another, and after he had severed the third, the others came undone too. He rubbed his sore wrists and removed his gag and the ropes around his ankles.

Of course all the doors were locked, and Tibor had no key. Since he could see nothing, he knocked against all four walls and concluded, from the echoing sound, that Kempelen had pushed two sides of the cabinet into a corner. So he wouldn't be able to slide the tabletop off. The only way out was the back door beside him. Tibor braced his shoulder against the wood. It creaked, but both the door and the lock resisted. Tibor knew how thick the sides of the cabinet were and that he had no chance of breaking them down. Perhaps the chessboard would give way. He crawled to the middle of the cabinet, lay down on his back, and pushed at the underside of the chessboard with his feet. Since he had no shoes on, the nails with the metal disks on them hurt the soles of his feet, and he had to twist the nails aside with his hand. Then he pushed against the chessboard again until the sweat stood out on his brow. But the marble wouldn't move. The chess machine was solidly built, to keep curious onlookers from stealing a look inside. He couldn't free himself by force alone.

He needed a key, and if he didn't have one, he would just have to make one. Crawling back, he reached a hand into the mechanism for one of the thin metal pins lying on the cylinder. He broke it off and pulled it out. Then he began bending the metal to fit the shape of the key as he remembered it. Since he had no pincers, he had to use his fingers, and as he could see nothing he had to work entirely by touch. He picked up one of the chessmen to help him and bent the wire around its head. When he had made a skeleton key, he inserted it into the lock. Now the real work began: he had to keep taking the key out to bend it a little more, sometimes just by a hairbreadth. A good hour later he managed to get it up against the little bolt inside the lock, which slid back with a faint sound. The door was open, and he crawled out of the cabinet.

Although Tibor had expected the atmosphere in the room to feel different, it was just as dark and stuffy there. There was only a faint line of light under the door leading to the workshop. Light. So it must be day. Of course that door was locked too, and he could have made another skeleton key for it, but he knew that the door also had bolts on the outside, and he wouldn't be able to open them.

He groped his way back to the chess automaton and touched the android's right arm, the wood and the fur-trimmed caftan over it. The cold wood did not give way to the pressure of Tibor's hand. He felt his way along the Turk's rigid arm, over its shoulder and throat, and up to its face. His fingers passed over its chin, mouth, and nose and reached the eyes. He touched those glass eyes with the tip of his thumb. The glass felt colder than the rest of the Turk. It was too dark for him to see its face. Tibor increased his pressure on the eye. There was a creak inside the Turk's wooden skull. The eye socket finally broke, and Tibor pressed the eye into the empty skull. Like a marble, it fell through the hollow body, struck wooden ribs and wires, and finally dangled from its optic nerve.

The Mechanical Turk would never play chess again. The eye that Tibor had pushed in was like a horn summoning an army to battle, like the scarf dropped as the signal for a tournament to begin, like the first shot fired in anger. If he was to die, then the damned Turk would go with him. Tibor twisted the android's right arm behind its back. The wooden bones cracked and splintered, and the silk of the caftan split all the way down. He pulled the arm out of the Turk's shoulder, broke it over his knee like firewood, and threw the remains into the corner. Then he broke the left arm, which contained the delicate pantograph mechanism and so shattered far more easily, almost like the hollow bones of a bird. Tibor took the hand that had moved the chessmen, with its ingenious mechanism that had taken so long to make, twisted it out of the wrist, and threw it on the floor, where he trod it underfoot. He tore the caftan and shirt off the now-armless android, leaving it naked in the dark. With both hands, Tibor seized the wooden ribs and broke them apart, ignoring the splinters that pierced his skin. He wrenched the cables out of the body with both hands, and the Turk nodded frantically one last time, but there was no one to be checkmated now. This was its own endgame. Tibor tore off the head, twisting the Turk's neck until it broke. He knocked the turban and the fez off the hairless wooden scalp and pushed in the second eye too, making it fall through the skull to the open throat and roll along the floor. Seizing the blind head, Tibor knocked its face against the wall again and again, until plaster was crumbling from the wall itself and the Turk's face was a grotesque mush of papier-mâché, splintered wood, paint, and false whiskers. Tibor wished he could see it.

He heedlessly dropped the head and turned back to the cabinet. He wouldn't be able to do anything to the wood, but he could wreck the false, deceiving clockwork. He broke the wooden post that had once been the android's backbone off the stool and rammed it into the cogwheels and cylinders. It made an absurd, tinkling melody, like someone kicking a clavichord. Tibor rooted about in the wound until the cogwheels broke out of their setting, and he smashed the metal teeth above the cylinder. What wouldn't he have given for some oil and a light, so that he could reduce the wreckage of the ill-starred automaton to ashes forever, leaving the whole of the mechanism just dirty, dull lumps of molten metal.

NIGHT WAS OVER, morning had come, and Kempelen had spent several hours sitting almost motionless at his desk, wondering how to kill Tibor where he lay bound in the machine on the other side of the wall. He couldn't think of a good way. Then Tibor had come around and started kicking the wood, and although the hollow hammering was barely audible, Kempelen couldn't stand it. He was unable to concentrate. So he put his topcoat on and rode through drizzling rain to the Royal Chamber, to go on thinking there undisturbed. It was still so early in the morning that he was the first official for whom the porter opened the gates. He told his clerk not to admit any visitors. Then he sat at his desk—just as he had been sitting in his own study earlier—staring into space and trying to think clearly. He couldn't do it here either. When the bell of the Town Hall struck nine, he remembered that he was expected at Jakob's funeral.

An hour later Wolfgang von Kempelen was tipping three shovelfuls of soil on his former assistant's coffin. He added Jakob's spectacles.

"Dust thou art, and to dust thou shalt return," he said, as the six Jews before him had done: Jakob's landlady, the junk dealer Krakauer, two members of the Jewish community, a Levite from the synagogue, and the gravedigger.

Kempelen had not followed a word of the ceremony. The whole funeral had passed him by like a dream. Jakob's grave was narrow and at one side of the cemetery, underneath a lime tree and next to the wall, in the shadow of a building. It had a plain tombstone. Kempelen remembered that Jakob had sworn, not long ago, to take the secret of the chess automaton to the grave with him. He had kept his word; here they both lay.

To his surprise, János Baron Andrássy was waiting for him at the cemetery gates. He was not in uniform, but he wore his sword and pistol as usual, and he smiled wearily. "I hoped to find you here," he said. "Sad, isn't it, that we so often meet in graveyards?"

Kempelen had stopped dead. The sight of Andrássy roused him from his apathy. "A graveyard is and always will be as inappropriate a place as anyone can imagine for an affair of honor, my dear Baron. I can only hope that's not what you're here for, because I take less interest in the matter than ever today."

"Oh, I don't want to fight a duel with you," replied Andrássy. "Not today or tomorrow or ever. I withdraw my challenge."

Kempelen blinked. "Why this change of heart?"

"I've had a certain kind of satisfaction since last we met, although it was by no means what I wanted. It was I who killed your Jew."

Kempelen was left at a loss for words.

"Let's walk a little way," said Andrássy, gesturing toward the mouth of Judengasse. "I'll be happy to tell you all about it if you want to know— but not here in the Jewish quarter."

AS THEY WALKED downstream along the bank of the Danube together, Andrássy told Kempelen that on the night of Jakob's death he had been in his barracks outside the city gates. He had been on the point of going to bed when a soldier of his regiment was shown in. The hussar, who had just ridden out of town, said that Herr von Kempelen's assistant was at the Golden Rose tavern on the Fischplatz, dressed up as the chess automaton and mimicking the murder of the late Baroness Jesenák—to the great applause of the guests—and he, the hussar, thought it his duty to tell the lieutenant what was going on. Andrássy had immediately had his horse saddled, sent for his corporal, and set off for the fishermen's settlement with Dessewffy. They had waited for almost an hour outside the tavern, then followed Kempelen's assistant in the direction of Judengasse. He had been rolling drunk, he still wore the Turk's costume, and he was singing a Yiddish song, none of it intelligible except for the name Ibolya. Andrássy and Dessewffy had caught up with him outside St. Martin's and addressed him. Andrássy had not at any point intended to kill the Jew, but the song and the impertinence of the man's costume had already enraged him so much that when Jakob greeted him with the words, "Off to slaughter a few pieces of furniture, then?" he struck him on the forehead with his fist. Jakob had fallen to the ground. As he lay there, Andrássy had given his companion his dolman, *kalpak*, sword, and pistol in its case and challenged the Jew to a fistfight, man to man, regardless of religion and social standing. The assistant, back on his feet, had taken his spectacles off and put up his fists. Andrássy had asked him whether he was ready, and as soon as the assistant nodded, he had punched him again. The fight was not a fair one: the first blow and in particular the large quantity of alcohol that Jakob had taken rendered him almost incapable of fighting. Andrássy was easily able to avoid his feeble blows. Once Kempelen's assistant had completely lost his balance and stumbled when Andrássy swung at him. However, the Jew had enough sense of honor not to give up and went on fighting to the end. A heavy blow against his ear had finally laid him low on the paving stones, with the turban fallen from his head.

Andrássy had bent over him and asked the question that had been tormenting him so long. "Who killed my sister? Tell me, Jew, was it the Turk?"

Jakob had taken his time over answering, licking the blood off his lips first. Then he had said a few toneless words. Andrássy had come closer to his battered face to make out what the Jew was saying. But instead of replying, Jakob, with sudden agility, brought his knees up and rammed them so forcefully between the legs of the unsuspecting Andrássy that a red mist came before his eyes, and he fell to the ground next to Kempelen's assistant, near fainting and writhing with pain. All this time Dessewffy, as instructed by the lieutenant, had not intervened. Jakob had risen to his feet, calmly put his spectacles on again, spat on the Baron's body, and said, "That's right, the Turk has your sister on its conscience. Only you Hungarians could be stupid enough to take such fairy tales seriously."

Thereupon Jakob had bent his unsteady steps in the direction of the Jewish quarter again. Andrássy had forced himself back up on his feet, wild with rage, snatched his sword out of the scabbard that Dessewffy was holding, and ran after Jakob with it. He had moved so fast that the blade went right through the assistant's body as if it were a piece of fruit. So there they stood: Andrássy horrified to see what he had done, Jakob incredulously feeling the bloodstained sword sticking through his chest. But he died before he could utter a sound, and as he fell dead, he slipped off the hussar's blade.

"We threw his body into the Danube, and no one saw us do it," Andrássy concluded. "I'm ashamed of what I did. He was a ne'er-do-well, to be sure, but he didn't deserve that death. It was not the act of a nobleman." Andrássy stopped and offered Kempelen his hand. "So I take back the gauntlet I threw down. You are free of our affair of honor. Enough blood has flowed in this business."

Kempelen took the offered hand and said, "Yes, it has."

"Pray for your Jew, because I certainly shall not." Andrássy touched his hand to his hat in farewell. "Goodbye to you."

The Baron had already gone a little way toward the city when Kempelen called him back.

"What else is there for us to discuss?" asked Andrássy, from where he stood.

Kempelen went toward him. "I'd like to make you an offer," he said gently. "If I tell you the name of your sister's murderer, the name you've wanted to know so long ... will you give me your word of honor to respect the secret as long as you live?"

Andrássy's eyes narrowed, but otherwise his face was set like stone. "I would respect the secret, yes—but not the life of the murderer, by God and all his saints!"

"I'm not asking you to," replied Kempelen.

WHEN ANDRÁSSY, with a loaded pistol in his left hand, used the last of the keys that Kempelen had given him to unlock the little lumber room and open the door, a strange sight met his eyes: there stood the chess cabinet with a wooden post sticking out of its clockwork. All that was left of the Turk was its legs, firmly screwed to the stool. The rest of its body was scattered piecemeal around the room. The wall had been damaged in a number of places, and holes in the plaster showed the masonry behind it. One glass eye lay on the floor. The scene looked as if a bomb had exploded, blowing the chess player into a thousand pieces.

In the midst of this chaos sat a small man, a dwarf, with his back to the wall. He blinked when the light from the workshop fell on him, and he raised one hand to shade his eyes. His forehead was covered with sweat, and splinters of wood, flakes of paint, and dust clung to it. When the dwarf was used to the bright light, he seemed to recognize Andrássy, and he smiled. Andrássy pointed the pistol and gestured to him to stand up.

"Was it you who killed my sister?"

Tibor nodded. "I didn't mean to," he said, but his dry throat made his voice crack so badly that it was hard to understand him.

"Did you molest her first? Did you indecently touch or kiss her?"

"I touched her."

"You'll have to atone for it. I am going to kill you. Now."

Tibor nodded again. He was too weak to defend himself or escape, and he didn't even want to anymore. He would sooner have Andrássy than any other executioner. Now the Baron would end what he had begun on the road to Vienna.

"Have you a last wish before you go?"

Unable to speak, Tibor pointed to a jug of water standing on one of the workbenches. Andrássy nodded. Tibor picked up the jug. The first sip still hurt. Then he greedily emptied the jug and put it back again. "Thank you."

"Kneel down," Andrássy told him, and when Tibor went on his knees facing him, "The other way around."

Tibor turned his back to the Baron. Andrássy put his pistol down on the table.

"Did you kill my friend?"

"I didn't mean to either," replied Andrássy. "Tell him that if you happen to meet him."

Tibor heard Andrássy draw his sword and weigh it in his hand, preparing for a single death-dealing stroke. He bent his head, folded his hands, and prayed.

"Hail Mary, full of grace, the Lord is with thee. Blessed art thou among women, and blessed is the fruit of thy womb, Jesus. Holy Mary, Mother of God, pray for us sinners at the hour of our death. Amen."

"Amen," said Andrássy too. Then he raised the sword in the air with both hands. Tibor closed his eyes.

Footsteps could be heard. They were not Andrássy's. The pistol on the table was picked up again as Andrássy spun around. Someone cocked the hammer of the pistol. Now Tibor opened his eyes and turned too. In the doorway stood Elise, in traveling clothes, grasping the pistol firmly and pointing it at the Hungarian. Since she was no longer trying to hide her pregnancy, her rounded belly showed. Andrássy lowered his sword. No one said a word.

Finally Andrássy took a step forward and put out his hand. "Give me that pistol."

But instead of retreating, Elise moved forward too, raising the pistol a little higher so that Andrássy could look down its muzzle. "I'll shoot you!" she cried, her voice breaking. "By God, I'll shoot you dead! Put that sword down!"

Andrássy looked at Tibor, then back at Elise, and finally put the sword down on the floorboards.

"Now, on your knees!"

Andrássy did not comply. "You're not going to kill me."

"I am if you don't kneel down at once!" cried Elise, taking another step toward him.

Andrássy knelt down. Tibor picked up the sword.

"Now what?" asked Elise. Tears were running from the corners of her eyes.

"I don't know," said Tibor.

For a while they all three looked at one another in turn, since none of them knew what to do next.

Tibor waited until Andrássy was looking at Elise again, then brought the pommel of the sword down on the back of his neck. Andrássy fell forward, but groaned, so Tibor struck him again. Then he jammed the blade of the sword into a gap between two floorboards and bent the hilt until it broke off. He threw the handle away. Elise was still pointing the pistol at the unconscious man.

"We won't kill him," said Tibor.

With shaking fingers, Elise uncocked the hammer again. The moment she had done it, she began sobbing out loud. The pistol fell from her hands. Her knees gave way, but Tibor was there to break her fall. She was weeping uncontrollably now, clutching his shirt with her fingers. He put one hand on her back and the other behind her head. He breathed in her scent. She smelled as she always had.

"Piano," he murmured, and, *"Tranquillo,"* because the German words suddenly wouldn't come to him.

She pushed him away from her and looked up with red-rimmed eyes. "You have no right to despise me! You ought to know better! You know what it's like having to sell yourself too! I sold my body, you sold your brain! What's the difference? What makes you a better person? Is it because I lied to you? You lied as well. You lied and cheated with your machine, and just because you say your prayers, it doesn't make you any better! You have no right to despise me," said Elise, adding rather more weakly, "I don't want you to despise me."

Tibor said nothing. He took her head in his hands and kissed her forehead. "Let's go."

They both stood up. Tibor took Andrássy's pistol. Elise dried her tears.

"Where's Kempelen?" he asked.

"I don't know. Not here. All the doors were open, but I didn't see him."

"I'm getting a horse this evening."

"Do you want to wait until then?"

"Yes. I'm not fast enough on foot."

"But where will you wait? Suppose Andrássy gets free and sends his soldiers after you?"

Tibor thought. "Jakob's room would be best. I'm collecting the horse not far away. I'll get my things."

While Elise dragged Andrássy into the lumber room and locked him in, just as Tibor had been locked in before, he put his belongings in a rucksack: the traveling chess set, his money, as well as Messerschmidt's pistol and Andrássy's, and the chessman that Jakob had carved for him. Then he put on his frock coat and tricorne and left his room and the Kempelen house forever. There was no sign of Kempelen there, or in Donaugasse either. But they went a long way around to Judengasse, across the Grüner Markt and the Kohlenmarkt, making sure more than once that no one was following them. They did not talk.

The key to Jakob's room was still under the tile, and no one had yet cleared the room itself. Jakob's clothes and papers lay on the bed exactly as Kempelen had left them. Elise looked at the yew-wood bust of herself, and Tibor looked at both Elises.

A little later footsteps came up the stairs, and there was a knock on the door. Tibor picked up one of the pistols and asked who was there.

"Herr Neumann?" asked the voice on the other side of the door. "Is that you, Herr Neumann? It's me, Aaron Krakauer."

Tibor pushed both pistols under the sheets on the bed and opened the door to the junk dealer.

"Shalom, Herr Neumann," said Krakauer. "I knew I'd seen you—and the beautiful young lady too."

"We're not here for long," Tibor explained. "We're soon leaving."

Krakauer nodded. "They buried Jakob just now. I didn't see you there."

"I wanted to come, but I was prevented."

"That's a pity. It wasn't the Curse of the Turk, was it?"

"What?"

"The butcher said the Curse of the Turk killed Jakob—the way it killed the Baroness and that teacher from Marienthal—because Jakob went to the tavern and dared to imitate it playing chess."

"No. No, it wasn't the Turk." Tibor thought of the Turk as he had left it: smashed beyond recognition. "Or if it was the Turk, then the Turk has paid for it."

Krakauer clasped his hands together. "Is there anything I can do for you, Herr Neumann? Or the lady? A *borovicka*?"

"No, thank you," said Tibor. "Just please don't tell anyone we're here. After all, this isn't our room."

"Of course. Well, goodbye, and I hope you have a good journey. May the Almighty be with you."

"Thank you very much, Herr Krakauer." Tibor closed the door behind the old Jew. It was early afternoon.

THEY HARDLY SPOKE during the hours until nightfall. Elise lay on the bed with her face turned away from Tibor, sleeping. Even when she was awake, she pretended to be sleeping. She was ashamed of her collapse in the workshop and afraid of the future. She wished so much that Tibor would sit down beside her and at least put a hand on her back. But Tibor kept his distance. He washed the sweat off himself, changed his clothes, and ate a little. Then he searched what Jakob had left behind. He collected his tools, tied them up in a piece of leather, and stowed them away in his rucksack. Jakob would have wanted him to have them. When darkness fell, Tibor drew the curtains and lit the seven-branched candelabrum.

"It's time to go," he said at last, putting on his green coat and three-cornered hat.

Elise sat up and slipped her shoes on. "Where are we going to ride?"

"Out of the city, and then . . ."

Tibor stopped in midsentence. A step had creaked on the stairs the other side of the door, and they had both heard it. There came the sound again. Tibor picked up a pistol in each hand, but as it was impossible to cock both at once, he tossed one to Elise. He aimed his loaded gun at the door. Elise moved a little farther up the bed, as if it had suddenly become a raft on a rough sea. The only sounds to be heard were creaking floorboards on both sides of the door.

Then the door was kicked in with such force that the old lock wrenched part of the frame out, and after that the door hung askew on its hinges. In the doorway stood Andrássy, and even before he saw Tibor the mouth of the pistol he held was aiming at his head. Behind Andrássy stood none other than Kempelen, also armed with a pistol. Tibor felt as if he hadn't seen him for an eternity. In defiance of Tibor's weapon, Andrássy stepped into the room and Kempelen followed him, his pistol also pointing at Tibor. When Elise, still sitting on the bed, cocked the hammer of her own gun, Kempelen briefly swung his around to her but then aimed at Tibor again, not sure who represented the greater threat—or which of the two of them he wanted dead most. Tibor took a step to one side so as to take aim at Kempelen better, whereupon Kempelen finally decided on him as his target. At that Elise aimed at Kempelen. Only Andrássy's pistol remained pointing at Tibor the whole time. This strange ballet was performed within a few seconds, without a sound, and almost decorously, as if it had been agreed in advance that no one would fire a shot before everything was in place.

Even now Andrássy couldn't suppress his aristocratic smile. "What fateful equilibrium!"

Tibor wasn't listening to the Baron. He looked into Kempelen's eyes. The black mouth of his pistol was like a third eye below them. Whatever happened in the next few minutes, this would be the last confrontation between the two men. Kempelen's gaze seemed to be trying but failing to avoid him, as if Tibor had bewitched him with an evil hypnotic spell, as if he were the rabbit and Tibor the snake. His fingers kept renewing their grip on his gun, as though it might slip out of his hand. He reminded Tibor of one of the magnetizer's patients in Vienna, a man who had tried to writhe out of his own body. Tibor's gaze moved on; he was still looking at Kempelen, but his eyes had fixed on a point behind him, as if it were possible to see right through the Baron's skull.

Everything seemed to suggest that this game would be a draw: if he shot Kempelen, Kempelen would shoot him, and they would both have lost. Even if they didn't both hit their targets, or their powder didn't catch, the other two would fire: Andrássy at him, the queen at Kempelen. Strategically, the queen was best placed, for the knight had turned his back to her. It was impossible for anyone to cry *"Gardez!"* for the queen was not in danger, and from her square she could take both him and the opposing king. Tibor couldn't move forward, because his opponent was blocking the way. To his right there was a table, to his left a wall. Behind him were a curtain, a window, and the door out to the roof of the adjacent building, but it was closed, and by the time Tibor had it open, the other two would have overpowered him. If only there was another piece of his own color on the board, even if it was only a pawn, for instance Krakauer, matters would look different. But as things now stood, there was nothing for it but for him to sacrifice himself. Then at least the queen would get to safety.

"Run, Tibor," said Elise.

Unless the queen sacrificed herself for him. The two men ignored Elise's cry. But Tibor saw Elise raise her arm with the gun and pull the trigger. The sound of the hammer striking the pan made Kempelen and Andrássy spin around, and by the time the powder exploded in the barrel, firing the bullet into the low ceiling, Tibor had picked up the menorah and hurled it at Andrássy. The candles went out at once. The candelabrum struck Andrássy, who cried out. All was dark, but Tibor had learned to move in the darkness. He pushed the table over, barring his pursuers' way. Someone stumbled. He heard Elise groan. Something fell to the floor. Tibor dropped his pistol. He couldn't use it now.

Shoulder first, Tibor rammed the narrow door to the rooftops. It broke away from the rotten woodwork around its hinges, fell to the roof next door, slipped clattering down the tiles, and stuck in a gutter. Tibor plunged after it and landed with a crash on the tiles, which gave way slightly. He immediately clung to the roof ridge. A shot was fired in Jakob's room, and the bullet whistled past Tibor, well above his head. "After him!" cried Kempelen. There was a scream from Elise, and then the sound of a loud blow. The curtain had fallen back over the doorway, and Tibor couldn't see what was going on behind it. Straddling the roof, he crawled forward over the tiles, which were still wet and cold with the rain left on them, until he reached the next roof. It was flat enough for him to cross it walking upright. In what little light the moonless night gave him, Tibor looked for ways of getting down to the ground, but there were none here: the paving of Judengasse lay on one side of the roof, the graveyard on the other. He had to go on and hope that he would soon be able to climb down a stairwell into a courtyard, or through the window of someone's dwelling. When he turned, Andrássy was looking out of the empty door frame. The Baron raised his pistol and aimed at Tibor, but he was too far away. Without putting his pistol back in its case first, the hussar leaped down onto the roof from the step outside the doorway and ran sure-footed as a tightrope walker over the gable that Tibor had been able to cross only on all fours. Tibor ran on and jumped to the roof of the next building, this time without even thinking of his safety: ultimately it made no difference whether he died of a bullet wound or by falling to the street below.

The chase over the rooftops was like a hunt in the undergrowth: chimneys stood in his way, gutters offered a sometimes deceptive hand-hold, tiles and rafters creaked and crumbled underfoot, mortar and fragments of tile, moss, and damp leaves dropped into the darkness below. Andrássy was not following the same route as Tibor—the network of rooftops branched often enough for that—obviously hoping to cut off his way of escape. An inner courtyard opened before Tibor's feet, a square black hole. He couldn't see the bottom of it any more than if it had been a well. Oil lamps were fitted here and there at various levels, but like will-o'-the-wisps they shone only for themselves, without illuminating their surroundings, and Tibor couldn't see any ladders or steps leading down. He wondered whether to shout for help, but there wasn't a human soul in sight, either in the buildings or down in the street.

As Tibor was crawling over another gable, Andrássy fired his pistol at him. The bullet hit a nearby tile, and red shards spurted in all directions. Tibor clambered on and clung to a chimney so that he could look around. Andrássy was only one building away, reloading his weapon in the dark. The high plateau of rooftops would soon come to an end where an alley intersected it like a ravine, with evening mist drifting along the bottom of it. Tibor was cornered.

"It won't end in a draw this time, chess player," called Andrássy.

Tibor tried to get into cover behind the chimney before answering. "No."

"Do you want to fight?"

"Not anymore."

"That's a pity," said Andrássy, lisping because he was holding his ramrod in his teeth. "Because you have about you some of those qualities of a nobleman that I value highly. All you lack is education. *Par exemple,* it was a capital mistake to break my sword. When you did that, you injured my honor."

"Then by your honor, Baron," replied Tibor, "don't harm the woman. She only wanted to help me. And she's in a delicate condition. Let her and her baby live."

"Have no fear. I would never in my life touch a hair of a woman's head." Andrássy loaded the gun and pulled back the trigger. "Unlike you, if I may say so."

Tibor didn't need to know anymore. To his left, the rooftop ended above the Jewish cemetery, and there was a lime tree growing not far off. If Tibor jumped far enough, he might be able to grab hold of its branches—and if not, then ironically he would die close to his friend. The idea of it made the palms of Tibor's hands break out in a sweat. He rubbed them dry on his trousers and then ran down the roof. Andrássy didn't fire, either because Tibor was a moving target or simply because this breakneck move had taken him by surprise.

With one foot, Tibor took off from the eaves and reached his arms forward in flight. Below him lay the cemetery, now entirely hidden in mist, its rising swaths like the smoke of the underworld. Twigs and damp leaves struck his face, but he forced himself to keep his eyes open. He managed to catch hold of a branch, but it was too slender. It bent under his weight and broke. However, he had reached for another, stronger branch just in time, and this one held. He immediately looked up, but he couldn't see Andrássy through the foliage—which meant that Andrássy couldn't see him either. He was safe for the moment. Quickly he began to climb down the tree, more by feel than by sight. Rainwater dripped around him, and the limp autumn leaves shaken off the twigs sailed down. Once he had spotted a gap between the densely crowded tombstones through the mist, he let himself drop the last part of the way. He landed like a cat on all fours. His old wound hurt. All he still had with him was his money, the clothes he wore, and the hat on his head. Now he had to make sure he reached Walther in good time, before Andrássy started searching the streets for him. He made for the gateway through the labyrinth of graves. Little pebbles fell from the sides of the tombstone slabs on which they were laid.

When Tibor jumped the cemetery fence and landed on the paved road, he began to run, first north to leave Judengasse, then down Nikolaigasse to the church. There were buildings on the left-hand side of the street, and a wall on the right-hand side. The church of St. Nicholas and its churchyard were on the other side of this wall. The church lay on the slope of Castle Mount, a little way above the road, and there were broad steps leading up to it from a gap in the wall. Walther was sitting on the bottom step. He rose with the help of his crutches when he saw Tibor coming. Tibor felt warm with the sheer relief of seeing his comrade there in the appointed place.

"*Sapperment*, where've you been, by Almighty God?" hissed Walther. "I was worrying about you. You're late!"

"I know," said Tibor breathlessly.

"And you're wearing half a tree on your head." Walther removed several leaves from Tibor's three-cornered hat. "Was that a shot just now?"

"Do you have the horse? I must make haste."

"Of course, of course. I tied the nag up by the chapel—only the devil can steal it there. It's a fine animal, Big Man."

"A thousand thanks, Walther."

"*Ça, ça,* one thank-you will do. It's your thousand kreuzers that'll fill my belly, not your thanks. Follow me!"

Nimbly swinging his crutches, Walther led the way up to the church of St. Nicholas, and Tibor followed.

But Andrássy was coming down Nikolaigasse from the other end. He had broken a dormer window, then got down to the street through an empty apartment and the stairwell to which it led. Leaving the Jewish quarter in the opposite direction from Tibor, he was now approaching from the Danube side.

IN THE SCUFFLE that ensued after Elise had fired her pistol and Tibor put out the candles, she had tried with all her might to hold on to Andrássy and prevent him from following Tibor. When the Baron failed to free himself from her clutches, he flung her away from him so violently that she fainted. Kempelen had seen hardly any of this. He had drawn back the curtain over the doorway and stood watching Andrássy set off over the rooftops after the dwarf. Only after he had lit the candles again with flint, steel, and tinder did he see Elise lying unconscious on the floor. He felt her pulse, picked her up, and laid her on the bed. Uncertain what to do with her, he next put the table back on its legs. Tibor's loaded pistol was lying under it.

Kempelen had paced around the room, breathing heavily, biting his nails and futilely striking the walls several times with his fist before he could bring himself to pick up the pistol at last. He sat down on the bed beside Elise gently, so as not to rouse her, and taking care not to touch her. All he could see was the back of her head. He wiped the tears from his eyes with the back of his hand, then picked up a pillow and put it around the pistol to muffle the sound. When the muzzle was against her head he groaned. His fingers closed on the trigger. He turned his head away from the sight—and looked straight into the eyes of Andrássy, who was standing in the doorway, whose return he hadn't noticed at all, and who was now aiming his own pistol at him.

"Put that gun down at once," said Andrássy, in a tone that could not be misunderstood, "or you'll be the next to die tonight."

Kempelen instantly obeyed this command; he dropped the pistol as a child might let go of a forbidden toy. Andrássy nodded and put his gun back in its case. He was holding Tibor's purse and tricorne in his left hand. He tossed both to Kempelen and let himself drop into the only chair, tired and no longer holding himself upright. He put his head back, closed his eyes, and sighed. Sweat gleamed on his skin.

Meanwhile Kempelen was examining the two objects that Andrássy had brought back. The purse was a few coins lighter than two days before but still heavy. Tibor's hat seemed a strange trophy, but when he put his hand to the brim, he felt that it was wet inside, and on taking his hand out again, he saw his fingertips covered with blood and fragments of something white. There was a hole at the back of the tricorne, hardly larger than a pinhead, and the felt around it was dark with blood. Kempelen immediately wiped his fingers clean on the sheet. Then he held the hat up to the candle, and the light falling in shone on the blood. Black hairs and splinters of bone stuck to it, and a white jellified substance that could only be brains. Nauseated, Kempelen dropped the hat.

"For God's sake, don't be such a hypocrite," Andrássy told him. "You wanted him dead, and death's a dirty business. Do you think my sister was a pretty sight when I found her on the terrace outside the Palais?"

"He's dead, then?"

"Yes."

"Where's his body?"

"On its way to Theben."

"What?"

Andrássy had run down the empty streets in search of the dwarf, furious with himself and the way his sister's murderer had just escaped him for the second time. Skirting the Jewish quarter, he had heard the clatter of hooves in Nikolaigasse. Tibor had come galloping through the mist toward him, his small body in his cut-down frock coat bending over the saddle. Andrássy had aimed at Tibor's head and pulled the trigger. The force of the bullet flung the body back on the horse, and then it slumped like a sack of flour and slipped out of the saddle but with one foot caught in the stirrup. Andrássy had stepped aside. The horse did not stop; the sound of the pistol shot had driven it on instead, so it had carried the corpse away, dragging it over the paving. In the process, first the hat and then, a little farther on, the purse had come loose. Then horse and rider had disappeared into the night, and Andrássy had picked up both purse and hat.

"You did well to avoid dueling with me," said Andrássy. "I'd have put a bullet through your brain just as accurately."

The bell in the Town Hall tower struck three. Kempelen shuddered at the sound.

Andrássy ran one hand through his hair. "Poor devil. The horse looked as if it would trot on forever. Somewhere on the road to Theben his foot will come out of the stirrup, or the girth will come adrift, and he'll be left lying on the road in the dust with a hole in his head."

Kempelen said nothing. He just went on staring at Tibor's hat. Andrássy rose, supporting himself with both hands on the chair, like an old man. "Let's go. It could be that some other Jew has worked it out that he heard pistol shots here, not claps of thunder, and has called in the constables."

Kempelen pointed to Elise. "She . . . she'll give evidence against you."

"Even so, sir, you can put that idea out of your head. This woman lives. She's carrying a child."

"What?"

"You heard me. She's pregnant. And she is under my personal protection. I gave my word, and so far I've always kept it."

Kempelen nodded. He picked up Tibor's purse again, weighed it briefly in his hand, and then put it down beside Elise where she lay on the bed. He was going to take Tibor's tricorne with the bullet hole through it away with him, but Andrássy advised him not to. "It's not a pleasant sight, but that way at least she'll know she doesn't have to look for him anymore, just pray for his soul."

So Kempelen merely picked up the pistols. Finally he put out the last three candles on the menorah and followed Andrássy out of the room.

As the two men passed Krakauer's shop, the junk dealer came out to collect his payment for informing Kempelen, as agreed, that the dwarf and his companion were hiding in Jakob's room. Once out of the junk dealer's hearing, Andrássy said viciously, "Jews!" and spat on the paving stones.

János Baron Andrássy and Baron Wolfgang von Kempelen said goodbye to each other for the last time as they left the Jewish quarter. "Promise me that the Turk will never play chess again as long as I live," Andrássy demanded.

"You've seen my chess machine. The dwarf destroyed it. It's wrecked. You have my word."

Andrássy went back to his barracks. Kempelen saddled his horse that same night, and despite the darkness he rode to Gomba to join his wife and child.

WHEN ELISE opened her eyes, the sun was shining brightly over the city rooftops. As soon as she saw the leather purse containing Tibor's money in front her, she knew that he was dead. The hat with the bullet hole on the empty table merely confirmed it. She fell back on the bed, shaking and in tears, and wished that Kempelen had finished what he came to do, and she had never awakened again—or at least not in this world.

Neuchâtel: Morning

"SO HOW DO YOU COME TO BE STILL ALIVE?" ASKED KEM-pelen. "Or are you a ghost or a doppelgänger? Or even an automaton that the bullet couldn't hurt, and your hat was wet with oil?"

TIBOR HAD FOLLOWED Walther up the steps to the church, and sure enough, there stood a fine strong horse tied to a tree. It turned to the two men on hearing the sound of Walther's crutches, its breath forming little clouds in front of its nostrils.

"*C'est ça,*" said Walther proudly.

Tibor took his hat in his hand and went up to the animal. He was in no haste now. He stroked the horse's warm flank. "Perfect."

"I put your provisions in the saddlebags. Take a look inside."

"I'm sure it's all there."

"No, do just take a quick look."

Tibor smiled and undid the string of one saddlebag, standing on tiptoe to look in. It contained a loaf of bread, some cheese, and several apples.

One of Walther's crutches fell to the ground, clattering. Out of the corner of his eye, Tibor saw a quick movement, and then something hard came down on his head with such force that he thought his skull was bursting into a thousand fragments.

When he woke up again—or at least when his mind woke up, for his body was numb and lifeless—he was lying facedown on the ground, and Walther was kneeling beside him, clumsily removing his coat. Tibor's face was pressed into the cold gravel, and warm blood was flowing into his hair from the top of his head. He could see the horse's hooves close to him.

Walther was talking to himself. "Clothes make the man, don't they? But without them, Big Man, you're only a hunchbacked gnome, a common boot-boy. You think you're something special just because you wear fine garments? And you expect Walther, who's lost his leg and has to beg his bread outside the church, to fawn on you like a dog if you just throw him a couple of guilders? But here goes Fortune's wheel turning around again. Now I'm wearing your clothes and your fine hat. Now Walther is the rich man and has a horse, and you're the cripple, and a fool of a cripple at that." Walther had finally got the coat off Tibor's arms, but had turned it inside out. Now he turned it back the right way again and put the little coat on himself. The seams split when he stretched. "There we are! Short in the arms and tight over the back, but *très élégant*. A thousand thanks!"

Tibor closed his eyes again. It was hard work keeping them open, and he didn't want Walther to see that he was conscious. He heard Walther hefting the full purse in his hand. Then his steps crunched on the gravel. He untied the horse, pushed his crutches into the saddlebags, and mounted, panting.

"I'll see you in hell, Big Man," he hissed at his comrade in farewell. Raising the three-cornered hat in mock respect, he spat on Tibor's back. "You go first!"

Then Walther clicked his tongue, and the horse trotted off with him. Tibor opened his eyes one last time to make sure that Walther had really gone. Then night finally enveloped him. He was sure that he would wake up again, sure that neither the blow from the crutch nor the cold of the night nor Andrássy would kill him. He didn't hear the deadly shot that Andrássy fired at Walther.

A woman coming to tend her parents' grave found Tibor in the morning. She roused him and offered her help, which he gratefully declined: he could walk—that was what mattered. He could do something later about the dried blood on his head and his shirt. Shivering with cold, and with faltering footsteps, he went back to Judengasse, ignoring the alarmed looks of those who met him. When he entered Jakob's devastated room, Elise was still weeping, and once he saw his three-cornered hat on the table and his purse beside the bed, he understood why. Elise fell silent for a moment when she caught sight of Tibor, only to burst into tears again more violently than before, but with a smile on her lips. She took him in her arms and wept. She put a hand on his sore head and rocked him like a child, and Tibor closed the lids over his own damp eyes and thought he was going to faint again.

TIBOR PUT HIS HAND over his eyes. He was tired. Day would soon dawn. In the meantime Johann had awakened, had found himself a blanket, and lay down again with it in front of the dying fire on the hearth.

"Of course you must hate me," said Kempelen, "and you never understood me, or perhaps you're sure you would have acted differently yourself. But you're perfectly happy now, aren't you? And but for me you wouldn't be here. I'm not asking you to thank me, only to be good enough to remember that."

"I'm not perfectly happy."

"Why not? You're a successful watchmaker, an accepted member of this community, you have a home, friends . . ."

"But not a day goes by when I don't remember that I killed Ibolya Jesenák. Inside the chess automaton. And I dream of it at night. No prayers or confessions have freed me of that, nor the passing years either. My guilt has followed me for thirteen long years, and it will follow me forever."

"I understand."

"I don't think you do." Tibor stood up. "I'm going to bed now. It's high time. We'll meet again in a few hours for the endgame."

Kempelen raised his hand. "Wait."

"What is it?"

Kempelen rubbed his brow. "Please wait."

"Are you thinking of finishing what Andrássy never managed to do?"

"No, devil take it. Just wait a moment."

Tibor waited but did not sit down again. Finally Kempelen looked up. His expression had changed. "I want to suggest a deal."

"A deal like your unspeakable bargain with Andrássy?"

Kempelen ignored this remark. "That guilt you spoke of . . . Ibolya's death . . . if I take it from you . . . then would you lose to the Turk?"

Tibor turned his head. He was frowning. "How can you take it from me?"

"But would you?"

"What do you mean by that question? Ibolya Jesenák is dead, and nothing can bring her back to life. No one can do away with my guilt."

"Tibor, just assume that I could. I'm offering you your soul's salvation. Would you lose the game in return?"

"Yes."

Kempelen took a deep breath.

"What do you have to tell me?" asked Tibor.

"Listen carefully: just as Andrássy didn't kill you but your comrade," he said slowly, word by word, "so it was never you who killed Ibolya."

Tibor sat down again.

"You remember how when we were in the Palais Grassalkovich, after Ibolya had fallen against the table, I put her on top of the cabinet to examine her? I felt her pulse . . . and it was still beating. I lied to you. She wasn't dead. She was only unconscious."

Tibor shook his head. "No."

"I swear it. Her fall was harmless. You went through much worse, and you're alive. You didn't kill Ibolya."

"But then . . ." Tibor stared at Kempelen, his eyes wide. "*Madre di Dio* . . . she was alive when you carried her to the balcony and—?"

"Yes."

"*You* killed her?"

"Yes."

"But . . . why?"

"Isn't it obvious? I could tell you I did it to protect you—but we haven't lied to each other all this night, and I'm not about to start lying now." He cleared his throat. "I did it simply because Ibolya would have given us away. You heard her. It would have been the end of me."

"She loved you!"

"She was bored," said the Hungarian, turning his eyes away. "Yes, yes, despise me! I don't expect much change in you there."

"Why—why didn't you tell me the truth at the time?" Kempelen made a noncommittal gesture, but Tibor was answering his own question. "To present me as the guilty man if anyone had found out . . ."

"Tibor . . ."

". . . and bind me to you forever with my fear of the gallows . . . to you and the automaton."

"You're exaggerating."

Tibor looked down at the floor. Then he unexpectedly—and savagely as a beast of prey—leaped over the table and seized Kempelen by the collar. Kempelen and his chair fell backward. Tibor stayed there above him, his left hand at Kempelen's throat. He had clenched his right hand and tensed his arm, ready to bring his fist down on Kempelen's face. Kempelen saw that fist quivering powerfully as the flesh of Tibor's fingers turned white. He didn't move. Tibor was breathing fast through his half-open mouth.

The noise had roused Johann. Drunk with sleep, he got to his feet and came over to the two of them. "Herr von Kempelen?"

"It's all right, Johann," said Kempelen, his voice distorted by Tibor's grip on his throat. "Stay where you are."

Tibor paid no attention to the assistant. He still couldn't make up his mind to strike; his fist was still clenched.

"My God, Herr Neumann! Please don't hurt him!" begged Johann pitifully. "It's only a game! I'll lose if you want me to so much!"

Tibor nodded. His features relaxed, and then so did his fist and his grip on Kempelen's throat. He took a step back.

"No," he said to Johann, "no, Herr Allgaier, that won't be necessary. Please forgive me for waking you so rudely from your sleep."

Tibor turned from Johann to Kempelen, who was still lying on the floor, and back again. Then he said, almost cheerfully, "Well, goodnight, gentlemen. We'll meet again in a few hours' time in the company of the Turk."

GOTTFRIED NEUMANN made eleven more moves, but his clumsy tactics left his king maneuvered into a corner from which there was no escape. And Kempelen's chess machine checkmated him there. The audience applauded. The President of the Chess Club said, "He never had a real chance of winning—how could he, against a machine?—but he played amazingly well."

Carmaux shook his head regretfully and kept saying, "Oh, what a pity, dear me, what a pity." Then he rose and opened his purse. "Well, the time has come—we promised to send the collection bag around."

Tibor, who was still seated, looked keenly at Kempelen—a glance that went unnoticed by the spectators—whereupon the Hungarian mechanician said, "No, no, *messieurs*, no money, please! Be good enough to forget yesterday's agreement. You've already paid for your entrance, and to have watched this excellent game is recompense enough for me."

Once again there was applause, this time for such magnanimity. "What a remarkable man!" said Carmaux. Only Kempelen's assistant Anton seemed dismayed.

Now Tibor rose from his seat, and turning to a boy who had been sitting in the second row both today and the day before, he said, "Come along, Jakob, let's go."

On his feet, the boy was already taller than the dwarf. Kempelen's mouth dropped open in surprise. The child was blond, fair-skinned, and extraordinarily good-looking. He had a small mole above the right-hand corner of his mouth. Tibor did not turn back again, but the boy looked over his shoulder and held Kempelen's gaze until he had disappeared among the throng of spectators.

. . .

"WHY DIDN'T YOU WIN? Jakob asked his father as they drove back to La Chaux-de-Fonds in their carriage.

"Because my opponent was better than me."

Jakob shook his head. "I don't understand the game, but I could see you weren't trying anymore. As if you didn't want to win."

Tibor smiled and ran one hand through the boy's hair. "How clever you are! Of course, you're right, I wasn't trying. I let my opponent win. But I would have lost anyway, believe me. I might have been able to go on longer and perhaps force a draw. But the other player was better."

"The Turk."

"Ah, yes. The Turk."

"You were wonderful, all the same! I'm going to tell Maman as soon as we get home."

They said nothing for a while. There was no wind, and the overnight snow had melted, but it was still bitterly cold. Jakob looked at the countryside, then at his father.

"Are you thinking of the machine?" he asked.

"No. No," replied Tibor. "No, I was just thinking of your mother. The mother who bore you."

"Elise?"

"Yes. It's a pity you never knew her better."

"She could have stayed."

Tibor sighed. "She couldn't stay in La Chaux-de-Fonds. Life as a mother in a little Swiss village wasn't for her. She wanted to move on. I promised her to look after you, so she set off for Paris to seek her fortune there. The summer after you were born."

"Did she find it? Her fortune?"

"No, I don't think so. She came back four years later, long after I was married to Maman."

"And she was sick when she came back to us."

"Yes, indeed. She said she wanted to stay with us to recover from her illness, but she herself probably knew she would never get better. She just wanted to see you one more time. And me. Because once she had what she'd come for, it was all very fast. You remember the day we took her to the churchyard?"

Jakob nodded. After a moment he asked, "Did you love her?"

"Yes," said Tibor. He took a couple of breaths and then went on, "Yes, I loved her very much."

"As much as you love Maman?"

"You can't compare these things."

"And did she love you?"

Tibor looked down and shook his head. "No. Not entirely, I'm afraid."

"Why not?"

"I don't know."

"Because you're small?"

"Perhaps. But then again, perhaps not. You know, Jakob, she told me something before she died. She felt sad that she had never loved as I did, she said, and sometimes that made her almost envious of me—particularly when she saw me and Maman together." Tibor looked into Jakob's eyes. "And then she said, 'I never really found out what love is, but I know I was closer to that feeling with you than with anyone I ever met.'"

Jakob dared not say anything in reply to that. He was grateful when his father, without another word, gave him the reins, and he could concentrate on driving the horses while his father looked at the landscape as he had done before.

The Purity Lodge

ON 2 OCTOBER 1770, IN A SOLEMN CEREMONY, THE HONOR-
able Gottfried von Rotenstein was admitted as an apprentice to the Purity
Lodge in Pressburg. In the following optional part of the evening, several
Freemasons gathered around Duke Albert, who told them that he was
thinking of doing something about the problem of the water supply to
Pressburg Castle at long last. All through the centuries projects for driving a well in the rock had failed, and they could no longer make do with
raising water to the castle by means of a mill, said the Duke. He was going to acquire an English steam engine to convey fresh water to Pressburg Castle. Now the Duke was looking for a civil engineer to supervise
the work.

Wolfgang von Kempelen spoke up. "*Mon Duc,* will you entrust the
task to me?"

Albert raised an eyebrow. "You, Kempelen?"

"I built the bridge over the Danube, and I used a steam engine to dig
a canal in the Banat."

"I don't doubt your talents, far from it," said Albert, "but I thought
your time was entirely taken up by your fabulous chess player."

"Not anymore, Duke. I have dismantled the automaton. The Turk
will play no more chess, *can* play no more chess."

A sound that was louder than a mere murmur went through the little group. There were vociferous protests, in which the Duke himself joined. The company positively begged Kempelen to reconsider his decision, to restore the automaton, beyond comparison the most wonderful invention of the century, and go on exhibiting it. Only Nepomuk von Kempelen and Rotenstein did not join in.

Kempelen raised his hands to calm the uproar. "*Messieurs*, the fame of the chess machine gives me no peace by day or night. My creature has become my master, and I don't want to spend the rest of my days presenting it to the public. I want to be free again. I'd like to make something new, new machines and inventions whose light, if I succeed, may one day shine even brighter than the renown of the Mechanical Turk."

So Wolfgang von Kempelen's decision was accepted. However, there were whispered suppositions that Kempelen's explanation was merely a pretext, and that the two mysterious deaths were the real reason for the dismantling of the automaton. That same year work began at the castle under Kempelen's supervision on the installation of a steam engine to raise water, and the chess-playing Turk that had cast the Habsburg Empire and Europe into amazement for a brief year gradually fell into oblivion.

Vöcklabruck

JUST BEFORE THE MAIN ROAD COMES TO AN ARCHED BRIDGE over the small but turbulent little river Vöckla, about halfway between Linz and Salzburg, a small wooden altar to the Virgin Mary stands by a tree a few feet from the verge. Tibor now stood in front of it. He removed the autumn leaves that had gathered at the Madonna's feet and stood on tiptoe to sweep an abandoned spider's web off the gable of the shrine.

The colors of the statue of Mary were faded, green moss was beginning to grow on her once blue dress, a steady drip of rain from the leaking roof had dyed her arm brown, and a woodworm had left its little pits in her body. But none of that had been able to cloud her gentle smile. Tibor looked at her as if she were an old acquaintance and remembered the words he once used in praying to her. He took the amulet from Reipzig out of his pocket and hung the chain over the cross. Some other traveler might take it away if he wanted. Tibor didn't need it anymore. He waited until the medallion had stopped swinging, kissed his fingers in farewell and then put them to Mary's feet, and went back to the road.

Elise was sitting on the box of the carriage and pair that he had bought in Hainburg for a large part of his wages. She was looking down at the waters of the Vöckla, for she hadn't wanted to intrude on Tibor's conversation with the Virgin. Her left hand was resting on her rounded belly. Through her dress, it felt like the warm side of a kettle.

"We'll soon be in Salzburg," Tibor called up from the road, and she turned to him.

"So are you going to drop me off there and go on alone?"

"What about your child?"

"Oh, it can be born in a barn or by the roadside if need be."

"These are the last warm days. It will get colder—it may even snow."

"Are you by any chance trying to get rid of me? Am I a nuisance to you?"

Tibor had come up to the carriage. He looked up at her, shielding his eyes from the sun with his hand, and shook his head.

"Then stop talking nonsense and get up here, you stupid dwarf, or I'll go on without you."

Tibor smiled and clambered up on the box. She took the reins and urged the horses on.

As the wheels of the carriage crunched over the stone bridge, Tibor reached into the rucksack behind him and from under his tools took out the traveling chessboard on which he had won that first game against Kempelen in Venice. With a casual movement, he threw it over the side of the bridge—too quickly for Elise to stop him—and didn't even look after it.

The chess set fell on a rock, and the two halves of the board broke. Thirty-two squares lay where the board had fallen, the other thirty-two slid into the water. The chessmen had fallen out: a bishop landed in the petals of a larkspur, a queen was caught between two stones, a rook stayed with the chessboard, but most of them had landed in the stream, or fell into it, and were washed away by the foaming water: pawns, officers, and royal highnesses in red and white set out on a wild journey over stick and stone, now drawn down by little whirlpools, now flung roughly against rocks, and quickly dispersed; their felt feet drenched, their wooden heads bobbing up: a horse's mane, a crown, a bishop's miter, a row of little pinnacles. The turbulent Vöckla carried them into its more mature sister the

Ager, which in its turn ran into the Traun, and the Traun took them to great Mother Danube, which would carry them on more sedately but ultimately just as swiftly past Vienna, Pressburg, Ofen, and Pest, through Hungary, the Banat, and Walachia, and at last, one day, it would bring them to the Black Sea.

EPILOGUE: PHILADELPHIA

Throughout the summer of 1783 Wolfgang von Kempelen displays his chess automaton in Paris. That autumn he crosses the Channel and stays in London for a year. This very successful tour next takes him to Amsterdam and then on to Karlsruhe, Frankfurt, Gotha, Leipzig, Dresden, and Berlin. At Sanssouci, Frederick the Great and his court succumb to the spell of the chess-playing Turk. In January 1785 Kempelen returns to Pressburg after almost two years' absence and ends the performances. The machine is put away in its room in Donaugasse again, and it stays there for the next twenty years.

As a result of the chess machine's performances on tour, and the publication of Karl Gottlieb von Windisch's *Letters on Herr von Kempelen's Chess Player*, a series of articles describing the playing of the automaton and trying to account for it appear in Germany, France, and England. Johann Philipp Ostertag surmises that supernatural powers operate the Turk. Carl Friedrich Hindenburg and Johann Jacob Ebert exclude anything metaphysical as its driving force but still consider the Turk a genuine automaton: they believe that the android works by means of electric or magnetic currents.

However, the skeptics are in the majority: neither Henri Decremps nor Philip Thicknesse is taken in by Kempelen's illusion, nor are Johann

Lorenz Böckmann nor Friedrich Nicolai, although their accounts of it
still go no further than hypothesis: none of them can demystify the illusion conclusively and beyond any shadow of doubt. Baron Joseph Friedrich
zu Racknitz is the first to show, by building a copy of the chess machine,
that it is possible for a human being to hide inside the cabinet—but that
is not until the year 1789, when the original has long since been gathering dust.

Kempelen ignores these accusations. He once again devotes himself
to his work as a royal councilor. He is charged, in particular, with the
removal of the governmental authorities from Pressburg to Ofen, otherwise known as Buda: from the old capital to the new capital of Hungary.
He still has plenty of time for his mechanical projects. Before his European tour he had built an adjustable health bed for the heavyweight Empress and a writing machine for the blind singer Maria Theresia Paradis;
now he designs the waterworks for the Fountain of Neptune at Schönbrunn. He supervises the building of a Hungarian theater in Ofen Castle.
In 1789 he patents his design for a steam engine to provide the energy to
drive flour mills, rolling mills, hammer mills, and sawmills. His last ambitious project, a plan for a canal to run from Ofen to Fiume, a waterway
from the Danube to the Adriatic, is never realized.

But he devotes most of his energy to his speaking machine, which is
finally able to utter short but clearly comprehensible sentences in French,
Italian, or Latin, *"Ma femme est mon amie." "Je vous aime de tout mon
cœur."* This is entirely without the concealed operation of any human
hand, although he is suspected of ventriloquism. In 1791 Kempelen publishes his book, *The Mechanism of Human Speech, with an Account of His
Speaking Machine,* which contains many illustrations of the machine and
becomes one of the fundamental works on phonetics. Finally, Kempelen
tries his hand as artist, poet, and dramatist. However, his play *Andromeda
and Perseus* has only one performance.

In 1798 Kempelen retires. Just before his death Emperor Francis II
withdraws his pension because Kempelen has expressed sympathy with
the ideas of the French Revolution. On 26 March 1804 Johann Wolfgang
von Kempelen departs this life at the age of seventy in his apartment in

Vienna. His last resting place is the churchyard of St. Andrew's in his native city of Pressburg. An epigram from Horace is inscribed on his tombstone: *"Non omnia moriar"*—I do not die entirely.

THE WATCHMAKER Gottfried Neumann, whose true name of Tibor Scardanelli is not known to any of his fellow citizens, dies the following year in La Chaux-de-Fonds. To the last he is making his popular *tableaux animés*, although he never lets himself be infected by the ambition of those of his professional colleagues who try to impress the world by constructing ever larger, more expensive, and more amazing clockwork devices. Most of Neumann's moving pictures show historical battles, or scenes from mythology or pastoral poetry. Whereas at first they are silent, he later makes musical boxes to provide music and sound for the spectacle.

After the French Revolution Neumann gradually changes the subjects of his tableaux and begins depicting scenes from everyday life and events from the Bible: Adam and Eve being tempted by the snake in the Garden of Eden and driven out by Gabriel; the birth of Jesus in the manger at Bethlehem, with the star in the sky and the arrival of the Three Kings, all to the tune of "Es ist ein Ros' entsprungen." His last work—as if he has guessed that his own death is near at hand—is the Ascension of Jesus: the Savior ascends into Heaven, the dark clouds open above him, and angels come flying down on a sunbeam to receive Christ.

Gottfried Neumann is carried to the grave in the presence of his wife, Sophia, his three children, the same number of grandchildren, and almost a hundred of his fellow citizens. His coffin is that of a fully grown man. Some of the local citizens remember Neumann as the man who almost succeeded in defeating the legendary Mechanical Turk. No one, not even his wife, knows that he himself was the first brain to operate the Turk.

Although Neumann has created countless images, no pictures of him are preserved, not even a silhouette. But his memory lives on in a doppelgänger: when Pierre Jaquet-Droz and his son Henri-Louis make their writing automaton, Neumann is their model for the android. The short-limbed writer is not a boy, as many believe, but a faithful likeness of Gottfried Neumann.

AFTER KEMPELEN'S DEATH, his son Karl sells the Mechanical Turk for ten thousand francs to the imperial and royal Court Mechanician Johann Nepomuk Mälzel from Regensburg, inventor of the metronome. When Napoleon Bonaparte occupies the city of Vienna in 1809, he wants to play a match against the chess automaton, and Mälzel arranges an encounter at Schönbrunn Castle. The French Emperor is known to be an excellent chess player, but he loses the first two games against the Turk, or rather Johann Allgaier. In the third game the Corsican repeatedly makes wrong moves, whereupon the angry android sweeps all the chessmen off the board with his forearm—to Bonaparte's great amusement.

In 1817 Mälzel takes the Turk on another European tour. Like Kempelen before him, he travels to Paris and London as well as many English and Scottish cities. Interest in the Turk continues unabated, although the chess automaton is not Mälzel's only attraction. His panopticum is enriched by some inventions of his own: a trumpeter automaton, a little mechanical female tightrope walker, and an automatic model of the city of Moscow presenting the great fire of 1812, as well as a small mechanical orchestra that plays an overture specially composed for it by Ludwig van Beethoven.

When the number of visitors to his show in Europe begins to decline, Mälzel sets off for the New World, and from 1826 onward he presents his works of art in New York, Boston, Philadelphia, Baltimore, Cincinnati, Providence, Washington, Charleston, Pittsburgh, Louisville, and New Orleans. Edgar Allan Poe is among the spectators in Richmond, and in his essay "Maelzel's Chess-Player" he writes an account giving reasons, based on meticulous detective work, why the Turk cannot be an automaton. By now it has also mastered the card game of whist.

After Johann Baptist Allgaier, Mälzel engages the local chess-playing talent in the places that he visits. In Paris he hires three regulars at the chess-club café De La Régence. In England he recruits young William

Lewis and Peter Unger Williams, in Scotland a Frenchman called Jacques-François Mouret. Years later Mouret is the first player to reveal the chess automaton's secret to the public. In America a woman operates the Turk for the first time.

The last person to act as the Turk's brain is Wilhelm Schlumberger, of Alsace. When Schlumberger is traveling to Havana in 1838 with Mälzel and the Turk, he dies of yellow fever. Mälzel does not return to the United States either but dies on the passage to Cuba. His body is buried at sea, in the Atlantic Ocean.

The Mechanical Turk is orphaned again. It finds a new home in Peale's Chinese Museum in Philadelphia, a collection of curiosities. But no one wants to see the chess automaton now that its mystery is gone. It is only an antique, the Trojan horse of the Baroque period, a relic from a time long past.

On the night of 5 July 1854 a fire breaks out in the Chinese Museum. The android cannot escape. Flames consume the cabinet, the clockwork, the entire artificial man: its wire muscles, its wooden limbs, its glass eyes. The chess-playing Turk dies in its eighty-fourth year of life, fifty years and a hundred days after its creator.

AUTHOR'S NOTES

While the public appearances of the Mechanical Turk in the nineteenth century are relatively well documented, much less is known about its early days. No one knows exactly when and where the premiere of the chess-playing automaton took place in the year 1770 or how many performances it gave after that before it was stored away for the first time. As little is known of whoever Kempelen hired as the first operator of the fake chess machine. (German has the verb *türken*, "to Turk," meaning "to fake," which does indeed derive from Kempelen's automaton.)

I have taken the liberty of making up my own story about the chess automaton, which I hope fits seamlessly into all that is known from that period about Wolfgang von Kempelen's career, his family, and his contacts in Pressburg, today Bratislava, the capital of Slovakia. As characters, I have made use of a number of well-known and less well-known people in the Habsburg Empire of the time, including Friedrich Knaus, Franz Anton Mesmer, Gottfried von Rotenstein, Franz Xaver Messerschmidt, Johann Baptist Allgaier, and the Hungarian nobility of Pressburg. Tibor, Elise, Jakob, and the Andrássys, brother and sister, are fictional characters of my own invention.

Finally a word in defense of the honor of Wolfgang von Kempelen: the murder of Ibolya Jesenák is fiction too. In real life Kempelen was ambitious but certainly not prepared to walk over corpses to further his career. His contemporaries describe him as a likable and unpretentious man with many talents—independently of the fact that his chess-playing Turk was only a conjuring trick. Today it is difficult to understand this attitude toward scientific fraud, but in the eighteenth century the dividing line between science and entertainment was not yet clear-cut, and Kempelen—like the magnetizers of his time—was more of a scientific entertainer than a cold-blooded con man. The verdict of Karl Gottlieb Windisch was that the chess machine was an illusion, "but an illusion that does credit to the human mind." And Kempelen himself, said Windisch, was "the first to admit modestly that its main merit was not as an illusion, but as an illusion of a completely new kind." Nonetheless Kempelen did his utmost to keep the deception a secret, and that secret was finally revealed only after his death.

IF THIS BOOK has aroused further interest in the chess-playing Turk—more particularly from its subsequent history in the care of Johann Nepomuk Mälzel to its immolation in Philadelphia—two nonfiction books that appeared a few years ago can be recommended: Gerald M. Levitt's *The Turk, Chess Automaton* (McFarland, 2000), and Tom Standage's *The Mechanical Turk: The True Story of the Chess-Playing Machine That Fooled the World* (Penguin 2002). Levitt's work is more extensive and richly illustrated, and it has an appendix containing original writings by Windisch, Poe, and others, as well as details of many of the games played by the chess automaton. Standage's book is more entertaining and brings the whole subject up to the present day, for instance covering the games played by the world chess champion Garry Kasparov against the chess-playing computer Deep Blue. (As it happens, Kasparov suffered his first defeat by Deep Blue in 1996 in Philadelphia, the very city where the Turk burned a century and a half earlier.)

A few copies of Kempelen's chess automaton exist in various parts of the world. The most recent (and fully operational) copy has been exhibited since 2004 in the Heinz Nixdorf MuseumsForum in Paderborn, as an indirect ancestor of the computer and artificial intelligence along with clocks, calculating machines, genuine automata, and genuine chess computers. The Paderborn Turk is sometimes given a "manned" performance.

The Technisches Museum in Vienna has a virtual three-dimensional chess computer in the form of the Turk, which lets visitors into the secret of the chess machine and challenges them to a game. The same museum also contains Friedrich Knaus's impressive Wonderful All-Writing Machine of 1760. The German Museum in Munich exhibits Wolfgang von Kempelen's speaking machine, although its voice is gradually failing. Copies of the speaking machine can be found in the Budapest Academy of Sciences and the University of Applied Art in Vienna.

Finally the three automata from the workshop of Pierre and Henri-Louis Jaquet-Droz, father and son—the writer, the artist, and the woman organ-player, dating from 1768 to 1774—are in the Musée d'art et d'histoire in Neuchâtel. These automata function as well as they did on the day they were first exhibited and show their skills to the public on the first Sunday of every month.

I WOULD LIKE to thank Dr. Stefan Stein of the Heinz Nixdorf Museums-Forum for revealing information about the interior of the Mechanical Turk, and Achim "Inside" Schwarzmann of Paderborn—the ghost in the machine, in succession to Tibor, Allgaier, and the others.

My thanks as well for their expertise to Professor Ernst Strouhal, Dr. Brigitte Felderer, Professor Andrea Seidler (Vienna), Siegfried Schoenle (Kassel), Swea Starke (Berlin), Dr. Silke Berdux (Munich), and Thierry Amstutz (Neuchâtel).

And not least, many thanks to Uschi Keil, Ulrike Weis, and Donat F. Keusch for their unstinting support for this story.